D0513734

THE
BEST OF FATHERS

THE
BEST OF FATHERS

Anne Baker

headline

First published in 2008
by HEADLINE BOOK PUBLISHING

1

Cataloguing in Publication Data is available from the British Library

ISBN 978 0 7553 4076 7

Typeset in Baskerville by Avon DataSet Ltd,
Bidford on Avon, Warwickshire

Printed and bound in Great Britain by
Mackays of Chatham plc, Chatham, Kent

Headline's policy is to use papers that are natural, renewable and
recyclable products and made from wood grown in sustainable forests.
The logging and manufacturing processes are expected to conform
to the environmental regulations of the country of origin.

HEADLINE PUBLISHING GROUP
An Hachette Livre UK Company
338 Euston Road
London NW1 3BH

www.headline.co.uk

THE
BEST OF FATHERS

PART ONE

CHAPTER ONE

March 1921

SUNDAY LUNCH was almost ready. The big kitchen was filled with appetising scents and the joint of beef cooked to a turn, but Mary Shawcross felt sick with anxiety. She knew a disastrous pit was yawning open at her feet and she must expect the most awful trouble.

Only half her mind was on what she was doing. Her mother had told her the apple pie and rice pudding needed five more minutes and asked her to take them out when they were done. She rushed to open the oven door. Searing hot air blasted up in her face as she jabbed a knife through the pudding skin. Yes, it was cooked. She was edging the enamel dish forward on the shelf when, with a gasp of horror, she felt it slip through the oven cloth. The next instant, it crashed to the stone floor and the clatter echoed through the house.

Mary let out a shocked scream as a pool of pudding spread round her feet. It had splashed over her shoes. Her brother Noel, with his white shirt half buttoned and his best tie loose about his neck, reached her first.

'Are you all right?'

He grabbed the oven cloth from her and righted the pudding dish to save what remained in it, and was about to kick the oven door closed when Mary wailed, 'Take the pie out, please, or it'll burn.'

'It looks scrumptious.' He slid it on top of the stove, his cheeks hot and his brown hair hanging over his forehead. Mary and her brothers shared a strong family resemblance.

Their mother Edith came hurrying downstairs in her Sunday best, a dark grey skirt and a pearl-coloured blouse. Shocked, she pulled up at the door, her mouth falling open as she took in the mess on the floor.

'What's happened? What have you done? Oh, Mary!'

'I've managed to save some of it,' Noel said helpfully.

3

'There won't be enough! Most of it is on the floor.' Edith's dark hair, now in middle age streaked with grey, had been freshly combed up into a bun, and her cheeks were scarlet with distress. 'You know how fond Pa is of rice pudding with his pie. Today of all days, we could do without an accident like this.'

'I'm sorry, Mum.' Mary knew her mother was seeing this as a major disaster, though compared with her own troubles it was just a pinprick.

'What am I going to do?' Edith cried.

'What about custard?' Noel asked. 'That goes better.'

'I'll make an egg custard,' Mary said. 'The oven's hot; it won't take long.'

She reached for a dish, while Noel hurried to the larder for eggs. Within moments she was whisking them up with sugar and mixing in the milk. Her mother sprinkled cinnamon on top and put it in the oven.

'That should do it,' Mary said, wishing her own dilemma could be so easily sorted. She and Jonty were in love; she'd thought everything was perfect, but now they had a problem and must decide how best to deal with it.

'Do run up and get changed, Mary,' Edith said, her voice fraught with tension. 'And Noel, you're only half dressed. Your father and his guest will be here at any moment. He'll be cross if you aren't all ready.'

Mary knew Pa had gone to church and would be bringing a guest home with him for Sunday lunch. He'd told them Mr Steadman was a fellow businessman who also owned garages. They were assuming Pa meant to further his business empire in some way.

'I haven't made the gravy yet,' Mary said.

Her mother was rarely irritable with her but she was this morning. 'What's the matter with you?' she snapped. 'You're walking round in a trance.'

That made Mary catch her breath. She couldn't possibly tell her. Certainly not now, when her mother was already in a tizz.

Edith added, 'You've got flour in your hair. Do go up and tidy yourself.' Father expected high standards; everything had to be perfect.

Mary ran upstairs and saw how woebegone she looked in the bathroom mirror. Her face was drained of colour, she looked scared and tears were welling in her eyes. If only she didn't feel so sick. She splashed cold water on her face, knowing she needed to pull herself together.

In her bedroom, she took her best dress from her wardrobe. Yes, in its full length mirror, she could see flour in her nut-brown hair. She must have touched it when she was making the Yorkshire pudding.

She brushed at it vigorously. Her hair had never pleased her; it was too straight, and over recent weeks it had looked lacklustre. She wanted to have it cut into the new short style but Pa had forbidden it.

Her blue wool frock, new at the beginning of winter, flattered her. It made her look tall and wand-like, which made her feel a bit better. A dab of powder on her nose now to stop the shine. She was reaching for her lipstick when she changed her mind; she daren't use any today though she certainly needed it. Pa would notice even the lightest touch and might send her to wash it off, even though she was nineteen. She was scared of his wrath, but then her mother was too.

Her father, Percival Edgar Shawcross, was an ambitious businessman. The war had ended sixteen months ago and now he expected his business to grow. He owned three garages in different districts of Liverpool, and employed mechanics capable of repairing the motor cars and motor bikes he sold. Petrol was not available in many places in the city, and Percy had added forecourts and petrol pumps to two of his sites. He had big plans to develop his third site in Childwall, where he had a sales showroom and plenty of space. Motor bikes were selling well; cars were less affordable.

Mary had three older brothers and Pa reminded them frequently that it was his intention to provide each of them with the means to earn a comfortable living. He was fifty-three, and she supposed at his peak. He was very much the head of the family and expected to control everything and everybody, both at home and in his business. He was scrupulously honest and a strict disciplinarian, ruthless with employees who broke his rules. He had a fiery temper; everybody did their best to follow his instructions and keep on the right side of him: employees, family, even Mum.

She was calling up the stairs, 'Len, please come down. Pa will expect you to be waiting for him. Have you got your best suit on?'

'Coming, Mum.'

Mary's two middle brothers, both lively, well-built young men, still lived at home; Mary herself was the youngest of the family. She followed Len down and went back to the kitchen, and was putting on her apron again when the front door knocker hammered through the house, followed by the scrape of a key in the lock.

'Here they are,' Mum was panic stricken, 'and we aren't ready yet.'

Mary was draining the fat from the meat pan. 'It sounds more like Dan and Barbara,' she said.

'Hello, anybody home?' Daniel was her eldest brother and, at twenty-eight, the handsomest of the three. He brought his wife straight to the kitchen.

Each of the brothers was nominally in charge of one of Pa's garages, though he oversaw very carefully everything they did. As the eldest, Daniel ran the largest and most profitable garage, in Sefton. Pa had made him wait three years before he'd allowed him to marry petite dark-haired Barbara, but now they had a little house of their own.

Mary brought her gaze up slowly to assess Barbara's expanding figure. She was expecting her first baby in four weeks. Shocked, Mary instantly looked back at the roux she was making in the meat pan. How long before . . . It didn't bear thinking about.

'Dan, get the boys to bank up the sitting-room fire, will you? I must make some mustard. Mary, I've saved this cabbage water for the gravy.'

A key was scraping in the lock again when Edith came out of the larder. 'Goodness, they're here,' she said, a split second before Percy's authoritative voice rang through the house.

'Edith, we're home.'

'Mary, come with me. Pa will want to introduce us,' her mother fussed. 'Take that apron off. We don't want Mr Steadman to see you looking like a kitchen maid, do we?'

Mary snatched off her apron. 'What does it matter what I look like?' she said in an irritable whisper to Barbara.

'What if it's you he's come to see?' her sister-in-law asked, raising her eyebrows. 'Perhaps he's looking for a bride.'

Mary giggled. 'Then he'll have to look elsewhere.' She peeped up the hall and giggled again. 'He's must be forty if he's a day.'

'Dan says thirty-seven. I'll make the gravy, shall I?'

Gratefully, Mary handed her the apron. Pa hadn't taken to Barbara, but everybody else had. She scurried into the hall.

'There you are.' Pa's eagle eye was looking her over. He was a big man, a commanding presence. 'My daughter Mary. Come, let me introduce you to Mr Arthur Steadman.'

Beside him, his guest looked almost weedy. He had a drooping straw-coloured moustache. Mary took the hairy hand he offered.

'Pleased to meet you,' she said. His grip was vice-like and made her wince.

'Charmed, my dear, charmed.'

Her mother ushered them all into their large and comfortable sitting room. She'd organised Len to offer the men sherry before their dinner. They only had sherry on special occasions, and even today it would not be offered to Mary. Pa thought it an unsuitable drink for young ladies.

The conversation was all about business. It seemed Mr Steadman owned two garages himself, one in Walton and one in Norris Green, far enough away from their own not to be in direct competition, and since her brothers were fascinated by motor cars, and knew every model on the market and all the technical details and prices, the talk soon became animated. Mary worked in the business too, but she did not share her brothers' obsession with cars and took no part in the discussion. Her thoughts were on her own problems, and never far from her boyfriend Jonty, who was twenty-three and had asked her to marry him. They'd been planning their future together for months.

When Mary had left school, she'd wanted to train to be a schoolteacher, but Pa had sent her to commercial college to learn typing and bookkeeping. Her job was to help him with the accounts and the paperwork. She shared an office with him above the Childwall garage run by Noel, the youngest of her three brothers. That allowed Pa to keep a very close eye on both her and his least experienced son.

Jonty was a motor mechanic and worked for her father too. As he was based in the same garage, Mary was able to look out of the window and sometimes see him going about his work. She could see his face before her now: kindly and serene with dark hair and intelligent brown eyes that wanted to play with hers. He always seemed to have a slight smile on his lips.

Pa called him Taffy, or sometimes 'that Welsh farm boy'. Jonty had been orphaned as a baby and brought up by an uncle on a hill farm behind Aberystwyth, but the uncle had died when Jonty was sixteen, and the farm was sold up.

'What happened to you then?' Mary had asked.

'I was offered a job on the biggest farm in the district and told I could live in, but the war had just started and I went to a recruiting office and volunteered instead. I told them I was eighteen.'

'Good heavens! And you fought in the trenches?'

'No, I didn't get that far. I was sent to an army depot and trained to repair army vehicles. I liked doing the cars and motor bikes best.'

'Yes, of course.'

'When the war was over, it stood me in good stead. I came to Liverpool and a distant cousin helped me find lodgings. I had to find a job but I had a trade.'

Mary smiled. 'And my father hired you. Dan says you're the best of the lot on motor bike repairs.'

'Because I've had one of my own for a long time. I bought it at a sale of army surplus army equipment. It's the sort used by army dispatch riders.'

Mary's father disapproved strongly of young ladies riding pillion. He was always sounding off about it to staff and family – although never to a paying customer – so Jonty had recently had a sidecar fitted so that he could take Mary out and about. They'd been courting for the last two years but had tried to keep it hidden. Noel had noticed, but Pa had not. Mary knew Pa wanted her to marry well; he'd talked to her about how important it was more than once. Unfortunately, she knew that he would not see Jonty as a suitable husband for her.

She hoped Mr Steadman would not stay late, because she always saw Jonty on Sunday afternoons. Impatiently, she sipped her non-alcoholic ginger wine, which was sweet enough to damp down any appetite. Barbara came to ease her bulk on to the chair beside her.

'Not much longer now,' she said softly. 'I can't wait to see my baby and hold it in my arms.'

Mary understood how she felt – she loved babies too – but it made her wince and she couldn't look at Barbara's bulging body. For the last few weeks she'd been worried stiff, afraid she was pregnant too, and with every day that passed she'd grown more certain.

She thought of how Jonty had held both her hands in his. 'Mary love, if you are we must tell your parents sooner rather than later, but we have to be absolutely certain before we do anything. You need to see a doctor.'

'Not Dr Davidson.' She had covered her face with her hands.

'No need to see your family doctor. I'll take you to see the one my landlady recommends to her lodgers.'

But when her pregnancy was confirmed, the certainty only made matters worse.

Last night she'd wept on Jonty's shoulder and he'd said, 'I'm so sorry it's happened like this. It's my fault. I blame myself – I should have taken more care.'

It wasn't that Mary was dead against having a baby. If she were married like Barbara she'd be anticipating the birth with pleasure too. But the timing was all wrong. How was she to tell Pa? She could guarantee it would bring his wrath down on her head. He'd be furious and she couldn't expect Mum to take her side, not about this. It had been drummed into her that having a baby before she was married was a mortal sin.

'We'll tell him together,' Jonty had said. 'I'll ask him for your hand in marriage. That's what we both want, isn't it?'

'He'll take against you,' Mary had said. Just thinking about it made her feel ill.

She was suddenly aware that Pa was leading everybody to the dining room. She got to her feet, meaning to head to the kitchen. It had always been her role to help get the food on the table, though Mum had not specifically asked her to do it today.

Now Edith said, 'Barbara and the boys will help me today. Father wants you to entertain his guest.'

Mary was shocked. Why her? What could she possibly say that would interest him? Besides, she was too wrapped up in her own worries to put herself out to be pleasant to a stranger. But Pa was steering her to the dining room and the chair next to Mr Steadman's.

'I'm proud of my clever daughter.' Pa's face was unusually benign. 'She keeps our books up to date; I'd be hard pressed to manage the accounts without her. She functions as my secretary too.'

Mary quaked. It sounded as though he was giving her a reference. The thought struck her with such force that it made her gasp. Was Barbara right? Was Pa matchmaking? Surely he couldn't be setting her up to marry this old man? He was going bald!

Pa was looking at her with such intensity in his eyes that it made her tongue-tied. It came as a relief to see Dan carrying in the joint for Pa to carve. She made a supreme effort. 'I understand you're in the garage business, Mr Steadman,' she said.

'Arthur, please.'

Oh, Lord! If he was the last man on earth, she wouldn't want to marry him. He had yellow rats' teeth and his hairy hands were playing with the cutlery.

9

'Yes. I have two at present, and hope to expand in the next few years.'

He outlined his plans while Mum and the boys brought vegetables to the table. When he had exhausted that subject, Mary asked him where in Liverpool his garages were. That kept him going until their plates were filled and they began to eat.

'Excellent tender beef,' Pa said.

'Wonderful Yorkshire pudding,' his guest added.

'Mary made it,' her mother told him.

'In that case I shall enjoy it all the more.'

Mary was pushing her food round her plate, unable to swallow. Did Pa see the two businesses being amalgamated into a much larger one? It was just the sort of thing he would think of. If so, he would be even more infuriated when he heard she wanted to marry Jonty. He'd go up like a fireball.

The meal dragged on. The boys did their best to join in the conversation but Mary switched off. The apple pie came to the table accompanied by a small rice pudding and the egg custard. Pa had chosen the menu and she could see him eyeing the size of the rice pudding with disfavour. Fortunately, Mr Steadman chose to have egg custard with his pie and so did Mary, her mother and her younger brothers, which meant there was enough rice pudding left for Pa to have a second helping.

Afterwards Mary handed round cups of tea while the boys set about the washing up, and at last Mr Steadman stood up to go. He was full of praise for the food and thanked them repeatedly. He looked Mary in the eye and told her he'd thoroughly enjoyed her company. Her father led the way to the front door to see him out. Her mother hooked her arm through Mary's and took her along too.

Arthur Steadman paused on the step. 'It would give me great pleasure,' he said, 'to entertain you to afternoon tea at my house next Sunday.'

His pale eyes were looking into Mary's. When her father accepted with thanks, she felt compelled to do likewise.

Mary knew her parents would settle down for their usual Sunday afternoon rest now; she was free at last to meet Jonty. Nowadays, he came on his motor bike to the end of Templeton Avenue to meet her, but she'd warned him she might be late today and she knew he'd wait.

She put on her best coat and outdoor shoes. Pa didn't like her going out without a hat, but few hats sat comfortably over her long hair and heavy topknot. Anyway, hats were out of fashion these days and she ran out without one. Len and Noel roared past her on their motor bikes as she hurried to the corner where she knew Jonty would be watching for her.

He'd told her he'd been christened plain John Jones, but at school, where there was another John Jones in his class, his friends had nicknamed him Jonty and he'd liked it.

To see him striding eagerly towards her, his head held high and a smile of welcome on his face, made her heart turn over. With his stocky build and bright red cheeks, he looked the picture of health and strength. He had soft dark hair combed neatly back and sapphire blue eyes. Everybody thought him a very presentable young man.

He took both her hands in his, then turned to fall in step beside her, pulling one hand through his arm. She'd asked him not to greet her with a kiss where the neighbours might see and tell her mother. They wouldn't get a chance to tell Pa because he discouraged what he called idle gossip.

'Are you all right, love?'

She clung to him tightly. 'Yes, just about. I've had a terrible morning – I think Pa's started matchmaking. He brought a man home for dinner to introduce him to me. It was awful.'

'What was he like?'

'Old, and going bald. But he owns two garages, so Pa thinks he's suitable.'

'He doesn't want you to be hard up. He's doing what he thinks is right for you.'

'But he never asks me what I want!' Mary was blinking her tears back. 'Anyway, it can't be, can it? It's your baby I'm having.'

His hand squeezed hers. 'I know, and I've put you in a terrible position. What are we going to do about it?'

She shook her head. 'I wish I knew. I've been thinking first this and then that, but . . .'

Jonty said, 'We're going to walk round Princes Park and make some decisions – we've got to. Putting it off is making you feel worse. We've agreed we want to get married, haven't we? So what's the next step?'

Mary got into his sidecar somewhat comforted. They often went to Princes Park; routine was comforting too. It was a bright blustery day. He linked arms and held her hand as they strolled towards the lake.

'I don't like to think of you on your own at home, trying to stand up

11

to your father. I want to be with you, really I do. You can't hide this for much longer. We have to plan for the future.'

Mary shuddered. 'I can't see what we can plan until we've told Father. So much depends on what he decides.'

'I'll ask him if I can marry you.'

'He'll be furious. I'm afraid he'll sack you on the spot.'

'That doesn't bear thinking about. We wouldn't be able to afford food and lodgings until I found another job.'

'He might also forbid you to come anywhere near me.'

'But he wouldn't do that,' Jonty said. 'He'd want to do his best for you, wouldn't he? He loves you. He wouldn't want you to be an unmarried mother.'

'He'll be mortified. He'll say I'm letting the family down. He sets great store on status.' Mary shivered. She could see no alternative to telling her father, except . . . 'Unless we just elope.'

'That would have the same effect. I'd have to leave my job, and when we came back your dad would be unlikely to take me back.'

'Couldn't you look for another job first, in a different district?'

'You know I've already been trying,' he said quietly. 'I'd need a lot of luck to get a similar position, especially if your dad won't give me a reference. The motor trade is so new, there aren't many jobs yet, and a lot of the people who've come out of the forces still need to find work. I've got to try to keep the job I've got, Mary.'

They walked on in silence for a while.

'Shall I come up to the office to talk to him?' Jonty suggested. 'Would it be better to do it there? Usually there's just you and him about.'

'What about Noel?'

'I'd make sure he was busy downstairs before I came up.'

'Perhaps if you came to the house,' Mary ventured. 'Mum would be there and we'd be able to tell them both together. I think she'll be on our side even if she doesn't say much.'

'Right. When shall I come? And what about your brothers?'

'Noel goes to night school on Wednesdays – he's learning bookkeeping – and our Len goes to his table tennis club on the same night.'

'Wednesday it is then. What time? I don't want to arrive while you're eating.'

'Not before half six. Better leave it till quarter to seven to be on the safe side.'

Jonty's brow was furrowed with worry. 'I must work out what I'll say to him. I've got to get that right.'

'Aren't you scared?'

'Yes, but we have to do it.'

Mary shivered.

'Come here,' he said, pulling her to sit down on a park bench and putting an arm round her. There were other people walking past, but nobody they knew. 'I love you and I want to marry you. Once we get this straightened out, we'll be a happy little family of three.'

His confidence made Mary smile.

'I won't let you down,' he said. 'I promise. I'm rock solid behind you on this.'

Mary swallowed hard. 'Three days to get through then.' She was afraid. She knew Pa better than Jonty did: he was going to be absolutely livid.

Every day Pa visited all three of his garages, and though Mary and her brothers cut sandwiches to take to work with them he went home for a hot lunch with Mum. Moreover, he drove a spanking new American Ford saloon which was always prominently parked, so everybody knew whether he was on the premises or not.

His unchanging routine had given her and Jonty the opportunity to get to know each other. They always ate their lunch together. That Monday, Tuesday and Wednesday they had plenty of time to talk, but they couldn't come up with a better plan than the one they'd settled on.

'I won't tell Pa you're coming until just before you arrive,' she said. 'Otherwise he'll be on at me wanting to know why. You won't be late, will you?'

'No, love.' He bent to kiss her cheek. 'I'll make sure I'm not.'

CHAPTER TWO

BY WEDNESDAY EVENING Jonty was nervous, knowing he should never have persuaded Mary to sleep with him. They both knew it was forbidden but he loved her with every fibre of his being and his feelings were growing stronger and stronger. By getting Mary pregnant he felt he'd let her down, and he knew he'd put her in a terrible position. He blamed himself and he had to do his best for her now.

That morning, he'd finished repairing a bike and Mr Shawcross had told him off for not putting away the tools he'd used. He'd tried to explain that he had intended to take the tools straight over to another bike with the same problem, but another customer had stopped him to ask for advice. The boss had told him not to answer back. It didn't augur well for tonight.

He'd gone home after work to wash and change into his best suit . . . well, his only suit. He'd scrubbed at his hands and nails until they were sore, in order to remove the last trace of oil.

It was dark when he switched off his bike's engine and cruised to a stop outside Mary's home. He felt for the small torch he'd brought and directed it at his watch. It was twenty-five to seven. He'd been so eager not to be late that he was a little early. He'd wait a few minutes. He had to give Mary time to tell her father he was coming.

She lived in a fine detached Edwardian house, which had a small but immaculate front garden. He'd driven past a few times to look at it, but he'd never been inside. Never been inside any house of this size. The electric light was on in the hall: he could see it through the fan light over the front door. It was on in the sitting room too, but the curtains had been drawn.

He shivered and checked his watch again: just gone twenty to seven.

The waiting was churning him up; better if he got on with it now. His shoes crunched on the white gravel drive. When he found the bell push, he heard it ring deep inside the house. Then Mary's footsteps came running to open the door and he knew she'd been waiting as anxiously as he had.

'I'm not late?'

'No. Come in.' She was agitated, but he thought she'd never looked more beautiful. She stood close to whisper, her hand on his arm. 'When I told Pa you were coming he said, "What's he want to come here for? He can say all he needs to at the garage." Mum said he'd better hear you out, but he's not in a good mood.'

Jonty followed her to the sitting-room door. It was an enormous room and a good red fire glowed in the grate. Mary's mother sat beside it looking shocked. It felt a bit like walking into the lion's den.

Mr Shawcross was standing stiff and erect in the window bay, looking every inch the boss. He glowered at Jonty, his face white and devoid of expression. Nobody spoke, and Jonty knew he had to break the brooding silence.

'Good evening, Mr Shawcross,' he said. 'And Mrs Shawcross.' He nodded in Edith's direction.

Percy came to life. 'I don't like my employees walking into my house. I see more than enough of you at the garage.'

'I'm sorry, sir, but I felt I had to. Mary and I . . .'

'Neither do I want my employees socialising with my daughter. In fact I forbid it, do you hear? I forbid it. I don't want you to speak to any of my family in future.'

'Father,' Mary said, 'Jonty and I are in love. We want to get married.'

A red tide swept up her father's neck and into his face. 'I guessed it would be something like this. The answer's no. Certainly not.'

'Mr Shawcross, I beg of you to hear me out. Mary and I have been in love for more than two years. I've come to ask for your permission to marry her . . .'

Percy Shawcross bellowed, 'Welsh farm boy, don't you understand English? I've said no. Get out of my house. I don't want you here. In fact, I don't want you at my garage either, after this. You're finished as of now. You can call round on Friday afternoon to collect the pay I owe you. Is that clear?'

'Yes, sir.' Jonty hadn't expected to be dismissed so quickly and so

15

finally, though Mary had warned him. He knew he must stand his ground. 'I'm afraid, Mr Shawcross, we haven't told you the full story yet. Mary is expecting my child.'

'What?' Percy roared. 'What? You dare to come in here and tell me you've made free with my daughter? You animal, I'm disgusted . . .'

He came at Jonty with fists flying, which took the younger man by surprise. The wham against his chin made his head reel and sent him staggering back. Mrs Shawcross gave a little scream. Jonty felt his anger rising; he could see Mr Shawcross coming back to give him more. He itched to hit him, give him some of his own medicine, but he knew it was the last thing he should do.

He caught his boss's wrists, one in each of his hands, and tried to hold them away from his own chin. He didn't know what else to do. The man was like a raging bull, jumping about, kicking at him and trying to free himself. But Jonty was thirty years younger and had the greater strength.

'Pa,' Mary shouted. 'Stop it. Please stop it.'

It made him turn on her. 'You little slut, going behind my back like this. Hiding what you're doing. For two years, you say?'

'Yes. Pa, we love each other . . .'

'No daughter of mine behaves like that. You can pack your things and get out too. I'm not having your bastard child in my house. Get out, go on, you can go with him now.'

'Percy, do calm down.' Edith had tears streaming down her face as she pleaded, 'You can't put her out at this time of night. Where can she go?'

'That's no longer my problem. I've done my best for her, brought her up to be respectable, and this is how she treats me.'

Jonty felt paralysed. His hopes has not been high, but he hadn't expected things to go so badly wrong.

'Of course it's our problem.'

'No. She's not fit to be our daughter. I'm not going to give her a roof over her head and food in her mouth any longer. She's got to go.'

Jonty made a greater effort. 'Please don't be hasty, Mr Shawcross. This is very important for Mary. Can't we talk it through?'

'You cocky little pup. What is it you want to talk about?'

'Mary is not yet twenty-one and will need your permission to marry.' Jonty took a form from his pocket and offered it to his boss. 'I enquired at the register office as to what was needed and they told me that if you signed this it would make it possible.'

'I'm not signing anything.'

'But sir, with due respect, you wouldn't want her to be an unmarried mother when I'm eager to be her husband? I want to take care of her.'

'You should have thought of that sooner. As far as I'm concerned, I no longer have a daughter.'

'Sir, it would make things hard for Mary. I do ask you to reconsider. Surely she'd be better off married to me than . . .'

'No, and that's final.'

Jonty felt desperate. 'Mrs Shawcross, will you please sign it so we can be married?' He could see her cringing back into her chair and knew she was afraid.

'No, she won't.' Percy leapt forward, snatched the form from Jonty's hand and tore it into little pieces. They fluttered down on to the Turkey carpet.

Jonty saw tears welling into Mary's eyes and realised how upset she was. 'Right,' he said. 'We'd better go then. There's nothing else for it.'

She ran to him. He put his arm round her and gave her his handkerchief, telling himself he mustn't lose his nerve.

'I hope you'll allow her to come back and pack her clothes and belongings tomorrow morning? Surely you won't turn her out without so much as a coat for her back?'

There was no reply but the request wasn't refused. In the hall cloakroom, he watched her put on her everyday coat and change her shoes. He picked up the slippers she'd been wearing, and she brought her umbrella and gloves. He put an arm round her waist to lead her out to his sidecar.

'Can you take me to your lodgings?' she whispered.

It wasn't going to be that easy. 'I'll ask my landlady, but she's strict and has rules about us taking girlfriends in.'

'Where can we go then?' He saw desperation on her pretty face.

'Let's get away from here, so we can have a think.'

Jonty drove a short distance and stopped round the corner in Penny Lane where it overlooked the playing fields of Liverpool College. It was a fine night and the moon was up, bathing everything in soft silvery light. This view had soothed him on other occasions, but nothing could calm him tonight.

'I'm horrified at what I've done,' he told her. 'We've both lost our jobs and you've lost your home.' Mary had nothing but what she stood up in. He had his clothes and his motorbike.

She'd recovered a little. 'I'm proud of you,' she choked. 'You behaved like a gentleman; you kept your wits about you and stayed calm.'

'It didn't do any good though, did it?'

'I thought Pa loved me. I didn't think he'd turn on me like that.'

'I held him down, physically restrained him. That meant I took away his power. It's not the sort of thing your father would forgive.'

'But what else could you have done other than take a beating?'

'I don't know. What can we do now?'

'Our Dan has a house. He and Barbara will put me up for a night or two, I'm sure.'

Jonty managed a smile. 'That's the best thing for you. It'll give us time to organise something. Where do they live?'

'On the other side of Sefton Park. You need to turn round.'

It was a two-bedroom terrace property. Daniel welcomed them and ushered them in. Barbara made a pot of tea while Mary told them what had happened.

Jonty knew Daniel, having worked at his garage for a couple of weeks the previous summer. They'd got on well as employee and boss, but he could feel the chill when the Shawcrosses heard about the coming child.

'Mary!' There was no doubting Daniel's disapproval. 'You're in a hell of a mess, but you don't need me to tell you that.'

'Go easy on her,' Jonty said. 'It's my fault.'

Barbara said, 'Of course you must stay here, Mary, but we have only two bedrooms and I've just finished fixing up the spare as a nursery. I've got a lovely cot, but it'll be no good to you. I'm afraid there's only that sofa, but you're welcome to sleep there until you can sort out something better.'

Dan sighed. 'We've got spare pillows and blankets, but hardly enough for two. What about you, Jonty? D'you fancy the floor?'

Jonty eyed the sofa. He didn't think Dan would want him to stay with Mary, and really they only had room for one. 'I can go back to my lodgings. My landlady would probably be worried if I didn't turn up and I hadn't told her.'

'You'll be all right?' Barbara seemed anxious.

'Yes, and I'll know Mary's safe with you. I'll come back in the morning to take you to get your clothes,' he told Mary. 'What time does your father leave?'

'About eight.'

'I'll be round just after eight then.' Jonty felt shy in front of Dan. He kissed Mary's cheek and left as soon as he decently could.

He was worried stiff as he rode to his lodgings. Before he'd gone to see Percy Shawcross he knew he was in trouble, but in his worst nightmares he hadn't imagined the result could be as bad as this.

He had a little money saved but not nearly enough to support Mary and the baby. With so few garages in Liverpool, he knew it would be difficult to get another job, and worst of all, they wouldn't be able to get married. He was afraid that would really upset Mary.

He had a terrible night as he tried to work out what it would be possible to do. In the morning he got up at the usual time and ate breakfast with the other lads who lodged in the house.

When they all left for work, their landlady usually sat down to have a quiet cup of tea. This morning, Jonty poured himself another cup and went to sit by her. She was stout and well on in life but, like him, had been born in Wales and had come to Liverpool in search of work. He'd been lodging with her all the time he'd lived in Liverpool and knew her to be kind-hearted, but she took only single men. He told her he'd have to leave and why.

She said, 'I'll be sorry to see you go.'

'Do you know anyone offering lodgings for married couples?'

'Maybe.' She recited an address where she thought a double room could be rented. He was going upstairs when she called him back to give him some recent local newspapers that advertised jobs and accommodation.

He went up to his bedroom and sat on his bed to glance through them. He needed to fix something up quickly. He and Mary would be all right so long as they were together, but the cost of rooms was frighteningly high. He could see no way of keeping up payments like that unless he found a job.

But he had to go. It was time to collect Mary and take her home to get her belongings. He took the rest of the papers with him; that was something they could do together.

Mary was pale and subdued when he picked her up. Her eyes looked red as though she'd been weeping but she said she hadn't. He thought she didn't want to admit to being scared, in case it upset him. In full daylight her home looked quite grand. Mary led him through the back door and into the kitchen. A woman he'd never seen before was doing some washing.

'Morning, Mrs Dobbs,' Mary said with forced brightness. 'Is my mother in?'

'Morning, love. Yes.'

'I'm here.' Mrs Shawcross had heard them arrive. 'How are you, darling? All right?'

'Yes, Mum.' The kitchen door was firmly shut behind them, and Jonty followed the two women up the hall. 'As well as can be expected.'

There was an ornate plaster ceiling in the sitting room. He'd noticed little last night.

'Jonty took me to Dan and Barbara's; I'll be staying there for a few nights. You mustn't worry about me.'

Edith was very fraught. 'How can I help worrying? What will become of you?'

Jonty knew she blamed him; how could she not? Only now did he realise that he was taking Mary away from a home, the like of which he had no hope of providing for her.

'I'll take good care of her, Mrs Shawcross,' he said. But he wished he knew how. Perhaps they'd be all right once they could be together.

Mary said, 'I want to take all my things.'

Her mother nodded, although she still looked worried. 'Of course.'

Jonty followed them up to Mary's bedroom. It was a beautiful room with a window looking over a huge back garden surrounded by trees. Mary must really love him to be willing to leave luxury like this. Her mother was bringing in a matching set of leather suitcases.

'Will you be able to carry two big cases?' Mary asked him.

'Yes, without you in the sidecar. Or I could make more than one trip.'

'Barbara said I could leave some of my things with her for the time being.'

Jonty was kept busy running up and down stairs with cases and carrier bags. He took two loads, the first to Barbara's house, where she fitted the cases under the stairs, and the second to his lodgings, where he spread the bags out across the floor of his room.

When he went back to collect Mary, savoury smells were coming from the kitchen. It reminded him that Percy Shawcross was expected home for his lunch. Mary and her mother were hurrying now to pack the last of her clothes in order to get them away before he came.

When they finally left, Jonty had another suitcase strapped behind him and there was only just enough room for Mary to squeeze into the sidecar amongst the rest of the packages. Her mother came out to see them off. Both she and Mary were close to tears.

'You will let me know how you get on? Even if you just drop me a card now and then.' Edith was biting her lip. 'I'll want to know about the baby . . .'

'Of course, Mum.'

'I'm sorry it has to be like this,' Jonty said. 'I know it's my fault . . .'

'My husband is very strict.' Edith was looking anxiously down the road in the direction he would come. 'I wish he hadn't stopped me signing that form. If you could be married I wouldn't feel so bad.'

Jonty almost suggested he bring another copy, but she wasn't offering to go against her husband's wishes. He kick-started his bike.

'We'll be married one day,' he said. 'I love your daughter very much and I know she's making a big sacrifice for me. I'll do my very best for her, you can be sure of that.'

Edith Shawcross looked so woebegone, he leaned over to kiss her cheek.

As Jonty drove to Sefton Park, Mary could feel tears scalding her eyes. She turned her head and pretended to be watching the houses they passed, so that he wouldn't see she was upset. She felt she was being torn away from her mother, her brothers, her home and everything she knew. She couldn't imagine what her future would be like, and she was bewildered by the speed with which the change had come about.

But she loved Jonty and he loved her; she had to hang on to that. It was another sunny but blustery day, and quite chilly for early March. There were fewer people about today than there were on Sundays.

'I've brought my sandwiches.' He took the packet from his saddle bag. 'We'll find a seat and share them. There won't be enough for us both, but we'll find a café and have a cake and a cup of tea afterwards. How's that?'

'Sounds fine,' she said, trying not to let her smile waver.

'My landlady gave me some newspapers too – we can look through the adverts while we eat. I've had a quick look and there aren't any jobs advertised for motor mechanics, but perhaps there's something else I can apply for. You see if you can find us a room where we can be together. It'll have to be furnished . . . or perhaps board and lodgings to start with. We can look for something permanent later.'

Mary opened one of the newspapers and bit into a sandwich. 'There's lodgings offered here in Menlove Avenue. *To share a double, south-facing room, with half board, thirty shillings a week each.* I know where that is – it's a nice area.'

'Mary, that's expensive. I pay a pound for a room to myself and I'm provided with a packed lunch on six days and a Sunday dinner.'

'There's another advert here for digs at a pound each, but it's Upper Parliament Street, not such a good district. And another – but that's in the Dingle.'

'It scares me when I think what your house was like. You won't be happy anywhere rough.'

'I'll be happy wherever you are,' she told him. 'Mum gave me fifteen pounds. She said that was all she had. Pa gives her money to pay Mrs Dobbs's wages, but he makes her account for everything she spends on housekeeping. That will help, won't it?'

Jonty nodded. 'That should keep us going for quite a while.'

'Mum told me not to tell you. She thinks I should keep a little on one side that you don't know about. She told me to go to my Aunt Dora's if we really get down on our uppers or if I wanted to leave you.'

'You've told me now.' Jonty's lovely smile lit up his face.

'I don't want there to be secrets between us.'

'Neither do I.'

'Mum also gave me some things she said I could sell if I had to. Jewellery and some small antique bits and pieces. I think she's afraid I'm going to starve.'

'No, love, I'll make sure you don't.' Mary was afraid he was keeping up this show of confidence to cheer her, but he went on, 'I've got forty pounds saved up too. We'll share everything and manage fine for a month or two. And this afternoon I think we should go to a jeweller's in town and choose a wedding ring for you.'

'We're going to pretend we're married?'

'Mary, no respectable landlady is going to take in an unmarried couple as lodgers. Especially when the baby makes itself obvious. The only way

22

is for you to wear a wedding ring, so we'll need to get that before we go round these addresses. Come on, let's have that cup of tea. It's cold out here and we can look through the rest of the adverts in the café.'

Jonty seemed more subdued now. He insisted on ordering iced buns for them and then opened a newspaper called the *Caernarfon Herald*. Surely he was not looking for lodgings in that? She saw the outlook as bleak and was afraid he was giving up.

But the next moment his cheeks were suddenly glowing and he was bursting with vitality. 'Mary, what d'you think of this? *To rent, Glan y Mor, an 18-acre smallholding, with cottage, barn and outbuildings, Anglesey coast.*' This was the bubbling eager Jonty she loved.

'A smallholding?' she asked cautiously. 'What's that?'

'A small farm. Eighteen acres isn't enough to make a living, and possibly it isn't good land, but we could survive on it.'

Mary was trying to take it in.

'Don't you see? I could run that. Even without a job we'd survive. I can milk cows and look after sheep and pigs and hens. We'd have a cottage to ourselves, not just a couple of rooms. I could grow potatoes and vegetables and I might be able to earn a bit of cash by mending motor bikes or cars in the barn. I might even find work on other farms during busy periods. I'm sure we'd be all right if we did that.'

His rush of high spirits was infectious. Mary laughed. 'We had a holiday in Anglesey at the end of the war. It was a lovely place. And it says it's on the coast.'

'We'd have to buy a lot of stock to set ourselves up . . .'

'I can sell Mum's jewellery. I mean, once we have cows we'd always have milk, wouldn't we? It's what you know, Jonty. You could do it.'

'The agent's address is in Bangor. We can't go tomorrow because I have to collect my last wages from your father.'

'It gives their phone number.'

'Let's find a post office and I'll try phoning them. We need to know if it's still available and how much rent they want.'

It took Jonty half an hour to discover that a tenant had not yet been found for Glan y Mor and the rent being asked was reasonable. He told the agent he'd come to see it on Saturday.

CHAPTER THREE

'AT LEAST WE can make plans.' Mary was feeling better now she could see some sort of future for them. 'And this is something you really want to do.'

Jonty was in high spirits. 'I'd made up my mind, d'you know? I was going to plead with your dad to give me my job back when I saw him tomorrow.'

'You'd do that?'

'I would, if there was no other way we could survive. I'd do anything for you.'

Mary was shaking her head. 'I doubt he'd give it to you.'

'I'd have tried. I'm a good mechanic, as good as any he's got, so he might. D'you want to stay in Liverpool? Because if so I'll still try.'

'Anglesey sounds more exciting. I'd prefer to go there and get right away from all this.'

'Good. So would I.'

'Pa won't believe we can do anything without his help. He'll expect me back with my tail between my legs.'

'Over my dead body.' Jonty smiled at her. That pleased Mary; she'd seen very few stand up to her father.

'Let's get your wedding ring next,' he said. 'But I'll need to go to the post office first to draw out some money.'

'How useful your bike is,' Mary said as she climbed back in the sidecar to be whisked to the post office and on to a good jeweller's in town. She was proud to go inside on Jonty's arm and hear him ask to be shown some wedding rings.

'The best you have,' he said. 'Twenty-two carat.'

The shop assistant sat them down and spread a black velvet cloth on the counter in front of Mary. While he was fetching the rings, Mary whispered, 'Twenty-two carat is a bit extravagant, isn't it?'

'Not for a ring I hope you'll be wearing for the rest of your life.'

The shop assistant encouraged Mary to try them on, and when she'd chosen the style he found one for her in the right size. He wished them every happiness as he put it into a small box, wrapped it up and gave it to Jonty, who slid it into his pocket.

'I don't think we'll look for a room after all,' he said as they went out. 'What we need now is a boarding house where we can stay for a couple of nights.'

Mary knew one. 'In fact there are a two quite close together. Pa and I passed them every morning on the way to work. They look quite nice but I don't know what they cost.'

'This might be the nearest we'll get to a honeymoon,' Jonty told her. 'So we won't quibble. Let's go and have a look at them.'

'Either would be fine,' Mary said. 'And yesterday they both had notices saying they had vacancies.'

'First we need to get our overnight things. We'll call at your brother's now to get yours.'

Barbara insisted on making tea for them and was thrilled to hear their plans. 'Dan will be pleased for you if this comes off.'

At Jonty's lodgings he introduced Mary to his landlady, and while he was upstairs she told Mary what a nice lad Jonty was. 'Quiet,' she said. 'But the sort you can rely on.'

By the time his bag had been manoeuvred into the sidecar it was late afternoon and beginning to get dark. The day had been a emotional roller-coaster, and Mary was tired.

'I'll be glad to check in to that boarding house,' she said. 'It's really cold now.'

'There's one more thing I have to do,' Jonty told her.

She was surprised when he pulled up again in Penny Lane, opposite the playing fields of Liverpool College. Tonight the view was very different. It was almost lost in grey murk.

'Is something the matter?' she asked when she saw him dismount.

'No, but I'd like you to get out too.'

Mary shivered. There was drizzle in the air, and she'd prefer to stay where she was.

'There's something I want to say to you.' He helped her out and put an arm round her shoulders to hold her close. 'Mary, love, this isn't how I'd have chosen to start our life together.' He leaned back against the sidecar and felt in his pocket for the little package containing the wedding ring. 'You asked if we were going to pretend to be married. As far as I'm concerned it won't be pretence. Getting married is an exchange of promises, isn't it? Well, I promise you that from now on I'll treat you as my wife.'

He took her left hand and slid the ring slowly on to her third finger. 'I consider myself totally committed to you, and I want you to think of me and rely on me as you would a husband. I'll try my best to be a good one and a good father to our child. We ought to be married now because of the baby. It's what we both want, but since we can't I don't want you to be worried about it. I promise we'll make it legal when you're twenty-one. I love you and I always will.'

Mary could feel tears of happiness prickling her eyes. His lips found hers and he pulled her closer while the evening traffic streamed past behind them.

'Thank you,' she whispered. It was a wonderful moment. She was sure that nobody could be more understanding or more loving than Jonty. 'You're quite a romantic.'

He smiled. 'I don't know about that, but we aren't going to let your father spoil things for us. I want us to start as we mean to go on. We're meant to be together.'

Mary knew that was true. She could rely on Jonty.

'Right,' he said. 'Now you're wearing my ring we'll see which of those boarding houses we prefer.'

Mary directed him to the nearest. Jonty ran his bike up the drive and got off to ring the bell. When he heard footsteps coming to the door, he whispered, 'Don't forget you're Mrs Jones now.'

'As if I could!'

Mary felt a little nervous as they were shown upstairs and she was very conscious of her ring making a little bump in her leather glove. The room was plainly furnished but clean. She couldn't take her eyes away from the freshly made up double bed.

'Thank you,' Jonty told the landlady. 'I think we'll be comfortable here.'

'Do you want an evening meal? It's pork chops.'

'Yes please,' he told her, though earlier he'd suggested going out for fish and chips.

'It'll be ready in half an hour. Come down when you're unpacked. There's a nice fire in the lounge.'

Alone with Jonty in this bedroom, Mary shed her gloves and coat and opened her case to unpack.

Jonty drew the curtains. 'We must try to relax and enjoy this,' he said. It was the first time they'd shared a meal that wasn't sandwiches or buns; the first time he'd seen the gaslight glint on her ring. Now they faced their first night together in a comfortable bed. Jonty had been looking forward to it ever since he fallen in love; he'd imagined an occasion filled with passion. They did make love, but he was very tired and Mary was asleep in his arms minutes later.

They were late waking up and spent most of the morning talking over their plans. When he was getting ready to go and collect his wages from the garage that afternoon, Mary asked, 'Shall I come with you?'

He said, 'It's up to you. You don't have to unless you want to. Your father said some very hurtful things.'

'He was horribly rude to me, and worse to you. But now he's had time to calm down, he may regret it.'

'I never thought he'd throw you out like that.'

'Neither did I, but now he has, I'm not sorry.'

'You're very brave, Mary. You've given up a great deal for me.'

'I will come with you, if you don't mind,' she said. 'Why would I want to hide here by myself? From now on we do things together.'

Jonty was not looking forward to seeing Percy Shawcross again, and rather hoped he'd have left the money with Noel and be out. They all worked a week in hand so he was owed a week and a half's pay; he couldn't afford not to pick it up.

However, when they arrived at the garage, Jonty could see his boss's car parked in its usual place on the forecourt.

'He's here,' Mary said. 'And I can see Noel under that car. Oh, there're two of them in overalls, and they seem busy. Pa's had to bring someone in to take your place.'

'It's Derek Fielding from the Childwall garage,' Jonty told her.

'Come on, let's get it over with.' She took his hand and they climbed the steps to the office. Her father was writing at his desk.

'Good afternoon, Mr Shawcross,' Jonty said.

He looked up and saw Mary. 'I wondered if you'd come too,' he said, sounding none too fatherly. 'I'm not going to offer you your job back, but if you want a couple of weeks' work to tide you over, you could come in to train someone else up.'

Jonty was pleased to see Mary straighten up. 'No thank you, Pa. I've come to pick up my things. I left a book I was reading in my desk, and there's my pen. Oh, and my macintosh.' She unhooked it from the peg.

Jonty could see a wage packet on the desk and knew it was his before Percy pushed it towards him. 'Thank you,' he said, and turned to leave.

'Aren't you going to ask for your job back?'

Jonty was taken by surprise, and for a moment he didn't know what to say. He saw Mary's mouth fall open; it seemed her father regretted sacking them after all.

He knew that to have a regular wage was the easiest way out of their predicament, but Percy Shawcross would be his boss again. He'd really shown his hostility the other day, and would he ever be able to forgive Jonty for taking his daughter?

Jonty knew he was dithering. A job here would provide a definite income, while the Anglesey smallholding seemed like an exciting dream. Perhaps that's all it was, just a dream.

'Well, lad, do you want it or not?' Percy's tone was belligerent.

'No, Pa,' Mary answered for him. 'He does not, and the girl you find to do my job will have to manage without help from me.'

Jonty clattered down the stairs with his money in his pocket, feeling very proud of Mary.

The next day, as Jonty drove the bike along the coast road to Bangor, he wanted to sing. He could see Mary smiling in the sidecar and knew she was enjoying it too. Yesterday, they'd burned their boats in Liverpool and it had given him a sense of euphoria that hadn't faded since.

'You were the brave one turning your dad's offer down like that,' he told her. 'I couldn't find the guts to do it.'

They'd spent the rest of the day sorting through their belongings and now had two manageable bags with enough clothes for a week. The rest of their belongings were being kept safe, either by Barbara or by Jonty's landlady.

Today felt like a holiday. They had no idea where they would sleep tonight. They were chasing a dream. The sun was shining; it was one of the first warm days of the year. The hills rose majestically in the background while the grass in the coastal fields was greening up, and lambs were gambolling everywhere they looked. Sometimes Jonty had wide views of the sparkling sea and at others the road snaked inland and there were only tantalising glimpses to be had of it through the trees. After the drab streets of Liverpool the countryside looked beautiful.

They had no difficulty finding the estate agent's shop among the ancient granite buildings of Bangor. Since Jonty had come across the advert offering Glan y Mor for rent, he and Mary had talked of little else. Curiosity nagged at him. Surely there must be some drawback, or there'd be a stampede to rent it? As they went inside the shop he could see a flush of excitement on Mary's cheeks.

The estate agent was occupied with another client. Jonty let his eyes wander round the notices and brochures pinned on the walls. Details of Glan y Mor seemed to leap out at him. There was a sketch of the house, a pretty traditional cottage with a porch over the front door. He drew Mary's attention to it.

It was said to be partly furnished. It had a kitchen with a coal-fired cooking range and a brown stone sink with a cold water tap. Also on the ground floor was a parlour and a dairy. Upstairs there were two bedrooms. The lavatory was outside.

'No bathroom,' he said, suddenly deflated. Why hadn't he thought of that? Had he ever seen a country cottage with a proper bathroom? He was afraid Mary would dismiss the cottage out of hand, used as she was to a warm and comfortable bathroom. Even he'd been allowed a weekly bath at his lodgings.

'Won't matter,' she hissed. 'We'll manage.' He squeezed her hand.

The eighteen acres of land was said to be fenced and consisted of eight acres of permanent pasture, two of arable and the rest was hill land. There was also a garden with fruit bushes. An annual tenancy was sought.

When the other client left, the agent came over to them.

'My name is Jonty Jones. I telephoned you from Liverpool,' Jonty said. 'We're interested in renting this.'

'Ah yes, Glan y Mor. It's in a very attractive position; the land runs right down to the beach and it's quite secluded. An excellent place for holidays.'

'We'd be living there permanently,' Jonty told him. 'What condition is it in?'

'Fair. It's a traditional stone-built property. Nineteenth century. The house was dry when I saw it, but it needs redecoration, I'm afraid. It's quite a substantial place – plenty of outbuildings.'

'And the furniture?'

'To be honest, not up to much. An old couple lived there for years, and when the husband died his wife went to live with her daughter.'

'How long has it been empty?'

'A year or two now.'

Jonty felt his spirits falling. 'And the land? How long since it was farmed?'

'That would be the same, but a neighbouring farmer has been putting sheep on it. To keep the grass down, you understand.'

'Yes.' Jonty knew it would be difficult to get back into good heart if it had been neglected for any length of time. 'We'd like to see it,' he said.

'Certainly, but I'm afraid it's rather a long way for me to come with you. I'll give you the key so you can look round yourself. You'll be sure to bring it back?'

'Of course.'

'I've got a little map of the area somewhere. Yes, here we are. It'll help you find the place.'

'Thank you. Would it be possible for us to get a night's lodging near by?'

'Well, I'm sure you could in Beaumaris or Benllech, and possibly nearer. In the holiday season there'd be no problem, but now it might be more difficult.'

'We're going to try,' Jonty said. 'All right if we keep the key until Monday?'

Mary bought two pork pies and some apples before they set off again and Jonty bought a copy of the Anglesey newspaper. 'If there's a local market it'll give the prices of sheep and cattle.'

Having learned more about Glan y Mor, he was feeling less hopeful about the future. He wondered if they'd have been wiser to accept the offer Mary's father had made.

They crossed the bridge and ran through several villages of grey granite cottages. The land looked less fertile here: perhaps a little bleak and windswept, and there were fewer trees. Mary had the map. He could hear her trying to tell him something but her voice was snatched away by the wind and the noise of the engine. 'What?'

'There it is up ahead,' she shouted.

The first sight of it took his breath away. Above them on a small headland, outlined against the sky, he could see the cluster of grey stone outbuildings, the cottage and the barn of Glan y Mor. There was an iron gate on the side of the road and a steep and rocky path climbing the hill.

'We have to go through there.' Mary scrambled out to open it. Jonty could see now that there wasn't a proper road up to the house; that could be one reason nobody wanted to rent it. The higher up the hill they went, the steeper the path. Now he could see the blue sea beyond the buildings stretching to infinity. It was a magnificent position but a real pull up; at last he chugged into the farmyard and stopped the engine. Mary was out of the sidecar in an instant and twirling round trying to take in everything at once. There was silence apart from the call of gulls carried on the breeze and the sound of the waves running up the beach.

'It's lovely.' There was awe in Mary's voice. 'Absolutely lovely. To live here would be paradise.'

Jonty could not have agreed more, but he was anxious about the state of the house. The key he'd been given was large and ornate. It was hard to turn in the lock, but the door creaked open at last.

It was colder inside than out and rather dark because the small windows were dirty and the curtains half drawn. The stone sink looked ancient. It was large and crusted with dust, dirt and dead spiders. He could see their webs everywhere he looked. He'd hoped it might be better.

'It'll clean up.' Mary turned on the solitary tap over the sink. Water gushed out, clearing a route to the plughole.

'At least there's water laid on.'

'Jonty, we can make this comfortable.' Mary's buoyant mood pleased and surprised him. He'd been afraid she'd be disappointed.

Within minutes they were rushing all over the house trying to see it all: opening every door, opening every cupboard and prodding at the sagging mattresses on the beds upstairs.

'I'd love to see all the outbuildings.' Mary's eyes were shining. 'But I'm hungry. Let's have a picnic here. Our first meal in our own home.' She ran her fingers over the big kitchen table that at one time had been scrubbed. 'I like this.' She laughed when she saw the trails she'd made in the dust and went to the sink to rinse her hands.

'It's filthy,' Jonty said. 'I doubt anyone's lived here for donkey's years. The agent said one or two but I reckon it's more than that.'

31

He spread the newspaper he'd bought in Bangor over one end. 'We'll use this as a tablecloth for now. Are you sure about this place?'

'I'm certain, Jonty. In the summer it'll be lovely here.'

'No electricity or gas. One cold tap and it's well water. The lavatory is a bucket down the garden.'

'I'll get used to all that. It's all ours – we can be independent. What could be better?'

'We haven't seen any shops or a school or . . .'

'They'll be in that village we went through. It isn't that far.'

'I grew up in a house where we had to carry our water from a stream, but you've had all mod cons. I don't know whether . . .'

Mary laughed. 'The alternative is one or two rooms in a back street in Liverpool. And we'd have to find work before we could afford that.'

'Yes,' Jonty said. 'Oh, I'm so relieved and pleased you feel like this.'

His eye was caught by an article on farming in the newspaper he'd brought. While Mary opened the bag containing the pork pies, he lifted up the page and began to read.

He'd never considered the economics of British farming as a whole, but now it was spelt out for him. Agriculture had been in decline for more than forty years except during the Great War, when prices of everything had doubled and trebled and scarcity of food meant that the country clamoured for everything the farmers could grow. For a short time farmers had enjoyed unparalleled prosperity, but now that inflationary bubble had been pricked; interest rates were being put up and government spending cut back. Prices were falling because nobody could afford them and cheaper food was being brought in from abroad.

In the markets, livestock was either failing to sell or bringing only a fraction of the price it had realised during the war. It was said that army officers returning to civilian life had used their savings to set up chicken farms and smallholdings and were finding it impossible to make a living. The article forecast a general full-scale depression, and that land which had been farmed for centuries would be abandoned.

Jonty pushed it in front of Mary. 'Now I understand why the rent here is so low.'

She surprised him again. 'If the price of cows and sheep is also low, that's an advantage to us when we want to buy, isn't it?'

'Yes, and we aim to feed ourselves on what we produce, so it's not all bad news. Though I'm hoping we'll have some surplus to sell.'

When they'd eaten, they went out to look round the outbuildings. Some were in a tumbledown state, though others appeared sound. There was wood in the woodshed and hay in the barn, but the hay was so old it was returning to dust.

Jonty strode round the fields. All the arable land was a mass of couch grass and docks. Some of the permanent pasture had fared better and there were a few rams on one field. On another, lower lying, rushes were coming up all over and bushes of gorse were flourishing, beautiful now with yellow flowers but a wicked waste of good land.

On the hill land, there were great outcrops of rock pushing through in places, and the layer of soil covering the rest seemed thin. A little scrubby grass was growing between the clumps of heather and bracken. It wasn't good news, but as he became infected with Mary's optimism Jonty felt an overpowering desire to put this little homestead back into good heart.

'We'll take it on.'

A surge of enthusiasm was sweeping him along. He could turn this into a productive little property. It would take energy and care, but he'd been brought up on a small hill farm and kept off school during busy harvest times to help. In the last years, when his uncle had been too ill to work, he'd been in charge of it all and he'd made a profit. Not a big one, but enough for them to survive.

He knew what to look for in a good cow. He'd buy two so they would not be without milk when one went dry before calving. He knew the best stock provided twice the profit of inferior animals, while they ate much the same amount and took only the same care.

Mary was just as keen as he was and it was getting dusk before he could persuade her to leave. They'd seen an inn in the nearby village of Moelfre and went there to ask if they could get a bed for the night. It turned out to be just a pub selling drinks and the answer was no, but they were directed along the village street to a house where a war widow took in paying guests.

They spent the evening in front of a spitting wood fire discussing plan after plan designed to put the smallholding to rights. Jonty couldn't sleep when they snuggled down in their feather bed. This was the biggest adventure of his life, and he could feel excitement raging through him.

They returned to Glan y Mor the next day to make lists of everything they'd have to buy. The first and most urgent need was to make it possible to live in the house. On Monday they went back to Bangor to see the agent and tell him they wanted to take it. They signed the lease and paid the first month's rent there and then.

They went round the shops after that, buying brooms and buckets, soap and washing soda. Mary pulled Jonty to a halt in front of a hairdresser's shop.

'I want to have my hair cut. Pa forbade it, but this bun is so old-fashioned, and it's a lot of work putting it up. What d'you think?'

'It's pretty hair,' he said regretfully. 'But you must do what you want.'

'It'd be short now if I'd had my way. A modern bob, then. I'll see if they can do it now.'

While he waited for her, Jonty noticed the next-door shop window was displaying furniture. He went in to have a look round.

Mary seemed transformed when she came out with short hair. 'It suits you,' he said. 'Yes, I think I like it.'

'It feels so much lighter.' Mary shook her head. 'I feel I've cut free from Pa.'

He took her arm. 'I've been in here.' He led her to the furniture shop. 'We'll have to have a new mattress. Come and see what they've got.'

They bought a flock mattress, added pillows and sheets and blankets, and were told it could all be delivered four days hence.

'We'll be keeping hens, and if I can find a market for them we'll also fatten geese and ducks for Christmas. That means we'll be plucking them, and in time we'll be able to make a feather bed to top it off,' Jonty said happily.

When the shops were closing for the night they began to look for lodgings. They passed a cinema and noticed that *The Four Horsemen of the Apocalypse*, starring Rudolph Valentino, was showing that night.

'I'd love to see it,' Mary breathed.

'Then we will. Tonight we'll treat ourselves. It's been a big day for us – we've rented not only a house but the means to support ourselves.' They found a boarding house offering bed and breakfast in a side street, and bought themselves fish and chips before going to the pictures.

They got up early the next morning and went back to the shops with their list. They ordered pots and pans, knives and forks and two easy chairs, to be delivered with the bedding, together with a few basic groceries, and then went back to Glan y Mor.

'This is like playing at house,' Mary laughed. 'It's great fun.'

The kitchen range appeared to provide an open fire and a means of cooking. There was an oven on one side and a tank that was meant to supply hot water on the other. From the chimney hung a hook on which a kettle could be swung over the blaze, and for saucepans there were several trivets which could be moved backwards and forwards over the flames.

'Let's try lighting a fire,' Jonty said. He started it with old hay, a few sticks and the wood in the shed. A few lumps of coal had been left by the previous tenant too. Soon it was drawing well and blazing up the chimney.

'It works. We'll be able to cook on it!' Jonty was thrilled.

'It's a bit shabby, and we forgot to get some blacklead,' Mary said.

'We're like kids with a new toy,' Jonty laughed. 'Once the bedding's delivered we'll be able to move in. It's beginning to feel like home already.'

'I can't wait.' Mary rubbed her palms together with satisfaction.

CHAPTER FOUR

A S FAR AS Jonty was concerned, going to bed with Mary was the best of times. Here in the boarding house he had to close their door carefully and make no noise. How much better it would be when they had their own home. He'd only to see her shyly unfastening her blouse to feel again the urge to show her how much he loved her. Deep in the feather bed Mary left him in no doubt that she loved him just as much.

Afterwards he'd hold her in his arms and they'd talk in whispers about their plans for the next day.

'We're spending so much,' Mary worried.

'It can't be helped at the moment. Once we're in our own place we'll be able to cut our expenses.'

'We're going to run out of money if we aren't careful. You want to buy livestock . . .'

'It'll be another two days before we get the mattress and can move in. I think we should go to Liverpool tomorrow to fetch our things.'

'We must find out how to sell the bits and pieces Mum gave me.'

'I hate to think of you doing that.' Jonty was frowning. 'They were given to you, to provide funds in time of need, but I'm afraid we'll have to. We'd better go to Barbara's tomorrow to get them.'

Barbara was all smiles and delighted to see them. They spent an hour drinking tea and telling her all they'd managed to achieve.

'I'm so pleased you're getting sorted,' she said. 'Dan and I have been worried about you, and so has your mum, Mary. Can I tell her about you? I'm sure she's desperate for news.'

'Of course,' Mary said. 'And Pa?'

'Dan says he's been in a foul temper since you went. He can't be civil to anybody.' She sighed. 'I just wish something was happening for me. I'm still waiting, as you can see.'

'It'll happen before too much longer, you'll see,' Mary told her. 'Now, the reason we're here is that Mum gave me some things I could raise money on and we need to do that now.' She dragged her belongings out from under the stairs and opened the bag in which she'd packed her mother's gifts. She, took out the silver trinket box which contained the jewellery, lifted out the pieces one by one, and handed them round.

'I'd like to see you wearing this ring.' Jonty examined it then pushed it on to her finger. It was a large octagonal Ceylon sapphire flanked by two graduated baguette diamonds. 'It's magnificent,' he breathed. 'You must only sell that as a last resort.'

'There's also a sapphire brooch,' Mary said. The blue stone was square cut and surrounded by rose diamonds. 'Mum said it was nineteenth century.'

'Somebody in your family was fond of sapphires.'

'My grandmother, I think.' Mary hesitated. 'I don't know whether I'd ever wear them.'

'I would if they were mine,' Barbara told her promptly.

'Mum says she never has; she's frightened of losing them. There are more rings here, an emerald one and this diamond solitaire. They're both quite handsome.'

'It's all lovely,' Barbara said. 'What a pity you have to part with it.'

'You don't have to, Mary,' Jonty protested. 'Not yet anyway.'

'There's some silver, too.' Mary went back to the bag and spread the pieces out on Barbara's dining table. 'These things are wine coasters – we'd never use them. Mum said they are George III and might be worth a bit.'

'A pair,' Jonty marvelled.

Mary unwrapped a silver cigarette case, a small silver clock, several fancy serving spoons and two snuff boxes, one of which was gilt.

Barbara was trying to help. 'There's a jewellery shop in Dale Street with a notice in the window saying they'll buy from you and give the best prices.'

'The trouble is,' Jonty said, 'we don't know what they're worth.'

'Take them round several shops. Most jewellers will buy – see who offers the most.'

'Right,' Jonty said. 'Let's sell some of this silver. We could put a few pieces in an auction, and also try that shop you were talking about to get some ready cash.'

Barbara made them lunch, and then Jonty packed Mary's cases into the sidecar, and stuffed it tight with her coats and shoes. That meant she'd have to ride pillion. Barbara insisted she borrow a pair of Dan's trousers rather than wear a skirt.

When they were leaving she gave Mary a little parcel. 'A present for your baby,' she said. Jonty saw a flush of pleasure run up Mary's cheeks as she unwrapped a baby's nightdress.

'I had a bit of white flannelette left over after I'd made all the nightdresses mine will need,' Barbara told her. 'So I thought of you.'

'It's lovely – the very first thing towards my baby's layette. Thank you.'

'You can start making more once we're settled in,' Jonty told her, feeling rather touched.

Going back through central Liverpool they arranged for the wine coasters and the snuff boxes to be sold at auction. And to raise some immediate cash, they sold the fancy dessert spoons to the Dale Street jeweller.

The following day Jonty ran Mary up to Glan y Mor before returning to Liverpool. 'If I go alone, I'll be able to pack the sidecar as well as strap baggage to the pillion seat and carrier,' he said. 'I'll collect the last of your things from Barbara's and bring everything back, so we'll have all our possessions with us.'

Mary was quite content. 'I can't wait to get on with the cleaning and polishing,' she said. 'I want everything to be shipshape when we move in.'

She threw open all the windows to let the fresh sea air banish any scent of age and decay and spring-cleaned as hard as she could. When she was too tired to do more, she went out into the fitful spring sunshine. There was still much to explore around her new home. She took with her the small map the agent had given them, hoping to pick out some of the local landmarks.

Once she left the shelter of the house and buildings, a blustery wind tossed at her hair. She climbed the gentle rise towards the headland, glad that the wind was off the sea. Had it been gusting from the other direction, she feared it might have blown her over the edge.

She peered gingerly down the sheer rocky cliff to where the sea was crashing and foaming against the rocks at the foot. It was a wonderful viewpoint, but she had to sit down on the thin wispy grass to feel safe. Out at sea, a few of the waves were being whipped up till they had lacy white tops. There were a few fishing boats out there and on the horizon she could see a large passenger vessel heading towards the Mersey and the port of Liverpool.

Below her to the left was a lovely beach of golden sand that seemed to stretch for a couple of miles. That was marked on the map as Hafren Sands but as the cliffs were high in that direction there was no quick way down to it. Some of the larger farms were named on the map too. Their nearest neighbour seemed to be Plas Hafren: a substantial white house under a blue slate roof, with a lot of farm buildings huddled round it. To reach that, they'd have to go down the track towards the road, halfway to where it forked and wound down towards Hafren Sands.

On her right Mary could see a small cove where the waves were running up a beach mainly of shingle. From here, she could see that their own land ran right down to the cove. Impossible to climb down this cliff to the beach, but from the house there was a grassy slope and a narrow path running down to it.

She got to her feet, and, wanting a closer look, went down. A smaller headland on the far side cut off the view along the coast, so they had their own, totally secluded little cove. Mary felt very lucky to have found a home in such a beautiful spot.

Here she was sheltered from the wind and in the full sun. She was tempted to look out her bathing costume, but it was still quite chilly. Instead, she climbed back up to the house to check on the curtains from the kitchen and what was to be their bedroom, which she had washed earlier and hung on the line she had rigged up in the yard. It was perfect drying weather, and they were now ready to go back.

Everything in the cottage was as clean as she could make it. Jonty had promised to bring blacklead back with him and he'd talked of painting the kitchen. Perhaps they could do with a little more furniture, but for the moment Mary was content with the state of her new home.

The morning after that, the new furnishings and kitchenware were delivered, with many complaints from the van driver about the state of the track up to the house. They laughed at him as they made up their bed together.

'Now we have our own home,' Mary chortled. She was thrilled and could see Jonty was too.

It was another sunny day, and the wind had dropped. There were no white horses out at sea and it was much warmer than it had been yesterday.

'I'm going to put my bathing suit on,' Mary told him, 'and I'll show you our private beach. To celebrate, we could have our first swim.'

Jonty found a pair of old shorts and they walked down together. 'I'm delighted with Glan y Mor,' he said. 'There's so much more here than I expected.'

Where the sand was dry it was warm. They spread out their towels and sat down to sunbathe, but the sea was Mediterranean blue and beckoned. Jonty couldn't wait. 'Let's have a swim.'

Mary raced him down to the water's edge and let a small wave lap over her toes. 'It's cold,' she gasped, jumping back. 'Really cold, ice cold.'

Jonty ran past her and dived headlong into the waves some yards out and began to swim. 'Come on, it's lovely once you're in,' he called.

Mary held her breath and edged in slowly, until eventually the water was deep enough for her to swim. But it was so cold they were both soon back on the beach towelling themselves dry, and making all haste to get back to the house and into their clothes.

'It's only March. It'll be really gorgeous when summer comes.'

'But I'll have a bump as big as Barbara's by then,' Mary protested.

'No need to feel embarrassed about that. There'll be only me and you here.'

When they were dressed again, Mary couldn't stop her teeth chattering. She shivered. 'I still feel chilled.'

'I'll light the fire now to warm us up,' Jonty said. Once it was going, it boiled the kettle for tea very quickly, and they sat round it until they felt thoroughly comfortable again.

'I'll be cooking our supper in this oven tonight,' Mary laughed. 'I hope I'll manage.' She scrubbed two large potatoes and put them inside to bake. Jonty had bought sausages in the village to go with them.

It was only when Mary opened the oven door an hour or so later to put the sausages in that she found the potatoes had barely warmed through.

'It's a slow oven,' she said. 'We'll never get our supper at this rate.'

Jonty used the enormous poker to push burning wood and hot coals under the oven and up the side. It warmed up after that but they were growing hungry. Mary put the potatoes in a saucepan and boiled them for fifteen minutes, then Jonty put them directly into the hot ash. Another half-hour and the sausages were just beginning to sizzle. Mary got out her new frying pan and transferred them to that. They were browning nicely in a minute or two.

'We could fry a couple of eggs to go with them,' Jonty suggested. 'I've got an appetite like a horse now.'

'Well, now we know we need to get the fire banked up well before we start to use the oven,' Mary said. 'At least we'll understand the technique next time.'

They ate on their knees sitting in the new easy chairs in front of the fire. 'It's lovely to be here alone with you,' she said.

When they came to washing up afterwards in what they hoped would be hot water from the range, they discovered it was barely lukewarm and needed a kettle of boiling water to top it up.

'We'd need a fire halfway up the chimney to get hot water as well as a hot oven,' Jonty said. 'Or I'll need to push the fire to the other side when we want a bath.'

'Not tonight.' Mary had been aware of a slight backache while they'd been eating, and now she had a dragging feeling in her abdomen too.

When she told Jonty, he said, 'Time for you to try out our new bed. Perhaps you've been doing too much. Go straight up now.'

Before doing so, Mary took the torch and went down the garden to the lavatory in the outhouse. It came as a complete shock to find she was bleeding. She shivered with fear. What did it mean? She was three and a half months gone. She rushed back to the house and threw herself into Jonty's arms.

'What's happening? Is something wrong?' he asked in alarm.

She told him.

'Come to bed, love. You must lie down. Perhaps if you can go to sleep, it'll stop.'

Mary got undressed and tried to sleep, but she was anxious and restless. The pain was getting worse not better and so was the bleeding. It was two o'clock in the morning when Jonty decided he must take her to hospital.

Jonty was exhausted and sick with worry about Mary. He'd not slept either; how could he when he knew she was in pain and trying not to show it? It had gone three by the time they reached the maternity hospital in Bangor and he had to ring the bell twice. When it was answered by the night sister, and he tried to explain Mary's symptoms, they were directed to another hospital across town.

He'd referred to Mary as his wife, given her name as Jones and claimed to be her next of kin. He wasn't sure whether he was breaking the law or not by doing so, but there was no one to challenge it.

At last a nurse led Mary away, saying she'd wake the doctor to see her. Jonty had been shown to this soulless room to wait. It was an hour or more later and dawn was breaking before the doctor came to tell him that Mary had had a miscarriage. He offered his sympathy and said they'd be keeping her in because she'd need a minor operation to clear out her womb.

When Jonty asked the nurse if he might see her before he went, he was asked to wait a little longer until they'd taken her up to a ward.

Jonty waited. It was less than two weeks since her father had sacked him and thrown Mary out. He couldn't decide whether he was relieved or sorry about the miscarriage, and wondered if it would have happened anyway. Or had it been because Mary was suddenly scrubbing floors and rushing round instead of sitting at a desk? It had been an anxious time for them; Mary must have felt on a knife edge, and perhaps he'd made love to her too often? Could that have caused it? But now, just when he'd got used to the idea of having a baby and they were settled in their own home, Mary had lost it.

When they let him in the ward, the nurse told him he could stay no more than five minutes because they needed to serve breakfast. Mary was inert on the bed, her face almost as white as the pillowcase, and she had been weeping. Her cold fingers groped for his. He felt full of love for her.

'I've lost it. I've lost our baby.' She was biting her lips to hold back her grief. He could see she was counting it a major loss. 'Just when we'd got ourselves organised, with a home of our own to bring it up.'

When he was leaving, she smiled wanly up at him from her pillow. 'I'd got used to the idea. I'd decided I'd rather like us to have a baby.'

He said gently, 'Don't you worry, we'll have plenty of time to make more babies. We've got our whole lives in front of us. When you're over this, and we've got our little farm producing food, we'll try again. Next time, we'll be ready.'

Jonty felt responsible. He loved her and wanted to take care of her, and yet he'd caused mayhem in her life. They'd both been shocked and rather horrified when she'd found she was pregnant, and as far as he was concerned, he'd have been over the moon if this had happened then. Mary might have been too, but apparently not now. Everything in their lives had changed over the last two weeks and it seemed everything was going to go on changing.

Jonty rode home feeling shattered after his sleepless night. Mary had given up so much for him and all he'd brought her was trouble. It was on his conscience that a little bit of him was relieved she'd lost the baby, while she was grieving.

Really he wanted to have Mary to himself for a long time, but he'd promised, and yes, if she still wanted it, they could think of a family later. He stopped to buy white distemper to paint the kitchen as a surprise for her homecoming.

After sleeping for two hours he got up and started painting. When he could do no more, he blackleaded the range. Without Mary, he felt lost. He worked on and on, not wanting to sit down and think of what he'd done to her. Her childhood home had been fresh and smart; he felt he owed it to her to make this house look as good as it could.

The next day at visiting time he returned to Bangor. Mary was still feeling dopey from the anaesthetic and kept drifting off. She couldn't really talk to him. He sat holding her hand while she dozed; even with mauve shadows under her eyes, he thought she'd never looked more beautiful.

On the way home, he bought a red and black rug to put down in front of their fire. When the painting was finished, it would add just the right touch.

He worked almost without stopping for the next few days because he didn't want to leave anything for Mary to do when she came home. On the last night, he stayed up late and finished painting both the kitchen and their bedroom.

On the way to the hospital to fetch her, he bought lamb chops and a cake. He wanted to celebrate her return. Once dressed, Mary looked more her old self. He carried her case and put one arm round her shoulders as he led her out to his bike.

'You've had a difficult time since you threw in your lot with me,' he told her. 'I hope you have no regrets.'

'No.' She smiled. 'No regrets.'

'I've missed you terribly this week. I couldn't stop thinking about how I took you from a comfortable home. Your parents would probably want you back now there's to be no baby.'

'Mum perhaps, but Pa wouldn't. He never relents. You must know that?'

'Couldn't your mum persuade him?'

'Nobody can persuade him. He has his own ideas and sticks to them. Anyway, I don't want to go back and share that office with him. I'm looking forward to helping you work on the farm.'

He pushed open the front door thinking of the pleasure she'd take in the freshly painted kitchen, but the first thing Mary saw was the envelope on the mat addressed to her.

'It's from Dan,' she said, tearing it open eagerly. 'He says Barbara's had a son weighing eight pounds four ounces and they're both well.' Her lip quivered. 'He's to be called Simon.'

Jonty held her tight. 'Your turn will come, love. I promise you.'

With the cottage in good order, Jonty turned his attention to his eighteen acres. He paced over the land several times planning how best to use it. The fields were divided by drystone walls that needed repairing in several places, but more urgently, if he was to grow their vegetables this summer and feed his animals next winter, he needed to plough and plant. But how could he do that without a horse?

Then there were the outbuildings. Before he could buy stock they would have to be cleaned out and repaired. There was a huge and ancient midden with a crust of green moss on top. He'd need to get that out on the land to clear the yard, though by now most of the nutrients would have been washed out by the rain. He mucked out the cow shed and found that, apart from broken hinges on the door, it was in fair condition.

He'd seen in the local paper that regular stock sales were held in Llangefni. He needed to find out what animals were being sold and what prices they made. He took Mary with him to give her a break from working in the cottage.

Mostly the cattle were Welsh Blacks, a breed he wasn't familiar with. His uncle had kept shorthorns and he'd prefer to have them. There were one or two in the sale but, with scarcity value, they were fetching higher prices. More, he thought, than they were worth.

A wiry man in his mid-thirties came up and introduced himself as Ted Evans. He wore a cloth cap, a tweed jacket with a tie and very serviceable wellingtons.

'I've seen you coming and going,' he told him. 'I'm your nearest neighbour; my land adjoins yours. The house is half a mile or so down the road – the white house. Plas Hafren.'

'Ah yes, I've seen it. It's a big farm, isn't it?'

'Just on three hundred and fifty acres. Some would say not all that big.'

Jonty knew it was big for this area and would be sufficient to make a good living. 'I've seen your cattle out on your fields. A breeding herd?'

Ted Evans told him he kept a pedigree Jersey cow to provide milk for the house, though his main herd was of Welsh Blacks. They brought up their own calves, which he then sold.

'Jerseys would be good for you,' he said. 'They're small and eat less than most breeds, and they're good milkers too: quiet and easy to manage.'

He told Jonty about a farmer near Holyhead who bred pedigree Jersey heifers for sale and that the price was usually less than for heavier animals. Jonty kept him talking and learned a great deal about prices and local conditions. He explained about his need to plough and confessed that he had no horse or equipment.

'I don't want to buy a horse I'd have to feed because I won't have enough work for it.'

Ted Evans said he was in much the same position. 'I got rid of my horses two years ago because times were hard and looking after them was work and expense. I bought a second-hand tractor from a firm in Holyhead, but it's broken down. I asked them to send someone out to mend it last week, but nobody has turned up.'

Jonty had no experience of agricultural tractors, but while he was in the army he'd worked on several different types of heavy engines. 'I think I could get it going for you,' he said. 'I'll do the job for nothing, if you'll let me borrow it. I want to plough two strips, one to plant potatoes and vegetables and the other for oats and mangels to feed stock.'

Ted Evans seemed pleased to agree. 'Will you come down and look at it tomorrow?'

'What about this afternoon?' Jonty wanted to get started on his land.

He found the tractor had come with a works manual, and within the hour he had it ticking over nicely. Delighted, Ted showed him a piece of cutting equipment that had ceased to work properly at the end of last season, and he repaired and serviced that too, ready for the next harvest.

Jonty was as well pleased as its owner as he drove the tractor and plough up to Glan y Mor ready to start work on his own land the next morning. Later that week, he took Mary on a trip to Holyhead and found the farm where Jerseys were bred.

The owner had two heifers for sale at the moment and as he liked the look of them, Jonty bought them both. They were delivered two weeks later when the spring grass was pushing through. He was glad he was starting at the beginning of the summer so that he could grow most of their foodstuff before winter set in.

The cows were docile and friendly and Mary took to them, so he taught her to milk them. They found an old churn in the dairy and after much scalding decided it was usable. Mary learned to make butter and what she had spare they were able to sell to the grocer in the village. Jonty bought some pullets on the point of lay, and soon they had a few surplus eggs to sell too. Mary also mastered the art of cooking in the range and began to turn out cakes and pastries.

On fine days, late in the afternoon when they'd exhausted themselves with work, they'd put on their bathing costumes and swim in their little cove. The sea remained fairly cold but they grew used to it. When it was wet, they'd pull on wellingtons and macintoshes and walk along the shingle picking up driftwood or anything else that would burn on their range. There was often a high wind, and on those nights they'd fall asleep to the sound of it howling round their chimneys and hurling the waves to crash against the rocky cliff.

Jonty and Mary worked the smallholding together and took pleasure in all they did. They found they didn't need to see much of their neighbours; they were all in all to each other and very happy. Nevertheless, they gradually got to know the people living near by. Some were quarrymen, some were farmers and many were inshore fishermen who earned their livelihood from the sea.

One, John Jarvis, walked up and asked for Jonty's help to repair the engine in his boat. He'd heard from Ted Evans that he was a good mechanic. Jonty obliged and, knowing that fishermen were finding it hard to make a living, refused payment, asking instead for an occasional gift of fish from John's catch. From then on, ten-year-old Howell Jarvis brought up a few herrings, mackerel or crabs from time to time. Jonty let it be known he could repair and service motor bikes, cars and most other engines, and found a little work that way.

As it became harder to make a living from the land, many farmers' children moved to the towns and cities, hoping to find work there. During busy periods of sheep-shearing and haymaking, Jonty was able to get casual work, often for payment. From Ted Evans he asked for no money, just the occasional loan of his equipment.

The smallholding was doing well. They were feeding themselves and had surplus to sell to pay for the things they couldn't produce. They both thought it was an idyllic life but Mary wanted a baby to make it complete.

'I think we should wait,' Jonty said. 'To have one now – well, legally it would be illegitimate and you know what a stigma that is.'

'Yes.' Mary sighed. 'But you said we must consider ourselves married. Don't you remember? It was the day you put this wedding ring on my finger and gave me your solemn promise.'

'Mary love, of course I remember.'

'I think of you as my husband.'

'I know, and I think of you as my wife, but all the same, to try for a baby now? Don't you think it would be wiser to wait until we've made it legal?'

'Wiser, yes, but you said we mustn't let Pa spoil our lives. I'd really love a baby now. Every letter I have from Barbara is about her baby and now she's pregnant again.'

'Mary love, I know how you feel, but . . .'

'Everybody here thinks we're married, so why not?'

Jonty was persuaded against his better judgement. 'If that's what you really want.'

By the spring of 1922, Glan y Mor had thirty sheep grazing on the hill land. Two Welsh Black calves had been bought to fatten on the milk Mary and Jonty had spare and two large white pigs were feeding on the buttermilk. Jonty planned to make one into bacon and sell the other. The fifty white Leghorn pullets were laying well and the two Jersey cows had been named Bluebell and Buttercup and seemed almost part of the family.

When Mary found she was pregnant again she was overjoyed. 'It'll make us a real family,' she said happily, and found time to crochet a shawl and sew tiny garments. They were both looking forward to having a child, and this time she was careful not to do too much or get overtired. Nevertheless, at three and a half months she suddenly found she was having another miscarriage. Mary wept and this time it took her longer to get over it.

Jonty was equally disappointed. 'We have everything else we could possibly want,' he said. 'We're happy here, aren't we?'

'Yes, I love being with you, but . . .'

'I know how much you want a baby, Mary. But we're still young. Sooner or later it'll happen, you'll see. We've all the time in the world.'

Mary nodded. 'We just have to be patient, don't we?'

CHAPTER FIVE

Summer 1922

IN MID-MAY, Mary received a letter from Barbara announcing the birth of a second son, who was to be called Tim. Since she herself was pregnant for the third time, she was able to write back and congratulate her sister-in-law without any of the envy she might otherwise have felt.

Her mother's birthday was in early June. Mary sent her a card and a letter with all her news. She'd sent cards each Christmas and birthday and had written regularly, but although her mother wrote too, Mary felt she heard more news of her parents from Barbara. Edith doted on her grandsons but had been unwell for some time with shingles. Percy was driving Daniel and his brothers harder than ever, and the family business was thriving.

Mary's birthday fell on the first of July and this year she would be twenty-one.

'You haven't forgotten we'll be able to get married then?' Jonty teased.

'Of course I haven't. But everybody here thinks we already are, so it'll have to be a very quiet wedding.'

'Let's do it quite soon.'

'That suits me. I don't want to look too pregnant on my wedding day.'

He smiled. 'But you're telling everybody you are. I wish we could have the wedding in Liverpool so you could have your family round you, but the cows need milking twice a day and there're the other animals to think of . . .'

'It'll have to be in Bangor, won't it?'

'That's a bit close. I've been thinking, if we arranged it in Llandudno on a Saturday afternoon, Dan might bring Barbara and your mother and meet us there. Would you like to write and suggest it?'

'It would be lovely if they could be with us,' Mary said wistfully.

49

'How about making it the first Saturday after your twenty-first?'

'Great. That'll give us the best part of a week for celebrations.'

Mary was bubbling with excitement when Barbara wrote to say Dan had asked Pa for the whole day off and been given it, though he hadn't told Percy why he wanted it. They would bring her mother too. Edith thought she was being taken on a trip to the seaside. Dan thought it wiser not to tell her the truth, because if Pa got wind of it he might forbid any of them to go. He was becoming more autocratic by the minute.

'Let's see if we can arrange to have it in the register office at midday. That will give us all enough time to get there.'

'Dan's got a car now,' Mary said. 'So it shouldn't be difficult.'

'And they're buying their own house on mortgage,' Jonty reminded her. 'Three bedrooms and a garden.'

'I'm not envious about that.'

'Good. I'll book a table at the Grand Hotel for us to have lunch afterwards.'

'Won't that be expensive?'

'We've got a good crop of early lambs to sell and prices aren't too bad just now. I think we can afford to splash out on our wedding day. I shall wear my one and only suit – it hasn't seen the light of day for ages but it's still all right – but I want you to buy yourself a new outfit.'

'I have my blue dress. I've always liked that, and . . .'

'No. I'm going to take you into Bangor on your birthday and you must choose a new one.'

'Are you sure? I mean . . .'

'I'm certain. And I'd like to buy you a camera too. You did say you'd like one.'

'Jonty! A camera is a luxury. Surely that's madness?'

'There's method in my madness, love. We'll be able to take our own wedding photographs, and we'll take some pictures of Glan y Mor – the lovely scenery and the animals – to send to your family. I hope they'll show them to your Pa. I want him to know you have a good life with me.'

'I have a wonderful life with you.'

'We have a wonderful life together.' He smiled. 'And I want to make it legal now the law allows it.'

'And it can be done well before the baby is born.'

*

By now they were growing their own potatoes, together with other vegetables to cook and more to put in salads. They had gooseberry and blackcurrant bushes and were hoping their raspberry canes would fruit. They'd discovered they also had apple trees but they'd come to nothing: the wind off the sea was too strong. However, a plum tree and a damson tree had survived and this year looked like bearing a fair crop.

Mary enjoyed her shopping trip to Bangor. For her wedding dress, she chose a simple style in cream silk, and a straw hat to wear with it decorated with blue flowers. Jonty bought an inexpensive camera and plenty of film, and as a treat they stopped on the way home for afternoon tea in the big hotel in Beaumaris.

'So elegant and so many lovely cakes to choose from.' Mary sighed with pleasure. 'I've had a lovely birthday. Thank you.'

On their wedding day Mary heard Jonty getting up at six in the morning as usual.

'You have a lie-in,' he said, but she didn't want to; she wanted to wrest the maximum pleasure from the morning. The sky was clear, the sea calm, and she knew they were going to have a fine summer's day. She helped him milk, let out the hens and fed the animals that didn't graze, just as she always did. They even had their usual boiled eggs for breakfast. As she washed up afterwards, she could see Jonty through the window, picking her a bouquet of wedding flowers.

He came in. 'There aren't enough of the white roses in flower at the moment,' he said. 'I'm going to wear one in my buttonhole, but I've found a good selection of other white and blue flowers for you. Scabious and iris and white honeysuckle from the garden, and I saw these white foxgloves in a corner of the far field.'

'They'll match the flowers on my hat,' Mary said.

'That's the idea.'

She watched him dress them up in a sheet of cellophane and tie them with white satin ribbon.

'Where did you get all that?'

'Bought it in Bangor. I knew I was going to need it, didn't I?'

'They look magnificent. I can't believe they didn't come from a florist.' She smiled. 'But it's much nicer to think they've grown here on our own land.'

They got bathed and changed. Before they set off for Llandudno, Jonty said, 'I need your wedding ring.'

Mary offered him her left hand. 'It hasn't been off since the day you bought it for me and put it on.'

'It'll soon be back where it belongs,' he said. 'Why don't you wear your sapphires? You'll never have a more suitable occasion and they'll even match your colour scheme. Besides, I want your mother to see you still have a little left of your dowry.'

Mary took them from a drawer and he pinned the brooch to her dress. 'Wear the ring on your right hand for today,' he said.

In the small space of the sidecar, Mary thought the scent of the honeysuckle and the roses was delicious. They went to the hotel where later they'd have lunch. Mary went to freshen up and then sat down with a cup of coffee to wait for her family. Jonty had chosen a table near both a window and the main entrance so they could watch for their arrival. The sun was fully up now and glinting on the azure blue sea. The sapphire and diamonds flashed on Mary's finger, reminding her that she hadn't seen her mother since the morning she'd given the ring to her. She felt keyed up; nervous about seeing her again after all this time, but excited too. She didn't have long to wait.

They were walking up to the door. Edith looked older, more gaunt; she and Daniel had Simon, now a toddler, swinging between them. Barbara was just behind, with her new baby in her arms, though all Mary could see was a lot of white shawl.

They came inside and she saw her mother's face light up. The next moment she was hugging her. 'Oh, Mary, you look so well. Absolutely radiant.'

'It's my wedding day. Brides are supposed to look radiant – especially pregnant ones.'

'I know, and I'm so pleased. Jonty promised he would marry you, and I can't tell you how delighted I am that it's happening at last. I do hope you'll be very happy.'

'We have been up to now,' Jonty told her.

'Lovely to see you, sis.' Daniel kissed her.

She'd always been closer to Dan than to her younger brothers. 'And you,' she told him.

When Barbara came forward to greet her, Mary gave her and the baby a joint hug and said, 'I'm dying to see him.' She folded back the shawl to look at the sleeping baby's face. 'He's lovely,' she breathed. To actually hold the tiny body in her arms and feel him breathing gave her enormous pleasure.

'So pleased to hear you're pregnant again,' Barbara said. 'It doesn't matter how much you have to go through, you'll find it's worth it once you have the baby in your arms.'

Mary laughed. 'I can't wait.'

Dan added his congratulations. Her mother joined in but said, 'I haven't told Pa yet. I thought it better to wait until you were married. You know what he's like.'

'Tell him we're both thrilled about it,' Jonty said.

Her family decided against having coffee. 'We've spent too long talking,' Edith told her. 'I'm so glad to see you still have your sapphires, that you didn't need them for . . .'

'No, we didn't,' she was proud to say. 'I'm keeping them for that rainy day.'

'There's room for you two in my car,' Dan said. 'Why don't we all go to the register office together?'

They had a short time to wait but Mary knew she had no reason to feel bridal nerves. She was totally sure of Jonty. She wanted to be his wife more than anything else in the world. Everybody was smiling at her. Edith said, 'I'm so relieved everything's turned out right for you. I was worried to start with.'

'Pa was wrong about Jonty,' Mary said. 'I knew he was and tried to tell him, but he wouldn't have it.'

They were shown into a small wood-panelled room, with flowers on the desk and on the windowsill, although none of them equalled her bouquet for scent.

Mary stood beside Jonty and heard him vow to love her, comfort her, and keep her only unto him for as long as they both should live. She knew he would – he'd already been doing exactly that.

Her eyes prickled with emotional tears. She knew her mother found it moving too because her eyes were wet when Mary looked up from signing the register. It was marvellous to be with her and Dan after such a long and sudden separation. She'd missed them. A lot of photographs were taken on the steps outside the register office and again at the hotel with the promenade and the sea in the background. They asked complete strangers to snap them so they could have pictures of all of them together.

Mary could count on one hand the number of times she'd eaten a full meal in a hotel, and there'd certainly been none over recent years. It was lovely to try different food. There was so much to tell her family about Glan y Mor, and so much news to hear in exchange, that the few hours they could spend together were gone in a flash.

'I have to get back for milking,' Jonty said, sounding apologetic. 'As it is, it'll be later than usual tonight.'

Dan fetched two gift-wrapped packages from the boot of his car. 'We didn't know what you wanted, but we hope you'll find these useful.'

Mum was crying again as she came to the sidecar to see them off. 'Don't let it be so long before I see you again,' she said.

Dan said, 'You could come and stay with us. We have a spare room now.'

'I can't leave the animals,' Jonty reminded him. 'Mary would have to come by herself.'

As soon as they were alone, Mary told him she didn't want to do that, not even for a few days. She had a little private weep as she was swept back along the coast to Anglesey in the sidecar, with her packages at her feet. She'd missed her mum and her brothers, especially at first, but now her life was with Jonty. She could see him sitting above her, concentrating on the road.

She twisted her wedding ring on her finger, finding the feel of it familiar and comforting. It was Jonty she wanted – and, of course, a baby. Seeing Barbara's newborn had made her more impatient than ever to have a child of her own. They'd joined the local library and she was borrowing books on baby care.

She prayed her third pregnancy would be absolutely normal and she'd have a strong and healthy baby. If she could have that, she'd have everything she could possibly want in life.

'You must be very careful this time,' Jonty told her, and he made her take more rest. He took over some of the jobs she usually did and made sure she went to bed early.

Mary was full of hope. When she went to the village, she couldn't help looking inside every pram she met on the pavement. Her eye was taken with every baby gown, matinee jacket or bonnet she saw for sale in a shop window. When she spotted something she particularly liked and she had the money, she bought it.

But one wet August Saturday, she began to feel the pains she dreaded and saw again the bleeding which meant the worst. Jonty took her to hospital where she had another miscarriage and stayed for a week.

On the afternoon he brought her home, she wept on his shoulder. 'Oh, Jonty, I can't bear it. Why has it happened again? I'm afraid we'll never have a baby.'

She felt his arms go round her and his light butterfly kisses all over her face and neck. 'I'm so sorry, love. I know you want a baby more than anything, but it seems to be the one thing I can't give you.'

They were both a bit low in the weeks that followed. Jonty was worried about Mary: it seemed she couldn't get over her third miscarriage. And August was a busy month for him. After a hot summer the grain harvest ripened early. He helped Ted Evans harvest his oats and then borrowed his cutter and tractor to work on his own crop. When the sheaves had dried, he took them down to Plas Hafren where they could be threshed at the same time as Ted's.

Towards the end of the month, the weather worsened. Ted Evans looked out to sea and shook his head. He told Jonty the glass was falling. There was often a stiff breeze at Glan y Mor, but now it gusted to gale force and brought heavy showers. The farmers caught with cut grass or grain out on their fields were counting their losses, and the inshore fishermen couldn't take their boats out.

That weekend started dry but overcast, and the wind dropped. Monday dawned brighter and there were short spells of fitful sunshine, but after lunch when Jonty went out to work on his stone walls it felt heavy and sultry and he noticed black clouds gathering in the distance. The afternoon grew steadily darker.

When he went back to the cottage for his usual cup of afternoon tea, Mary was gathering in her washing from the line. 'It's not all that dry,' she called, 'but I'm bringing it in because it looks as though it's going to teem at any minute.'

'We're in for a storm,' he said. 'A bad one. Put the washing indoors and come up on the headland with me. I bet it'll look very threatening from there.'

Sure enough, on the horizon the sky was spectacularly black and silver. Jonty looked down the hundred-foot drop to the huge waves crashing against the rocks below, throwing up white spume high enough for them to feel it. The wind was buffeting them one moment and raging the next. Jonty hung on to Mary, half afraid she'd be blown off her feet.

'It looks ominous,' she said.

'Don't let's make the tea just yet. I'd rather get the animals fed and shut in for the night before it gets any worse. I'm going to fetch the cows and milk them early.'

'I'll see to the hens,' Mary said. 'We'll get the outside work done so we can stay inside snug and dry.'

The cowshed seemed airless. Jonty tethered Bluebell and Buttercup. The tabby cat prowled at his feet meowing to remind him to fill the old sardine tin he kept there, something he did every milking. Apart from that the cat lived on the mice she caught and often brought to the cottage window to show them.

The sheep usually spent their nights out on the rough hill land. There was only the breeding flock left now; the lambs had all gone to market. The old ewes sensed the coming storm too and had gathered at the gate. Jonty opened it and they all streamed into the more sheltered field behind the house. He carefully closed every door and window and battened down everything he could.

When the work was done he and Mary went back to the headland to take another look at the gathering storm, but visibility was closing in. All was gloom and darkness.

'We've not had a really bad storm like this before,' Jonty said. 'I'm glad we're on dry land and not out there.'

He felt Mary shiver. He took her hand and they ran back to the cottage, stopping only at the woodpile to collect an extra armful to take inside. He lit the oil lamp, and piled more wood on the range, while Mary made dumplings to add to the pan of stew for their supper.

'It's going to be a wild night.' Jonty felt uneasy, and after the meal he went round his animals to make sure all was well. By ten o'clock, when they were going upstairs to bed, a screaming gale was rattling round the cottage and hurling sheets of rain against the windows. Usually they were lulled to sleep by the sound of the sea running up the beach, but tonight the waves were thundering against the rocks.

Mary was restless and Jonty couldn't sleep either, worried that so violent a storm might cause damage to the outbuildings. He was in the process of refurbishing one where he could store foodstuffs for his animals, and he'd re-roofed the calf shed only last spring and was not too sure of his own workmanship.

Then, above the wild cacophony of the storm, he heard a new sound. He lifted his head from the pillow to listen and tried to decide what it might be. Suddenly, he shot out of bed and felt for his clothes. He started to pull them on in the dark so as not to disturb Mary, but she was already awake. 'Where are you going?'

'Out. Can you hear that noise?'

Mary struck a match to light the candle. 'I can hear something.'

'I'm afraid the wind's catching the calf-shed roof. Something's banging up and down.'

Down in the kitchen, Jonty lit his hurricane lamp. Outside, the wind took his breath away, and the noise was twice as loud. He'd used new zinc sheets to roof the calf shed, and after nailing them down on the old beams he'd not been completely satisfied that he'd made a good job of it, so he'd stretched a wire across the roof a foot up from the gutter to hold them in position.

Now, in the light of his lantern, he was horrified to see the corner of the roof lifting six inches or more in the gale, and thumping back when the gust was spent.

With his heart in his mouth, he let himself inside. His two calves should have been curled up asleep on their straw, but they were up and nervously pawing the floor. 'It's all right.' Jonty held his lantern high and tried to soothe them. 'Nothing for you to worry about.'

Cold rainwater sprayed into his face as the roof lifted again. No wonder the calves were edgy. He'd fastened the wires on to the beams on the inside, so it should be possible to tighten them here to hold the zinc sheets more firmly. He knew he'd have to, or risk some of the sheets blowing off; that would almost certainly twist and damage them and result in further expense. He'd need his stepladder from the barn. He went to fetch it, and on the way back the gale-force wind caught the end of the steps and almost turned him round.

He saw Mary's hurricane lamp coming towards him. 'You're never going up on the roof?' she shouted.

'Not in this. I can do it from the inside.'

She helped him carry the ladder to the calf pen. When he tried to open the door the gale almost snatched it out of his fingers, but they managed to get inside and close it against the worst of the elements.

'Poor things,' Mary said. 'You can tell they're frightened.'

'Yes.' Jonty put the stepladder in position and climbed up. 'Can you hold the light higher?'

He waited until the zinc sheets thumped down again and then tightened the wire as quickly as he could before he felt the wind tugging at them again. It was the best he could do, though they were still moving slightly. Less rain was spraying inside now, but the calves would need dry straw in the morning. No point in trying to bring it across the yard tonight: the rain was still coming down in sheets and would soak it in seconds. Mary was stroking the nose of one of the calves and making soothing noises.

'They won't settle until we go,' he told her. 'We'll leave the steps here so I can have another go in daylight.' He had wire left over from the original job, and could add another strand. 'I'll need to go up on the roof when this wind drops.' He took her arm. 'Let's go back to bed.'

When they left the shed, the wind caught them in the back and sent them scurrying towards the cottage. In the shelter of the porch, Jonty turned round to marvel at the rain slanting across the farmyard. There was a small river crossing the yard now and the lower part was turning to mud.

'Ugh,' Mary said. 'I'm soaked through.'

'Shush. Did you hear that?' The gale raged on but again Jonty could hear something different. 'Is there a boat out there? That sounded like a distress gun.'

Mary shook her head silently.

'There it goes again. I think it is. You go in – I'm going to see.'

'I'm coming with you. The cliff could be dangerous.'

'The wind's off the sea. An on-shore wind can't hurt us.'

But he knew that with this torrential rain the grass would be slippery, and the cliff edge could be weakened. Jonty leaned into the wind as he climbed, towing Mary by the hand. By now, he should be high enough to see the lighthouse at Lynas Point, but though he strained his eyes into the murk he could pick out nothing. With low cloud and heavy rain stinging his face, it was almost impossible to open his eyes.

And yet ... Nearer, in the other direction and out to sea, was he looking at a weaker light?

Mary was jerking at his arm. 'Gosh, look, there must be a boat out there. Is it a fishing boat?'

Jonty was shocked. Gigantic breakers were thundering over the rocks at the foot of the cliff. 'Bigger than that. It could be a yacht. It'll get blown into our cove if they aren't careful. It must be terrible out there.'

Mary was tugging at his arm and yelling to make herself heard. 'Look, they're in trouble.' They both saw the blue glow of the flare, but it was soon blotted out by the swirling rain. 'Would the coastguard be able to see that from Lynas Point?'

'I doubt it. We can't see their light tonight, can we?' Another blue flare showed for a few seconds. 'I'm afraid this wind is blowing them in. They could be smashed against the rocks.'

'Will they have called out the coastguard?'

'If they have the means to do it. I hope they have an engine.'

'Surely they're bound to, a vessel of that size? It's quite big.'

'It's drifting closer. I can't hear anything.'

'We wouldn't be able to in this howling gale. Is there anything we can do to help?'

Jonty shuddered. 'I'll go up to Lynas Point on my bike and tell them. They could call out the lifeboat at Moelfre.'

He ran with Mary back to the porch. 'You go indoors, love.' He dropped a kiss on her cheek. 'Make some tea. I won't be long.' He saw her indoors, wanting to make sure she was safe.

It was a dangerous night to ride a motor bike, and he was glad of the sidecar to give it stability. At Lynas Point the coastguard on duty had seen nothing and was immediately concerned. 'I'll send a signal to the coastguards at Bangor.'

'What about the lifeboat at Moelfre?' Jonty asked. Moelfre was much nearer.

'Might be too rough to launch it tonight,' the man replied. 'But I'll ring John Jarvis and tell him you've seen distress flares.' To his consternation, however, he found it wasn't possible. 'The storm must have brought the lines down.'

'I can ride down and tell him,' Jonty said.

'Would you? I'd be grateful.'

Jonty had to pass the bottom of his own hill path to get to Moelfre and he could see the light shining in his kitchen window. As he drew near the lifeboat station he realised it was a scene of bustling activity as the crew prepared to launch their lifeboat. One of them had seen the flares too.

'It looks as though the boat is being blown onshore,' Jonty told them.

'If it's just driven up on the beach, all might be well.'

An older man said, 'If they can see the beach and if they can steer the boat. But there are rocks out there. We have a lot of wrecks along this coast.'

'What sort of vessel is it?'

Jonty couldn't tell them. He'd seen nothing but the light.

He decided to go home. He didn't like leaving Mary on her own on a wild night like this. She was relieved to see him. 'You've been a long time.'

The tea was stewed. Mary made some more and Jonty cut himself a slice of home-made sponge cake. It felt strange to be hungry at half two in the morning, but he was ravenous. The raging energy of the storm seemed to transmit itself to him, and he knew he wouldn't sleep if he went back to bed.

He made up the fire again. 'I'm going to see what's happening out there,' he said. 'You go to bed.'

'I'm coming with you,' Mary told him. 'I don't like being left here by myself wondering what's going on.'

CHAPTER SIX

MARY RE-LIT both of their hurricane lamps and put on her damp oilskins and sou'wester. Once outside, she had to hang on to Jonty. The wind seemed stronger than ever, and she felt it could blow her off her feet.

They went up on the headland. Everything had changed in the hour or so since they'd been here. There were lights under the cliff and Jonty held Mary round the waist as she looked down, shocked by the scene of devastation on the rocks below.

'Heavens, just look at that! They've run aground down there and the boat's breaking in half.' The coastguard cutter was already there, shining a searchlight on what remained of the doomed vessel.

Mary caught snatches of sound on the shrieking gale that was whipping at her sou'wester: screams of horror and splintering woodwork as the boat scraped against the rocks.

'It's already in two pieces.' Her legs felt weak. 'People will be drowned.'

'It's some sort of yacht. Look, there're more lights out there.' They clung together watching for a while. 'It looks like the lifeboat from Moelfre coming to help.'

There were several figures on the rocks, looking in danger of being washed into the sea by the waves.

'We can't do anything up here,' Mary shouted. 'Let's go down to the cove. We might be able to help.'

They were sheltered from the worst of the gale as they went down the path, but as soon as they reached the beach they realised they wouldn't be able to get round the headland to reach the wreck. It could only be reached from Hafren Sands. Even in fine weather and at low tide it wasn't easy to cross those rock ledges, but tonight great waves were sweeping over them and it was only too clear that if they tried to scramble to the neighbouring cove they would be washed into the boiling sea and drowned.

As for their beach itself, Mary hardly recognised it. The shingle had all been lifted higher by the breakers and the whole geography had changed. Now a steep bank shelved down to the angry waves.

'What's that?' Jonty sounded horrified and she couldn't immediately see what had caught his attention. There were pieces of wood being swept in on the tide, together with a bucket and a spar of some sort. But Jonty was slithering down the bank and wading into the foam towards what looked like a bundle of clothes. Mary held her breath, afraid the next wave was going to wash him out to sea. But he was dragging the bundle back with him. Only then did she realise it was a human being. She left her lantern beside his high on the bank of shingle and started sliding down to help.

'Don't,' he screamed. 'Stay back. It's a woman, but I'm afraid she's dead.'

Mary felt sick with horror, but she went on, knowing Jonty would never get the body up the steep bank if she didn't. They were both puffing when at last they laid her down out of reach of the waves. Mary fetched their lanterns. As soon as the light fell directly on the woman they knew she was beyond any help. Her face was badly cut and grazed where the waves had dashed her against the rocks. She was wearing a pearl necklace. One of her arms was missing from the elbow and her left leg was twisted into a strange position.

'She's definitely dead,' Mary choked. 'She's got terrific injuries.' She felt cold with horror and knew Jonty was as shocked as she was.

'She's young, not much more than a girl. There could be others, some we could help. I'll go round by Plas Hafren and wake Ted Evans up. They're going to need all the help they can get.'

'I'll come with you.'

'No, love, I want you to go home where I know you'll be safe. The beach is no place for you tonight.'

She took a deep jagged breath. 'No place for you either.'

They reached the two lanterns they'd settled into the shingle. Jonty snatched his up and moved away. She knew her voice would never carry above the wind and he'd take no notice even if he heard. He knew there were people needing help and he meant to give it if he could. Even through her shock and distress, Mary felt a surge of pride in this husband of hers.

Her nerves jangling, she began walking back to the foot of the path back to the house. All manner of oddments were being washed up along the tide line; nobody could be in any doubt as to where they'd come from. She could see the flotsam swirling in the breakers as they crashed on the shingle, but it was almost impossible to know what the objects were until the waves retreated leaving them high and dry.

A contraption made of wood landed a few yards ahead of her. She pulled it higher and saw it was part of a steamer chair, twisted and damaged. It made her think about life on board the yacht that was now being smashed to bits against the rocks. As she moved on, her wellington kicked at something else: a woman's silver dance shoe. Her stomach contracted violently. It might have belonged to that poor dead woman; probably did, like the hairbrush that landed in front of her next.

When Mary first heard the baby's cry, she thought she was imagining it. Babies had been much in her thoughts recently. She stumbled over what seemed to be a snaking hawser and stubbed her wellington against something solid. She held her lantern higher and saw a boxlike object. The weak whimper coming from it was unmistakable even above the booming of the waves. Her heart turned over and began to thud. It was a baby!

The small wooden cradle with a wooden hood had been washed up on the shingle with the baby still inside. The child had been held in place by some net contraption, perhaps meant to prevent the occupant from being tossed out in rough weather. Mary tore away the netting and lifted the baby up on to her shoulder, the strength ebbing from her knees. It seemed only just alive; it was a miracle she'd found it in time.

'You poor little mite.'

It felt very cold and was soaked to the skin. Its cry was a feeble mewl so piteous it tore at her heart. Why had Jonty gone? She needed help. Mary would have liked to pull the cradle with its wet bedding higher up the beach, but she couldn't manage that as well as the child and her lantern. She hesitated for a moment at the woman's body, thinking she could be the child's mother. But she had to hurry. She set off up the path at a slow jog. She feared for the baby, it was too still and far too cold. It must have warmth and dry clothes as soon as possible.

Once in the cottage, she turned up her oil lamp and took the infant to the fire to strip off its sodden clothing. It was a little girl, stiff and blue with cold, silent now and hardly moving. Mary wrapped her hurriedly in a towel and hugged her, so filled with pity it brought tears to her eyes.

She blinked them away impatiently; she knew what she had to do. She'd seen Jonty bring in the occasional lamb lifeless and cold that had been born outside on a wet night and rejected by its mother. Slow, gentle warmth brought them back to life.

She put the baby down and put more logs on the fire, then put the kettle on to heat water for a bath. She needed to find clothes that would fit the child and make her more comfortable, so she went to her bedroom and fetched the nightdress Barbara had given her, and one of the matinee jackets and pairs of bootees that she'd knitted herself. She cut up a flannelette sheet to make napkins and a shawl to wrap the baby in.

Then she rinsed out the washing-up bowl, filled it with warm water and brought it close to the fire. She held the baby in it, hoping it would both warm her up and wash the sea salt from her skin. As she dried her, Mary was beguiled to find she was holding one of the most beautiful little girls she'd ever seen.

She had very little hair, just a few reddish brown curls close to her scalp. Her limbs were rounded and plump. As far as Mary could judge, she'd be under three months old, perhaps just a few weeks. Mary dressed her as quickly as she could and held her against her own body. Gradually the baby began to warm up, taking on a better colour and no longer feeling flaccid. Now she was warm and dry, her big brown eyes stared intently up into Mary's face. Mary bent to kiss her neat little nose and gave her a hug of joy.

The little whimpers had strengthened to more normal baby cries. Mary wondered if she was hungry and what she could feed her on. She had plenty of fresh milk from tonight's milking so she diluted that with hot water from the kettle and put in a little sugar. Barbara had told her once that that was what she did for her babies. Then she fed her a teaspoonful at a time, and to see her open her tiny mouth for the spoon brought tears to sting her eyes again.

Mary had fed a pair of weak lambs in the spring when their mothers had not had enough milk. She'd used any old bottles – one had held tomato sauce and the other lemonade, she remembered – and Jonty had bought tough strong teats to fit them. She'd need proper baby teats now.

She nursed the baby until the child's cheeks were pink and her eyes closing, then popped her in the middle of their own bed and stood watching her while she slept, fascinated, thrilled and feeling full of love for this helpless scrap of humanity. All her dreams of having a baby of her own one day were forgotten; what she wanted was this baby to care for now. It seemed she was meant to have her; the child had been washed up in their cove almost at her feet.

The baby had been wearing a matinee jacket of finest wool as well as a woollen vest. If they weren't hung out to dry very soon they would surely shrink and be spoiled. Mary rinsed the clothes through, wrung them out and pegged them on the line in the open-fronted barn, where she knew the wind would dry them whatever the weather.

Then she began thinking of Jonty and of what might be happening to the boat that had been driven up on the rocks beneath their cliff. After making sure the baby was asleep, she pulled on her oilskins again and went to see what was going on. There were lights in their cove now so she ran down there. She met Jonty and Ted Evans coming up, carrying a stretcher between them. A sheet covered the body on it.

Mary's heart missed a beat. 'Is that the poor woman we pulled . . . ?'

'No, it's a man,' Jonty told her. He looked exhausted.

'We're taking the dead to Hafren Chapel where they can rest in peace,' Ted told her.

Mary shivered as she saw them hoist the body on to a cart.

'We're landlubbers,' Ted went on. 'We're leaving the work on the beach to the fisher folk – they understand the sea better than we do.'

'We've already taken two women up,' Jonty said. 'You go back to bed, Mary. There are plenty of men helping here now. Things are under control.'

Mary was glad to go back to the baby knowing Jonty was not in any danger. She'd meant to get into bed beside the sleeping child, but when she went in with her candle she saw the baby's brown eyes solemnly looking up into hers. While she got undressed, she heard the infant start to whimper, so she scooped her up for a cuddle and crooned soft words of comfort until she went to sleep again.

Jonty was going to love this baby as much as she did. They must think of a name for her. She'd decided on Rosemary for any daughter she and Jonty might have, but this baby didn't seem to suit it. She wondered about her parents. It seemed likely that both had perished in the shipwreck, which was a tragedy, but one that might, just might, mean that Mary could adopt her and bring her up as her own.

It was daybreak when Jonty walked back from Plas Hafren. He'd declined the cup of tea Ted had offered, wanting only to get home and sleep. He was so tired he could hardly put one foot in front of the other, but he'd need to milk the cows before going to bed.

Three of the people on board the yacht were known to have drowned and three more were said to be missing, but he'd heard six had been rescued from the back part of the boat, wet, cold and shivering but with only minor injuries. They'd been taken to hospital. He felt sickened by it all.

He rested his forehead against Buttercup's flank for a moment, taking comfort from the smell of warm milk. The tabby cat was lapping up her breakfast in the corner of the byre. At least his world had not changed.

When he'd finished, he let the cows out and opened the gate so they and the sheep could go back up on the hill. The grassland squelched under his feet after such a heavy downpour, but the rain had stopped now though heavy clouds still raced across the sky.

Jonty took the two buckets of frothy milk to the dairy, and poured it into the flat pans from which, later, Mary would be able to skim the thick cream to make butter. The fire in the range had died back, so he threw more logs on and swung the kettle on its chain over the flames. He'd love a cup of tea now.

Upstairs he opened the bedroom door softly. The curtains were still drawn, and in the semi-darkness he could see Mary curled up asleep; she'd had a broken night too. Trying not to disturb her, he stripped off his clothes. They'd been soaked but had now dried on him. He saw Mary stir.

'Hello,' he said. 'Have I woken you?'

She sat up with a jerk and seemed instantly wide awake and jubilant. 'Jonty, look. A baby girl. Isn't she lovely?'

'A baby?' He noticed the child for the first time, and his mouth fell open.

'She was washed up in the cove in her cradle. She was wet and cold but she's fine now.'

'Mary, you should have said. The coastguard were trying to check who's survived and who hasn't. They need to know.'

'I want to keep her.'

'Keep her?' He was astounded. 'We can't, she's not ours. Her relatives . . .'

'But her parents have been drowned. That woman we dragged out of the surf . . . And you said there was a man. Surely they were her parents?'

'We can't know that.'

'They must have been,' she insisted.

'One of the dead women was wearing a nanny's uniform. It was a big luxury yacht.'

'Oh!' He saw the anxiety in her eyes. 'But the other woman was her mother.'

'She might have been. The dead man was wearing uniform too. He looked like a ship's officer. But six men were taken off the wreck alive, Mary – one of them could well be this child's father.' Mary was hugging the baby to her as though afraid he'd prise her from her arms. He said, 'We have to tell the coastguard she's survived and she's here.'

'No, Jonty, no. I can't give her up. I found her . . .'

'That doesn't make her ours.'

'She was stone cold and soaking wet. She'd have died if I hadn't brought her to the fire.' Mary was in tears and he could see she was distraught. 'Please, please, Jonty. I want to keep her. She's absolutely beautiful. Just look.'

Jonty suddenly remembered he'd set the kettle to boil. He shot downstairs and found the living room full of steam, but luckily there was enough water left to make a pot of tea. He had to think this through and he'd never needed a hot drink more.

For him, life here was marvellous. It had given him independence, he'd escaped from being tied to an employer, he was his own boss. They had plenty to eat and he could make enough money to pay the rent and buy petrol and other necessities. He sought nothing more and felt grateful to Mary for making it possible.

She'd given up her family and a comfortable home to come with him. In a way he felt he'd forced her to, by getting her pregnant. He'd often wondered whether, if that hadn't happened, he'd have been able to persuade her to come. In view of her father's attitude towards him, he suspected she'd have stayed at home until she was twenty-one and of age to marry without her parents' consent.

So getting her pregnant that first time had given him two extra years here. Mary, poor love, had been worried stiff back then. But it had made her think about bringing up a child, and her repeated miscarriages had made her long for one. He understood how much having a baby meant to her, and he'd wished many times he could give her her wish.

And he was indebted to her in other ways. It was the money realised from the sale of the silver her mother had given her that had allowed them to buy the animals and set up the smallholding. Mary had enabled him to return to his roots and the sort of life he'd lived as a boy. For her, brought up in Liverpool where she'd enjoyed the theatre and the big shops, it must have seemed very alien at first.

He was glorying in life at Glan y Mor. It permitted him to have Mary all to himself, all day and all night. He loved and needed her and she was the one who had made it all possible. But while she seemed happy to be here with him, she wanted more.

He wanted to give her the world but what she wanted was a baby and despite their best efforts they'd not been able to achieve it. He felt ready to worship the ground Mary walked on. There was nothing he wouldn't do to make her happy.

He poured two cups of tea and took them up to the bedroom. Mary had hardly moved; she was still nursing the baby. Her eyes were suspiciously bright. 'Can't we keep her?' she pleaded.

He said slowly, 'If that's what you really want.' How could he deny her what she wanted most? But his conscience was heavy.

She was smiling. 'We'll tell everybody she's ours.'

By full daylight the sky had cleared and the wind had dropped. The air was sharp and damp after last night's storm. Jonty was aware of unaccustomed activity around his smallholding.

'Come out and see what's going on,' he suggested as they ate breakfast. Mary was reluctant to leave the baby, but he persuaded her to walk up to the headland with him and look down on the scene of devastation below. It was low tide now and they could clearly see what remained of the yacht. The stern section was solidly impaled on the rocks with a tilt of thirty degrees to the deck. In front of it, little of the bow remained. It had been pounded to bits against the rocks by the force of the waves. Pieces of it littered the rocky ledges. On one, they could see the name *Priscilla* picked out in gilt lettering.

'It must have been a grand yacht,' Jonty said sadly. 'The tide's on the turn. It'll break the wreckage up completely when it's full in.'

Flotsam had been washed up everywhere and was strewn along the two-mile tide line of Hafren Sands for as far as they could see. Their little cove was full of it too.

'I can't see that cradle you mentioned from here,' Jonty said. He'd made a makeshift one from a drawer taken out of their chest. 'Could it have been washed out to sea again?'

'I don't want that,' she said vehemently. 'Her relatives would recognise it, wouldn't they? I don't want anything that would identify her.'

'No, no . . .'

'I want people to think she's ours. When I was pregnant I told a lot of people.'

'Yes,' he agreed, 'you were so pleased about it.'

'Don't you see, that'll make them believe she's mine?'

Jonty felt his heart roll over. Mary would be heartbroken if she had to give this baby up. 'I don't know. We might not get away with it.'

'We will,' she insisted.

He was afraid she was going to be disappointed over this baby too. Afraid they'd both end up in trouble.

Several boats were patrolling just off the coast, and photographs were being taken. Both tourists and local people were on the beach, come to see the shipwreck for themselves. The Anglesey police had parked a vehicle on the edge of Hafren Sands and were combing the shore. The coastguards were there too, from Port Lynas and Bangor.

'Such a lot of people about,' Mary said nervously. Jonty knew she was worried somebody might start asking questions.

'I'd better go and talk to them,' he said.

'You won't tell them, will you?' Mary was pulling at his arm. 'About the baby, I mean.'

He shook his head silently.

'I'm going back to her.'

Jonty wanted to find out more about the survivors of the wreck. He particularly wanted to know if anyone had mentioned the baby. He set out towards Hafren Sands, but before he reached the beach he saw Jack Jones, their local policeman, leaning on the gate leading to Ted Evans's farm.

He nodded at Jonty. 'A shocking storm last night,' he said. 'Terrible the havoc it caused.'

'Yes.' Jonty didn't know how to ask about the baby. He hesitated for too long.

'I hear you alerted the coastguard at Lynas Point. You saw the vessel heading for the rocks from your place?'

'I knew it was in trouble. It was sending off distress rockets, calling for help.'

'Yes, well, with four dead there'll have to be an inquest. You raised the alarm and helped at the scene, so you'll be called to give evidence.'

'Four dead? I thought there were only three?'

'Early this morning the coastguards found another body washed up on Hafren Sands.'

'That's awful.' Jonty had to ask. 'Is that everybody accounted for?'

'No, there's another adult and a baby still missing.'

Jonty's heart turned over. He ought to tell him now that they had the baby safe and sound.

'About the baby . . .' But how could he? Mary would never forgive him if he did.

'Yes, there was a two-month-old baby on board.'

He caught his breath. 'So . . . so sad for the family.' He was desperate to find out more. 'The captain had his wife and child on board?'

'No, the son of the owner did.'

Jonty's heart was thumping. He had to know. 'Did he survive?'

'Yes.'

He felt sick. So the baby had not been orphaned. That made what he was doing ten times worse.

'Poor man,' he managed. 'Losing his baby like that.'

'Lost his wife too. He picked a bad day for a pleasure cruise.' The policeman kicked at a dried cowpat.

Jonty thought of the young woman wearing the pearl necklace and felt tears of agony burn his eyes.

'I think I helped Ted Evans take her to the chapel last night.' What had he done? It was too late now to mention the baby. He was committed to stealing another man's child.

One of the coastguards was walking past, and stopped when he saw them. 'Did you know another ship ran aground last night?' he said.

'Where?' asked the police officer.

'Not ten miles down the coast beyond Red Wharf Bay. A small coaster loaded with Cardiff coal, called the *Elsie Wainwright*.'

'Any loss of life?'

'No, thank goodness. Didn't do herself much damage either; she was driven up on the beach. There's a tug sent for to try to pull her off on the next tide.'

He went on his way and the policeman turned back to Jonty. 'You'll get a letter from the coroner to let you know where and when the inquest will be held.'

Jonty swallowed hard. 'Yes,' he croaked.

'Just to give evidence about what you saw and did.'

Jonty was scared. The last thing he wanted to do was give evidence. He'd be expected to tell the truth, the whole truth; after all, a coroner's court was a court of law. But for Mary's sake he'd already suppressed the truth about the baby. Now he would have to do it again, and this time he would be under oath.

CHAPTER SEVEN

I N THE DAYS that followed, Jonty's conscience troubled him. He'd been brought up to be honourable and truthful and throughout his life he'd prided himself that he was. But now he'd turned his back on that. He couldn't stop thinking about the baby's real relatives and what they must be going through. A few days ago he would not have considered himself capable doing such a thing. He felt sorry for her real father, believing himself to be doubly bereaved. He told himself the baby had to stay for Mary's sake; he'd had no choice.

She'd always seemed a happy person contented with her lot, until her last miscarriage. That had devastated her. She'd been overwhelmed with sadness and afraid any future pregnancy was doomed to failure. But now, with this baby she was all smiles and literally sang as she went about her daily work. Her thoughts were largely about the child.

'We must decide on a name for her,' she said. She'd changed her mind once or twice but now seemed to be settling on Charlotte Mary. To Jonty, however, another problem seemed painfully obvious.

'I'm worried about how we're going to pass her off as our own,' he said. 'Will they believe us? A baby goes missing in that storm and suddenly we've got one.'

Mary seemed to be pushing difficulties like that to the back of her mind. 'Nobody saw me bring her up from the beach. I didn't see anybody to speak to that night.'

'You did. You saw me and Ted Evans in the cove, when we were taking that poor man up to the church.'

'So I did.'

'Was that before or after you found the baby?'

'After. She was asleep then.'

'If you'd given birth around that time, you wouldn't have been out in that storm. It's bound to come as a surprise to Ted.'

'I hardly see him. I haven't been out much recently, and if he's seen me I've probably been wearing my coat.'

'In July and August?'

'My mac then. It was often wet.'

'It's been a long hot summer, Mary. And what about Enid, his wife? What's she going to think?'

'I told Enid I was pregnant ages ago, and I never told her I'd had a miscarriage. I couldn't. She went away, didn't she?'

'That's right, she did. She went to Aberystwyth because her mother was ill, and was gone for several weeks. But other people must know about it.'

'I didn't go round telling everybody.' He saw her shudder. 'Would they know? Bangor hospital is a long way away.'

Jonty tried to think back. He'd taken Mary to hospital in the middle of the night. She'd been kept in for five days. He always felt pressed for time when she was in hospital, what with looking after the animals and visiting her; he didn't think he'd talked to anyone very much during that week.

Mary had been very low when he'd brought her home. She'd rested, just pottered about the smallholding. She'd needed a quiet time to get well again and get over the third disappointment. He was quite sure none of the neighbours had seen her to speak to after she came out of hospital until the night of the storm.

She asked, 'Did you tell anybody? That I'd had another miscarriage?'

He couldn't remember. He'd been miserable too because it looked as though Mary couldn't carry a baby to term. He'd not deliberately hidden it, but he'd seen it as a medical problem they couldn't solve and had tried not to dwell on it. He didn't think he'd talked about it to the neighbours, but he wasn't absolutely certain.

'I spent a lot of time with Ted on the night of the storm. If you'd had a baby then, surely it would seem odd for me not to say so?'

'You had other things on your mind, and so did the neighbours. What did you talk about?'

'Just the storm; what we should do next to help. We were all on edge.'

'There you are, then. It won't seem odd that you didn't talk about the baby. We all live in our own worlds.'

'But the dates don't tie up. Your baby wasn't due till November. Did you talk about dates to Enid Evans?'

'No, I don't think so.'

'But you're not sure?' He could see she wasn't. 'If you tell anybody you're pregnant, surely they ask when it's due?'

Mary sighed. 'I remember her asking how I was keeping, and we talked about pregnancy and babies in general. It was the same with the Jarvises at Moelfre and Mrs Roberts at the library. No, apart from you, I have no close friend here.'

'Nobody you've confided in?'

'No . . . yes! Barbara asked about dates, and afterwards I wrote and told her about the miscarriage too.'

'Then we'll have to tell her truth. What about your mother?'

'I told her I was pregnant. I don't think about the other . . .'

'Barbara will have told her.'

'But the neighbours won't hear about it from them,' Mary said. 'We'll have to swear them to secrecy.'

'Mary!' Jonty covered his face with his hands. 'How can we?' He didn't think any of this would be as easy as she seemed to think.

'If we have to, we can.'

Mary started a letter to Barbara right away.

'It'll have to be a tissue of lies,' Jonty worried.

'I'm going to say that I was so upset by yet another miscarriage that we've decided to adopt a motherless baby girl from the village. That's all right, isn't it?'

'And when this baby girl is growing up, what are we going to tell her? That she's adopted?'

'No.' Mary sighed. 'Not if we've led the neighbours to believe she's ours. Anyway, I want her to think she's ours too.'

'Then you'll have to say more than that to Barbara, otherwise in the future she could let it out without realising. Then there's your mother; you'll have to write the same to her. I don't know whether all this is going to work. We might be digging a great big hole for ourselves.'

Mary continued to write. 'I'm asking Barbara if she told Mum about the miscarriage. I don't think Mum wrote to me about it this time. Previously, she sent me the sort of note that was meant to comfort, saying I can always try again.'

'Here's the postman coming across the yard,' Jonty said. 'I've got a stamp. Give it to him now.'

Three days later, the postman brought her Barbara's reply.

I can quite understand why you want to adopt. After three miscarriages you must be feeling it's pretty hopeless. Of course I'll say nothing if that's the way you want it to be.

I don't think I did mention your last miscarriage to your mother. At the time, she was away in Preston helping your Aunt Dora who'd just come out of hospital after her operation. Anyway, Mary, I believe that's the sort of personal news that is best left strictly to you to tell.

There was a postscript. *I was forgetting that I always give Dan your letters to read. So he knows, but he promises silence too, if that's what you want.*

'You see, it'll be all right,' Mary said, hugging the baby to her.

'Then I suppose we'd better start taking her out. We'll go down to the village shop tomorrow.'

It was Mary's turn to be anxious now. 'Will they put two and two together? Will they guess she's the missing baby?'

'We'll have to risk that, won't we?'

They didn't sleep much that night. They discussed the baby's first outing over and over, and when they did finally drop off she woke them up in the small hours, which was unusual. By the time they were ready to go out the next morning, Mary was getting cold feet and wanted to stay at home.

'We mustn't look as though we're hiding her,' Jonty said, though he was feeling nervous himself. 'The sooner everybody knows we have a baby, the sooner they'll accept it.'

Mary dressed Charlotte Mary in the best outfit she had and wrapped her in a big shawl. Then she climbed into the sidecar, and Jonty settled the baby in her arms. At the post office and general store in Moelfre Mary took a deep breath and went inside holding the child close.

The postmistress, another Mrs Jones, hurried from the back region wearing a floral crossover pinafore. 'Oh, you've had your baby?' she said. 'Congratulations, Mrs Jones.' She was round from behind the counter in an instant. 'Let's have a look at her.'

Mary kept the shawl pulled close and allowed her only a glimpse. 'The ride down has put her to sleep. She gave us a wakeful night last night.'

'Don't they all? She's big, isn't she? What was her birth weight?'

Jonty saw that the question had thrown Mary off balance. They'd given no thought to her birth weight. 'Just on nine pounds,' he said.

'Didn't you do well? She's lovely.'

'Charlotte Mary,' Jonty said, and added before she could ask, 'Aged three weeks.'

'A lovely name too.'

The postmistress rang up the till, then came back and pushed a florin into the baby's hand.

'Cross her palm with silver and she'll never be hard up.'

'Thank you,' Mary said. 'That's very kind of you.'

'She's a very bonny baby.'

Jonty bought a newspaper and some sugar and tea. Two other customers came in and made a fuss of the baby. He got Mary outside to his bike again and whispered, 'That went well. I don't think anyone was suspicious.'

'She looks older than three weeks.'

The difficulty was, Jonty thought as he kick-started his bike, he didn't know very much about babies.

Jonty heard by letter that the inquest was to be held in Holyhead ten days later. Because she couldn't possibly take Charlotte there, Mary would have to stay at home to look after her.

'I wish I could go,' she said. 'You'll find out all about the baby.'

'I'll take a notebook and pencil,' Jonty told her, 'and jot down all the relevant details for you.'

He knew she was also worried about what he might feel compelled to say in evidence. The body of another man had been washed up in the days following the wreck, having been carried by the currents to a beach up near Lynas Point. When it was identified as that of Joe Kelly, a deckhand on the *Priscilla*, all on board had been accounted for except the baby.

As Jonty hadn't known how long it would take him to get to Holyhead and find the hall in which the inquest was to be held, he arrived much too early. He sat studying the other people as they came in and took their places. His stomach was churning; these were not the sort of people he lived among. He knew the *Priscilla*'s home port was Liverpool, but they were not like the people he'd known when he'd worked there. They were the rich and powerful; they looked important.

The inquest was half an hour late starting because they had to wait for one of the main witnesses, who had been on board at the time of the accident. At last a party of three arrived, a couple in late middle age and a man Jonty took to be their son. The mother was tall and slim, a good-looking woman, fashionably dressed. The father was shorter and plumper than she was, with a lot of grey hair. Jonty heard someone behind him whisper that this was the owner of the *Priscilla*. The son, then, was the witness who had survived the wreck – and Charlotte's father. He looked haughty, and appeared unconcerned at having held proceedings up; almost as though he expected things to wait until he was ready.

The inquest started by naming the six who had lost their lives. Jonty jotted two of them down in the little red notebook he'd brought: Alicia Barrington Brown and her daughter, Abigail Elinor Barrington Brown, whose body was missing, presumed drowned. The baby had been born in Liverpool on 21 June 1922.

Then Roderick Barrington Brown was called, and the late-arriving son stepped forward to give evidence. He looked little older than Jonty himself, perhaps in his mid-twenties. He stood tall and broad-shouldered, with a pencil moustache and elegantly trimmed hair that was growing a little thin on top. He had rather a lordly expression as he agreed he'd identified the dead. They had all been known to him.

He told the court that when he'd last seen his wife and child, they'd been in the owner's day cabin which on the *Priscilla* had been up in the bow. The woman he employed as a nanny, Olga Maud Price, had been with them. The two women had been frightened by the storm and it had seemed the safest place for them.

Jonty felt transfixed by the man. He'd stolen his child, Abigail Elinor Barrington Brown aged nine weeks. He swallowed hard, awestruck that Mary had even dared to think of keeping her and that, even worse, he'd agreed.

Barrington Brown went on to say he'd been in the wheelhouse at the stern of the vessel with Captain Robert Merryhew, a helmsman and a deckhand when the yacht ran aground on the rocks.

'I tried to reach my wife and child.' Jonty could see the man's face working with emotion. 'But the *Priscilla* had broken her back and a rift was opening between the two halves. The bow was being pounded against the rocks and was breaking up. Joe Kelly, one of the deckhands, was on the bow half and tried to throw a rope to me. I wanted to establish a means by which we could get everybody to the stern of the vessel, but the gap was widening. The sea began rushing between the two parts and it was impossible for me to reach my family.'

Everybody in the hall was moved by the sight of his anguish. He went on to tell the court that his wife had been a little run down after the birth of their daughter and had needed a holiday. They had been down to the Isle of Wight for Cowes Week, a voyage that had lasted a month, and were on their way home to Liverpool when the incident had occurred.

He told them that the ship's cook, the deckhand Joe Kelly and the captain had also perished. Captain Merryhew had been employed by his family for many years, and had thirty years' experience of the sea.

Roderick's father Jeremy Barrington Brown was called to give evidence about the vessel. He was an older but softer version of his son with all the polish that authority, fine clothes and great wealth can give. He said the *Priscilla* was not a racing craft; his son had gone to Cowes Week for the social scene. She was an auxiliary motor yacht that had been owned by his family since she had been built in their yard in 1889. She was heavy and old-fashioned, but sat well in the water and had safely ridden out many storms in the past.

Jonty's mouth felt cinder dry as he studied the man, who described himself as the owner and manager of the Barrington Brown ship repair yard. Jonty knew of the business: two of his fellow lodgers in Liverpool had been riveters working there. It was a vast concern, employing many hundreds of people, and not very far from one of Percy Shawcross's garages. Jonty had passed the gates many times and heard their hooter sound at five thirty in the afternoon. Once he'd been on hand to see the workforce come out in a never-ending stream.

Jonty had thought his wife's family successful and rich but they were small fry compared with the Barrington Browns. He felt sick. He ought to stand up and admit he'd stolen this man's granddaughter. But he couldn't.

Then William Farrow, the mate of the *Priscilla*, was called. He was the most senior member of the ship's crew to survive and was asked to describe the circumstances leading up to the accident. He was nearing retirement age, an old Liverpudlian sea dog, and was on crutches having broken his leg in the wreck. The scars of recent grazings could be seen on his face and head.

'During that afternoon,' he said, 'we sailed up through Cardigan Bay on our way to Liverpool. The weather was grey and sultry and the sea was flat, but it looked as though a storm might blow up. By the time we were approaching Anglesey at six that evening, the wind force had risen and the barometer was falling. I was acting as helmsman when I heard Captain Merryhew suggest taking shelter in Holyhead harbour, but Mr Roderick Barrington Brown was anxious to get home and get back to work. We'd started the journey home four days earlier than intended because he'd heard that his father was ill and he was needed to manage the business. With that in mind, it was decided we should go on. The wind was from the south-east and growing stronger. We were heading north and were making fair headway under sail. All seemed well till we rounded the Skerries.'

He was asked to explain what the Skerries were.

'A group of small rocky outcrops off the north-east coast of Anglesey. We rounded them and turned in a wide circle across Liverpool Bay.'

He paused, and let out a juddering pent-up breath, obviously distressed and in some discomfort. He was told he might sit to give the rest of his evidence and an usher brought him a chair and a glass of water.

'Captain Merryhew ordered some of the sails to be furled, but Mr Roderick wanted to get as much speed out of her as he could, so we proceeded under full canvas.'

Roderick Barrington Brown leapt to his feet and interrupted to say, 'Nobody was much concerned at this point. The *Priscilla* was a soundly built heavy-weather boat and had survived storms at sea under Captain Merryhew before. The problems only began when the wind direction changed from south-east to north-east, which meant the gale was blowing us back against the coast of Anglesey.'

'Thank you, Mr Barrington Brown,' the coroner said. 'Would you agree, Mr Farrow, that the change of wind direction was the main cause of this accident?'

'Yes, sir.'

'Please proceed, Mr Farrow.'

The mate had been distracted and it took him a moment to pick up his tale. 'The captain ordered the engine to be started. Normally we used it only when there was insufficient wind for the sails or when we were manoeuvring in or out of a berth where we had little room. It was old and not nearly powerful enough, and it made little difference. The gale was still blowing us on land when we needed to get out into the Irish Sea.

The boat was rolling and heeling over, and by now making little headway against the mountainous waves rushing in towards us. The wind was really up and the mainmast must have been carrying too much canvas because it suddenly snapped and fell. The weight of the mast and canvas damaged the deck ribs and all but smashed the wheelhouse to smithereens, injuring Captain Merryhew.

'Mr Barrington Brown took charge after that. There was a huge sea running and we were taking in water through the structural damage. Heavy seas were breaking over the vessel, and water was running down the companionway hatch. The forehatch had been torn away and water was pouring through that and going down into the engine. From the moment it died the *Priscilla* was out of control and being swept before the storm.

'Mr Roderick ordered the anchor to be put out in the hope it would hold and prevent us drifting on shore. It dragged. We were moving with the wind and the tide, more slowly now, but we were still being swept closer to the coast. It was very dark and we could see nothing. I was ordered to send up distress flares. The first went up but the wind was so strong it was immediately blown down into the sea before anybody would have seen it. While I was watching it, two other flares that had been packed with it got wet, and wouldn't go off at all. I did manage to get another one up but I knew we were in big trouble by then.'

Jonty could hardly breathe. This was what he'd been watching from the safety of the headland. The old man was visibly tiring now. He blew his nose and went on.

'We all knew when the worst happened. The first jolt almost threw us off our feet. There was a terrible scraping and tearing noise as the hull kept pitching against the rocks. The gale and the incoming tide were still driving us forward and shattering the timbers until the *Priscilla* was split and broken in two. I saw Joe Kelly, a deckhand who happened to be in the bow section, trying to swim the few yards to shore, but the rollers threw him mercilessly against the rocky outcrops and he was drowned. Nobody who'd been in the bow section survived. The Moelfre lifeboat eventually arrived and took me, Mr Roderick and the remaining crew off the stern section.'

Roderick Barrington Brown was recalled and asked what experience he had of handling the *Priscilla*.

He held his head high and said in his authoritarian manner, 'I consider myself a competent master of the vessel. I've been sailing it since I was a boy; Captain Merryhew taught me to handle it and I often did. I knew the vessel inside out. Sailing is a family hobby.'

The keeper of the Lynas Point lighthouse then took the stand. He confirmed what the mate of the *Priscilla* had already told them. He'd logged the wind strength and confirmed that it had changed direction at about twenty-three fifteen to become a Force Ten north-easterly storm.

An officer of the coastguard then told them it had been a dark night and little could be seen in the murk and flying spray. The *Priscilla* had run aground on the headland, the worst possible place. Had they been able to steer her a few hundred yards to the west, she'd have been able to run up Hafren Sands, or in the other direction lay Moelfre Beach and the long stretch of Red Wharf Bay. Many other vessels had foundered in these waters.

After that, Jonty heard his name being called and got to his feet. He felt he was barely coherent as he tried to describe how he'd seen the flares and alerted the coastguard of the approaching disaster. Then he'd returned to the beach near the site of the wreck to see if he could do anything to help.

He was asked to describe the scene and said, 'It was horrific. Pandemonium. The wreck was close inshore but nobody could reach it. Gigantic rollers were washing across the wreck and the rocks, and pounding everything to bits. We'd have been washed into the sea if we'd tried. We had to wait until the Moelfre lifeboat and the coastguard cutter came.'

'Then as far as you were concerned it was over and you went home?'

'No, I helped Edward Evans, a neighbour, to move the bodies washed up in the cove to Hafren Chapel.'

'Do you know the names of those you took to the chapel?'

'I didn't at the time, but now I believe one to have been Mrs Barrington Brown. The other woman was wearing a nanny's uniform and the man appeared to be the captain.' Jonty could feel his gut churning. He was afraid the next question could be about a baby's body.

'Thank you,' he was told. 'You may step down.'

Jonty could feel himself shaking as he did so. He couldn't take his gaze from Roderick Barrington Brown. The man's head was bent, his hands covered his eyes, and he looked the picture of grief. Jonty was overwhelmed with guilt.

Not only had he wronged Barrington Brown and his family, but he'd also wronged the baby. Instead of growing up as Abigail Elinor Barrington Brown in a wealthy family with every advantage, she'd be plain Charlotte Mary Jones, the daughter of a subsistence farmer. Jonty tried to comfort himself with the thought that Mary would love her and care for her every bit as well as her natural mother would have done, but he could not suppress the feeling that he had done a terrible wrong.

He found it difficult to concentrate on the court proceedings after that, but before it rose he heard the verdict. For the adults, it was accidental death by drowning. As a result of the same accident, Abigail Elinor was missing, presumed dead by drowning.

Jonty went home feeling wrung out, and gave the notebook to Mary. He'd written down all he could about the shipwreck and the names of the different members of the Barrington Brown family, together with everything he'd learned about them and their circumstances.

Over the following days, he went out and bought several newspapers, all of which gave accounts of the wreck and the inquest. He kept cuttings of everything that was relevant and folded them inside the little red notebook.

He was very troubled by what he'd done and was glad Mary had not been with him to hear the heart-rending tale. She seemed to think that now Abigail was legally presumed to be dead, nothing would prevent them keeping her.

Jonty couldn't help saying, 'Her father will miss her. He looked agonised.'

'Yes, but it's not easy for a man to look after a tiny baby when he has no wife.'

'She has a grandmother, and she was near to tears at the inquest. They employed a nanny anyway. It wouldn't be that difficult for them.'

'But would Charlotte be better off than with us? I'll love her more than any paid nanny would.'

Chapter Eight

A S THEY LEFT the hall where the inquest had been held, Roderick Barrington Brown couldn't stop trembling. He felt cold and stiff and he had a thumping headache. His father walked beside him staring straight ahead, his face white with anger. Roderick knew he must expect more trouble.

Damn, damn, damn Bill Farrow for opening his mouth so wide. It hadn't occurred to Rod that the old fool would tell the coroner that Captain Merryhew had suggested they take shelter in Holyhead harbour on the night of the wreck, and that he had insisted on going on. Or that the captain had wanted to furl the sails and he'd persuaded him not to. Or that Farrow had heard him tell Merryhew that his father had been taken ill and he was in a hurry to get home to run the business. Rod hadn't even realised Farrow had been near enough to hear what they were discussing. Farrow had made it sound as though the accident was all his fault.

For God's sake! All he'd wanted to do was to give old Merryhew a reason to go on. It had been an innocent white lie. But for Farrow to repeat it in court in Pa's hearing when he knew it to be untrue! Rod knew that was guaranteed to bring Pa's wrath down on his head again. It had been bad enough having to give evidence and relive the horrific details of what had happened on that awful night, without the mate, stupid fellow that he was, making matters worse. He wished Bill Farrow had perished with the rest of them.

Dorking, his father's chauffeur, leapt out of the car to hold the door open as soon as he saw them approaching. Rod watched his parents get in.

'I'll sit in the front with Dorking,' he said. 'It'll give you more room.'

'No.' His father rapped out the word. 'Get in here with us. I want to talk to you.'

He did so reluctantly. His father's word was law.

'Dorking, please take us back to that hotel at Beaumaris,' his father ordered. 'We'll need a meal and a rest before we can travel home.'

Rod watched his father carefully close the glass partition to prevent the chauffeur from hearing what they said. He sank back in the leather cushions and closed his eyes. He knew what was coming.

His father turned on him. 'Why did you have to interfere with Bob Merryhew's orders? He was in charge, and if only you'd let him decide what should be done, you'd all have been safe. You always think you know best. You were lucky not to be held to account for causing that accident.'

'Jeremy dear, don't . . .' his mother put in softly. 'I'm sure Rod blames himself for what happened.'

'I doubt it, but he certainly should. And why tell the crew I'd been taken ill and you were in a hurry to get home? That was a pack of lies. I was as fit as I've ever been. I should have stood up and told the coroner so as soon as I heard Farrow say it. And as for taking over the yard, Rod, you've a long way to go before you'll be doing that.'

'Why were you in a hurry?' his mother asked. 'We thought you and Alicia would enjoy a few weeks on the boat.'

Rod stiffened. He and Alicia had had a tiff and they were both fed up with the boat. They were living on top of one another and the crew were always underfoot and in the way. Most meals had to be taken with Captain Merryhew who would report back to Pa. He'd wanted the trip over and done with, so he and Alicia could be at home on their own. He'd thought it would be easier to sort themselves out there where they had more space.

Pa was still moaning at him. 'You always have to lie to justify what you do.'

'I'm sorry, Pa. The last few weeks have been an ordeal. Things are on top of me at the moment.'

'I'm sure they are.' His mother was more sympathetic. 'It must be agonising losing Alicia and the baby like that. We loved them and miss them. How much worse must it be for you.'

Rod was blinking hard. He mustn't give in to tears again, but they'd been perilously close ever since the shipwreck. He had loved Alicia, and now she was gone for good. He felt bereft without her. He couldn't stand any more of Pa rubbing his nose in this mess.

'If it's all the same to you, I'll take the train home,' he said. 'After Dorking drops you at the hotel, I'll get him to take me to the nearest railway station.'

'Right,' Pa said. 'Perhaps it would be better if you did. We might say things in the heat of the moment we'd regret later.'

Clarissa Barrington Brown was fighting to control her tears as they went up the hotel stairs. They did not intend to stay the night; Jeremy had booked the room so they'd have somewhere private to rest before the drive back to Liverpool.

'Such a tragedy. Such a terrible loss of life.' She took off her hat and coat and lay down on the bed.

'I should have known old Merryhew would never have put the *Priscilla* in danger.' Jeremy was angry. 'I shall miss him, miss the boat too. Roderick countermanded his orders. What a stupid fool the lad is.'

'Alicia was such a sweet girl, and her lovely lovely baby, both drowned. It'll take me a long time to get over this.'

'Six dead. All his fault and he won't admit it. He's looking for excuses, damn it.'

Clarissa sighed. 'Don't push him too hard, Jeremy. You know what he was like when he had that mental breakdown.'

'That was ages ago. He was just a lad.'

'In his teens.'

'He's grown up now.'

'I'm not so sure about that. Just go easy on him.'

'He's no common sense, doesn't use his brain, but he thinks he knows it all. Give him a choice and he'll always make the wrong decision.'

'He needed Alicia to lean on. There's no stability about him.'

'Never has been.'

Clarissa closed her eyes. 'Don't you have the feeling he's on the brink of another?'

Jeremy gripped the rail at the foot of the bed. 'A mental breakdown, you mean?'

'Yes. He's done a truly terrible thing, hasn't he? He must blame himself, surely?'

*

An hour later, Rod wasn't so sure he'd done the right thing. He'd got away from Pa, but he'd had to wait on a windswept country station for the local stopping train to Bangor. From there he'd just missed a train to Liverpool and had another two hours to wait for the next. If only he'd known what to expect, he'd have got Dorking to run him straight into Bangor. It wasn't that far. As it was, he thought they might all be back in Liverpool before he was. If his father knew, he'd no doubt say, 'Par for the course. You've taken yet another bad decision. Better if you'd stayed with us and let me organise it. Then you could have travelled in comfort.'

Rod did manage to get a second-rate meal at a hotel in Bangor, and that passed some of the time. But he felt exhausted by the time the Liverpool train was setting off. It had been a terrible day and he hadn't slept well since the shipwreck.

He got a first-class carriage to himself and settled himself into a corner seat. It was getting late, and there was nothing to see on this dark night. He dozed during the journey; truly tonight nothing could have kept him awake.

He might have known he'd have that dreadful nightmare again. He'd hardly had a night's peace since the *Priscilla* foundered. Alicia was there before him again, with her lovely dark red hair and her clothes streaming with seawater.

Her face was twisting with bitter feeling. 'It's your fault. I blame you. You drowned me and our baby. How could you be so heartlessly stupid? Why didn't you put into that safe harbour?'

Everybody was blaming him for it, even the dead.

From the moment Mary had found the baby on the beach she'd been sure it was providence that had brought them together. She was meant to bring this child up as her own. She knew Jonty was edgy about keeping her because, as always, his conscience was pricking him. He told her it was morally wrong. Mary was feeling pangs of guilt herself and was equally edgy. She was also afraid they would be found out and forced to hand Charlotte back. She doted on the baby. She was enjoying her company and ready to play with her at any time of the day or night. One evening she saw Jonty watching her sing some silly nursery rhyme that had ended with her tickling Charlotte and making her laugh, and said, 'I feel she's part of our family already. You love her too, don't you?'

He took the baby from her arms and studied her with a mixture of doubt and concern on his face. Charlotte's big brown eyes stared up into his. Then Mary heard the baby chuckle again. She saw her give him a big smile, showing her rosy gums and tiny tongue. His arms tightened round her in an involuntary hug.

'You're right,' he said. 'She's adorable. We'll do our very best for her. We'll give her a good home and the best start in life we can.'

But later, when the baby had been put to bed and they were eating their supper, Mary knew all his doubts had returned.

'We ought to register her birth,' he said, frowning. 'Everybody needs a birth certificate. It bothers me that she won't have one.'

'She won't need one for ages yet,' Mary told him. 'Can't we say when it comes up that we've lost it?'

'No. If we lose ours we can ask for a copy, but for her there'd be nothing in the registers to copy. That could be one way she might find out that she really belongs to somebody else.'

'Then we'll have to do it.'

'Dare we?' Jonty was worried. 'I know we'd have to go to the registrar of births, marriages and deaths, but do we need proof that the baby is ours? I don't know much about that sort of thing.'

'If we take Charlotte with us, she's the proof we've got a baby, isn't she?'

'I don't know.'

'If we had her birth certificate, that would make her really ours. Isn't that legal proof she belongs to us?'

Jonty shook his head. 'I know nothing about such things.'

'We must do it.'

He kept her awake for a long time that night, as he tried to decide on the best date to give as the baby's birth date. Not her true one: that would link her with Abigail Elinor. Anyway, it was nine weeks ago, far too long for proud new parents to have kept her hidden at home without saying anything to the neighbours. Neither did they want to give the date of the shipwreck. That was indelibly inked on everyone's mind here and they didn't want that date associated with Charlotte.

'We'll do it today,' Mary said as she helped with the morning milking and the feeding of the stock. She knew she had to be the strong one in matters like this, and she'd read somewhere that a baby's birth had to be registered within six weeks, or parents could be fined.

Jonty seemed nervous as he drove them to Holyhead that morning to look for the registrar's office. They went inside as a family.

'I want to register our daughter,' Mary told the clerk, and gave her name as Charlotte Mary Jones, born at home on 20 August 1922. That made her three weeks old. She kept her well wrapped up in her shawl, so nobody could get a good look at her and think she must be older. Outside on the steps Jonty took the baby from her because she was getting quite heavy.

'There's no turning back now,' he said, giving Mary the manila envelope containing the essential birth certificate.

Mary was pleased. Jonty had accepted that Charlotte was with them to stay.

'I need to buy a dozen nappies and a couple of vests for her while we're here,' she said.

He sighed. 'Ought we to be thinking about a pram?'

Mary saw the years that followed as the happiest in her life. She had everything she wanted except a larger family. She was beginning to acknowledge that repeated pregnancies could ruin her health without ever giving her the baby she wanted so much.

As she grew older, Charlotte became more responsive. She walked and talked at an early age, and they both adored her. As a toddler she was just as likely to be at Jonty's heels as he went about his farm work as she was to be in the kitchen with Mary.

During the summer of 1924 Charlotte had her second birthday. Dan wrote to say he was due for his annual week's holiday and would like to bring his family to Anglesey and see something of her and Jonty. Would Mary book them into a nearby boarding house?

Mary wrote back to say she was sorry she hadn't room for the four of them in her little cottage. She'd booked for them to have bed and breakfast in a guest house in Moelfre and she would provide their other meals at Glan y Mor. She was longing to see them.

She was even more thrilled when Barbara wrote to say Edith wanted to come with them. Mary wrote back by return to both Barbara and her mother saying she'd love Edith to stay with them at Glan y Mor. They had only two bedrooms but she could easily move Charlotte's cot into their own room. They would buy the single bed she would soon need and her mother could sleep in it first.

Mary was so looking forward to it that she persuaded Jonty to act on his plan to put a push-pull lavatory into the woodshed adjoining the house and knock a way through to it. It was finished in good time and he was able to help her repaper the second bedroom so it would look its best when Edith came. Mary spent the day before cooking and baking in readiness.

Dan drove them down in his car. He now looked a prosperous family man and Barbara was beginning to look more matronly. Mary thought her mother looked older and somewhat dispirited when she arrived.

'I've brought my old sewing machine for you,' she said to Mary. 'I don't use it now, but when you children were small I used to make all your clothes.'

'Oh, Mum, thank you! I'll find it very useful. I'll be able to make Charlotte's clothes, and some for myself too.' Mary had been taught to sew as a teenager and had used the machine from time to time to make dresses for herself.

Edith said, 'I've told your father he was wrong about Jonty and that you're happy here helping him run his farm. I've also told him you have a little daughter.'

'What did he say?'

'"Only one? I'd have thought they'd have a string of children by now."'

Mary smiled ruefully. 'I wish I had.'

The family made a big fuss of Charlotte. 'She's full of life and a real chatterbox,' her mother said, watching the toddler playing with Dan's two little boys. Jonty showed them all round his smallholding, and they were very impressed with it. The sun shone and the sea sparkled.

'You did the right thing, Jonty,' Dan told him, 'to get clear away from our garages. It must be lovely to live in such a beautiful place.'

Mary wanted to hear all the family news.

'Len is planning to get married early in April next year. Pa has agreed to increase his wages so he can. We all like Ruth. I've brought some photographs for you to see.'

'I've met Ruth,' Mary said. 'He was walking out with her before I left.'

'Of course. Noel has plenty of girl friends, but doesn't seem to find any of them special. Probably just as well, as Pa would say he was too young.'

'And Pa?' Mary asked. 'How is he?'

'Just the same.' Her mother sighed. 'I told him I was coming to see you and asked him to come too, but he wouldn't.'

Mary's thoughts went back to the day he'd told her to leave his house. 'He hasn't forgiven me then?'

'I'm afraid not. He's a proud man, Mary, and he has to be right about everything. He never backs down.'

'I want you to remind him I'm very happy with Jonty. Let him know we have a much better life here in the country than we would have had in Liverpool.'

'And with your own little cove too. It's a lovely spot. I can see why you enjoy it so much.'

The weather was wonderful all that week, one of the best weeks of the summer, every day warm and sunny. Mary loved having her family round her again. They spent a lot of their time on the beach but Dan's two little boys loved the farm and the animals, and were more than happy playing about the fields and the farm buildings. They and Charlotte seemed to get on well together, and they all loved the picnic lunches down in the cove, or out on the headland. Much nicer than sitting at the kitchen table, they said, as they did for high tea.

Mary was sorry when her visitors had to return to Liverpool. 'Come again, Mum,' she said, giving her a hug. 'And make it soon. I don't want us to lose touch.'

Having Charlotte made festivities at Christmas much more fun. It was at Christmas 1925 that Mary realised she was pregnant again. Jonty had persuaded her that they should try to prevent it happening in case she miscarried again, but it had happened despite Jonty's precautions and Mary was not sorry. She'd love to have another baby now, to complete her family. She lived in hope for three months, but had another miscarriage in March.

'I'm so sorry,' Jonty whispered, holding her close. 'I must be more careful.'

'It's me,' Mary said. 'There's something wrong with me. I can't carry a baby through to term.'

'We all have to accept what we can't change,' Jonty told her. 'We'll not let this happen again, it brings nothing but grief. We have to be content with what we have.'

For Mary, that made Charlotte doubly precious. 'I was right to persuade you to keep her,' she said.

Charlotte started at the village school in the September following her fourth birthday. She was not in the least anxious about it, but Mary knew she'd miss having her about the house all day. On the first morning Jonty ran them down in his sidecar, but it took him away from his morning routine with the animals, so after that Mary walked down to the school each morning while Charlotte danced ahead of her.

She was a very pretty, lively child. Her thick hair had a slight curl to it and was a lovely deep auburn colour. For school, Mary anchored it in two bunches with elastic bands. Every afternoon, she met her at the school gates and was drawn into conversation with the other mothers as they waited. By the end of the first term she knew Enid Evans and the family at Plas Hafren much better than she had.

Ted and Enid had four children, the youngest, Glyn, was four months older than Charlotte. Mary usually walked part of the way home chatting to Enid while the children streamed ahead.

That Christmas, Mary was drawn into sewing costumes for the nativity play and baking fairy cakes for the children's party. The school fascinated her. It was very different from the one she'd attended. There was one large classroom heated by two coal fires, with a glass partition closing off one end. For the first two years the youngest had their own teacher, Miss Jenkins. Charlotte loved her and learned a lot from her and it was some time before Mary realised she had no qualifications to teach. Miss Williams taught the rest of the school and she was both qualified and experienced.

Every morning, Mary cut a sandwich for Charlotte's lunch and filled a tomato sauce bottle with fresh milk to put in her school bag.

Charlotte soon became friends with a little girl in her class called Megan. Her father kept the Red Lion pub in the village, and Mary became friendly with her mother.

'Charlotte is very good for our social life,' Jonty told her. 'We know many more people than we did.'

'I must say, I get out and about more, but all the same I'm looking forward to the school holidays when I'll have Charlotte at home,' Mary said.

Enid stopped walking Glyn to school after one term. 'What's the point when the older ones are going? Our Glenys is nine – she'll keep an eye on him. She can keep an eye on your Charlotte too, if you like.'

Mary was reluctant. 'I enjoy the walk and meeting the other mothers,' she said.

'If I feel like a walk in the afternoon I meet them coming out. In the morning, I get my work done while I have the house to myself.'

Mary soon realised Charlotte was more than happy to go with the other children. She took to walking down to Plas Hafren with her, and when the children moved out in a noisy bunch Enid would offer a cup of tea and they'd sit down for a chat.

In the school holidays Charlotte wanted to help about the farm. She loved the animals and grew up knowing how to manage them. Jonty taught her to milk the cows and make butter and by the time she was ten years of age she had a ewe and lamb of her own.

The year she turned eleven, Charlotte brought home a note from Miss Williams saying her school work showed promise. The teacher believed Charlotte to be capable of passing the scholarship exam for the County School and recommended that she should sit it in the spring. Mary was pleased and Jonty even more so.

'If she can get in it would be wonderful,' he said. 'She'll get a decent education.'

Mary knew he still worried that because they'd taken her from her rightful family Charlotte was losing out. That year, three of Miss Williams's pupils managed to get scholarships: Glyn Evans, Charlotte and her friend Megan Lewis.

Both Jonty and Mary were thrilled and set about collecting her new school uniform. It meant a much longer journey to school, but Enid told Mary that though there was a bus going from Moelfre she'd found the simplest and cheapest way was to provide a bicycle and let her children make her own way there and back. Glyn's older siblings, Kevin and Tegwen, had now left school, but Glenys, his second sister, had been cycling to the County School for the last three years. Glyn already had a bike and he'd be going with his sister.

Jonty found a second-hand bicycle for Charlotte and worked on it until it looked like new. From that September, she rode down to Plas Hafren to pick up Glyn and Glenys and they cycled to school together through the country lanes.

Every summer Mary invited her Liverpool relatives to Glan y Mor. Her mother came by train and stayed for a week. Barbara's boys Simon and Tim came with their grandmother and stayed on to spend several weeks during the school holidays. They thought it a great adventure to sleep on top of the hay in the barn and play about the farm. Charlotte loved having them around, and they enjoyed helping with the animals.

On some days, Jonty would arrange with John Jarvis to take them out fishing in his boat. On others, the Evans children came to play. They'd collect driftwood along the beach and when they'd dried enough they'd light a bonfire there and cook their lunch on it. Mackerel if they could get it, or Enid provided home-cured bacon.

Jonty's motor bike had always fascinated Charlotte, and by the time she was in her teens she was begging Jonty to teach her to ride it. During one summer holiday when they had a long spell of dry weather and the bike wouldn't cut up the turf on his level field, he taught her and Dan's boys to manage the bike and sidecar. At the end of the holidays Dan and Barbara would come for a few days and take them home.

Mary thought of them as halcyon days. They were for her and her family, but in the wider world storm clouds were gathering. Jonty bought his first wireless so they would know what Hitler was doing in Europe.

CHAPTER NINE

THE YEAR CHARLOTTE and Glyn turned sixteen, Hitler's armies were surging across Europe and there was talk of another war. Many people could remember the horror of the last one and lived in dread of another. Even though the Prime Minister had been to see Hitler and promised peace for their time, people were afraid it was coming.

Both Mary and Jonty were anxious that Charlotte should train for some sort of career. They tried to discuss it with her.

'You must make your own choice,' Mary told her, remembering how her father had mapped her future out without consulting her. Charlotte talked about her strengths and weaknesses and where her interests lay. She was doing well at the County School and it seemed she'd have a wide choice.

Glyn Evans had already made up his mind he'd like to be a teacher and that he'd apply for a place at the Bangor Normal College when the time came. Mary knew Charlotte was toying with the idea of teaching too. But eventually she said, 'I think I'd rather be a nurse.'

Jonty was pleased because it was the one career for which training did not cost money. Almost anything else would have proved difficult for him to finance.

Glyn's sister Glenys was already training to be a nurse at the hospital in Bangor, where their older sister Tegwen was a staff nurse. Charlotte went over one day when Glenys had come home for her day off and had a long talk with her in the big kitchen at Plas Hafren. Glenys was happy there and full of anecdotes about life on the wards. Charlotte decided she'd like to train at Bangor too, though Glenys would have finished her training by the time Charlotte was ready to start.

'I'll be able to come home every week for my day off,' she told Mary when she got back, and both Mary and Jonty approved of her choice.

Then her friend Megan decided she wanted to be a nurse too. Mrs Lewis was friendly with one of the ward sisters at Liverpool Royal Infirmary, who said the training given there was considered superior and carried more status. Megan was planning to go to Liverpool. Charlotte changed her mind. She wanted to go with Megan.

'I'd have a friend to go with and to live in a big city would be an adventure.'

Mary tried not to let her see that she was upset, 'But we won't be able to see so much of you.'

'I'll come home as often as I can, Mum,' she said. 'You know that.'

Jonty said, 'If it's true the training is better there, perhaps she should go.'

Later, when they were alone, he said to Mary, 'Another reason Charlotte should go is that she'd have been brought up in Liverpool if we hadn't . . .'

'Jonty, that's all ancient history now!' Mary didn't want to be reminded. 'We've made Charlotte ours. She's a country girl.'

'Yes, but she ought to see something of city life while she's young enough to enjoy it.'

Mary wrote to Barbara to see if she knew anything about the Liverpool Royal Infirmary.

'It has an excellent reputation as a training school,' her sister-in-law wrote by return. 'And Charlotte can come here or go to your mother's on her days off. It's not as though she knows nobody here.'

Mary still didn't like the idea, though she could see the sense of it.

'She's growing up,' Jonty said. 'At her age I was coping on my own. Charlotte must learn to do that too. You mustn't wrap her in cotton wool.'

'I know,' Mary agreed, 'though I'd like to keep her close. I'll miss her if she goes to Liverpool.'

All year, war loomed ever closer and shortly after Charlotte's seventeenth birthday they were shocked when war was declared with Germany.

'War changes everything,' Charlotte said over their Sunday dinner that day. 'I don't want to spend another year at school. I want to do something to help.'

'No,' Jonty insisted. 'You need to get your higher school certificate first.'

'I can do nursing without that.'

'But they won't let you start until you're eighteen so you might as well spend the time in school.' Charlotte was smouldering. Jonty went on, 'I'd like to help too, but I'm too old to be called up.'

'Thank goodness for that,' Mary said firmly. 'I want to keep you both safe. Anyway, I couldn't possibly manage the milking and everything else here by myself.'

So that autumn Charlotte and Glyn returned to school and watched their friends and relatives being called up. Charlotte's cousin Simon went into the army and Tim announced his intention of volunteering for the air force as soon as he could.

They both grumbled about staying on at school. 'We'd be better off helping the war effort,' Charlotte said.

'My sister Glenys is determined to join the QARANC as soon as they'll have her,' Glyn told Mary. 'But they're asking for two years' postgraduate experience and she only sits her finals this October.'

His brother Kevin wanted to join the air force, but his father said he couldn't manage the farm work without him because he'd already lost the farm boy he'd employed for the last two years. He applied for exemption for Kevin and got it. Kevin wasn't pleased.

The question of Charlotte's nursing training came up again.

'I don't think you should go to Liverpool,' Mary said firmly. 'Not with a war on. It's dangerous – the children there have been evacuated out here.'

Megan's parents said the same, that she must train at Bangor. Megan rebelled. If she couldn't go to Liverpool she wouldn't do nursing. She wouldn't stay on at school either; she was going to leave home and find herself a job.

She went to live with an aunt in Bangor who helped her become a telephone operator, but Megan wasn't happy there. She came home whenever she had time off and told Charlotte it was a boring job and did nothing to help the war effort.

Life went on pretty much as it always had in Anglesey, except that Charlotte was developing a social life of her own. All that year she'd been going with Glyn, and his brother and sisters if they happened to be at home, to cinemas in Llangefni and Holyhead. At weekends they teamed up with a group of school friends and went to dances held in village halls across half the island.

'I don't like her going out so much,' Mary said to Jonty as they were left together by the fire. 'She's too young to have a boyfriend.'

He laughed. 'Mary, love! We were courting when you were her age, and you were only nineteen when I persuaded you to come here with me. She'll not go far wrong with Glyn Evans.'

They were not sure what the relationship was between Glyn and Charlotte. They'd always been friendly as children and now they were certainly seeing more of each other, but when Jonty asked about him Charlotte laughed and said she didn't think of Glyn as her boyfriend.

Enid, Glyn's mother, chatted about it to Mary. She thought he was serious about Charlotte. Knowing that Enid thought it was a good thing helped to reconcile Mary to the idea.

Charlotte was surprised to find the first year of the war passing quietly. Everybody was worried about rationing but she knew they'd have few problems because Glan y Mor was a subsistence farm that produced most of what they ate. There was as much milk, butter, bacon, ham and eggs as they'd always had. Potatoes and other vegetables grew in profusion.

Her mother had always bottled, preserved and cured. She made jams and chutneys, cakes and pies. She complained about the scarcity of sugar, but the proprietor of the village stores offered her extra if she didn't take her rations of margarine, lard and bacon. Shop butter was known as box butter on the farms and used to make cakes. When Mum had surplus fresh butter she sold it to the shop. If anything in short supply came into the shop, it was kept under the counter and offered to farmers' wives like Mary.

They'd fattened a herd of thirty geese for Christmas, keeping one for themselves and sending one to Edith in Liverpool. All their customers had praised the tender succulent meat. Charlotte knew nobody went hungry on a farm, even if they couldn't get as much sugar and tea as they would have liked.

Megan Lewis came home saying she was fed up with Bangor and spent her time helping her parents run the Red Lion pub.

'I don't want you to drop out of school like Megan,' Jonty told Charlotte. 'It's important to take the exams to prove you've had a good education.'

'Glyn's thinking of dropping out,' she told him. 'He'll be eighteen at

Easter. He says he'll get his calling up papers then. He wants to join the air force.'

Christmas was over but school had not yet reopened. Charlotte loved dressing up and going to a dance. Tonight, she was going to wear the new dress Mum had made as a Christmas present from a length of blue and white striped taffeta. It had turned out very well and Charlotte was delighted with it. She wore her dark auburn hair in one fat plait to school, but she'd washed it today to get rid of the kinks, as she wanted to wear it loose tonight. She brushed it until it shone and then held it back with a tortoiseshell Alice band. Having applied a little face powder and lipstick, she went to twirl her new dress in front of her parents.

'You look lovely,' they told her.

She was looking forward to her night out as she wrapped up her dance shoes and pulled on her wellingtons and macintosh to run down to Plas Hafren. It was cold and had been raining most of the day. Tegwen and Glenys were both home for their night off. Both were small and slim with dark curly hair. Glenys was the prettier of the two. She was wearing a blue skirt with a white peasant blouse. Tegwen had made herself a green floral dress with a wide skirt.

Ted, their father, often said that he didn't get on well with machines and was sorry he hadn't kept his horse and trap. Kevin had become the main driver in the family and was teaching Glyn to drive. If he could save enough petrol from their allowance he was permitted to use the family's Ford. Tonight, they'd decided to go dancing in a church hall in Amlwch. There were still a few visitors on the island and the local youngsters were out in force to dance to the five-piece band. When they arrived it was playing a bouncy quickstep that set Charlotte's feet tapping.

'Let's dance this one,' she said to Glyn and he had her circling the floor within moments. She thought herself lucky to have a choice of partners, and it was accepted that they'd each dance with other friends during the evening. When the tune finished, Glyn started to talk to someone else.

Kevin had a girlfriend who lived in Amlwch and she had joined the group. Charlotte was chatting to a girl from her school when she noticed a man watching her from across the room. She smiled, and he immediately came across and asked her to dance.

She knew who he was and where he lived. She knew almost everybody living nearby at least by sight. Alun Jarvis and his older brother Howell used to bring fish up to Glan y Mor to repay Dad for maintaining the engine on their father's boat. He had dark hair with a slight wave and dark eyes that were trying to flirt with hers. He was quite a bit older than she was, and although she'd chatted to him from time to time he'd never been part of her circle.

Now, she couldn't take her gaze from his face. He was like a magnet drawing her senses. She felt his arms go round her as they moved off in unison to the beat. Charlotte believed she fell in love with him at that moment.

The suddenness of it made her tongue-tied. She felt an urge to put her head down on his shoulder and she had to make an effort to sound normal as she asked him if he was still fishing with his father.

'No,' he told her. 'Howell usually goes out with him. It's a small boat and two men are enough to manage it.'

'I heard you were going out in the other local boats.'

'I did for a few years, but now there's a war on, I decided I'd join the merchant navy.'

Charlotte was impressed.

'I thought I'd do it while I still had a choice,' he said. 'My friends are getting their call-up papers. The sea is what I know, and I'd rather this than the Royal Navy.'

He was tall and stood very straight; his strong broad shoulders made the boys of her age look mere striplings by comparison. He told her he was twenty-six. Alun was a man in his prime. He stuck to her side like a limpet all evening and she drew him into the circle of her friends. He got on well with the older Evanses and danced first with Tegwen and then with Glenys.

Glyn asked, 'D'you like him?' Charlotte could tell he wasn't pleased.

When the last waltz was over and they were preparing to leave, Alun said, 'Can I take you home? I've come on my motor bike and I could, if you're willing to ride pillion.'

'Yes.' Charlotte was quite at home on a motor bike. She often rode pillion behind her father. With Mum in the sidecar, it meant the family could go out together.

'No,' Glyn objected, scowling at Alun. 'Your dad made us promise we'd always see you got back to the gate at the bottom of your hill. He'd kill us – wouldn't he, Kevin? – if we didn't take you back.'

'Yes, that's right.'

'Oh! I didn't know that,' said Charlotte, startled.

'So you'd better come with us,' Glenys said. 'Anyway, you'd only get oil on your dress from his old bike.'

Alun smiled at her and whispered, 'There's no reason why I can't walk you up the hill, though. I'll walk you to your door.'

Kevin had to make a detour to take his girlfriend home. After Charlotte had said good night to her friends and thanked Kevin for the ride, she got out of the car at the gate leading up to Glan y Mor. She watched its rear lights disappear up the empty road and felt a shaft of disappointment. Alun had started out ahead of them and she'd expected to find him here waiting for her.

She turned towards the gate to go home. Now her eyes were used to the dark she could see Alun opening it for her from the inside.

'I've left my bike against the hedge here where nobody's likely to see it,' he said, throwing his arms round her in a bear hug that swung her off her feet. He was planting little butterfly kisses all over her face, 'You're so beautiful,' he whispered. Then his lips found hers in a kiss like none she'd ever known. She could feel his passion, and felt her own heart fluttering. This was the sort of love she'd read about.

He lifted his mouth from hers just long enough to whisper, 'I've been longing to do this all evening.'

Charlotte was thrilled and wanted it to go on all night, but she knew her parents would be waiting for her to come home. They might even have watched the car lights come up the road and know she was on her way up the path. It was she who started them walking with their arms round each other.

Never had the journey up the hill been so enjoyable or taken so long. Alun kept stopping to kiss her again, and run his fingers through her hair. 'I've never seen anyone else with hair this colour. You have wonderful hair.'

They'd almost reached the cottage. 'Can I see you again tomorrow?' he asked. 'Will you come out with me?'

'I'd love to.'

'I'll come for you. Early. How about three o'clock?'

'I wish I didn't have to go in now.'

He'd pushed his arms inside her macintosh and was holding her tight. His body felt strong against hers.

'Charlotte? Is that you?' It was her father's voice.

She sprang away from Alun as she saw Jonty's lantern coming across the farmyard.

'Hello, Dad,' she said, straightening her mac and buttoning it up.

Mary put aside the cardigan she was knitting for Charlotte. She was beginning to think Jonty had been mistaken about seeing the Plas Hafren car go up the road, but no, here was Charlotte safe and sound. It surprised her to find she hadn't come alone.

'I've brought Alun in to say hello.' She was pulling him by the arm, and she sounded exhilarated.

Mary stood up. 'Hello, Alun. It seems a long time . . .'

'Yes, I'm just home for a holiday. I've joined the merchant navy.'

Jonty shook his hand. 'Good for you. As an officer cadet?'

'No, they've scrapped all that now we're at war. Anyway, they couldn't get enough lads to join at sixteen and be indentured for four years. They're taking on men now. I've been on an induction course and I'm joining my first ship in Liverpool on Monday.'

'Alun's going to help the war effort,' Charlotte said proudly. 'There's been a lot of talk about the Germans starving us out by stopping our cargo ships getting through with supplies.'

'Well done,' Jonty told him.

'I'm hoping it'll give me a peacetime career too,' he said.

Mary took a deep breath. He must have known the Germans were attacking British ships. Had it not occurred to him that they might sink his?

'Good idea,' she said. 'Very wise.'

She knew Alun, of course. He was a very nice lad; both John Jarvis's boys were. She remembered opening the front door and finding Alun on the step with a parcel of fish. The Jarvises' cottage was next door to the postman's in Maelfre. Nowadays, he brought the fish along with their letters.

'Where will your ship be going?' she asked.

'They don't tell me that, I'm afraid. It's all hush-hush now we're at war.'

'Of course. I shouldn't ask.'

'Probably an American port.' He looked ill at ease, so Mary offered him a cup of tea and a piece of cake.

'No thank you, Mrs Jones. It's getting late and I must get home. I'll be on my way.'

She watched Charlotte show him to the door, and heard them whispering in the porch. Did this mean Charlotte saw him as a boyfriend? Alun had grown into a good-looking man, but he must be nearly ten years older than Charlotte. Mary thought him altogether too grown up for her.

'How's the cow?' she asked Jonty, who had been out to the byre because Pansy, his newest Jersey, was nearing her time to calve.

'She's all right. It doesn't look as if anything will happen until tomorrow.'

It was only when they were in their own bedroom with the door carefully shut that he said, 'That's a turn-up for the books. Little Charlotte with a grown-up boyfriend.'

'I'd rather it was Glyn,' Mary said.

'Oh, Mary.' He smiled. 'You're getting like your father. Surely you aren't matchmaking for your daughter?'

The next afternoon, Charlotte spent a marvellous time on the beach at Red Wharf Bay. It was a better day of fitful sunshine and cold blustery wind. At the top of the beach Alun made a little hollow in the sand and spread out a groundsheet he'd brought in his saddlebag. It sheltered them from the cutting edge of the wind, which was sending the clouds scudding across the sky.

Charlotte lay down beside him. Soon Alun's gentle touch was sending shivers of ecstasy up and down her spine. She could feel herself responding; she'd never felt so alive. He was opening up a whole new world to her. His eager kisses raised her to unimagined heights of pleasure and made her cling to him. Her heart raced as she smoothed his dark windblown hair back into place. She thought him very handsome.

The gulls called and the waves pounded on the beach, but she was only aware of his touch. It grew colder as darkness fell, and the only source of warmth was the heat of his body. Soon the beach was bathed in silvery moonlight, making the white-tipped waves sparkle. Charlotte was touched by love and thought it was the most romantic evening of her life.

At last he said, 'Come on, you're getting cold. We can't stay here for ever. Let's go.'

She felt dazed, and didn't want this to end. 'Where to? Everything closes on Sundays.'

'I know, there's not a pub or a café open anywhere round here. Liverpool's much better.' He took her hand and pulled her to her feet. 'I could take you to my sister Margaret's. You know her, don't you?'

Charlotte dusted the sand off her clothes. 'Sort of. Not well.'

'She's married now and has a house in the village. She usually gives me a welcome.' He put his lips on hers again and his kisses tasted of sea salt. 'We can get warm by her fire and she'll make us a cup of tea.'

Charlotte knew it was that or ask to be taken home, and she wanted to stay with him for as long as she could. Mum and Dad would do the same for them, but their presence would inhibit her.

Margaret was very hospitable. She sat them at her table and gave them a supper of soused herrings with bread and butter followed by Christmas cake. Her husband wanted to hear about Alun's life in Liverpool, which sounded exciting compared with their humdrum existence here. Charlotte couldn't drag her eyes away from him. She thought he was wonderful.

Afterwards, he ran her home on the back of his motor bike. At the bottom of the hill he took from his saddlebag an envelope containing a photograph of himself in his new uniform.

'You might like to have this,' he said. 'It's a spare. My mother wanted me to have it taken. She had nothing but childhood snaps of me.'

'Thank you.' Charlotte held it near his dimmed headlight so she could see it. 'It's lovely. I'll get a frame for it and keep it by my bed.'

'I'd like to have a photograph of you.'

'Of course. I'll look one out.'

'I think I'm falling in love with you,' he whispered. 'I wish I wasn't going away.'

'I wish you weren't too,' she sighed. 'Just when we've found each other.'

They strolled up the hill with their arms round each other and said a lingering good night, and only when they were both getting cold again did he turn to run back and she go indoors. When she viewed his picture in a better light she thought him incredibly handsome in his peaked merchant navy cap.

She found it hard to settle back to her school work after that. She felt she'd grown up overnight and life seemed suddenly flat without him. She wrote to him almost every night when she'd finished her homework. He wrote to her every day but in diary form because he wasn't able to post anything until he reached port. It was a red letter day when she received one of his thick envelopes.

His life at sea seemed very different from anything she'd known. He was filling the position of third mate on the *Ocean Prince* and admitted he found a day divided into watches difficult to get used to, and was confused by the eight bells. One of his duties was keeping the able seamen chipping off rust on outward voyages and red-leading and painting when homeward bound.

Alun was always in her thoughts. His ship was sailing with the Atlantic convoys bringing food and fuel into Britain. Often there was dreadful news on the wireless about the number of ships being sunk by Hitler's U-boats.

She resented the war and wished it could all be over. She feared for Alun's life. To think of him out there in the Atlantic under constant threat of death by enemy action was almost more than she could bear.

She kept his photograph on her bedside table and every night sent up a silent prayer that he'd come home safely. More than ever, she itched to do something to help the war effort in order to fill the time they'd be separated and make it seem shorter.

In the letters Aunt Barbara and her grandmother wrote, they said there was little sign in Liverpool that they were at war. Nothing much was happening on the home front except that there was less in the shops. Even the evacuees were heading back home in large numbers. Charlotte told her parents she could see no reason why she couldn't go to Liverpool in September to do her training.

She received a letter from Alun just after Easter letting her know that, he'd been given shore leave, and telling her when he'd arrive. Charlotte was thrilled and excited that he was coming home sooner than he'd expected. He looked tanned and healthy when she saw him and seemed very happy to be home. He clasped her in a hug of welcome.

'For how long?' Charlotte wanted to know. He never stopped smiling and his eyes were wicked as they searched into hers.

'A week. My ship's in dock for repairs. It was damaged by enemy action.'

'How awful! What happened?'

He seemed reluctant to talk about it. 'It was terrifying,' was all he'd say. 'They sank two ships from our convoy. We were trying to pick up survivors when we were hit.' He smiled at her. 'But we made it back to Liverpool.'

Jonty suggested Charlotte invite Alun up for supper one night, so they might get to know him better. In the meantime, he took her out and about. It was bliss to feel his arms round her again and his lips on hers. Although the summer season hadn't really started the attractions were opening in readiness and they found plenty of places to go, but Charlotte enjoyed most the hours they spent on the empty beach at Red Wharf Bay.

Alun took her to dinner at the Buckley Arms Hotel in Beaumaris. Charlotte knew its reputation. It was expensive and her friends at school thought highly of it.

He took her home to have Sunday tea with his parents. They made a fuss of her and Charlotte felt both families seemed to accept that they were serious about each other and one day, when the war was over, they'd be married. He told her often that he loved her, but he hadn't proposed. Charlotte was sure it was because the war was making it almost impossible to plan anything, but she thought about it all the time.

Last summer, Jonty had been given a few duck eggs by Ted Evans; he'd put them under his broody hen, and she'd reared seven ducklings. Four were female and he meant to keep them to start a flock of his own, but one of the males was now fat enough to eat. He suggested they have it the night she brought Alun home for supper. Charlotte helped Mary prepare a magnificent meal of roast duck with baked apples. Alun was full of praise for the meal, but by then his leave was virtually over.

'I do wish I didn't have to go back tomorrow,' he said, and Jonty noticed that his gaze lingered on Charlotte.

'Your ship wasn't badly damaged then?' he asked. 'I suppose they repair them as quickly as possible these days.'

Alun sighed. 'No, it'll be in dock in Liverpool for a couple more weeks. I'll be part of a skeleton staff they keep on to look after it.'

'Are you allowed time off?' Charlotte asked.

'Yes, as long as we take it in turns so there's always someone on board.'

'Could I go to stay at Aunt Barbara's for a few days?' She turned to Jonty. 'She has asked me.'

'But you go back to school tomorrow, and your exams will be on you before you know it. Once those are over, you'll be able to do other things.'

'But Alun would be there if I went now. We'd be able to go out in the evenings.'

'Just be patient a little longer,' Jonty said. 'It's important to do well in your exams.'

'I don't think people bother much about exams any more,' she protested. 'Not with the war and everything.'

He could see patience was the last thing she had at the moment. 'Which yard is your ship in?' he asked Alun to change the subject.

'Barrington Brown's.'

Jonty tried to suppress a gasp of amazement.

'It's that big place down beyond Huskisson Dock.'

'Yes, I know. I used to lodge with a couple of riveters who worked there.'

Jonty's head was spinning. He couldn't look at Charlotte. He saw again the hordes of workers streaming out at five thirty in the afternoon when the hooter sounded. It brought the guilt of what he'd done to her flooding back. He could almost feel the lordly presence of Roderick Barrington Brown standing over him.

CHAPTER TEN

CHARLOTTE WENT back to school to sit her exams, and, persuaded by his parents, so did Glyn. Both grumbled about it, feeling school was for children and they'd outgrown it. Charlotte felt swept off her feet by the intensity of her feelings for Alun and couldn't concentrate on her school work. He was her first boyfriend, her first adult experience of love. She was quite sure it was love that would naturally progress to marriage and last for ever, as it had for her parents.

As before, she wrote to Alun every night and expected a daily letter in return as he was now in Liverpool. She was disappointed when it didn't always come. He apologised for not being a good correspondent, and said he was kept so busy he found it difficult to find time to write. Eventually, the *Ocean Prince* put to sea again, and she received a diary-type letter posted in Scotland as the ships sailed north to gather into a convoy before crossing the Atlantic. She worried about his safety now he was back at sea.

The summer visitors were arriving in Anglesey and were to be seen on the beaches, swimming and sailing their dinghies. Charlotte thought it made everything seem normal, though really it wasn't. During those summer evenings of 1940, Jonty would switch on the wireless and the family would listen to accounts of fighter pilots engaged in dog fights in the skies over Kent. The action came to be known as the Battle of Britain and was very frightening, but here further north it remained quiet, and life went on pretty much as it always had.

With her exams now behind her, Charlotte began to think of her next step. She was determined to train in Liverpool. It was the home port of Alun's ship and she'd be able to see more of him if she were working there. She applied to Liverpool Royal Infirmary and was accepted on a training course starting in September.

With Glyn at home to help his father run their big farm, Kevin Evans had finally got his way and joined the air force. Charlotte could see Glyn wasn't pleased; he'd set his mind on a flying career as well.

'I suppose somebody has to produce the food,' he grumbled to Charlotte. 'Dad's worried about how he'll manage if he has no help. I've agreed, but I'm going to miss out on all the excitement. Oh, and have you heard? Megan's off again. She's joined the WAAF.'

In August, Charlotte first heard reports of bombings on Merseyside. Her mother tried to persuade her to apply to Bangor instead but she refused to change her plans. If Alun could do his bit for the war, so could she. She meant to be where she could see something of him when his ship was in port.

In September, when Charlotte went to Liverpool to start her career, she could see little sign of damage. She'd been to Liverpool before. On two occasions she'd stayed for a few days with Uncle Dan and Auntie Barbara and been whisked round the museums and art galleries and enjoyed trips on the river with her cousins. She'd thought it great fun, but now Liverpool was sombre with the sky full of barrage balloons. The hospital was a vast Victorian edifice the like of which she'd never seen before.

There were eight other girls starting their training that day. Two were from Wales and two from Ireland, and the remaining four had always lived in Liverpool. Charlotte found she was to share a room with Shirley Mathews, one of the local girls. Charlotte liked her wide smile and thought she could take to her.

First, they were all taken up to the sewing room and fitted up with uniforms: striped dresses and stiffly starched aprons. They were given what appeared to be gauze tray cloths or table runners and a sister taught them how to fold them into caps. She told them no nurse must allow her hair to touch her collar or fly about. Hospital rules of hygiene said it was essential to keep hair controlled and covered.

Dressed in her new uniform and addressed as Nurse Jones, Charlotte almost felt like one. This was a very different world from what she was used to. They were to spend their first weeks in the preliminary training school but school didn't start until nine o'clock. They were roused with the rest of the day staff at six o'clock, in time to dress, have breakfast and be up on a ward by seven thirty.

They all crowded into the ward office to hear the staff nurse read the night report. Charlotte tried to concentrate and hoped all the medical terms would soon mean something to her. Then a third-year student was detailed to show her what needed to be done. Every patient had his bed made; all sheets, blankets and counterpanes had to have neatly folded corners and many patients needed clean linen. Charlotte struggled to keep up with the brisk movements of the other nurse.

Next she had to help serve breakfast to the patients and clear away. After that came the bedpan round for those patients not allowed out of bed. The orderlies took over at that point but the junior nurses were expected to help, and then empty the flower vases in the sluice room and take them back to the ward with fresh water. With everything made tidy, Charlotte had to ask Sister's permission to leave the ward in time to be in the classroom by nine o'clock.

It all took a bit of getting used to.

Mary missed having Charlotte about the house. 'She's gone despite all our advice,' she mourned.

'That's youth,' Jonty told her. 'She needs to try her wings. We mustn't stop her.' All that summer Jonty had not been feeling too well. He'd said nothing to Charlotte because he didn't want to make that an excuse to keep her with him, when she was so keen to go.

'But just when Hitler has started bombing in earnest, and Liverpool has all those docks and munitions factories. She could be killed.'

'So could everybody else who lives there. We have to trust that she won't.'

When Jonty and Mary were in bed, they could sometimes hear planes flying overhead, and couldn't help wondering if they were on their way to drop bombs on Liverpool. Mary would pull the blankets over her ears to shut out the ominous drone. She hoped against hope that none of her family would be hurt.

In the mornings, they'd listen to the news bulletins and hear that bombs were battering London. A few weeks later it was Coventry's turn to be flattened. Mary worried that soon Liverpool would get its share of attention.

Charlotte began to feel she could cope with the routine. While she was in the school she had every Sunday off, and spent most of them at Auntie Barbara's because she could only afford the fare home once a month.

She was sure she'd have settled down and enjoyed her new life if she hadn't had the bombings to contend with. The wail of the air raid warning was enough to strike terror into anybody. There was an emergency routine to practise on the ward in case there was a fire or a direct hit and patients had to be evacuated. All nurses were told to stay calm whatever the crisis, and think first of their patients and not their own safety. As Liverpool was one of Britain's biggest ports, inevitably the Luftwaffe began to give it attention. There were lots of small air raids that started small fires.

Charlotte's group completed their preliminary schooling. She was sent to work full time on a women's surgical ward and was appalled at the horrific wounds she saw – a result of the bombings. She was getting very anxious about Alun. His letters had become fewer and suddenly they stopped altogether. She listened to the news bulletins in the nurses' home whenever she could, and the number of ships lost on Atlantic convoys seemed enormous, but the vessels were not identified by name.

She felt cold inside every time she thought about his ship and was terrified it might have been torpedoed and sunk. That he might have been injured or drowned filled her with every sort of dread and fear.

She wrote to his sister in Moelfre asking for news, but received no answer. She wrote to her parents asking if the Jarvises were all right. Nowadays people were in closer contact than they used to be, and news of a bereavement could travel fast. But they'd heard nothing. She continued to write to Alun but it was no longer every day.

Her roommate, Shirley Mathews, thought she might be able to find out for her, as her father was employed in the shipping industry. Anything like that could be hush-hush, but he'd probably say yes or no. She came back from her day off with the news that there had been no reports of any loss of life on the *Ocean Prince*, nor had it been sunk. It was somewhere in the Atlantic. Charlotte was relieved but more confused than ever.

'Are you sure he hasn't given you the old heave-ho?' Shirley asked. 'That seems the most likely. Has he found another girlfriend?'

Charlotte laughed. 'How could he find another girl when he's at sea?' Anyway, Alun was so genuine and honest, he wouldn't do such a thing. She loved him and he'd sworn undying love for her. She expected to spend the rest of her life with him. She decided to go home for her next day off, and she'd make a point of seeing Alun's parents while she was there.

When she arrived at Glan y Mor, her father wasn't well. It rather shocked her to hear he'd been feeling ill for a long time but hadn't been to the doctor's. He didn't seem to know what was bothering him, and when he described his symptoms she had no idea either.

'I work it off,' he said. 'Attending to the animals makes me feel better, so what's the point of bothering the doctor?'

'I'm a nurse now,' Charlotte told him, 'though a very junior one, and I think it's time you did.'

Her mother told her, 'By the time he's done his work he's exhausted, and he doesn't feel like getting on his bike and going to the doctor's.'

They had no telephone. Charlotte said, 'Dad, tomorrow I'll borrow your motor bike and go and ask the doctor to call, and I'll pop in to see Margaret Jarvis while I'm out.'

'Margaret Williams, she is now,' her mother said. 'A good job Jonty taught you to ride that bike.'

'A pity you never learned,' Charlotte returned. 'How do you manage?'

'With difficulty,' Jonty groaned.

'I can walk to the village shop. And Enid – you know, Glyn's mother – takes me into Llangefni when she goes. Did you know Glyn is doing the egg round now?'

'No! I thought he was going to help on the farm.'

'He says he's doing the egg round in his spare time,' Jonty said. 'The lad who used to do it joined up and there was nobody else.'

'It's quite handy,' Mary went on. 'He's told me I can have a lift with him whenever I want. I go to the village on the days I know he works, and he brings me and my groceries home. I just have to fit in with his timetable.'

Charlotte was desperate for news of Alun. It was almost as though he'd vanished off the face of the earth. After calling at the doctor's surgery, she went into Moelfre to see his sister. Margaret answered her knock and came to the door with a small baby in her arms.

'Hello,' Charlotte said. She knew by the look on Margaret's face that she wasn't pleased to see her. 'How are you? I'm sorry if I've come at a bad time, but I've not heard from Alun for some time and I'm getting worried.'

A woman's voice behind Margaret called, 'Is that our Polly?'

'He hasn't been taken ill or anything?' Charlotte had imagined him injured and in some hospital on the other side of the world.

'No . . . he's well.' A pink flush was spreading up Margaret's cheeks.

Charlotte said, 'He didn't tell me you had a new baby.'

'No,' she faltered. 'It's not . . .'

'Hello.' Another woman bounced up behind Margaret and proceeded to take the infant from her arms. 'He'll catch cold out here on the step. He's mine. I've called him Alun, after his dad.'

Charlotte froze. She knew the woman by sight, as she knew most people in the district.

'This is Gwyneth Pugh,' Margaret said awkwardly.

Charlotte blinked at the other woman. 'Yes . . . I know you, don't I?'

'Yes, and you're Charlotte Jones, Glan y Mor.'

'He should have told you,' Margaret said, looking embarrassed.

Gwyneth smiled and said, 'Alun will be home on leave in three weeks and we're going to get married. The banns are being called.'

Charlotte felt shocked to the core. 'I didn't know.'

'And I didn't know he had a bit on the side. We've been walking out for three years.'

She couldn't get away quickly enough. She felt utterly betrayed. How could she have been so mistaken about Alun? She'd believed him when he'd said he loved her. She loved him. How could she have been such a fool? Tears were streaming down her face as she rode home on her father's bike.

Charlotte went back to Liverpool feeling thoroughly churned up. She couldn't stop thinking about Alun, that he'd already had another girlfriend when he'd taken up with her. He'd got Gwyneth Pugh pregnant but hadn't found the guts to write and tell her. He'd just dropped her and all the time she'd been worried stiff about his safety. Charlotte couldn't understand why nobody had seemed to know about his affair with Gwyneth Pugh – even his parents had seemed to think he was serious about her. She could only conclude that he must have been as underhand in his dealings with Gwyneth as he had been dishonest with her. For heaven's sake . . . Common sense told her she was better off without a man like that, but all the same she felt cut to ribbons.

'There're more fish in the sea,' Shirley told her. 'Better to find out now than later.'

She took Charlotte home and introduced her to her brother. He seemed nice enough but he wasn't interested in her and Charlotte didn't want another boyfriend. No thank you. She was going to devote herself to her career.

She went shopping and to the cinema with Shirley when they could get time off together. She was friendly with the other girls in her group, and joined in activities with them, but it took her a very long time to get over Alun. Even her fear of air raids couldn't keep him out of her thoughts for long.

The blitz was stepped up in the days before Christmas. A raid would start about seven in the evening and finish about ten. But then another wave of bombers would come in about midnight and keep up the bombardment until four in the morning. The hospital normally ran with a small night staff but in a raid they couldn't cope with the steady influx of injured.

The day staff were sleeping in cellars and shelters. They were organised into teams, some of whom were woken and brought on duty while others were allowed their turn of a full night's sleep – if the noise didn't disturb them. Time off was cancelled and holidays postponed.

Charlotte was horrified at the damage she saw spreading all round the hospital; St George's Hall and many other notable landmarks, together with hundreds of houses, were in ruins. Food warehouses were set alight and there were big fires on the docks. Exchange Station was closed and all railway traffic brought to a standstill. By Christmas Day, all were exhausted.

In between the raids everybody tried to live in the way they normally would. Charlotte had her days off and often went to see her Aunt Barbara. If one of her cousins had a few nights' home leave, he'd take her out dancing or to a theatre.

She met her Uncle Noel there, the youngest of her mother's brothers, and also her Uncle Len and his fiancée Ruth. They'd been engaged for several years, because his father felt they shouldn't rush into marriage. They should save for it first.

Now that they'd waited for the time he'd stipulated and his blessing might be expected, they were unable to find a house to rent, as the bombing raids had reduced so many houses to rubble. And as Percy pointed out, nobody wanted to buy property when the next raid could raze it to the ground.

Eventually, Edith invited Dan and Barbara to bring Charlotte to supper one night.

She went feeling on edge. She'd never spoken to her grandfather but she'd heard a great deal about him. Her mother had told her he'd been a very strict father, that he'd refused to allow her to marry Jonty and had disowned her as a daughter. That was why they'd never taken Charlotte to see Mary's childhood home.

Her first impression when she got out of Uncle Dan's car on the drive was that it was a rather grand house. Edith opened the door to them and seemed fluttery with nerves. She led them into a big sitting room, and Percy Shawcross put aside his newspaper and pulled himself to his feet.

'This is Mary's girl,' her grandmother said, her voice hardly above a whisper.

'Hmph. Not much like her.' His face was lined, and his dark eyes aggressive. He looked bad-tempered. He put out his hand and she took it.

Charlotte wondered if she should kiss him as she had her grand-mother, but he didn't seem to expect affection. She'd prepared a few words of greeting.

'Hello, Grandpa. I'm glad to meet you at last. Mum has told me about you.'

'She won't have said anything good, I'll be bound.' He collapsed back into the armchair with a grunt.

'She says there's good in everyone if you look for it,' Charlotte replied. Gran was ushering her to a seat. 'Mum says you were good at providing for your family. You wanted them all to have a comfortable life.'

'I don't suppose your father was a good provider.'

Charlotte smiled. 'That's exactly what Mum said you'd say. She told me to be sure to tell you she's had a wonderfully happy life with him and she hasn't gone short of anything.'

When 1941 started other cities were being pounded with bombs. In March and April the Luftwaffe stepped up the number and ferocity of the raids. On the first eight nights of May, Liverpool had the worst bombardment of all.

Ships were sunk in the Mersey and the warehouses on the docks blazed for days. A heavy bomb fell on Mill Road Infirmary, demolishing three hospital buildings and damaging the rest. Patients and staff were trapped in the debris and fire broke out among the cars and ambulances in the courtyard. Seventeen members of staff lost their lives as well as fifteen ambulance drivers and thirty patients. The Royal Infirmary was asked to send experienced staff to help, and three hundred and eighty patients were safely evacuated to other hospitals.

It took many days to put out all the fires, repair gas mains, and restore electricity supplies, telephone wires and railway lines. Everyone dreaded further raids and fully expected them on fine bright nights, but after May they virtually ceased, though it took years to recover, repair and rebuild.

To Charlotte it seemed a miracle that none of her relatives were killed. Her Uncle Len had his arm broken when a wall collapsed on him while he was helping dig bomb victims out of a cellar. The windows of their houses had been blown out more than once, but otherwise they received only minor damage, though the garage in Sefton received a direct hit and the petrol stored there caused a fire that burned for two days and razed some of the surrounding property to the ground.

Over the following two years Charlotte was able to concentrate on her studies and enjoy her time off. She went home more often because Jonty wasn't well and she could help him do jobs about the farm.

This last spring, Glyn had driven his father's tractor up to plough and harrow three acres for them. He planted an acre of potatoes and an acre of oats, with half an acre of swedes. Charlotte had planted out carrots, cabbage and salad vegetables during her holiday in April. It was important that they produce enough food for the animals as well as themselves.

She was worried about her father, who was becoming increasingly breathless. The doctor had told him he had farmer's lung, caused by breathing in dust from old hay many years earlier. Jonty was very low after that. He knew that his Uncle John, who had brought him up, had suffered from the same disease.

Charlotte had only been back from her holiday for a month when Uncle Dan's birthday came round. Barbara was getting tickets for the Empire Theatre for themselves and Edith, and she asked Charlotte if she would like to go with them. It was an old-fashioned music-hall show and George Formby and his wife Beryl were topping the bill.

Charlotte jumped at the chance, and as she'd managed to get her day off the next day, Barbara suggested she should stay overnight in their spare room. They all enjoyed the show and had a good laugh. They were all in high spirits when Dan dropped his mother off on the way home.

Barbara made a hot drink and Charlotte fell into bed, looking forward to her weekly chance of a long lie-in the next morning. But at half past six she was woken by the telephone bell's shrilling through the house. She heard her Uncle Dan thump sleepily downstairs to answer it, then turned over, expecting to settle back into sleep.

Though she couldn't hear what Dan was saying, the horror in his voice told her something was very wrong. He came racing back upstairs to talk rapidly to Barbara, his voice shrill with shock, and she knew both were dressing quickly. Charlotte got out of bed to find out what had happened.

'Is something the matter?' she called on the landing. Barbara came to her bedroom door.

'That was Grandma. She says she can't wake Percy up. She sounded frantic – we're going straight round.'

'I'll come with you,' Charlotte said. 'Perhaps I can help.' She was a nurse after all. She ran back to her room to start throwing on her clothes. They were there within twenty minutes. The house was in an uproar. Noel was still in his pyjamas.

'The doctor's just come. He's up there now.'

'What's happened?'

'I think Pa's dead.'

'Dead? Surely not?'

'I think Mum woke up to find him dead beside her. He must have died in the night. Passed away in his sleep.'

'Oh, my goodness!'

Len, who had left home at last and married his Ruth, arrived at that moment, and they had to go through it all again.

'Tea,' he said and went to the kitchen to make it. 'We could all do with a cup. I can't stay long, not when Ruth's supposed to be on bed rest. Her blood pressure was up last week.' Her first baby was due within the month.

'Do you think I should go up?' Charlotte asked. 'Grandma will be in a state of shock.'

'I'll come with you,' Barbara said.

'Perhaps we should all go.' Dan made for the stairs.

The doctor was glad to see them. 'A heart attack, I believe, but we'll have to have a post-mortem to be sure. I'll arrange for an ambulance to come for him. Look after your mother.' He was looking at Barbara.

'I'm a nurse,' Charlotte said, and went to give her grandmother a comforting hug. 'I'll look after her.' Edith's eyes were red, swollen and wet.

'It's given her a dreadful shock,' the doctor said, 'to wake up and find him dead in bed beside her. What could be worse?'

'But, if it's any comfort,' Charlotte pointed out, 'it was good for Grandpa. He felt well and was working right up to last night.'

Edith blew her nose into a wet handkerchief 'I kept telling him he should retire and make the business over to the boys. He drove himself too hard, but he wouldn't listen.'

'How old was he?'

'Seventy-four.'

The doctor noted it down. 'Mrs Shawcross, I'll leave you something to help you sleep,' he told her, closing his bag.

'I'll see you out,' Dan said. When he came back he said to his brothers, 'We'll have to open up the garages this morning. It's what Pa would want – and, don't forget, we'll be taking over his work too.'

Charlotte knew sleep was the last thing Edith would need at the moment. She was convulsed with grief and still wearing her nightdress and dressing gown.

'A terrible thing to happen,' Charlotte said, giving her another hug. 'I'll run a bath for you and when you're dressed we'll see about a bit of breakfast. Then perhaps a breath of fresh air? We could go for a little walk.'

Barbara lit the fire and produced the meal, though nobody ate much. Charlotte told her grandmother they'd stay all day. She sent a telegram to Glan y Mor. Edith had put her feet up on the sofa after lunch when the phone rang. Charlotte swept out to the hall to answer it, and found it was her mother ringing from the post office. She was upset and wanted to know all the details.

'I ought to be there,' she worried. 'But Jonty isn't well enough to do the milking and stay here by himself. If they could time the funeral for about midday, I might be able to get there and back for it.'

The conversation left Charlotte very worried about her parents. They must be having a hard time of it at Glan y Mor and she couldn't be there to help. It was all she could do at the moment to cope with things here.

After some thought, she rang the hospital and asked to be put through to the matron. She'd had few dealings with her and from afar thought her strict and rather awesome.

She explained about her grandfather's sudden death, and was given two days' compassionate leave so she could stay with her grandmother. Matron told her she'd be allowed extra off duty on the day of the funeral in order to attend.

Charlotte put the phone down with relief. She'd see her mother at the funeral and be able to talk things over with her.

PART TWO

CHAPTER ELEVEN

November 1943

CHARLOTTE HAD been worried about her father's failing health for some time. Letters from her mother were becoming shorter and she didn't write so often: she was clearly finding it hard to manage. Charlotte knew she was badly needed at home and wanted to be there to help.

But at the same time, she knew it would be quite a wrench to leave Liverpool and the life she'd made for herself here. As nursing was classed as essential war work she had to apply for permission to leave her employment on compassionate grounds. As soon as she heard she'd passed her final exams and was entitled to call herself a State Registered Nurse she did so. Once she'd received permission, she gave in her notice. She was on her way home for good.

It was raining and the afternoon seemed bleak when she got off the long distance Crosville bus in Bangor. Buses and trains didn't run to time any more – it had been late starting, and she knew she'd have about an hour to wait for a connecting bus to Anglesey. She thought her best plan would be to find a café and get a cup of tea, so she'd have somewhere warm and dry to wait.

The driver had opened up the luggage compartment and was pulling the baggage out on to the pavement. Charlotte was waiting in the crush of passengers to collect her suitcases when she heard a voice she knew well.

'Charlotte? Hello, how are you?' Glyn Evans threw his arms round her and swept her into a quick hug. 'How about a lift home?'

She gave a little squeal of pleasure. 'That would be marvellous. I'm so pleased you noticed me in this crowd.'

'Notice you? With hair like yours, you stand out in any crowd.' No longer in uniform, she was wearing it loose for a change, hanging down her back. He smiled. 'Actually, I was looking out for you. Your mum told me you were coming today.'

'You've come to meet me? That's very kind.'

'I was in Bangor anyway. I have to bring the eggs across.'

'Thank you. I heard you'd taken over the egg round.'

'There was nobody else, and it gets me out and about round the farms. I'm a bit pushed in the summer, but it's all right at this time of year.'

Charlotte had seen Glyn every time she'd come home and they'd gone to the pictures or dancing just as they always had, but now she realised that in the last three years her old friend had grown to manhood. He was taller and broader yet still totally familiar, and already she felt as though they'd never been parted.

'Here, let me give you a hand with your luggage.'

He took both her cases and led her to a large white van pulled in to the kerb round the corner. The words Egg Marketing Board were emblazoned on its side. He opened the back door and heaved her belongings inside.

She studied Glyn as he drove. His dark hair seemed to wave more than it used to and his skin was bronzed with being outdoors in all weathers, but his ready smile was just the same.

'How's my dad? You must have seen him?'

'Yes. I'm afraid he's not getting any better.'

'I've come home to look after him,' she said sadly. 'Mum's finding it hard. It's the animals too, you see. Dad can't manage them or do the milking any more.'

'I know – he's been bad for a long time. I cut the hay for him in the summer, and that patch of oats he grows for the hens.'

'Thank you. We're all very grateful for your help, Glyn.'

'My father says we owe him a lot. He's always helped us with our machines. Even our old tractor is still going, thanks to him. D'you know, the last time it broke down, he came to fix it but he was struggling so hard for breath he he had to sit next to me on a chair and tell me what to do, step by step until we got it going. Dad said I shouldn't have let him stay that long – it could have harmed him.'

'He's like that.'

'I'll never forget it. It taught me a lot. Perhaps I'll be able to fix it myself next time.'

Charlotte blinked back her tears. She'd always felt very close to her father. It was agonising to hear his health was failing like this, and typical that he'd push himself to the limit for other people.

She asked about his family. 'How's Glenys? She became an army nurse, didn't she?'

'Yes. She was sent out to Cairo but now she's following our forces in Italy. Tegwen joined up too. She's working in a military hospital in London.'

'And what about Kevin?'

'He's stationed at an airfield in Cambridge, making bombing raids on Germany.'

'Your mum and dad must be proud of them, all doing their bit for the war.'

'Except me.' He turned to give her a wan smile. 'I'm doing the egg round and milking the cows.'

'Somebody has to, Glyn. I remember you saying that.'

'I'm beginning to wish it was somebody else's turn. I'm at home safe and sound, while everybody else . . . I feel I should be doing more to help the war effort.'

'The troops have to be fed.'

'So everybody tells me.'

'Sorry . . .'

'I hear the Germans have stopped dropping bombs on Liverpool?'

'Yes, thank goodness. We've had no raids all this year.'

He pulled in at the gate from where the path wound up to her home. 'Sorry, can't get this any nearer.'

'I know. This is fine, and you've got me here much earlier than I expected.'

'If there's anything else I can do, you know where to find me.'

'Thanks.' Charlotte sniffed, still not far from tears. 'Thanks for everything.'

She swiftly climbed the last half-mile home despite being weighed down with her cases. It had stopped raining, and she could hear the sea running up the shore though she could see little through the thick mizzle. The seagulls were weaving and calling over the grey stone cottage and outbuildings.

She reached the front door, which was never locked, pushed at it and made it creak open. She stepped inside and immediately felt surrounded with love. The familiar scent of wood smoke was here too. No other house had such an atmosphere of peace and caring.

'Mum,' she called. 'I'm home.'

'Charlotte.' It was her father's frail voice calling from the next room. 'In the parlour.'

It was a room they'd rarely used. It used to be cold and smell of damp; now there was a fire in the small grate and it had the fetid atmosphere of the sickroom.

Her father was trying to pull himself up the bed and was breathless with effort. She ran to help him and kissed his grey and sweating cheek.

'Dad, how are you?' It shocked her to see how much weight he'd lost since her last visit. She shook up his pillows to make him more comfortable.

'Better for seeing you.' He was trying to smile. 'So glad you've come to stay this time.'

'You've had your bed brought downstairs, I see.'

'Easier for your mum, and . . . I still feel I'm in the thick of what's going on.'

'Where is she?'

'Upstairs. I sent her to rest. It's taking a lot out of her.'

'Now I'm home, things will be easier for you both.'

'I know. It's lovely to see you.'

It went through her to see him so ill. This household had been run on his energy and enthusiasm. There was nothing he hadn't enjoyed doing, whether it was looking after his animals and growing vegetables or even cooking in the kitchen, and now . . .

'I'll go and find Mum.' But she didn't need to: she could hear her footsteps on the stairs. A moment later she was wrapped in her mother's arms.

'Charlotte love, I heard your voice. It's lovely to see you looking so well.'

Mary looked tired and drawn. She said, 'I'll put the kettle on. You sit with your dad for a bit. He's been so looking forward to having you back with us.'

Charlotte sat down and took her father's hand between both of hers.

'Like old times,' he said, 'now the family's together again. The best of times. I want you to know, Charlotte, that having you, watching you grow up, gave Mary and me much pleasure.'

124

Today Charlotte felt her tears were ever present. She blinked them back again. It sounded as though he was saying his goodbyes. He was only forty-five; he ought to be in his prime. By rights, he should with them for years and years yet.

'About this farmer's lung . . .'

Mary had written that he'd been upset by the diagnosis. Charlotte remembered him telling her that he'd been orphaned as a baby. On her last visit he'd said, 'Uncle John brought me up on his hill farm behind Aberystwyth. He never married. I had to look after him in the end, as well as do what I could on the farm. He died of farmer's lung when I was sixteen. It makes me realise . . .'

It had made them all realise that the disease could cause his death too. Charlotte had asked a medical consultant at the hospital what exactly farmer's lung was, as it didn't seem to be on the curriculum. She told him about her father.

'I think it's what the text books call pneumokoniosis,' the doctor had said. 'It's the term given to changes in the lungs resulting from inhaling certain dusts. Old hay dust? I gather it's not uncommon in the farming community. We don't see it much here.'

Dad managed a wan smile from his pillows. 'After Uncle John died, I had nobody of my own before I had Mary and you.'

Charlotte said as cheerfully as she could, 'I bet you and Mum had some smashing times before I came on the scene.'

'We both wanted a family. For us, Charlotte, you were the jewel in the crown. I'm glad you're here. There's something I want to tell you.'

He looked blue about the lips and she could see he was getting more breathless. 'What about a puff of oxygen?'

'Perhaps I'd better.'

She wheeled the big cylinder closer and helped him fit the tubes that fed the gas into his nostrils.

'Thanks. That's better.'

When her mother returned with the tea and sat down on the other side of his bed, Charlotte couldn't help but notice the way they looked at each other. After a lifetime together, Dad's eyes were full of adoration as they followed Mum about the room. The marvellous thing was that they'd always had so much love left over for her. They were a happy family bound tightly together with affection. Everything was perfect, or it had been before Dad became ill.

'There're things you should know.' His voice was growing fainter. 'Things I want to tell you . . .' He was finding it an effort to speak.

'No hurry for that,' she said. 'You need to rest now.'

She held her father's tea while he sipped at it. 'Tell her, Mary,' he murmured. 'I want her to know.'

'Know what?' Charlotte asked.

'About us.'

She smiled. 'Dad, I've come home fairly often. There can't be much I don't know.'

'Mary . . .?'

'All right, Jonty.'

'Start at the beginning . . . how you had to run away with me and we came here.'

'Mum.' Charlotte smiled. 'I've been seeing quite a lot of Grandma and Aunt Barbara while I've been in Liverpool, so I've heard all about that. It was very romantic to run away with Dad when Grandpa refused to let you marry.'

'We were married as soon as I was twenty-one,' Mary said defensively.

Charlotte smiled. 'Yes, I know.'

In her mother's day, living with a man without the benefit of marriage was considered beyond the pale for respectable girls. Now, in wartime, things were changing. Charlotte knew girls were having to say goodbye to their boyfriends without knowing whether they'd ever see them again. In that situation, many girls did what Mum had done.

'Grandma said that after you'd gone, your father realised he'd pushed you into what he was trying to save you from, but he wouldn't admit it. He'd never admitted being wrong in his life, never admitted making mistakes, and never said he was sorry for anything.'

Jonty had a quavering smile. 'He was so dogmatic, all fireworks and drama. I could hardly believe it when he died so quietly.'

Her mother felt for Charlotte's hand and said, 'I'm glad you were able to be with your gran when that happened. Poor Pa, he was so strict with us, we were all scared of him.'

'He meant well. It was his way of taking care of you,' Jonty said.

'Yes, but he didn't trust you to look after me in the same way.'

'I couldn't in the material sense.' Jonty sighed. 'You've never had a house as comfortable as the one he provided. We've always been near the breadline.'

'I love Glan y Mor,' Charlotte said. 'I can think of nowhere nicer to live.'

'Nor can I,' Mary agreed. 'And you did your best to make it comfortable, Jonty We're still one of the few houses out in the Anglesey countryside to have electric light. You figured out how to run it on wind power and managed to fix it up.'

'With a little help.'

'And once we had electricity you put in a proper bathroom with hot, running water.'

'But only just before the war. You had to manage for years with the old stone sink in the kitchen and one cold water tap.'

'You were always keen to make improvements. Always reading up about the latest domestic appliance.'

'Yes.' Jonty was cheered by chatting about the old days.

'The neighbours came up to see how you'd done it, and marvelled,' Charlotte remembered. 'And most still use oil lamps and candles.'

'It takes a brisk breeze all the year round, like ours, to make it possible,' Mary said. 'And not many have that. You did all you could to make life easy and comfortable for me.'

Charlotte noticed that her father was sinking back into his pillows and his eyes were closing.

'Dad's dozed off,' she whispered. 'Let's leave him to rest. That's what he needs.'

Her mother tied a dark cloth over the shade of his bedside lamp to dim it, so the light wouldn't bother him. Then they tiptoed to the kitchen and closed the door softly. Mary couldn't hold her tears back any longer.

'I hate to see him so weak and suffering like this. I'm afraid he's going to die and how can I possibly manage without him?'

'That's why I've come home. There are decisions to be made.' Charlotte saw fear on Mary's face. 'I'm afraid you need to prepare yourself for it, Mum.'

Mary thumped the table with frustration. 'Why does it have to be Jonty? Life's so unfair. He's always done his best for everyone. He's kind and generous to a fault and he's finding it such a struggle to get his breath, while Pa . . .'

Charlotte said gently, 'That's the way of farmer's lung, Mum. But the oxygen helps.'

'Dr Williams has been very good. Poor Jonty, he tried hard to fight it. For a long time we thought he'd win, too.' Mary gave a little sob. 'But now . . .'

'I don't think he can come back from this.' Charlotte held her mother in a tight hug. 'He's too ill.'

She had been near to tears ever since she came home, and seeing her mother like this she couldn't hold them back. They clung together and wept.

Mary pulled away first and mopped her eyes. 'I should be getting you some supper. You must be hungry.'

Charlotte felt too churned up to eat. 'No. What about the milking? You haven't done it yet? Then I'll go out and do that now.' She lit a hurricane lamp and pulled on an old coat of Mary's that hung behind the back door. 'You make us some supper and I'll do the outside work tonight.' She knew it was all getting too much for her mother.

The cows were waiting at the gate to be let into the byre, which showed they were used to being milked earlier than this. At this time of the year, they usually went out for a few hours on fine days but in bad weather they stayed indoors. Mum could not have noticed the rain. Charlotte fed them some hay and a few nuts. There wasn't much grass for them on the fields now.

There was a new creamy white and tan Jersey cow called Posy, but Dad had had Marigold for five years and she was like an old friend. Charlotte started with her. She enjoyed milking and usually found the rhythmic spurt of milk into the bucket relaxing, but nothing could relax her tonight.

Her parents had always been strong. They'd always supported and nurtured her, but now Dad was so ill they were desperate for her help. She'd spoken of coming sooner, but Dad wouldn't hear of it until she knew she'd passed her finals.

This little farm had been a joy when she was growing up, but Mum wouldn't want to cope with it on her own. Probably couldn't. Charlotte knew she would have to point things like that out to her, and hated the idea. Mum wanted Dad to live until he was eighty and didn't want to change anything, certainly not yet. She couldn't think of a future without Jonty and had no plans.

It would be impossible to sell some of the animals and keep the rest. The cows made the workload as they needed milking twice a day, and then there was the cream to churn into butter, but the calves were reared on the skimmed milk, and the pigs fattened on the buttermilk.

She took the warm milk indoors to the dairy. The savoury scents coming from the kitchen made her stomach rumble. She put the milk through the separator to remove the cream.

'Would you feed the calves, love?' her mother called.

'Yes. What shall I mix with the milk?'

Charlotte knew her father was buying in calves at ten days old to rear and sell for beef because their Jerseys provided so much milk. They had their own calves too, but the Jersey male was said not to provide good beef: the fat was too yellow, and the housewives wouldn't buy it. It had fetched a poor price until the war brought such a shortage. Dad had always been delighted when a calf turned out to be female.

The calves were all lovely. One licked her hand, its tongue like sandpaper, and their milky feed smelled tasty enough for her to drink. Not so the pigs' buttermilk and boiled potatoes: that was sour. The pigs got most of the household scraps too. Finally, Charlotte crossed the field and shut the hens in for the night.

The chores had taken her an hour and twenty minutes. Impossible for Mum to do that morning and evening and look after Dad, and cook and clean. In addition, she had butter to make three times a week and the byre, the other pens and the henhouse to muck out once a week. The sheep had to be fed daily in winter, and there were lots of other jobs like scalding the separator and the milking buckets.

The ewes had been put to the ram and the lambs would be born next spring. But with Dad unable to help, she was afraid she and Mum would not be able to cope with lambing. Trying to do too much had already worn poor Mary out.

Charlotte thought the only logical step would be to sell up, but it was their only means of earning a living, and it was a very difficult subject to bring up while Dad was lying there so ill.

The following evening, Charlotte was sitting on one side of Jonty's bed with her mother on the other when he asked again, 'Mary, have you told her? I think Charlotte should know.'

She felt a shaft of curiosity as Mum shook her head in misery. 'Are you sure we should? It'll change . . .'

'She must know,' he insisted.

'Know what, Dad?' Charlotte could feel his tension.

'There was a shipwreck here . . .' He paused to get his breath.

'Dad, there are shipwrecks all along this coast. I was reading about another only last month. A coastal tramp called the *Leonora* . . .'

He held up his hand for her to stop. 'I'm talking about one back in 1922.'

'The year I was born?'

'Tell her, Mary,' he panted. His eyes were glazed.

'It might be better not.'

'Please. I can't rest until this is off my mind.'

'All right, don't fret yourself.' Charlotte could see her mother struggling to recall days long past. Her drawn face went slack. 'It was a motor yacht called the *Priscilla*. She broke her back on those rock ledges at the foot of our headland.'

'Yes?'

'Five were drowned and their bodies retrieved, but a baby was missing and presumed dead.'

Her mother came to a stop. There was silence.

'You were that baby,' her father whispered, his sunken eyes staring up at her.

'Me?' Charlotte felt confused. 'How d'you mean?'

She had to strain to hear what her mother said. 'You were washed up in our cove in a wooden cradle. It acted like a boat. You were wet through and very cold but otherwise unhurt.'

'We kept you,' Jonty choked.

'I'd been longing for a baby for a long time. I couldn't carry a child through pregnancy. I'd had three miscarriages.' Mary's blue eyes were craving her forgiveness. 'When you were washed up in our cove, you seemed like a gift from heaven. I wanted you so much. You were a gorgeous baby. I made Jonty agree to keep you, and I know it's been on his conscience all these years. He feels he has to do the honest thing.'

Charlotte felt tight with tension. What were they telling her? 'Are you saying you aren't my parents?'

Jonty let out a shuddering breath. 'We aren't, Charlotte.'

'But you are, Dad.' What they were saying didn't seem possible.

'No, love.'

The whole world as she knew it was falling away. 'My parents were drowned so you adopted me?' That much made sense.

130

'No, Charlotte. Your mother was drowned in the wreck but not your father. We didn't adopt you, we stole you.'

'Dad,' she said impatiently. It seemed such a tall story. 'How could you steal me?'

'It's a terrible thing we did. The world, and your real father, believe you perished in the wreck.'

'You were such a sunny-natured child,' Mary told her. 'A delight to bring up. We've loved you so much, but now I'm afraid you'll hate us.'

'Hate you? How could I? You've been the best of parents.' But to hear them say they were not took a bit of getting used to. 'I mean, who am I?'

The questions went on and on, over and round, until they could tell her no more and Jonty was tired out. His exhausted pain-filled eyes made Charlotte insist they must stop. She warmed some milk for him, helped him drink it and said goodnight.

While she was making cocoa for her mother and herself, Mary brought her a small red notebook crammed with newspaper cuttings.

'Jonty made notes about your family and what came out at the inquest,' she said. 'It's all in here. I wish he hadn't told you. I knew you'd be upset.'

'Well, I know now.' Charlotte kissed her cheek, and felt it wet with tears. 'Go to bed, Mum. Perhaps things will look better in the morning.'

She sent her upstairs with her hot drink and sat down at the table to read Jonty's neat script and the faded newspaper cuttings in the little red book. Yes, she was upset. She found it astounding, almost impossible to take in. She couldn't see herself as Abigail Elinor Barrington Brown. How could she not think of Jonty and Mary as her parents? All her life she'd felt their love for her. Always it had surrounded her, bound her to them and made them a close little family that had kept her safe and secure. She'd loved them and had relied on them. It was them she wanted, not some strangers.

Mary had been sleeping on a camp bed in Jonty's room so she'd hear him if he wanted anything during the night. Last night Charlotte had slept downstairs on the camp bed and she intended to do it tonight so her mum could have another undisturbed night and hopefully feel better in the morning.

Last night Charlotte had pulled the bedclothes over her and gone out like a light, but tonight she couldn't get to sleep. She could hear Jonty tossing and turning restlessly, and then there was a soft buzz as he turned his oxygen on. She felt overwhelmed with pity.

She'd nursed many dying patients and felt compassion for them, but this was very different. For the last three years, she'd seen Jonty fighting this disease, while it made slow but inevitable progress. She was going to miss him when he died. He'd always been part of her life, but how much worse it must be for Mary whose life had pivoted round him. She had deep emotional ties to both of them and to have this happen seemed tragic beyond words.

She heard him reaching for the glass of water they left near to hand and knew he wouldn't disturb her unless he was desperate for something else. He was like that. She slid out of bed and pushed her feet into her slippers.

'Dad, I know you can't get to sleep. Neither can I. Is there anything I can get you?'

'No, love, I have everything I need.' There was a pause. 'I'm sorry.'

'Why sorry?' She slid on to the chair beside his bed and felt for his hand.

'Such a selfish thing to do. You'd have had a far better start in life with your natural father. He was a rich man.'

'Don't be sorry. You gave me a wonderful childhood,' she told him.

'I knew I was doing wrong and it's been on my conscience ever since.'

'Oh, Dad!'

'Seeing you grow up strong and healthy brought us great happiness, but it wasn't the best thing for you. I regret that. But now I've told you, I'm not sure that wasn't selfishness on my part too. I wanted to confess to ease my mind; I wanted to explain it to you before I died.'

'Dad, don't . . . It's all right.'

'But now you don't know who you are or where you belong. I've destroyed your feeling of belonging here.'

'I belong here,' she said firmly. 'It would take a lot more to destroy that. And I've always realised I don't look like you or Mum. I mean, I'm taller than either of you.' Charlotte gave a nervous laugh. 'Do you remember I asked you once why I had this red hair and you told me it must be a throwback to our forebears? That in the past there had been others in our family who had hair like mine.'

'I lied. I'm sorry, Charlotte. I wanted to do my best for you and I tried, but it hasn't done you any favours. A rich man could have given you everything. A good education . . .'

'I did all right at the County School.'

'You're cleverer than me. I only had to explain a thing once for you to grasp it.'

'It doesn't matter what you say, I'll always think of you as my dad. I'm going to miss you.'

'Look after Mum for me.'

'You don't have to ask that – you know I will. I'll want to. I've always been proud to call her Mother.'

Her feet cold, Charlotte crept back to her own bed and tried to sleep. It came fitfully at last; at one in the morning, Jonty roused her to say his oxygen cylinder seemed to be running out. She got up to fetch another from the porch and changed them over. She made them both some more hot milk but he took only a few sips of his. She sat holding his hand for about half an hour. When he dropped off she went back to the camp bed and tried to get some more sleep, but it wouldn't come.

She lay listening to the soft buzz of the oxygen but it didn't seem to ease his breathing, so she got up to increase the flow. He was grunting and growing more restless. She could hear him struggling to get his breath and knew how distressed he was. She got up and, in the hope it would help, gave him another pillow from her camp bed and sat him more upright.

He whispered, 'Feels like there's an iron band round my chest so it can't expand to take in enough air.' She increased the flow of his oxygen yet again.

'Is that all right, Dad?' He didn't reply. Charlotte stood looking down at him for a few moments. 'Dad, are you all right?'

'Just tired, love,' he panted and relaxed back against his pile of pillows. His face was blue and clammy, and he hardly seemed to know she was there. It was four in the morning when she tiptoed upstairs to wake her mother. Mary had made her promise she would if there was any change. She was wide awake in an instant.

'How is he?'

'Failing, I'm afraid.' It seemed as though he'd waited to die until he could make what he'd called his confession. It had been there on his mind all these years, a heavy weight he had to deal with.

Once downstairs again, she said, 'Mum's come to sit with you, Dad.'

'Good.' The word came out on a hiss of breath. He sighed. 'I'm a trouble . . . to you, Mary.'

'Of course you're not,' she told him. 'You lie back and rest.'

They sat one either side his bed, each holding one of the hands that were now cold and blue. The smile Charlotte knew so well quavered on his lips for a moment.

'Look after . . . Mary for me,' he said again, and she felt the gentlest squeeze from his fingers.

They were the last words he spoke before he slid into unconsciousness that grew deeper and deeper. Mary was in tears most of the morning and Charlotte couldn't persuade her to eat or drink. Jonty's breathing became more laboured until it seemed each one must be his last.

It was early afternoon when Mary lifted her red and swollen eyes to say, 'He's gone.'

CHAPTER TWELVE

CHARLOTTE FELT drained by the harrowing few days she'd had since coming home. If only she'd been able to come sooner, she could have seen more of Jonty, said goodbye to him properly. She was dog tired and wished she could have a sleep, but there were things she must do.

'You go upstairs and rest on your bed,' she said to her mother. 'We were up so early.'

'Rest? I couldn't, I'm all churned up inside.' Mary was agitated, unable to keep still.

'I have to let Dr Williams know.' Charlotte knew she had to be strong for her mother now.

'Don't leave me by myself. I don't feel . . .'

'No, no.' Charlotte could either run down to Plas Hafren to use their phone or take Jonty's motor bike and go to the surgery. But it was a long time since she'd ridden the bike and she didn't feel up to trying it at the moment. 'Would you like to walk down to Plas Hafren with me? A breath of fresh air might do us good.'

'They were good friends to Jonty. Yes, we have to tell them.'

It was a raw afternoon. Charlotte found warm scarves and gloves and set off, linking her arm through her mother's. There were a thousand things she must do, a thousand things to discuss with her mother and decisions they must make, but at the moment they were so overwhelmed by their loss they could think of nothing else.

Enid Evans was alone in the house. She'd been baking and the house was fragrant with the scent of it. She ushered Charlotte to the phone and Mary to the fire. Then Mary rang her mother in Liverpool. Tea was made and sponge cake offered.

'Ted and Glyn have gone to market to buy some new rams, but they'll be back any minute now.'

Enid was a kind person and was providing the sort of comfort Mary needed. Charlotte asked her advice about the funeral.

'I have a cousin,' she said. 'He owns the funeral parlour at Menai Bridge and people speak highly of him. He'll come to your house to talk to you. Shall I ring him and ask him to call?'

'Yes, please. That way Mum can decide on everything.' Charlotte felt it was one thing off her mind.

She began to feel better when she'd had the tea and cake, but what she craved was time on her own so that she could quietly think through their options. A long lonely walk along Hafren Sands was what she needed. She told Enid where she was going, and asked if she could leave Mary with her for a while.

'Of course, love,' Enid said. 'We all have our own way of coming to terms with our troubles.'

Charlotte set off. The wind was sharp against her cheeks and the sky was dark. It was high tide and waves were rushing furiously up the beach. Walking on sand was heavier going than she'd remembered, and try as she might she couldn't clear her head. Did it make sense for her and her mother to stay on at Glan y Mor, or should they return to Liverpool?

She'd gone perhaps half a mile when she heard a shout and turned to see Glyn hurrying after her. She was always pleased to see him and walked back to meet him.

'I thought you'd never hear me,' he panted. His arms went round her in a hug. 'You poor thing, you haven't had time to draw a breath, have you? Losing your dad straight after coming home. I'd no idea the end was so close.'

'Neither had I.'

She put her forehead down on his shoulder, felt his arms tighten round her and immediately felt comforted. She'd thought she had her tears under control but at the first sign of sympathy they were burning her eyes again. She tried to stem the flow against his rough coat.

She'd grown up with Glyn. Through her childhood years he'd commiserated with her when she was in difficulties, helped her celebrate her successes, and been her friend and support throughout.

He said, 'It must have come as a dreadful shock.'

'Yes, and not the only one.'

Before she knew what she was doing she was telling him that Jonty and Mary were not her natural parents. All the details she had read in that little red book came out in a rush.

'And you didn't know?' He looked astounded.

'No, never even suspected. It all came out last night. That was the first I heard of it.'

'You poor thing.' With his arm round her waist they were walking slowly back.

'Sorry,' she said. 'I had to tell somebody. There are questions I'd like to ask Jonty and now it's too late.'

'Your mother . . . you can still ask her.'

'Mum didn't want me to know.'

'Perhaps that was her way of protecting you. And herself too, of course. She wanted to keep her daughter and to go on being a mother to you.'

'That isn't going to change, Glyn. I need her, especially now.' She blew her nose and wiped her eyes. 'They've been the best of parents to me – they loved me. I find it hard to believe they aren't.'

'Keep thinking about them that way. They gave you a happy childhood?'

'Very happy.'

'All the same, it must make you feel your whole world has changed.'

'As though I've had the ground cut away at my feet,' she said.

He kissed her forehead and continued to hold her tight. 'I hardly know how to help you with this. It goes way beyond my experience,' he said.

'And mine,' she said. 'But you already have. The best thing for me is to continue thinking of them as my parents.'

'Aren't you curious about what and where you'd be if they hadn't kept you?'

'Very,' she told him. 'Dad . . . Jonty, I mean . . . thought I'd have done much better. He said they were rich.'

'I suppose you'll be off looking for them?'

'I don't know where I'm going any more. I suppose it depends on what Mum wants to do. I don't think she'd be able to run Glan y Mor by herself.'

'But with your help she could. I'd come up and plough for you and cut your hay . . .'

'You're very kind.' She hesitated. 'But I'm a nurse. I'm used to that life now. I know I can cope with it, but there'd be things I could never do here, ploughing and buying stock and all that.'

'I'd do that for you.'

Charlotte was not convinced. 'I'll have to talk it over with Mum; it has to be her decision. She's got relatives in Liverpool, her own mother, and I think she might prefer to go back.'

Glyn sighed and said awkwardly, 'I rather hoped you'd stay, and we could be friends again.'

'We'll always be friends, Glyn.'

'More than friends, I mean. You know . . .'

Charlotte said slowly, 'Yes, I do know. You've shown it, doing so much for me. Don't think I'm not grateful, Glyn, but Jonty dying and finding out . . . it's thrown me sideways.'

'Charlotte, love.' He put his arms round her in a hug. 'I should have had more sense than to mention it now. It's too soon for you; you still feel raw. It's just that you're going away.'

'I don't really want to but I might have to. If it's best for Mum.'

'I do understand.'

She sighed. 'I'm shattered, and it's high time I took Mum home and we got on with the milking.'

Mary felt in dire straits. Jonty's death had catapulted her into unknown territory. She didn't know how she could manage without him. She hung on to Charlotte's arm to climb the hill on the way home. She was grateful to have her here to help in her hour of need, and it seemed churlish to say it was really Jonty she wanted.

The neighbours at Plas Hafren had gone out of their way to be kind to her, and were doing things for her she should be doing for herself. Except just now she seemed to have lost the energy to do anything.

It was growing dark when they reached home and Charlotte hurried her inside to change into her wellingtons and work clothes. Mary had always done her share of the chores, and Charlotte said, 'It'll do you good, Mum, to be out looking after the animals.'

But Mary didn't feel like it; she wanted to curl up and die. Charlotte insisted and hurried to shut the hens in before the foxes came on the prowl. Mary stood watching her until Charlotte pushed a basket into her hand and pointed out that the eggs hadn't yet been collected.

She followed a few paces behind Charlotte as she forked hay into the cow's stalls next. They were waiting at the gate; she had only to open it for them to come in to get their supper.

When Charlotte gave her a milking pail she sat on the stool to milk Marigold. It was something she'd done morning and evening for years, and tonight it was comforting in a way. Restful, almost soothing.

Charlotte had finished milking Posy in half the time it took her, but that didn't matter. It gave Charlotte time to see to the pigs and the calves. She was washed and changed when Mary took Marigold's milk to the dairy.

Once she'd washed and changed herself, Mary wanted to be with Jonty. She sat by his bed and studied his well-loved face, listening to Charlotte in the kitchen preparing something for their supper. After a while, Charlotte came to sit down on the other side of the bed.

Mary felt anguished. 'I hardly know what I'm doing and I'm leaving most of the work to you. D'you think I'm spending too much time with Jonty now he's dead?'

'No, Mum,' Charlotte said gently. 'I'm going to miss him too. Very much.'

Mary felt burdened with all the things she needed to do, but she couldn't think and couldn't move from the chair. Time seemed to be standing still, though Charlotte always appeared to be busy and the house was full of visitors. The doctor came, and the undertaker, the clergy and the neighbours, one after the other. They talked gravely to her and then took over.

The death certificate and the coffin arrived, the funeral date and time were fixed. People brought flowers, casseroles and cakes: so much food it overflowed the larder and was laid out on the dresser and the kitchen table. They said such nice things about Jonty. Everybody had loved him.

Dan was planning to bring Barbara and his mother down for the funeral. Mary had seen much more of Edith recently. Since Percy's death, she'd needed comfort and support and Mary had asked her down to stay several times over the summer. She felt they were much closer and was very glad to have it so now.

The postman brought Mary a letter from her mother.

Would you like me to stay on for a few days to help you sort things out? At a time like this, it's hard to know whether I'd be a help or more of a nuisance to you. Feel free to say no, if that's what you want.

She handed the letter to Charlotte, who immediately said, 'Tell her you'd like her to stay. We have to make some decisions, Mum, and she'll be a help.'

By now, Jonty had been dressed in his suit and put into his coffin and the parlour was filled with the fresh sharp scent of chrysanthemums. Mary still went to sit with him. She thought about the life she'd had here with him and tried to take stock. Here she was at forty-two feeling her life was over. How was she going to fill the rest of it?

On the morning of the funeral, Charlotte rushed through the outside work by herself; Mary couldn't think of helping. It was Charlotte who prepared the breakfast, tidied up and urged her to get ready. Fortunately, Mary already had a black coat and skirt, and her white blouse would do. She and Jonty had never bothered with fine clothes.

Her family arrived in their mourning clothes and it drove the finality of the occasion home to her. She took them in to see Jonty but when Charlotte led them back to the kitchen for a cup of coffee, she stayed to say her last goodbye to him. The undertakers arrived shortly afterwards to fasten the coffin lid down.

The neighbours were arriving by then, including the family from Plas Hafren. They needed six strong men to carry Jonty's coffin the first half-mile down the steep path to the road. Glyn and his father with two men from the village helped the undertakers and the rest of them walked behind.

It was a mild and sunny November day and the little church was full. Jonty was popular; he'd always been willing to help anybody. It was a simple service but Mary could hardly take it in. She didn't want to be here watching this, she wanted to be with Jonty. Knowing that in future she never could made her feel bereft, and she couldn't stop her tears welling up and running down her cheeks.

It was all over at last. She'd thrown a spadeful of soil down that gaping hole on to his coffin, and Dan and her mother were helping her back to the car. She hardly knew or cared what would happen now. Jonty was gone for ever.

Enid had insisted on holding the funeral tea at Plas Hafren, as some of the mourners were too old or infirm to walk up the hill to Glan y Mor. It was Charlotte who took Mary upstairs to Enid's spare room where she could have a few minutes alone to pull herself together. On the way up they'd passed the bathroom that Jonty had helped convert from a bedroom. Mary looked at herself in the mirror and thought she looked a travesty of her normal self. She bathed her eyes with cold water and hoped it would help.

A few minutes later, she went unsteadily downstairs in this much larger house to find her way to the crowded parlour. Many people, some she hardly knew, told her how much they had respected and liked Jonty and were going to miss him.

For the first time, she noticed how much at ease Charlotte was with this family. Glyn had driven her to the church and back with his parents, and he was being very attentive to her now. He was showing deep affection, perhaps even love, and Mary was glad for Charlotte's sake. Jonty had liked Glyn; he would approve of an alliance there.

It was Glyn who rode his own motor bike up to Glan y Mor to fetch Jonty's, which had the sidecar. He took Mary home first, and it seemed all wrong to see him perched beside her where previously there'd been only Jonty, but she'd have to get used to it.

On her doorstep he kissed her cheek, and said, 'If there's anything I or my family can do to help, you know you have only to ask.'

That brought the tears flooding down her face again and the house seemed empty and cold. She made up the fire, which was nearly out, and by then Glyn was delivering her mother and Charlotte. He stayed to help Charlotte with the evening milking.

For Mary, the days ahead stretched empty and forlorn. Despite having her mother and daughter with her, she felt lonely. Charlotte thought she should go out and do things. Edith was ready to accompany her, but her mother couldn't easily manage that half-mile walk uphill, and walking on the beach wasn't easy either, especially now there was a sharp cold wind off the sea.

Mary wanted to be left to sit and think of Jonty in the room where he'd died. But Charlotte and Edith spring-cleaned it vigorously and turned it back into the parlour she'd hardly used, talking all the time of the future and urging her to think of where she'd like to live. She told them in a fit of impatience that she wanted nothing except to be left in peace, alone here at Glan y Mor. Charlotte held her hand and went through the pros and cons over again.

'You couldn't manage the work here by yourself. You'd be cut off without transport through the dark days of winter when you'd hardly see anybody.'

'I know what it's like. I've spent many winters here.'

'But not on your own. How would you sell your butter and eggs? I'd be very happy to stay with you, Mum, at least for a year or so until we can see ahead more clearly.'

'Charlotte could do the day to day work with the animals,' Edith added. 'But planting potatoes is hard work. So is lifting them, and she can't cut hay. Farming is heavy work for a girl.'

Charlotte sighed. 'And I don't know what to look for when buying and selling stock.'

'Besides,' Edith went on, 'Charlotte wanted to be a nurse and has trained for it. She'll find it easier to earn her living that way, but if she stays here for a year or so she'll lose her skills, won't she?'

There was no answer to that.

'Why don't you come back home and live with me, Mary? I need you now. Being a widow and facing old age is no fun. You know I'd love to have you, and Liverpool used to be your home.'

Mary felt her mother really wanted her to go, but she said, 'It would be like turning my back on the home Jonty set up.'

'But would you be happy here without him?'

'He was everything to me.'

Edith said, ''Tis better to have loved and lost than never to have loved at all.'

'What do you want to do, Charlotte? Do you want to go back to Liverpool?' Mary asked.

Charlotte gave a gusty sigh. 'Like you, Mum, I hardly know what I want.'

Mary shook her head. Everything here reminded her of Jonty. 'We'd be better off in Liverpool, wouldn't we?' she said.

Charlotte had spoken the truth when she'd said she didn't know what she wanted. Now that she was faced with selling off the animals and the crops they'd gathered, together with the odds and ends of equipment needed to run a smallholding, she wasn't at all sure it was the right thing to do. Even when she'd moved to Liverpool, she'd seen Glan y Mor as a place of peace and security where she could forget her problems.

She wanted to keep Jonty's motor bike. He'd taught her to ride it before she was sixteen, and even made her pass her test, but she'd not ridden it since the petrol shortage began to bite. Glyn offered to take her out for couple of practice rides. He rode pillion behind her, or sometimes in the sidecar, and usually managed to see to his own affairs at the same time. She visited a farm where he wanted to pay for the six-week-old ducklings and geese he'd bought, and was now fattening for Christmas. He and his father regularly visited the market in Llangefni where stock was sold, to keep abreast of prices, and Glyn took her there. Once they stopped at a café for a cup of tea.

She'd always seen Glyn as a friend and welcome companion. Now he was coming up almost daily with gifts from Plas Hafren; they'd killed a pig and he brought a joint for her to roast. A day or two later, there were chitterlings, and after that he brought up one of his mother's home-made loaves and then a sponge cake for them.

He often stayed to give her a hand with the milking and if one of her animals seemed off colour he'd give his advice. Should treatment be needed, he could usually provide that too.

When Mary made the decision to sell up and move to Liverpool, she turned to Glyn for help. He brought his father up to discuss it later the same day and they sat down with a cup of tea in the kitchen.

'I've been wondering whether you'd want to leave,' Ted Edwards said. 'If you're giving up the tenancy, I might see if I can buy the place. Our land adjoins it and it would be easy to run alongside Plas Hafren. I'll buy your sheep and your poultry flocks from you. If you're happy to do that, Glyn and I will look them over to set a fair price.'

'Thank you,' Mary said. 'I'd be grateful if you would.'

'I think you'd be better selling the pigs and calves in the market as fattening stock. I can arrange that if you're agreeable.'

'What about the cows?' Charlotte asked.

'I run a suckler herd and Jerseys aren't suitable for that, but there are plenty of small farms that would want them. You could telephone the place where Jonty bought them; they may know of somebody. Or you could put an advert in the paper.'

The cows were sold the following week, more quickly than Charlotte would have liked. Soon only the sheep and the poultry remained.

'I'll miss you,' Glyn told her when the house too was beginning to look a bit bare. 'Since the night you wept on my shoulder and told me you were washed up on the beach after a shipwreck, I haven't been able to stop thinking of you. Now you've found you have an exotic background I suppose you want to find out more about it?'

'I'd rather it was more ordinary, but yes, I am curious.'

'Of course you are. That's only natural, but I hate seeing you getting ready to leave. Promise you won't lose touch?'

'I won't.'

'And come and see us once in a while. Mum would be only too pleased to put you up.'

Charlotte nodded. Now they'd got to this point, she wished they weren't going.

Mary found packing up her home of more than twenty years not only depressing but hard work. Charlotte helped her crate up the things she wanted to take with her and arranged for them to be collected by carrier and delivered to Edith's address in Templeton Avenue.

Three days before they were due to leave, they put Edith on the train so she could get her house ready for them. She took with her a box packed with one of their prime cockerels, dressed and ready for the oven, several pounds of fresh butter and two dozen eggs. Dan had promised to meet her train at the other end.

'I'm glad that you want to keep Jonty's bike,' Mary said. She'd parted with so many of his things, she was beginning to hate it. 'We'll use it; it'll mean we don't have to rely on public transport.'

Charlotte shook her head. 'We won't be able to get a petrol ration,' she said. 'We have a few coupons left because Dad couldn't use it over the last months, but when they've gone that'll be the end of it.'

It brought home to Mary that she was facing a very different life. She felt a bit nervous in the sidecar with only Charlotte's slim frame perched above her, but she remembered Jonty saying she was very capable. Glyn helped Charlotte check the bike over before they set off, though he said he was an amateur compared with Jonty.

Charlotte was out late with him the night before they left. Mary began to worry that she'd not get enough sleep before the journey and she'd never ridden the bike such a long distance before. But Charlotte was full of energy the next morning and up early; they got off on time.

For Mary, to leave Glan y Mor was the sad end to an era. She felt she was leaving Jonty too, because no longer would she be able to take flowers to his grave. She got into the sidecar amongst the possessions Charlotte had already packed in, determined to think of the future, and fought the urge to look back as the bike bumped down the hill.

It was a week before Christmas and a clear and pleasant day for December. Mary was beguiled by the beautiful, ever-changing views of mountains and sea as Charlotte drove along the coast road. It was mid-afternoon when they reached Merseyside and daylight was already fading.

In the grey dusk, she saw the destruction in the centre of the city and was appalled. All of Liverpool looked shabby and run down. There were bomb-damaged buildings everywhere, half-houses with half-staircases hanging on the walls. Rooms without floors but with fire grates up on the second floor, and paper curling off the walls. The air seemed smoke-laden and heavy.

It was not her first glimpse of war-torn Liverpool; she had come for her father's funeral, but she'd stayed only one day because Jonty was ill. She'd noticed nothing of this devastation then. It seemed an unpleasant place compared with the beauty of the Welsh countryside.

But her home was very much as she remembered it. Like everything else it needed a coat of paint, and there were vegetables growing in the back garden. Her mother gave them a very warm welcome and the scent of roasting chicken filled the house. Mary slept that night in the room that had always been hers, feeling she'd done the right thing by coming home.

CHAPTER THIRTEEN

IT WAS THE fifth Christmas of the war, but the news from the front was encouraging. Germany was no longer sending its planes over to bomb British cities. Its army was being driven out of Russia and there was much speculation about the Allies opening a second front. Charlotte was missing Glyn, but Gran had wanted to get back to the rest of her family for the festive season and it had seemed selfish to keep her mother at Glan y Mor when half the furniture had already gone. Gran needed all her family round her and Charlotte thought her mother needed it even more.

She understood Gran was going to provide a quiet Christmas in deference to the two recent deaths in the family, but all her relatives living in the city were invited round for Christmas dinner. Mary seemed quite excited when she met her younger brothers again. 'I'm looking forward to seeing much more of you now I'm back home, and getting to know my sisters-in-law, too.'

The family had expected Noel to remain a bachelor but earlier that year he'd met Valerie and quickly become engaged. He said at their age it was ridiculous to put off getting married, particularly as she was living alone in the small house in which she'd been brought up and she wanted him to move in with her. They did it quietly and without fuss, because his father had so recently died.

Valerie was a plump jolly woman in her mid-thirties. She was a secretary who used to work for the Mersey Docks and Harbour Board, but since Percy had died she'd been employed in their business so that the three brothers could take over more of their father's work. Charlotte took to her right away and she thought her mother did too, and Mary had never been more in need of a supportive circle of relatives.

146

They had a very enjoyable Christmas at Templeton Avenue although fires had to be kept low because of shortage of fuel. Nine adults and Len's little daughter, Jenny, sat down to eat, and the turkey and plum pudding were large enough to feed them all. They raised their glasses and drank to the future, to Simon and Tim and a quick end to the war.

Charlotte looked round at their smiling faces and could see a vague family likeness between them, but she definitely didn't share it. Everything about her was different. It drove home to her that she was Abigail Elinor and that started another surge of curiosity about the Barrington Browns.

When the Christmas holiday was over, Charlotte thought her mother was settling down in her old home, but for her things were falling a little flat. She'd felt close to Glyn during the weeks she'd spent at Glan y Mor. She'd confided her problems and uncertainties to him and he'd always been ready to help. They'd talked and talked and without him she felt lost. She remembered her friend Shirley Mathews from her training days, and thought it would be nice to see her again. She rang her home number, but her mother said her boyfriend had persuaded her to go to Edinburgh to do her midwifery training because he was stationed up there. Charlotte got her address and wrote to her but what she'd wanted was her company.

The war seemed much closer in a big city, with the blackout and power cuts. There was less food available here, where few could augment their rations. Nobody looked as smart as they used to; clothing was getting shabby and only utility styles were to be had with their clothing coupons.

Charlotte couldn't stop fretting about Jonty. She thought again of how he'd told her she wasn't his daughter, and saw once more his pain-filled eyes looking into hers. She'd cried about that more than once – and Mary's distress too – although she hadn't wanted her mother to know. There had been many nights when she had been so tormented with questions she couldn't get to sleep. If she wasn't Charlotte Jones, who was she? And if Jonty wasn't her father, who was? She took time to read through the little red notebook Jonty had given her again. He'd painstakingly written down the names and address of her family. Of course, that was more than twenty years ago, but he'd told her he knew men who'd worked at their shipyard. She had to take a look at that; she had to find out more about them.

Gran gave her a street map of Liverpool that had belonged to Percy, and she set off along the Dock Road on Jonty's bike. It would have been impossible to miss: the name Barrington Brown appeared on a pair of huge gates in foot-high letters. She stopped to take a closer look. Underneath, she read *Ship Repairers*, and then *South Gate*. The size of the place made her gasp. She rode on. The eight-foot stone wall seemed to stretch for ever, but eventually she came to another large gate, labelled *North Gate*, with the same wording above it.

This was not a family business like the Shawcrosses'. She knew Jonty had been impressed by the status of the Barrington Browns; her curiosity about them was growing. Suddenly, the works' hooter let off a piercing wail. The gates were opened to let a horde of workmen stream out, some cycling, some running for buses, some walking.

Charlotte looked at her watch. It was twelve thirty; it must be their midday break. She could find out no more here, so she turned the motor bike round and went home.

After lunch, she set out again, this time to look for the Barrington Browns' house. Burford House was some way out in the direction of Ainsdale. She found Lutters Lane without trouble and passed the entrance to a farm. Round the corner she came to the house. It was the only one on this lane and hardly a house. It was more of a mansion. Her heart began to hammer. There was so much unknown territory here. Again there were large gates, but these were ornamental and of wrought iron. She couldn't get close enough to see much of the house, but there was a drive and a wide stretch of lawn which seemed well cared for. The house itself was half hidden by trees, some of them evergreens, but it was undoubtedly of substantial size.

She got off the bike and walked back hoping to see more, but all she could do was marvel at its grandeur. She felt desperate to know more about the family from which she'd originated. But what else could she do? She could look at the electoral list in the public library to find out the names of those living there now. She'd do that, but was there any way she could see them? She wondered if she had a family resemblance to them. She was seething with a hot and burning curiosity and couldn't sleep that night for thinking about them.

She made herself think seriously about going back to work. She needed to earn her living and she ought to be helping the war effort. Mum and Gran urged her to have a few weeks' rest before returning but they'd be fine now they were together. Her presence was no longer essential.

Over the next few days, Charlotte tried to decide where she wanted to work. She quite fancied joining the Queen Alexandra's Royal Army Nursing Corps like Glyn's sisters, but they were asking for a minimum two years' experience after qualification. She was almost sure they'd take her back at Liverpool Royal Infirmary as a staff nurse and thought she might work there for two years.

Or she could see if they wanted more staff nurses at Bangor Hospital. If she went there, she'd be able to see more of Glyn. Though Mum wouldn't like it when she'd just persuaded her to come to Liverpool and it would feel a bit like letting her down.

She went down to the local library and looked through the adverts in the nursing press. Clearly, she was spoilt for choice; nurses were needed everywhere. Then her eye was caught by a private ad. With a gasp of astonishment, she sat up straighter.

Required, qualified nurse for elderly lady who has had a stroke. Husband may also require minor help. Also, occasional babysitting. Full time, live in, other staff kept. References required.

The name given was Barrington Brown, and the address Burford House with a phone number.

Charlotte felt her heart turn completely over. Would she dare? Anyway, it was not the sort of job she should consider. She needed to work on a busy hospital ward where she'd gain experience . . . but this was *her family*.

It frightened her to think of applying for a job with the Barrington Browns but to be amongst them, see what sort of people they were, was what she craved. But would she have the nerve to do it?

She was intrigued by the need for babysitting. She got out the red notebook again but it was no help. If there was an elderly lady who'd had a stroke, it must be the child's grandmother.

Charlotte didn't sleep well that night. She kept changing her mind about whether she should or shouldn't apply for that job. Full of qualms, by morning she'd decided she must. It wouldn't do to get the wind up and be put off; she'd never get another chance to meet them like this. It might come to nothing anyway, but what had she to lose?

*

Charlotte was a bag of nerves by the time she dialled the number. A piping girlish voice answered. 'Burford House, Mrs Meriel Barrington Brown speaking.'

Out came the few words she'd rehearsed about seeing the job advertised, finishing with 'I'd like to apply'.

'Oh!' The girl sounded pleased. Charlotte was asking herself who Meriel was. 'Can you come along and see us?' They agreed that two o'clock that afternoon would suit them all. Charlotte was about to put the phone down when the piping voice asked, 'You are a trained nurse?'

'Yes. State Registered.'

'Will you please bring your certificates to show us?'

Charlotte put the phone down with shaking fingers. Meriel sounded young and almost as nervous as Charlotte felt herself. But who was she? Her father might have married again, or possibly there were other members of the family she didn't know about. No point in bothering with electoral lists now; she'd find out soon enough.

Mum had made her some warm trousers to wear when she rode the motor bike, but she wanted to attend this interview wearing her best skirt. But she had no idea which bus to take, and as she'd been once she knew she could find it. She'd manage to ride there in her skirt. It was a cold but dry afternoon.

Alongside the mammoth wrought-iron gates she'd seen before was a small gate for pedestrians. She pushed her bike through and rode nervously up the drive. It was a large Victorian house, not terribly handsome but one of the few buildings she'd seen that was not desperate for a coat of fresh paint. The flower beds and shrubs were neatly kept.

Where should she leave her bike? There was nobody about to ask. Stone steps bounded by stone balustrades led up to an enormous front door. She slipped off her headscarf, oilskins and heavy shoes, rolled them up and popped them in the sidecar. She brought out her best court shoes and handbag and ran a comb through her hair. The brisk breeze immediately tossed it about again and she twisted it briskly into a pony tail. She'd have preferred her French pleat for this interview, but had been afraid the bike ride would mess it up and it was hard to repair.

Having made herself look as respectable as she could, and leaving the bike propped against the stone balustrade, she climbed the steps. Sick with apprehension, she rang the door bell. She heard it ring somewhere in the depths of the building but nobody came. She waited and stamped, her feet icy in the cold shoes. She rang again and kept her finger on the bell. A moment later she was relieved to hear light steps hurrying to open it.

'Hello? Are you the nurse come about the job?' The girl's face was tight with tension; she seemed very little older than Charlotte was herself.

'Yes, I'm Charlotte Jones.'

'Come in.'

The girl's hair was almost white blonde, fine, flyaway, short and untidy. She wore a stained grey cardigan over her wool dress.

Charlotte looked round the enormous entrance hall. It had a black and white tiled floor and larger than life marble heads on stone plinths. It was almost as cold inside as it was out. A bit spooky too. Charlotte felt goose pimples break out on her arms and shivered. She told herself she was being silly. There was really nothing scary about the place, it was all in her mind. She must look at this as a straight job interview, and not get nerve-racked about being related to the owners.

'This way.' The girl set off rapidly down a wide passage. Charlotte caught glimpses of immense rooms as she hurried past open doors. It was all rather grand and formal and anything but homely. She had to jog in order to keep up, and she could hear babies crying before the girl flung open a door and shot inside.

Charlotte was close behind and saw her rush across the room and unstrap a distressed and howling infant from a high chair.

'There, there, pet. I told you I wouldn't be a minute.' An enamel mug hurtled past Charlotte's head and bounced against the wall.

'He's getting quite heavy to carry about,' the girl said to Charlotte. 'Yes, do come in. I'm Meriel Barrington Brown – we spoke on the phone.'

An older child was climbing out of a playpen and balancing precariously on the top rail. Charlotte went to lift her to safety, but the girl screamed louder at her approach. 'No, no, not you.'

The first child, now quiet, was pushed into her arms and the mother threw her arms round the older one and pulled her on to the sofa.

Now it was quiet enough to make herself heard, the girl said, 'That's Robin you're holding, he's ten months old, and this is Rebecca, she's three and a half.' They were attractive children with their mother's pale, flyaway hair, but they looked unkempt, their clothes surprisingly stained and shabby. Meriel spoke too fast and could barely control her wriggling daughter.

151

Charlotte felt confused. Had her father married again and was this his new family? She found it hard to believe; the girl looked too young and hardly seemed to be coping.

'Won't you sit down?' she asked.

There were toys everywhere. Charlotte moved a doll, a ball and a stuffed rabbit to make room at the other end of the sofa. But it was making her feel better: she couldn't feel scared or nervous in the midst of this chaos. Robin gave a sniff and a whimper, and big wet brown eyes stared up at her.

'I understood it was an elderly lady I was to look after,' Charlotte said.

'Yes, yes, of course, my mother-in-law. My nanny left before Christmas and I've not been able to get anybody else. Bridget used to do a lot for Mother too . . .'

The older child started to cry again and fight to free herself from her mother's arms.

'Becky love, do be quiet while I talk to this lady.' Meriel jerked the little girl up and down vigorously until she broke loose and scrambled over to a large stuffed dog on wheels and started towing it round the room.

'It's almost impossible to get any help with this war on,' Meriel complained. 'And living here is impossible too. We can't get enough coal to heat more than one or two rooms. I shouldn't be telling you things like that, should I? Not when I want you to come and work here.'

She gave Charlotte no time to say anything. 'I must thank God for Mrs Shipley. She's the cook and she's been here for fifteen years, so we can have hot meals when she can stretch the rations.'

Charlotte thought Meriel was never going to start interviewing her. She reached into her handbag for her certificates, pushed them towards her and said, 'I trained at the Liverpool Royal Infirmary, and I qualified in October last year.'

'Yes, yes. Robin's going to sleep on your knee. Here, let me take him.'

Charlotte rubbed at the damp patch he left on her best navy skirt. 'I've had some experience of nursing stroke patients. How is your mother-in-law? Has it left her badly handicapped?'

'It's left her weak down her left side. She can't walk very well.'

'But she can do things for herself?'

Meriel looked bewildered.

'Feed herself, I mean? Wash herself, comb her hair, that sort of thing.'

'Grandpops helps her a lot. She has to take loads of pills and gets confused. Rod, my husband, says I must tell you that you'll need to make sure she takes the right ones.'

'I'll certainly do that,' Charlotte said. So this was Roderick's second wife. If she'd remained here as Abigail, this girl would be her stepmother! The thought shocked her. She struggled on, trying to give more details about her training and background.

'So you will you take the job?' Ingenuous blue eyes searched into hers.

'Well, I'd like to know more about it before I . . .'

'Of course. Rod said I was to ask you how much you were paid in hospital and offer half as much again.'

Charlotte blinked. 'That's very generous . . .'

'He doesn't want you to leave to get a better paid job, like Bridget. That upsets everybody's routine, you see.'

'Yes. Perhaps I ought to meet my patient before we go any further? She'd have to want me to look after her, wouldn't she?'

'Yes. Yes, of course. Just one thing. Rod wants you to keep an eye on his father but we don't say that to him. Grandpops is not very steady on his feet but he's very independent and wants to run things as he used to. The trouble is, he's eighty-one now, and doesn't always know what he's up to. We've told him we're looking for a nurse for Mother. Please don't say anything about his needing help himself.'

'Right, I won't.'

'I'll take you up, then. Becky, you'd better come too.' She lowered the sleeping Robin to the floor of the playpen and covered him with a rug. 'He'll be all right there for a few minutes.'

Becky was scampering ahead; her mother was talking over her shoulder as Charlotte tried to keep up.

'Isn't it cold and draughty in these hallways? Rod is trying to do something about it but it's almost impossible to get enough coal. We were bombed out of our house and there was nowhere else for us to go. We've tried so hard to find . . .'

Charlotte felt she should try to remember the way back to the main hall and front door, so as not to get lost in this vast house. If the doors were open, she couldn't resist peeping into the rooms as she passed. They all looked over-furnished and very Victorian: lots of dark paint and too many tables and chairs of polished mahogany. The heavy window drapes made them dark; the ceilings were ornately plastered with leaves and cherubs and the walls were decorated with gilt mirrors and paintings.

Up a handsome curved staircase. 'Our flat is in the east wing. Rod's parents have a flat here on the west side in the main part of the house and it's upstairs. We had a chairlift put on the servants' stairs for Grandma – it was easier because they're straight. Steeper too, of course, but that's a good thing for a chairlift because it can be shorter.'

Becky and her mother were rushing past another open door. 'Meriel,' a voice called. 'Meriel?'

'Oh, you're there, Grandpops.' Meriel turned back.

'Grandpops,' Becky screamed in delight, hurling herself at his legs.

'I think we have a nurse for Grandma – I was just bringing her up to meet you both. This is Nurse . . .' Meriel looked at Charlotte and faltered.

'Charlotte Jones.' Her heart was racing. She put out her hand and went forward, very conscious that she must be greeting her grandfather. This was her family. This house might have been her home. It was an awesome thought.

'Jeremy Barrington Brown. No, my dear, my hands are dirty, so I can't shake yours at the moment. As you can see, I'm regilding my picture frames. Can't get anybody else to do it these days.'

He was working on the huge ornate frame of a dark oil painting, laid flat on a table covered with newspaper.

The toddler pulled at his trouser legs and jumped up and down. 'Want to paint. Want to paint with Grandpops.'

Her mother grasped the child's hand firmly. 'No, Becky, don't touch. That's gold leaf, not ordinary paint.'

He said, 'Of course, the picture itself is badly in need of a clean, but I fear I don't have the skill for that.'

Jeremy Barrington Brown was a well-rounded rather dumpy figure, and was wearing a white apron splattered with gold leaf over his Harris tweed sports jacket and cavalry twill trousers. Charlotte noticed he was supporting himself against the table, and a walking stick had been left within reach.

'We shall be very glad to have the services of a nurse,' he said and smiled at her.

'A trained nurse,' Meriel added.

'Good. You take her up to see Clarissa. Tell her I'll be along in a few minutes.'

His head was a bald shiny dome fringed with neatly trimmed white hair round the back. He was a dapper man with round pink cheeks and wiry grey brows. As she followed in Meriel's wake, Charlotte decided her first impression was that she liked her grandfather.

'Here we are.' Meriel knocked and led the way in. 'Grandma,' she said. 'I've brought Nurse Jones to meet you.'

Charlotte crossed the carpet to the woman slumped on a green fireside chair. Once she must have been tall and slim, because there was an elegance about her still, but her patrician-looking features were heavily lined and sagging with pain. Her faded blue eyes sparked with irritation.

Meriel said, 'We think Nurse Jones will be able to help you.'

She said impatiently, 'I'd be very grateful if somebody would. I do wish you wouldn't all disappear and leave me sitting here by myself.'

Charlotte said, 'What can I do for you, Mrs Barrington Brown?'

'I need to go to the bathroom. I've been wanting to for the last half-hour, and you know, Meriel, I can't get up by myself.'

Meriel was rushing to bring out a wheelchair. 'Where's your bell? It's supposed to ring down in the kitchen.'

'I've been ringing till I'm blue in the face, but nobody comes.'

'Sorry,' Meriel said. Charlotte helped to get the patient – her grandmother! – into the wheelchair. She didn't seem to have the ability to do much for herself.

'Which way?' she asked and manoeuvred the chair in the direction Meriel indicated. 'It must be very frustrating for you, to be dependent on this sort of help from others.'

Once in the bathroom she got the old lady to her feet. 'You'll have to tell me how much help you need,' she told her. 'I'll gladly give it but people value their privacy in the bathroom. Do you want me to stay or to leave you?'

'Stay,' she said imperiously. 'I can't manage without.'

'Right. How long is it since you had this stroke?'

'Last year. It's been eight months of hell. There are so many things I used to do. Sometimes I wonder if life's worth living any more.'

'You need more time to get over it, then you'll find it will be.'

'I spend so much time waiting. Meriel isn't much good with the sick and infirm. It's too much to expect her to look after her mother-in-law as well as her two babies. Not that she seems to have much patience with them either. She was such a pretty girl before Roderick married her.

'Bridget wasn't too bad, a cheerful soul, but even she got fed up with me. Now there's this young fourteen year old, Marjorie. She's useless, absolutely useless. Too small and frail to bear my weight. I'm afraid I'll fall on her and squash her. Of course, she's got other duties too, she's supposed to do the housework. Heaven only knows where she is at this time of day. Probably cleaning downstairs.'

Charlotte said gently, 'Did you know stroke patients can continue to improve for two years? You could get more use back in your limbs. Are you having physiotherapy?'

'Not any more.'

'With the right exercises you might be able to do more for yourself. Then you wouldn't be quite so dependent on others. That would make life easier for you.'

Charlotte could see from her pursed lips that Clarissa didn't believe she would get much better. 'Of course,' she said, 'improvement is quicker over the first few weeks, but I've seen patients come back to clinic two years later doing more than they could a few months before.'

'You've really seen that?'

'Yes, I have.'

Clarissa was looking at her with more interest now. 'I do admire women who train for a career. You're really needed now there's a war on.'

'The first need is to earn my own living.' Charlotte smiled. 'That's why I did the training. Did you never work?'

There was another gusty sigh. 'I did voluntary work, helped raise money for the hospitals and the seamen's mission. Brought up my family and ran this house. Now I'm useless. Really, it's Jeremy who does most for me. I'm a terrible burden to him.'

'I'm sure he doesn't think that.' Charlotte wheeled her back into the sitting room, feeling unexpectedly sorry for her. What could be worse than suddenly finding you're partly paralysed and can no longer do things you took for granted?

Clarissa Barrington Brown sighed. 'I hope you're right.'

Charlotte found that her grandfather had joined Meriel and Becky and was playing with the little girl. She was aware of the warmth and light in the room, which had been modernised and made more comfortable than the others she'd glimpsed in this house. Three huge windows looked over a pleasant garden to farmland.

She couldn't help but notice the photographs. They were everywhere, and all seemed to be of the same man. Hanging on the sitting-room wall were two large ones, one taken in boyhood, the other when he was a grown man. There were several more in silver frames on the mantelpiece, the desk and the bookcase. She felt her heart miss a beat. It must be her natural father. She had to ask Meriel, 'Is this your husband?'

'No.' The girl shook her head, looking bewildered again. 'That's his brother. I must go back in case Robin wakes up.' She gathered up Becky and took her leave.

'It's my elder son, Nathaniel,' Clarissa said. 'He was killed on the Somme in the Great War.'

'I'm so sorry.'

'He was just twenty-one and had everything to live for. He was very brave. I do miss him so.'

'We all do,' his father said sadly. 'He had so much ability – he was on top of everything.'

Charlotte looked round. There seemed to be no photograph of Roderick, the younger son, and neither did they mention him. Yet it seemed he'd taken his brother's place in the business. Was it that they didn't regard him with the same favour?

Jeremy Barrington Brown started asking questions about her circumstances and training, and outlining what her duties would be. He covered everything efficiently in a very pleasant manner. Charlotte was reminded that before retiring he'd run a large and successful business.

He smiled at her and said, 'You seem to be the sort of person we're looking for, and I think Clarissa's taken to you. We'd both be very pleased if you'd come and look after her.'

Almost on the spur of the moment, Charlotte said, 'Thank you, I'd like to.'

She hadn't expected to be offered the job immediately, but perhaps there were no other applicants. Perhaps Clarissa was desperate and they'd have offered it to almost anyone.

She gave him the name of the matron at the Royal and told him, 'She said she'd be happy to give me a reference should I need it.'

Suddenly, she was worried about what she could be getting into. What if they found out why she'd applied for this job? She'd intended to come for the interview just to meet the family and satisfy what she saw as natural curiosity. She hadn't seriously considered taking up private nursing as a career, or even if she'd be allowed to with the war on.

'We've been given official permission to employ a nurse,' Jeremy told her, when she voiced this concern. 'It seems for Clarissa it is deemed a necessity.'

He stood up to get the document from a drawer, and she was shocked to see how difficult he found it to walk. He leaned heavily on his walking stick and held on to furniture with his other hand. He handed the document to her to read. Sure enough, the Barrington Browns were permitted to employ 'a person to carry out nursing duties'.

She might well be considered over-qualified for that description, but she wasn't going to ask. She quite liked her grandparents and felt very sorry for Clarissa. She wanted to make life easier for both of them. Besides, she hadn't yet come face to face with her father and her curiosity was by no means satisfied. If anything, knowing a little made her yearn to know more about the family.

When she was leaving, Clarissa Barrington Brown put out a gnarled hand to her.

'I'm not really cantankerous. I do hope we'll get on.'

'I'm sure we will.'

Charlotte could see the pale eyes examining her face. Clarissa said, 'You know, you do remind me of someone.'

She felt the blood rush to her cheeks; they were burning. She hadn't thought this through. Why hadn't it occurred to her she might resemble her natural parents? Was that what Clarissa had recognised?

CHAPTER FOURTEEN

MARY FELT uneasy and somehow rudderless. Jonty was rarely out of her thoughts for long. She was glad she'd come to Liverpool, but it was giving Charlotte the opportunity to search out her natural father and she didn't like her doing that. She didn't want her to replace Jonty in any way.

Last night, Edith had heard them talking together and been stunned to gather that Charlotte had been adopted. When she asked, Mary had told her the truth about the shipwreck and how she'd insisted on keeping Charlotte. Edith couldn't believe Mary had dared to do it. She had found the whole story as upsetting as it was shocking and had had to retire to bed early.

With the whole business in the front of her mind again, Mary was worried about Charlotte. She didn't trust these wealthy strangers. Charlotte belonged to her and Jonty; they'd brought her up and she was their daughter. Mary hated all this talk about another father. She'd pleaded with Jonty to say nothing to Charlotte about the circumstances of her birth, and she'd truly believed it would be better for them all if Charlotte hadn't known.

Jonty's conscience had always been troubled by what he'd done. He was sure it was a sin and had only gone along with it because she'd wanted it so badly. He'd believed that suppressing the truth about anything was wrong, and also worried that Charlotte would have had a better life with her natural family.

Mary couldn't blame him for trying to put the record straight. Jonty had believed Charlotte was strong enough to take the truth in her stride, but it couldn't be that easy for her. Mary was afraid that, now she was grown up, Charlotte might say she'd have preferred to stay with her birth

159

family as they'd have been able to give her so much more of this world's goods. She was certainly filled with curiosity about them and Mary didn't like that at all. She couldn't bear it if Charlotte turned her back on her; she needed her more than ever now she'd lost Jonty.

Now she was in Liverpool again, Mary could feel herself being drawn back into the life she'd known as a young girl. Her three brothers and their wives were making a big fuss of her and that helped.

Tonight, she was in the kitchen with her mother helping to prepare the evening meal. Edith was a good cook and enjoyed stretching the rations. When Charlotte came home they could hardly wait to hear what she thought of her other family.

'How did you get on?' Mary wanted to know. Charlotte was all smiles as took off her coat.

'Fine. They've offered me the job, and I've said I'll take it.'

'Charlotte!' Mary was appalled. She hadn't expected things to happen so quickly.

'I know you don't like what I'm doing, Mum. I'm sorry, but . . .'

'What's he like? Your natural father?'

'He was at work. I haven't met him yet.'

Mary gulped down her distress. 'It's just that I want you to think of Jonty as your father.'

Charlotte put an arm round her. 'Mum, I do, believe me. I always will. Nobody will ever take his place.'

'You say that, love, but you seem . . .'

'I'm just curious.'

'Desperately curious, I'd say.'

Charlotte understood how she must be feeling. 'Yes, but it makes no difference to what I feel for you and Jonty. You'll always be my mum and dad, the best in the world. I'm starting on Monday morning.'

'So soon? That's only three days away.'

'They really can't manage without help, Mum. They want me to wear uniform, but I'll have to buy it.'

'They should be paying for that.' Edith was indignant.'

'They said they'd refund the cost if I took them the bill. It's the coupons . . .'

'I can spare you a few.'

'Thanks, Mum.'

'So can I,' Edith added.

Charlotte kissed them. 'Thanks. You're both very generous.'

'I have a wardrobe full of clothes, Charlotte. I don't really need more. Tell us about the job.'

'I'll be sleeping there. I'm to be given one day off each week, but not always the same day. I said I didn't want it always to be Sunday. I'd like to be able to go shopping sometimes. So I'll be coming home the evening before my day off and then spend that day with you.'

'We won't be seeing all that much of you then?'

'No, Mum.'

Mary was biting her lip. It shouldn't threaten her position, because Charlotte's birth mother had lost her life, but somehow she felt it did. Mary was afraid Roderick Barrington Brown would be delighted to have his daughter back alive, and that he'd oust Jonty in Charlotte's affections. Jonty had been a loving husband and father and she wanted nothing to tarnish his memory.

Charlotte's arm was still round her shoulders, and now she gave her a little squeeze.

'I have a blood link with this family. Whether they know it or not. I'm what I am partly because of them, and . . .'

'Haven't you told them who you are?'

'No. To be honest, Mum, I don't know how to begin.'

Charlotte's mind had blazed with doubts as she'd ridden back to Templeton Avenue. There was something underhand about taking this job with the Barrington Browns and not telling them why she wanted it. But what alternative did she have if she wanted to make contact? She could hardly ride up to their front door and announce herself as Abigail Elinor their long lost granddaughter.

She could see that both Mum and Gran were getting worked up about it, and thought the best thing was to be open and truthful about what she was doing. But she hadn't told them she'd taken to her grandparents. She was afraid they'd find that hurtful.

Having to acquire uniform bothered her. As a student nurse at the Royal, she had been provided with three dresses, three caps, and fourteen aprons so she could wear a clean one every morning. They'd all been crisply starched in the hospital laundry, and she didn't know how she'd manage that at Burford House. Fourteen aprons seemed a prodigious number to provide for herself and would no doubt take a lot of coupons.

When she'd qualified, she'd been given a permit to buy her own uniform and the address of a Liverpool stockist. She went there the next day to see what they had for private nurses. The assistant told her they had white dresses in stock, which were popular because aprons were not needed. Charlotte bought three, and three small caps; she didn't think she could manage on less even though she'd be washing them herself.

Glyn telephoned her that evening, wanting to know how she was getting on. Charlotte was full of what she'd been doing and let her news pour out.

'I knew you'd be fine once you got to Liverpool,' he said rather sadly. 'I'm missing you. I'm stuck in my usual furrow and rather lonely. Couldn't you come back for one of your days off?'

'I'd love to, Glyn,' she'd said. 'I'm missing you too, but I've got so much on just now. I'll come later on.'

'In the summer? You'll get holidays then?'

'Yes, I expect so.'

'Come for your whole holiday, Charlotte. We can put you up here. I'd love to have you all to myself.'

Daniel and Barbara called in to see them one evening when Charlotte was there and Mary admitted that sometimes she felt at a loose end.

'You need more to fill your day,' Charlotte told her. 'You've always been busy and now suddenly everything's gone slack for you. Besides, all women of working age are expected to have a job in wartime.'

'Even married women,' Barbara added, 'unless they have children under school age.'

Dan, being the eldest brother, had taken overall responsibility for the business. Now he said, 'There's no problem about that, Mary. You can always come back to work in the garages again.'

Mary shook her head. 'In the twenty odd years I've been away I've forgotten all I knew about your office work.'

'Give yourself time,' Dan urged. 'You need a good rest first – I'm sure it doesn't apply to recent widows. But keep an open mind. You may change it.'

'Office work was never Mary's choice,' Edith said. 'She's more a homemaker.'

Charlotte said, 'You'd prefer a job looking after children, wouldn't you, Mum? That's more the sort of thing you'd enjoy.'

But for some reason, Mary couldn't make up her mind to do anything.

*

When Monday morning came, Charlotte was ready to start work at Burford House and was quietly excited at the thought of meeting her father. She went on the bus, taking her suitcase. It meant quite a walk at the other end but at least she knew where to find the house.

She was on the doorstep by nine o'clock, and saw a large black Jaguar parked on the forecourt at the bottom of the front steps. Nervously, she rang the bell, worried she'd be recognised as Abigail Elinor. The front door was snatched open almost immediately by a man in a formal office suit carrying an umbrella and a briefcase.

Charlotte felt her heart skip a beat. This must be her father. 'Good morning,' she said.

He glowered at her. With the help of the little red book, she'd already worked out he'd be forty-seven; he was tall and thin and took after his mother. With his dark hair, pencil moustache and strong features, he'd be good-looking if he didn't have such heavy lines of dissatisfaction round his mouth. She searched his face for a resemblance to herself but could find none.

'You must be the nurse,' he said impatiently. Without waiting for a reply he turned and roared, 'Meriel. Meriel!' When nobody came he jabbed his finger on the doorbell and kept it there until the fourteen-year-old housemaid came running.

'The new nurse, Marjorie. See to her, will you?' He was already descending the front steps to his car as he spoke.

Charlotte was left gasping. He'd hardly glanced at her. Clearly, if that was her father, she'd not made any impression on him. She shivered with disappointment. She'd imagined their first meeting as an important and exciting moment and it had fallen flat.

Marjorie was shy and frail-looking. She took Charlotte to the vast old-fashioned kitchen, which smelled strongly of burnt toast. 'This is Mrs Shipley,' she said.

The cook was a stout middle-aged woman, with a vast white apron tied round her girth. Her white cap covered all but the front tuft of her grey hair. She smelled of burnt toast too.

'I'm about to take breakfast up to the seniors,' she told her. 'I'll take you at the same time.'

Roderick Barrington Brown flung his briefcase and umbrella on the back seat of his Jaguar and set off down the drive on his way to the shipyard.

He felt out of sorts. The baby had woken him twice in the night and it had left him feeling dozy this morning when he knew he'd need all his wits about him.

It hadn't stopped there, either. Rebecca had crept into their bed at six o'clock this morning, waking him yet again. She knew better than to come to his side and put her cold feet on him. She'd got in on Meriel's side; she could twist her mother round her little finger.

Yesterday Meriel had bought her a new party dress, and of course she'd left it hanging on her own wardrobe door instead of putting it away.

'I want to see it again, Mummy.' Becky had started to nag as soon as she saw its pale outline in the semi-dark.

'No,' Meriel had grunted, but just as they were drifting off again Becky had got up and taken it down.

'It's lovely. I want to wear it now.'

'No, you'll get it dirty. You want to keep it nice for tomorrow's party, don't you?'

'Please, Mummy, let me,' she'd wheedled.

'No. You can wear your red pinafore dress this morning.'

'I don't like that one.'

'Don't be silly.' Rod had had to roar at the child before she took the slightest notice. 'Rebecca, go back to your own bed and leave us in peace. It's too early – we don't want you here now.'

The peace had been short-lived; her noise had woken Robin. When Rod got up to go to the bathroom, Meriel was changing Robin's nappy. When he came out, Becky was pirouetting round in her pink taffeta frills.

Meriel laughed when she saw her. What more stupid way was there to treat a child? No wonder both their children were running wild; Meriel let them do whatever they wanted. Any discipline had to come from him. He'd swung the child round to face him and got down to her level.

'Don't you understand?' he'd said forcibly into her face. 'Do as you're told. Go to your room and get dressed in your everyday clothes.'

Her face had crumpled and she'd thrown herself down on the floor, rolling and screaming in a tantrum, crushing her frills. Even properly managed children might have tantrums when they were two, but Rebecca had not grown beyond that stage at three and a half.

'Do as you are told,' he'd shouted.

That had produced louder screams and much drumming of heels, until he could stand no more. He'd given her the good walloping she'd been asking for, but within minutes Meriel had picked her up to kiss and comfort her. So the child never would learn to behave.

Meriel was worse than useless. She had no idea how to bring up children or how to make a comfortable home for him. The place was always in a mess. His parents were too forgiving, saying Meriel was young and hadn't given up girlish things. But she only looked young. She was twenty-nine and it was high time she grew up.

She'd been a pretty little thing when she'd first caught his eye: a young secretary who was temporarily filling in while his permanent middle-aged lady was on holiday. At that time, everybody felt very sorry for Meriel. Her parents had gone to the cinema and been caught in an air raid on the way home. An ARP warden had marshalled them to the nearest air raid shelter but it had received a direct hit and they'd both been killed.

What had possessed him to believe he loved her? She wasn't his class; he should have known she wouldn't do. She was living with her sister in their family home, a prewar three-bedroom 'sunshine semi' in Woolton.

She hadn't been up to much as a secretary. She was like a butterfly, more ornament than use, a fluffy sort of girl who couldn't cope with anything. Why had he not realised that before he'd married her? Life had played him some cruel tricks. He'd barely said boo to her over breakfast this morning but she'd dissolved into tears. It was no way to start a working day.

He reached the shipyard gates, where it pleased him to see the gateman recognise his car and run to throw them open for him. He drove inside and up to the main office building. He'd been coming here man and boy and knew the place like the back of his hand. This was his heritage, as it had been his father's before him.

'Good morning, sir.'

'Good morning.' Everybody acknowledged him.

The yard was busy. The hammers were clattering and the welding torches flaring, and had been for an hour or so already. They'd been working overtime since the Battle of the Atlantic had started. It was providing endless repair jobs for them.

He mounted the wide staircase with its mahogany balustrade to his first-floor office. Miss Kent, his secretary, was already typing hard in the outer office. Her given name was Pixie, but she'd been sadly misnamed. Rigid waves of iron-grey hair covered her head and ended in tight curls.

She usually wore black with a white collar, looked super-efficient, which she was, and had a phenomenal memory. She'd worked for his father before him.

'Mr Graham from the Admiralty has telephoned to apologise,' she said. 'He won't be able to keep his appointment this morning. He wants to know if you can see him tomorrow?'

'Er – let me think.'

'You'll be free between eleven o'clock and two.'

'Ask him if he could come about twelve thirty. If he's free, we could talk over a spot of lunch.'

'Yes, Mr Barrington Brown.' Her face was an inscrutable mask, her manner always formally polite. He didn't know what Pixie thought about anything, whether she liked him or loathed him. She kept him organised just as she had his father; she was almost part of the office furniture.

His father had retired in 1927 and handed the management over to him. He couldn't have taken over at a worse time. Every business was in the doldrums then and the ship repair yard was no exception. Nothing had gone right for him. The yard had started losing money immediately and had lost more as year succeeded year.

According to Pa, it was the first time in its history that the business had failed to make a profit. But all Pa's old cronies were still in post and wanted things done just the way they always had been. Rod had felt he had to fight them to change anything. Pa had insisted on coming out of retirement to help him turn the business round, which had been a terrible indignity. He hated to think about it; he'd been the first Barrington Brown to need that sort of help.

It was only now, because of the war, that Rod had managed to get the profits up to the level he wanted and the family expected, but he knew Pa wouldn't approve of the way he was doing it. Neither did he know how long it would last. Really, it was a case of making hay while the sun shone.

Charlotte waited nervously beside her suitcase in an echoing kitchen that looked like something out of a history book. She felt uneasy, worried that Clarissa might have remembered who she reminded her of.

Marjorie, the little housemaid, rushed past her several times with covered containers that looked as though they contained hot food. The back stairs went up from the passageway near the kitchen door and Charlotte could see her loading the seat and footrest of a chair lift. At last she pressed a switch and sent the food climbing slowly to the top of the stairs.

'I'll show you up now, dear,' Mrs Shipley told her. 'They have their breakfasts at this time, you see.'

The back stairs were steep and very narrow now that some of the space had been taken by the chair lift. Charlotte was hampered by her suitcase and Mrs Shipley by a tray. The suddenly warmer atmosphere made her realise they'd reached the suite that was being lived in.

'This is to be your room.' Mrs Shipley nodded towards an open door. 'We've got it ready for you. Pop your suitcase in and I'll let them know you're here.'

The room was smaller than any other Charlotte had seen in this house, with space for little more than a narrow bed and a small dressing table. She shed her coat and within moments was in Clarissa Barrington Brown's vast bedroom to find her still in bed. There was no sign of Jeremy.

Charlotte saw a backrest, lifted it in and helped her sit up against it. Marjorie set her breakfast in front of her on a tray with legs. It was egg and bacon with toast and marmalade. Mrs Shipley was setting out another breakfast on a small table beside the bed.

'My husband's been sleeping in our guest room since I had the stroke,' Clarissa told Charlotte.

She understood now. The room she'd been given was the original dressing room to this main bedroom. The connecting door was through a small lobby with her bedroom on one side and a splendid bathroom on the other.

While the couple were eating, Charlotte changed into her nurse's uniform and discovered a walk-in wardrobe off her little room with two full length mirrors. When she re-joined the Barrington Browns, Jeremy offered her a cup of coffee from his pot. When she looked round for a cup and saucer, she found there was also a small kitchen in their suite. Everything was to hand, and it seemed the couple were as comfortable as they possibly could be.

'Is your room all right for you?' Jeremy asked.

'It'll suit me down to the ground, thank you. There's a lovely view from the window.'

'Across the garden, yes. We put you there so you'd be within call. If my wife wants to get up in the night, she needs help.'

'Yes, I realise that.'

'And you don't mind being woken?'

Charlotte smiled. 'No. I want you to feel I'm worth the salary you're going to pay me.'

Later that morning, Charlotte helped the old lady to shower and dress. It gave her the chance to see just what Clarissa could do for herself and what she found difficult. Charlotte thought about the help stroke patients had received in the Royal and was sure it would benefit Clarissa. If she could, she wanted to help her improve.

The couple then sat together in their sitting room talking softly. Charlotte was afraid they were discussing her and wondered if she should tell them who she was. Would it be better to be open with them now rather than risk having it surface later? She felt she was walking on eggshells.

At about midday, Dr Staples called to see them. Marjorie brought him up, a rather bent old gentleman weighed down with a large medical bag. He was clearly on friendly terms with the Barrington Browns, and Charlotte was pleased he'd come because she wanted to ask about the treatment they were having.

'Alas, there's nothing he can do for me,' Jeremy said. 'And little enough for Clarissa.'

'There's always something,' Charlotte said and asked the doctor whether a regular exercise programme would help them both.

'Yes,' he said, 'most definitely.'

Later, Charlotte saw him down to the front door where his Austin Seven waited at the bottom of the steps. He said, 'Mrs Barrington Brown went on a rehabilitation course, but found it hard going and wanted to come home. They both thought she'd do better in the bosom of the family. Unfortunately, she's on her own a good deal and doesn't have enough stimulation. I think she's bored. Being restricted in the way she is must make for a dull life. If she could learn to do more for herself, I'm sure she'd feel better. Anything you can do in that direction would help.'

Charlotte's thoughts were already on what she meant to suggest to her patient when her eye was caught by a painting of a yacht hanging on the wall in the entrance hall, a watercolour. Next to it was a large frame holding several photographs of the same vessel. She stopped to examine them more closely, and found, as she'd expected, that this was the *Priscilla*, the boat that had foundered on their headland back at home.

The sight of it left her shaken. This was her connection to the Barrington Browns.

She took a couple of deep breaths and tried to put it from her mind. She felt haunted by her history. It would be so much easier to settle into this job if a job was all it was. Upstairs again, she sat down to talk to her employers.

'Dr Staples thinks you would benefit from doing regular exercises,' she said gently to Clarissa. 'And it might get the left side of your body to function a little better so you could do more for yourself. Would you like to try it?'

'Yes,' she said immediately.

'Do you know what exercises she should be doing?' Jeremy asked.

'Only vaguely,' Charlotte admitted. 'But I know some of the physio-therapists at the Royal; they'll know. They're doing work like that all the time. I could ask if one would be willing to come and see you. She'd know what muscles you need to work on and devise a routine for you to follow.'

'You can't lose, Clarissa,' her husband said. 'I think you should try it.'

'I was shown some exercises before I left hospital,' she said, 'but I'm afraid I didn't keep them up. I got a bit lazy.'

'More like disheartened,' Charlotte told her. 'It's not easy to keep going on your own. I'll be able to keep you at it now, but first I'll have to find out what you need to do. Right, then. I'll try to telephone the hospital.'

Jeremy showed her to his study and pointed out the phone on his desk. She pulled it towards her and asked the operator to put her through to the Royal Infirmary. It took a few minutes to get through to the physio-therapy department and speak to the person she knew.

When Charlotte explained what she wanted, the physiotherapist said, 'Do you remember Polly Carr?'

Charlotte tried to think. 'I don't recognise the name.'

'Polly worked here for about eight years, even after she was married. Her husband's away fighting with the Eighth Army so she's living with her mother and saving for a house of their own. She had a baby last October and with him to look after she can't come back to work full time, but I think she might welcome temporary work such as you're suggesting.'

'Is she on the phone?'

'Yes. Hang on a sec, I'll find her number for you.' Charlotte scribbled it down. 'Polly was one of our best; she's very keen. I feel I can safely recommend her to you.'

Charlotte rang the number straight away. Polly lifted it up. 'Yes,' she said, 'I could find time to do that sort of a job. I'd like to, thank you. It'll keep my hand in.'

When Charlotte mentioned the Barrington Brown name and address, she said, 'That's only a ten-minute bike ride from where I live, so it's handy for me. When would you want me to come?'

'If you tell me when it's convenient for you, I'll talk to the patient and see what would suit her.'

Charlotte went back to the sitting room, and told them what she'd agreed.

'My goodness,' Jeremy said. 'You don't let the grass grow under your feet.'

'The thing is, this girl thinks she'll need to come daily for a little while to get us both started and she's suggesting she stay for an hour each time. She says she can come around eleven in the morning or about three in the afternoon; either would fit in with her baby's schedule. She wants to know which you'd prefer?'

'Mornings, I think,' Clarissa said.

Charlotte mentioned her hourly charge.

'Don't worry about that,' Jeremy said. 'If Clarissa could be more her old self, it would be worth every penny.'

'Shall I ask her to start tomorrow?'

'Yes. You've nothing else on, have you, Clarissa?'

'You know I never have anything on these days.' She sounded a little impatient.

Charlotte said, 'Then I'll ring her back and let her know.'

She knew Clarissa was pleased at the idea of having more physiotherapy. It was giving her hope that she might recover more use of her left arm and leg. She seemed to be looking forward to meeting Polly Carr.

When the doorbell rang just before eleven the next morning, Charlotte ran down to answer it. As soon as she saw the girl on the step, she recognised her brown curly hair and tip-tilted nose.

'I do know you,' she said. 'You were always about the wards.'

'And your face is familiar to me.' Polly smiled.

Charlotte told her about the Barrington Browns as she led the way upstairs. 'I'm sure Jeremy would benefit from your help too,' she said, 'but he won't admit he needs it. You're here to work on Clarissa. I've got her dressed and out of bed so she's ready for you.'

She took Polly into the sitting room and introduced her to Clarissa and Jeremy. Polly took a white coat from her bag and put it on.

'I'm really glad to have this job,' she told them in her bubbly, outgoing manner. 'I've always worked, and being at home with the baby makes me feel quite cut off. My grandma's keeping an eye on Bobby at the moment, so I've no worries about him.'

Charlotte was impressed by the way she got Clarissa to do everyday things and jotted down her observations in the notebook she'd brought. Then she massaged the muscles in Clarissa's left arm and leg and explained some starter exercises. Charlotte knew she was making sure both she and Clarissa understood what needed to be done and why. With Charlotte's help, Polly soon had her walking round the room.

'I'll work out a programme for you,' she told Clarissa. 'If you do it twice daily, you'll find you have more strength in your limbs. Charlotte can put you through your paces this afternoon. You'll probably see an improvement in a month or six weeks.'

She turned to Jeremy. 'I've noticed that walking gives you a problem too . . .'

Within a week, she was giving him massage and exercises every day as well, and the hour she'd planned to stay had stretched to an hour and a half.

Polly always seemed happy; she bubbled with delight when she talked about her baby son. He mother was the district nurse and when Polly's grandmother had been bombed out her mother had taken her in as well as Polly and Bobby. Soon Clarissa was asking after Polly's family.

Charlotte knew that by comparison she said very little about her circumstances. She was beginning to feel oppressed by her secret.

CHAPTER FIFTEEN

THE BEDROOM door closed softly behind Charlotte and Clarissa settled down for her afternoon rest. She needed it these days and often had a little sleep, but she was no longer dozing on and off all day as she used to. Charlotte and Polly made her work at her exercises and she was feeling much better for it. She blessed the day Charlotte had come to look after her.

If Clarissa woke in the night, she usually felt she had to get up to the bathroom. She'd hated having to wake Jeremy and really he wasn't all that steady on his feet himself.

'Just ring the bell if you want help,' Charlotte had told her and left it within reach of her right hand. 'I'll leave the connecting door open so I'll be able to hear it. Ring as hard as you can.'

She'd rung when she'd had to, and always Charlotte appeared, a silent wraith in her camel-coloured dressing gown, her dark red hair hanging down her back. It made her look younger, not much more than a child. During the day she had it swept up in a French pleat with her white cap perched on top.

She would leave Clarissa in the bathroom for a few moments and come back to straighten her pillows and sheets. Last night had been very cold, and she'd shivered as Charlotte was getting her back into bed.

'Shall I refill your hot water bottle for you?' she'd asked. 'You'll never get back to sleep if you're cold.'

'Yes, please.'

'As I'm boiling the kettle, what about a cup of tea?'

Charlotte had brought tea for herself too and sat by her bed to drink it with her. She'd been babysitting Rod's children in the evening and had said, 'They're lovely. Very sweet and well behaved.'

Clarissa was surprised. Rod was always complaining that Meriel had no control over them and they were half wild. 'Did you get them to bed all right?'

'Yes. Becky wanted to play in the bath but agreed to get out when I promised to read a story.'

'You're used to looking after children?'

'No, I've never had a lot to do with them. I'm an only child. Robin was asleep before I'd finished *The Three Bears* but Becky wanted *Little Red Riding Hood* after that. They didn't wake up at all.'

Clarissa thought it was Charlotte's friendly manner and willingness to play that had won over Becky. She and Polly were so full of enthusiasm and energy. They'd even persuaded Jeremy to let them work on him, and he was doing exercises too now. Charlotte said she was going to sort them both out.

Polly wanted to take Jeremy out to buy a new walking stick. She said the silver-topped cane he used was very elegant but too short for him. It had belonged to his father before him so perhaps she was right.

Today, Polly had asked her what she'd enjoyed doing before she'd had this awful stroke. Clarissa had told her she used to play bridge at least once a week, but she'd had to stop because she couldn't hold her cards in her left hand, let alone deal them out.

'We'll have to see if we can get you going again,' Polly had said. 'Luckily, you're right-handed.'

Polly had been massaging her fingers for some time and was always coming up with more exercises for her hand. One day, she'd said, 'I want you to start using a knife and fork again at mealtimes.' Clarissa had been having her food cut up and using a spoon. Polly stayed one lunchtime, positioning the implements in Clarissa's hands. Clarissa had found it quite hard to lift the loaded fork to her mouth, but every mealtime now Charlotte expected her to try. She didn't let her give up until she was tired.

'You're getting better at it,' they encouraged her, but getting her paralysed left hand to work was a slow business. The girls now had her practising getting in and out of bed with less assistance, and washing and dressing herself, but Charlotte was always there, ready with a helping hand when she needed it.

On one or two mornings each week, Polly stayed later and they played cards. Jeremy made up the fourth and the Barrington Browns were teaching the girls to play bridge. Everyone laughed at the mistakes they made, but Clarissa knew they were doing it to help get her back into the routine of playing. Jeremy was very keen that she should.

'Clarissa used to be a very good player,' he told the girls. 'If she could play with our old partners again, I'm sure she'd love it.'

One wet afternoon the following week, she was listening to the radio with Jeremy when Marjorie showed in her old friend Doris Spalding. Clarissa was glad to have visitors these days; it made her feel more her old self. She asked Charlotte if she'd make them a pot of tea, and when she brought it into the sitting room Clarissa introduced her to Doris. 'At one time,' she'd said. 'Doris used to come regularly to make up a bridge four.'

Charlotte seized the chance as she always did. 'We're trying to encourage Clarissa to play again,' she'd said. 'I wonder, would you mind if we tried a few hands when you've finished your tea?'

'Not at all. I miss coming here for our bridge sessions.'

Clarissa didn't feel she was up to it yet, and had protested, 'I can't hold my cards and I won't be able to deal.'

'Somebody else can deal for you, that won't matter,' Jeremy said quickly. 'And didn't Polly bring you a stand on which to spread your cards out?'

'I'll get it,' Charlotte said. 'You tried it and it does help.'

'So you play too?' Doris asked Charlotte.

Jeremy said, 'We're teaching both her and Polly so they can make up a four.'

'But I'm not very good yet.'

'You're not bad for a beginner and certainly good enough for this.' Jeremy was setting up their card table.

'I'm afraid I still have a lot to learn.'

Clarissa smiled. 'Practice will help, my dear. If you keep trying you'll find you improve. Isn't that what you're always telling me?'

Charlotte had to laugh. 'I can't bid as you do.'

'Bidding was always Clarissa's strong point,' Doris said.

'I've grown rusty and I'm slowing everything up.'

'You really do need another player of your own standard,' Charlotte told her. 'It would make it more interesting for you, and you'd soon get your old skill back.'

Jeremy said, 'We could ask Walter or Veronica to make up a four. They used to come with Doris sometimes.'

'Next week we will,' Clarissa said.

A week later, Jeremy took Polly down to the front porch to show her the collection of walking sticks he already owned. A large Victorian umbrella stand held an assortment of eleven that had been used by his forebears. Polly measured them up and chose a strong bentwood stick with a wide comfortable handle.

'You'll be able to lean on this one,' she told him. 'It's a little too long for you, so I'll take it with me and have it cut to your exact size and get a rubber ferrule fitted.'

He watched her walk down the drive twirling the stick with the wind ruffling her brown curls. When she reached the gate at the bottom she turned and waved. Polly was working wonders on his leg and Clarissa was improving too.

Jeremy turned away, wishing his own family were as capable as she and Charlotte were. His eye came to rest on the painting of the yacht *Priscilla* and beside it the framed collage of photographs. In two of them, Roderick was standing proudly in the bow. Jeremy sighed. Rod was driving him to despair.

Even before the terrible wreck of the *Priscilla* Jeremy had had his doubts about his younger son. He seemed unable to make a success of anything, whether he was sailing the yacht or running the company. But losing Alicia, his wife of three years, as well as his baby daughter in the shipwreck had been a blow for the whole family. They'd all loved Alicia; she'd fitted in well.

He and Clarissa had worried that Rod must blame himself for their deaths and had tried to be supportive. Truly, he'd seemed unstable and unable to cope with anything then. It had taken them all a long time to recover.

Jeremy had been just thirty when he'd taken over the management of the ship repair company from his father, and he'd made an excellent living from it. He was rightly proud of the firm built up by his forebears over the last seventy years, and had always planned to hand over the running of it to his children when the time was right.

Roderick had been a much longed for second son. Perhaps he and Clarissa had indulged him as a child. If so, they'd indulged his older brother Nathaniel too, but Nathaniel had grown up a normal happy lad keen to learn the ropes in the family firm.

Rod had always been jealous of Nathaniel. He thought their parents favoured the older boy, but they'd always tried to treat them both alike. Nevertheless, whatever they gave Rod it was never enough.

Jeremy was afraid Rod's school hadn't suited him. Nat had been happy there but Rod had not. The school was aiming to turn out pillars of society and had tried to make Rod fit the mould. It had given him to understand that he was a leader of men, capable of achieving almost anything, who had a good brain and could think quickly. Rod had left school believing success should come automatically. The problem was that, for him, it had not.

Rod saw himself as a superior being, and rather looked down on the common man. He said he was disgusted by their stupidity. He had no tact and could be abrasively arrogant and had always been unpopular with their employees. He was a loner, with absolutely no aptitude for dealing with other people; he had no empathy with them.

He appeared to be self-confident, but Jeremy thought it was all a stance, and that in fact he was unsure of himself and couldn't stand criticism, especially not from him. Neither could he admit to needing help. Jeremy also thought him extravagant. He seemed to have no money sense and believed he could afford anything. On top of all that, he always wanted his own way, convinced he knew best. He was inclined to shout the opposition down and could be argumentative. More than once he'd shown a volatile temper if crossed.

He and Clarissa had talked about him countless times over the years. 'Rod takes after my family, not yours,' she'd said many times. 'Doesn't he remind you of my Uncle Simon?'

Jeremy had to admit that he did. In 1885, when he'd first met Clarissa, she'd been twenty years old. Orphaned at eleven years of age, she'd been brought up by her widowed grandmother. Her father, James Calvin, had built up a business from small beginnings. At his death, he'd owned five modern iron steamships that were engaged in transporting coal from the coalfields of South Wales to Merseyside, where it fed the new industries. One vessel had been named the *Clarissa Calvin* in her honour and she still had a photograph of it.

As well as this successful business, Clarissa was sole heir to a fortune which was being held in trust for her until she reached the age of twenty-five. In the meantime, her Uncle Simon, her father's younger brother, had taken over the management of her financial affairs and was running the business on her behalf.

By the time Clarissa came into her fortune, there'd been little of it left. Her grandmother had accused Simon of fraud, but Jeremy had combed through the accounts and believed the fault to be largely mismanagement.

'It's only money,' he'd consoled Clarissa. 'Don't worry. As my wife, you won't be short of that.'

But it hadn't turned out to be only money. A week or so later, Simon had committed suicide, bringing greater grief to his mother and his niece.

Roderick even looked like the Calvins. He was balding while all the Barrington Brown men had thick heads of hair into old age.

Jeremy sighed and turned away from the pictures of the *Priscilla*. He'd been sixty at the time she'd sunk. He'd intended to retire when he was sixty-five, but he'd hung on for an extra year before promoting Roderick to managing director and giving him full responsibility. Rod had needed time to get over the shipwreck and get his confidence back.

Jeremy thought he had by then, but Rod hadn't coped with the job. In 1932, when Jeremy turned seventy, he'd had to go back to work part time for a year or two to help get the business back on track. After that he'd kept an eye on Rod and never been entirely happy with what he was doing.

In 1940, when ships were being sunk in the Atlantic and many others damaged by torpedoes and bombs, Jeremy had gone back again for a couple of days each week, to help with the extra work. But by then he'd been seventy-eight and felt the power he'd once had had dissipated. Rod had grown used to being in charge and no longer took notice of his suggestions. On his eightieth birthday, Jeremy stopped going into work altogether. What was the use? It was high time he left Rod to run the business his way.

In recent years, many of Jeremy's former colleagues had retired and Rod had chosen their successors. He'd insisted on promoting men to senior positions whom Jeremy felt were unsuitable. In particular he distrusted Miles Morrow, who was now their chief accountant.

When Morrow had been just another of their senior accountants, Jeremy had read a report in the *Liverpool Echo* about his being charged as a middleman in a black market. He'd bought five thousand tins of soup from the manufacturer at six shillings and sixpence a dozen. He hadn't moved the soup from the warehouse, but eventually it reached the shops having been sold to them at fourteen shillings and sixpence a dozen. Morrow had been found guilty of profiteering and given a modest fine.

'He's a wide boy, a spiv,' Jeremy had said to Roderick. 'He shouldn't be working for us. He's lining his own pockets unlawfully.'

Rod's violent temper had blown up at that. 'He's good at his job so he's lining our pockets too,' he'd said. 'Times have changed since your day. Stay out of it, Pa. It's time you backed off.'

When he'd heard that Rod had promoted Miles Morrow to chief accountant, Jeremy had been angry and voiced his objections again, but Rod wouldn't listen. He'd said, 'These days, we can't afford the paternalistic attitude that you and our forebears had. We aren't philanthropists. You just look after yourself and Mother and leave the yard to me.'

Jeremy was afraid Rod saw him as a nuisance and was pushing him aside. Rod wanted him to stay at home and keep out of his way. He was eighty-one now and troubled with arthritis. He felt he'd been put out to grass and was too frail to do anything about these problems.

The next day, Polly brought back his walking stick and told him to try it. He went up and down the sitting room with Clarissa and the two girls watching him. He turned to smile at them all.

'Polly, you're right. It's comfortable to use and it makes walking easier for me. It does make a difference.'

'You owe me a shilling,' she said. 'I had to pay for the ferrule and having an inch cut off.'

'Is that all? Thank you, Polly.'

He was thankful he had these two sensible girls to look after him. He felt they spurred him on, made him feel younger. He mustn't be an old codger and sit back doing nothing. Not yet. He ought to get off his backside and go on doing his best for the business. He had to try to keep Rod on the straight and narrow.

Later that week, Jeremy was just completing his afternoon physiotherapy exercises when the phone rang. He went to answer it and Charlotte sank down on an armchair to rest. She'd found the best way to keep the couple working at their exercises was for her to do them too. She told them it was fun, but privately she considered that the double session every day was likely to drive her into an early grave.

He came back looking serious. 'It's for you, Charlotte. It's your mother.'

She asked, 'What's the matter?' but he was shaking his head. Full of trepidation, she ran to his study. Mary had never rung her here before. Family opinion was that she was here to work, not talk to them.

'Mum?'

'Charlotte, love . . .'

'What's happened?'

'Glyn's just phoned. He wanted you to know, his brother . . .' She gulped. 'Kevin's plane was shot down over Hamburg last night. It was seen to go down in flames.'

Charlotte felt tears spring to her eyes. 'Oh, goodness. Oh, Lord!'

'He's very upset. Well, the whole family is.'

'How awful,' she choked out.

'I think you ought to ring him, dear. To say how sorry you are.'

'Yes, of course. Thanks, Mum, for letting me know.'

She put the phone down and sat looking at it. Kevin killed! She thought of him as she'd seen him last, when he came home on a forty-eight-hour pass last summer. Tall, handsome, with dark curly hair. Full of high spirits, wanting to wrest the utmost pleasure from his leave.

She knew the Evanses had been trying for years not to think of this possibility, though planes were being shot down all the time and they all knew what the death toll was like in Bomber Command.

For her, his death was a painful shock, but how much worse for his family. She knew how they must be feeling. When Jonty died it was the Evanses who had comforted and supported her and Mum. They'd all rallied round: Enid had put on the funeral tea and Ted had helped them sell up at Glan y Mor. When she'd first heard about the shipwreck of the *Priscilla*, it had been Glyn she'd confided in. He'd helped and comforted her.

She went slowly back to the living room. Jeremy and Clarissa looked up, their eyes full of sympathy.

'Has something happened?' Jeremy asked. 'To one of your family?'

'Not my family exactly.' She'd hardly mentioned her family to them, being wary of saying she'd grown up in Anglesey, in case they asked which part and were reminded of the *Priscilla*. She told them now, and about their neighbours, Ted and Enid Evans.

'Their eldest son, Kevin, was a navigator flying with Bomber Command. His plane was shot down over Hamburg last night.'

'Your boyfriend?' Clarissa was aghast.

'I've know him all my life; we were close to the whole family. Glyn, their youngest, was my special friend, but Kevin was like a big brother to me too.'

'Would you like to ring them?' Jeremy asked. 'Use my phone.'

'Thank you. Mum said Glyn sounded overwhelmed. The whole family will be stricken.' Charlotte had clasped both hands to her face. She hesitated, but made herself turn and face them. 'I'd really like to go and see them. They were so kind to me, but I hardly like to ask when I've only been working for you for a few weeks. Would you mind?'

Jeremy said, 'Now, you mean? Right away?'

She nodded.

Clarissa said, 'Of course we'll spare you, if you really want to go.'

'Yes. Yes, please, I would.' She wanted to comfort Glyn now while he was hurting and needed her.

Jeremy said, 'Do you want to go this afternoon and take your day off tomorrow? Would that be long enough?'

'Yes, thank you, I think it would. I'll ring them and see.'

Charlotte went back to the phone and lifted it with shaking fingers. Glyn answered so quickly, she thought he must have been sitting near it.

'Glyn, I'm so sorry. Mum's just told me about Kevin. How are you?'

'Terrible – we all are. I wish you were here. I could do with a shoulder to cry on.'

'I can come. Just for one night.'

'Now? Please do, Charlotte. I really want you.'

Charlotte took a deep breath. 'But what about your mother? She mightn't want visitors at the minute.'

'She wouldn't count you as a visitor. Tegwen is in Italy and can't come. Glenys has applied for compassionate leave but has to wait until it's approved.'

'Can I speak to your mother? Could you put her on?'

A few moments later she heard Enid's voice. 'Do come if you can, Charlotte. Glyn needs you. Things are a bit chaotic here – none of us seems to know whether we're coming or going. Kevin had flown on so many raids, we'd come to believe he led a charmed life, but . . . oh, dear. Please come, Charlotte. I have to go now.'

Jeremy took charge. He rang the Crosville bus station and learned that the last bus of the day to Anglesey would be leaving in an hour and five minutes.

Charlotte tried to think. 'I need to go home to pack.'

'No time,' Clarissa said briskly. 'You have night things here and a change of clothes; just put them in a bag and go.'

'First ring Anglesey again,' Jeremy said, 'and tell your friends what time you'll arrive. Then I'll ring for a taxi to take you to the bus station.'

'Thank you. You're very kind.'

'And hadn't you better let your mother know what you're doing?'

With the taxi waiting on the gravel outside, Jeremy pressed some money into Charlotte's hand. 'If you're coming back late through town tomorrow,' he said, 'be sure to take a taxi. All right?'

Charlotte felt fraught after the mad rush, but by the time she was sitting on the bus watching the green fields flow past the window she had begun to feel calmer.

She'd been selfish, taking Glyn for granted. For months, he'd been telling her he loved her. She'd seen it in his eyes and felt it in his kisses, and yes, it had sparked thrills that had made her lift her mouth to his. But she'd left him before Christmas accepting everything and giving little in return.

Had she been too full of grief over Jonty's death to take in what Glyn was offering? When she'd heard of the shipwreck and her origins, she'd been overwhelmed with feelings of fear and curiosity. She didn't know who she was any more. Her head was full of anxiety and she'd felt compassion for her mother too, not to mention the urgent need to help her make important decisions. Since then she'd been trying to find her feet in a new job and to come to terms with the fact that she had real relatives she hadn't known about. There was still so much she had to sort out. Perhaps in the midst of all that, it was understandable that she'd made the mistake of confusing friendship with love.

She'd been heartless, not telling Glyn how much he meant to her even though it wasn't so long since she'd turned to him for comfort. Now she felt an urgent need to be with him to help and comfort him. Of course she loved him. Why had it taken a tragedy like this to make her see how important he was to her?

As the bus pulled up in Bangor she could see him waiting at the stop. He looked woebegone and pale. As she came down the steps he said nothing but took her into his arms in the tightest hug she'd ever had. When he released her, she feasted her eyes on him. Everything about him was achingly familiar.

'I'm glad you've come,' he said. 'Mum's in a terrible state. So's Dad really, but at least he does come out and help with the animals. We've spent most of the day sitting around and we can't stop talking about Kevin.'

'You're all in a state of shock, you're bound to be.'

'You've brought only that small bag? Good, it'll fit in my saddlebag. I came over on my motor bike.' It was raining. 'I've brought an oilskin for you.' He helped her put it on.

Charlotte completed the journey with her arms wrapped round his waist and her cheek pressed against his back. It was cold but it didn't matter. How had she not seen that she loved him? She'd always loved him.

He drove straight into the barn where he kept his bike. Enid was opening the front door, her face wan and tear-stained.

'I was so sorry to hear about Kevin.' Charlotte held her close.

'I can't stop crying.'

'This is a time for tears.'

Enid wept on her shoulder. 'All those happy childhood years and now he's gone. He'll have no funeral and no grave that we know of.'

'There'll be a memorial service in the church,' Glyn said. 'The vicar's been to see us.'

Ted said, 'I thought he'd take over the farm from me. It's hard to think of Kevin's life being over.'

It was Glyn who got them all up to the supper table. 'It's cold, so I could get it ready before I went to Bangor.'

'I've gone to pieces,' Enid said, her eyes wet with tears again.

'Mum and I were just the same when Jonty died.'

Glyn said, 'I was envious when Kevin left home. I thought he was having all the fun while I was stuck here. I only realised I had the easy option when he came home last time. He had black shadows under his eyes and looked exhausted. When I asked what was the matter, he said, "I'm feeling a bit low at the moment. My friend Malcolm . . . well, his plane was shot down over enemy territory last week. It seems every friend I make buys it, while I seem to lead a charmed life."

'He was scared, you know. Scared stiff his turn was coming. He said he couldn't say that to anyone on the airfield. They were all scared, but they had to put on brave faces.'

'That must have upset you.'

'It made me feel quite emotional. When he was going back, he said, "I've got to get over Malcolm, get back on an even keel and get on with the job." I told him he was brave. "Not really," he said. "It's what everybody has to do. I mean, what alternative is there? If we stopped to think of all the friends who've bought it, we'd all be paralysed with fright."'

'Whatever Kevin thought, he was very brave,' Charlotte said. 'He gave his life for his country. We should all be grateful to him.'

Charlotte persuaded Enid and Ted to go to bed while she and Glyn washed up and reset the table for breakfast. She spent most of the night in Glyn's arms. It was very late when they went to sleep. Late, too, when they got up the next morning.

As Glyn had to work outside with his father, Charlotte helped Enid prepare the usual big Sunday lunch. The meal was ready and they were all about to sit down when the telephone rang. Glyn answered it and came back looking happier. 'That was Glenys. She's getting the next train up. I've told her I'll meet her at Llangefni station at six thirty.'

'How long can she stay?' his mother asked eagerly.

'She has a forty-eight.'

'It'll be lovely to see her. That'll lift us out of our misery, won't it?'

It had gone three o'clock when they'd finished eating. Charlotte helped to wash up and they sat down again with a cup of tea. It seemed no time at all before Glyn had to take her to Bangor.

'You haven't had a very restful day off,' he said, as they went out to his motor bike. 'It'll be late before you get home.'

'I'll be able to go straight to bed. Everybody else should be tucked up by then.'

The Liverpool bus came in and the passengers were checked on board. Charlotte stood with Glyn till the last possible moment.

'I'm very glad you came,' he said. 'You've made me feel better, but the time has flashed by.'

'I wish I'd asked for an extra day off now, but I couldn't bring myself to do it. They were so kind and I haven't worked there long. Never mind, you'll have Glenys now. Isn't it time you went to meet her?'

'Yes, I mustn't keep her waiting at the station.'

Charlotte tried to smile. 'You didn't cry on my shoulder after all.'

'But Mum did.' The driver got in and was ready to go. 'Come again soon,' Glyn said, as he gave her a final kiss.

CHAPTER SIXTEEN

THIS MORNING, Jeremy had invited two old friends to come round for a rubber or two of bridge after supper.

One of them, Walter Collingwood, had spent most of his working life in their office. He'd been a friend as well as a colleague and Jeremy had eventually made him chief accountant. He'd retired before the war, but when Jeremy had asked him he'd come back to help. Jeremy admired Walter and knew him to be hard-working and trustworthy.

The other, Veronica Terry, was almost family. She was Alicia's mother, and they'd supported each other through some very bad times. Roderick wanted nothing to do with her, nor she with him, but Jeremy and Clarissa both liked her and they kept in touch.

It had been a strange afternoon getting Charlotte off to see her boyfriend in Anglesey. It made him compare what that family was doing for the war effort with his own. A navigator son flying bombing sorties over Germany, two daughters who were Army nurses and a father and son producing much-needed food.

Already Clarissa was missing Charlotte's gentle presence, although Meriel, who usually stood in for her, had said she'd come up to help Clarissa into bed tonight.

When Walter came, Jeremy thought he looked even older than he did himself. He had sparse white hair and a heavily lined face, but his dark eyes seemed to miss nothing. He was tall; once he must have been a six-footer though now he was somewhat stooped, but he still moved with ease and said he'd walked here tonight.

'It's downhill,' Jeremy teased. 'I bet you won't walk home.'

'No.' Walter had a good brain and had lost none of his ability. He and Veronica were good company. Jeremy felt the evening went well. He enjoyed it, and it pleased him tremendously to see Clarissa play a real game of bridge and enjoy it too.

Jeremy helped her to her feet when Meriel came up at ten o'clock. 'Goodnight,' she said, stifling a yawn. 'You'll have to excuse me, but I need my bed. I'm afraid I tire easily these days.'

'You've done very well,' Jeremy told her as she went off. 'I'll look in to say goodnight later.'

'She is so much better,' he told their friends. 'Now, how about a nightcap before you go? I managed to get some brandy.'

'Brandy!' Walter said. 'Thank you, that would be a treat, but may I ring for a taxi first? I'll tell them to come in fifteen minutes but it's bound to take them half an hour. I'll drop you off, of course, Veronica.'

She nodded her thanks. 'Clarissa was in good form tonight. What a help that card stand is to her.'

'Yes, Polly produced that. It means Clarissa can play again. We're both very grateful to Charlotte for introducing Polly to us. Grateful to both of them really.'

'Clarissa's moving her hand and arm much more than she used to,' Veronica said, accepting a glass of Madeira. 'And she's much more cheerful.'

'We're hoping she'll continue to improve. And with all these exercises to do, time no longer hangs heavily for her.'

Walter rolled his brandy round his tongue. 'So things are looking up all round?'

Jeremy sipped his drink. Roderick was still a worry, of course, but Walter knew what a problem he'd been to them, and he didn't want to talk about it tonight. Not when they were all feeling cheerful.

'Yes, the physiotherapy is doing us both good. You're lucky not to need it, Walter.'

'No worries on that score, but have you been down to the yard recently?'

'No. If I go to the yard, Rod feels I'm interfering.'

'The *Atlantic Voyager*, a freighter, is refitting in the yard at the moment. My grandson Charles is her second officer and he's on board. It was damaged by German planes. He says . . .'

'I think this is our taxi.' Veronica was by the window. Jeremy joined her and saw the headlights.

'Yes, it is. I'll see you both down. What did your grandson have to say, Walter?'

'Quite a lot. I meant to tell you, but it's a long story and it's too late now. Why don't you call round to my place? I won't be able to offer you brandy, but how about tea and biscuits one afternoon?'

The following Friday, Charlotte was making the mid-morning coffee when Meriel came up looking rather apologetic. She heard her ask Clarissa, 'Can Charlotte be spared to look after the children for a couple of hours this afternoon?'

Charlotte had already agreed to babysit for her that evening as Rod wanted her to partner him at the golf club dinner dance.

'I feel such a mess,' Meriel explained. Her fine flyaway hair reminded Charlotte of a dandelion clock. 'I really need to get to a hairdresser. I badly need a trim and a wash and set.'

Clarissa smiled. 'As far as I'm concerned, yes,' she said, 'as long as you don't ask too often. But you'd better ask Charlotte yourself.'

'Of course,' Charlotte agreed. 'What time do you want me to come down?'

Half past three meant she had to rush through the exercise sessions, but she brought the children back to Clarissa's rooms and they all spent a pleasant afternoon playing with them until it was time to take them down to eat the tea Mrs Shipley was preparing. Meriel returned with a much neater head, her white-blonde hair transformed to a style that became her.

Charlotte returned to find Jeremy and Clarissa having a drink before their earlier-than-usual supper, which she ate with them. She knew how successful their bridge evenings were and that Jeremy had set up another for tonight. 'It's giving Clarissa a bit of a social life again,' he told Charlotte. 'A reason to ask our old friends round.'

Marjorie brought up the plate of sandwiches Mrs Shipley had made and Charlotte set out the cups and saucers in the kitchen so the bridge players could make a hot drink. Meriel had told her she and Rod wanted to leave about seven thirty. When it was time for Charlotte to go down, she said, 'What time would you like me to come back to help you into bed?'

'Not late, say about ten,' Clarissa said. 'Better ask Marjorie to sit with the children while you're up here. Becky sometimes plays up if her mother's out.'

Charlotte called in the kitchen on the way, but the housemaid was nowhere to be seen. Mrs Shipley told her, 'I've had to send Marjorie to bed early; she didn't feel well. She thinks she's starting with a cold. Don't worry, I'll sit with the children later on.'

As she approached the younger Barrington Browns' living quarters Charlotte could hear raised voices. The living-room door was ajar. She heard Meriel give a little cry of distress. Then her voice, querulous and anxious. 'Please, Rod, stop it. I'll see to it. Please.'

It stopped Charlotte in her tracks. She took a few backward steps, not wanting to walk in on them in the middle of a row.

'You see to it?' Roderick roared. 'You silly bitch, you never see to anything.'

Charlotte stopped again, shocked that any man would talk to his wife like that.

'She doesn't know the word no. You let that child run wild. If you don't discipline her, somebody has to. Come here, Becky.' He was clearly in a foul temper.

'No, Daddy, no!' It was a cry of panic. The next moment she screamed and Charlotte heard the slap of flesh against flesh.

That drove her forward to push the half-open door wide. He had the child across his knee with her nightdress up and her pink buttocks bare, and was bringing his hand down hard against them, again and again. The little body was squirming and struggling to get away. Meriel was crying too.

'No, Rod, please,' she begged, wringing her hands.

Charlotte couldn't believe her eyes. She strode across the room and caught hold of his arm just as it was coming down heavily once more. The child's bottom was showing red weals where it had been slapped. Roderick leapt to his feet outraged and the child seized the chance to scramble away to her bedroom.

'What the hell do you think you're doing?' he shouted, spinning round to face Charlotte. She was so shocked at what she'd done, she could hardly get her breath. 'Who are you to come bursting in here like this?'

Meriel was standing open-mouthed, her breasts heaving in her low-cut scarlet evening dress.

'What right have you to interfere?'

Charlotte's mouth was dry, and she had to force herself to speak. 'No father should treat his child like that.'

'You . . .' He was apoplectic. 'How I treat my child has nothing to do with you. It's none of your business.'

'I'm sorry,' she said, 'but I feel it is.'

'She's my child and I decide when she needs to be corrected.'

Charlotte felt a spurt of cold anger. 'I don't see that as correction. You were venting your anger on her, and she's a fraction of your size and strength. I'd call behaviour like that barbaric.'

Meriel's gasp of horror attracted their attention. When she saw them both staring at her she turned and fled after her daughter. Rod turned back to Charlotte, his face frozen with anger.

'Get out of here,' he grated. 'Now, this minute.'

For Charlotte, everything stood still for a long moment. She thought she might faint.

'I've come to babysit,' she said, as calmly as she could. 'So you and your wife can go to a dinner dance. I'll go along to the nursery, shall I? See if the children need anything?'

She went swiftly. Meriel was sniffing into her handkerchief, her eyes wet with tears as she tried to rock Becky in her arms. The child's screams had subsided into great sobs that made her whole body shudder. Charlotte felt desperately sorry for them both.

'Do you want to get ready?' she whispered.

Roderick Barrington Brown was behind her. 'When I tell you to get out of here, I mean it,' he thundered. 'We won't need anybody's services as a babysitter tonight. Go, and don't ever come back.'

'Aren't you going to go out?'

'No,' he roared. 'How many times do I have to tell you? Get out of my home.'

Charlotte turned on her heel and fled. She felt sick. What had she done? This was her father too. She couldn't go back upstairs to his parents, not before her hammering heart stilled a little. She wanted to go outside to the garden, but she mustn't let the great front door close behind her. It would be impossible to ring the bell and face Roderick should he answer it.

She went instead to the kitchen. Mrs Shipley was almost horizontal in an old armchair pulled up to the hearth. 'Is something the matter?'

'Roderick's in a bad temper,' she choked. 'He's decided not to go out after all. You won't be needed to sit with the children tonight.'

'Good. I'll have an early night then.' Charlotte's eye was caught by the brown earthenware teapot standing on the hob, and Mrs Shipley noticed. 'Fancy a cup, do you?'

'Yes, please.'

'Help yourself.'

The hot tea was comforting, and it helped to revive her. She'd been there five minutes when a bell on the wall clanged. Mrs Shipley shot upright, she was cross.

'I can guess what he wants now,' she fumed. 'Mr Rod's changed his mind about going out to dinner and wants a meal here.'

She lumbered off down the passage and was even angrier when she came back.

'I've told them there's hardly anything to eat in the house. "You can rustle up something, Mrs Shipley," he says as though he doesn't know there's a war on.' Still grumbling, she disappeared into the pantry.

Charlotte heard the front door bell and went to answer it, but Jeremy was already down in the hall. 'That'll be our visitors,' he said. 'I'll let them in, Charlotte.'

She knew she wouldn't be needed for a while and returned to the kitchen. Mrs Shipley had lit the oven.

'He's no thought for anyone else, that one. He expects me to cook another dinner for him and Meriel now when I've got everything cleared away. And there's nothing but a bit of fish pie that was meant for Marjorie's supper. She didn't want anything and I'd have eaten less myself if I'd known they were staying in.' She reached for a pan. 'I've said I'll do Welsh rarebit to follow.'

Charlotte helped where she could, resetting the trolley that had been made ready for breakfast, and making coffee. While the meal was being delivered she made more tea for Mrs Shipley, then stayed to help her clear up again and listen to her chatter. When at last Mrs Shipley decided to go to bed, Charlotte took the back door key.

'I'll go out for a breath of fresh air,' she said. Her mind was still racing.

It was a bright moonlight night, just the sort they used to dread at the time of the Blitz. What had possessed her? She should never have said things like that to Rod. She'd made an enemy of him, an enemy of her natural father. She crunched down the gravel drive and out to the road.

And what to tell his parents? That she'd had a terrible row with

Roderick? It made her cringe every time she thought of it. Should she just leave and forget all about the Barrington Browns? But her roots were here and she couldn't walk out on Clarissa and Jeremy, not now. They relied on her and she was growing fond of them. Fortunately, Rod had ordered her out of his home, not theirs.

There was nobody about. Everywhere was still and silent except for the call of an owl and the distant bark of a dog. She turned back. By the time she was climbing the stairs again she felt a lot calmer.

Should she tell Jeremy and Clarissa the whole truth? She'd be worried about it until she did. Better to get it over with.

As soon as Charlotte went in, Clarissa struggled to her feet. 'I'm glad you've come,' she greeted her. 'I feel exhausted tonight.'

'I'm sorry, have I kept you waiting?'

'No, we've only just finished the game.'

Clarissa's visitors had not yet gone. The man was adding up the scores and the woman was chatting about the poor hands she'd had.

Clarissa said to them, 'I'll say goodnight now. Do excuse me.'

'I'll pop in to say goodnight later,' Jeremy told her, 'after I've seen our guests out.'

Charlotte took Clarissa to her bedroom. She could see she was past being able to take in the complicated tale of the shipwreck. It would have to wait for another night.

Clarissa yawned as she was getting undressed. 'Did you get the children off to sleep all right?'

'Rod changed his mind,' she said. 'He decided not to go out, so I didn't babysit after all.'

'What made him do that? After Meriel had had her hair set, too.'

'I upset him.' Charlotte's voice shook. She was nervous about telling Clarissa, afraid she'd side with her son, whatever she did. 'Well, Becky and me. She recounted what had happened. 'He said I was interfering in what wasn't my business and ordered me out of his house. He was too angry to go out after that.'

'Don't you upset yourself, Charlotte,' Clarissa said. 'Rod can erupt like Mount Vesuvius on the spur of the moment.'

'He really was thrashing little Becky. That bothers me. And Meriel, too – she's scared of him. I didn't realise things were so bad between them.'

Clarissa groaned. 'I'm afraid Rod is a problem to us all,' she said wearily. 'We all worry about him.'

*

Charlotte found sleep hard to come by that night. She was worried that she'd got off on the wrong foot with Roderick. She could hardly expect fatherly affection from him after what had happened last night, but neither could she see him as a father figure. In fact, she didn't like him.

The next morning, when she went down to return the breakfast dishes to the kitchen, she saw him drive off in his Jaguar, so she ran down the passage to see how Meriel and Becky were.

Meriel's eyes were red and her cheeks white. She looked as though she'd been crying half the night. She drew Charlotte through the living room to a playroom beyond. Both children were there, still in their nightclothes; Becky seemed happy enough playing with her dolls. 'I think she's forgotten about it,' Meriel said quietly, then took Charlotte back to the living room. 'Thank you for what you did last night. I'm sorry Rod was horrible to you.'

'He wasn't nice to you.'

'That's his way.' She sniffed into a handkerchief. 'But it's hard to take.'

'What had Becky done to upset him?'

'I suppose . . .' Meriel had to think. 'She wanted to see me get dressed in what she calls my party dress. I let her stay in our bedroom while I put on my make-up and things. But Rod came in before I was ready and ordered her to bed, and as I'd said she could stay she didn't immediately go. Disobedience, Rod called it – it blew up from that.' Big blue eyes raked Charlotte's face. They were puffy underneath.

Charlotte said gently, 'I'm told Rod is known for his temper.'

'It isn't just Becky, it's me too.' There was a catch in Meriel's voice. 'I get on his nerves.' The red eyes were wet with tears again. 'I'm not from his class, you know; he looks down on me. My dad was a primary school teacher and I grew up in a new semi-detached in Woolton. Rod thinks it's an awful place. I'm not a good wife for him.' Charlotte put her arm round the quaking bony shoulders. 'He's not happy with me. He thinks it was a mistake to marry me.'

'He doesn't say that . . .'

'He does.'

Charlotte took a deep breath. 'People sometimes say things they don't mean, Meriel.'

'I don't think I'm cut out for motherhood either, but I do love them. They're sweet kids really, but it tears me in two. I'm just too tired to cope.'

'They're getting on top of you. You'd feel better if you could get a break from them.'

'I know,' she sobbed. 'But I can't get a nanny and now Marjorie's given notice.'

'Has she? Why?'

'She says Rod frightens her.'

'Oh, dear.'

'I'm not surprised really. She says she's got another job as an usherette at the Odeon in town. She thinks she'll like it better and she'll be able to live at home.'

'Who can blame her?'

'Nobody wants live-in jobs any more. Not since the war. Mrs Shipley says she'll try to get another housemaid, but she doesn't hold out much hope.'

'There must be somebody who'd like to look after the children,' Charlotte said. 'A mother's help to take them off your hands for a few hours each day. An older woman, perhaps.'

She thought of her mother. Mary would love a job like that and it might help her over the loss of Jonty. She'd be the ideal person, except that the Barrington Browns knew nothing of her connection to them. It was hardly practical, and anyway Mary would be scared and wouldn't want to come anywhere near here.

'We must try to find someone to help you,' she said. 'Maybe I could take them off your hands for an hour in the afternoons, until you get fixed up. But I'll have to ask Clarissa first.'

'Thank you.' Meriel lifted an anxious face to look at her gratefully. 'You're very kind.'

The next time Charlotte went home for her day off, she told Mary about Meriel and her children, and how badly she needed someone to look after them.

'I know you believe every mother should care for her own children, and that it's a labour of love, but Meriel isn't coping. The Barrington Browns have always employed nannies. Meriel had one for a year or two when Becky was a baby. She's not used to dealing with children, and she's on an emotional knife edge.' She paused. 'You know, it's something you could do. What do you think?'

193

'Oh, Charlotte, no. I couldn't. How could I?' But Charlotte could see she was half tempted. 'I'd like to earn my living again, and everybody's expected to have a job in wartime. But I wouldn't want to live in like you.'

'I'm sure Meriel would jump at the chance of having any help, and Gran could manage without having you here all day.'

'No,' Mary decided suddenly, 'I couldn't. It's too complicated. I'd like to if it was any other family, but not the Barrington Browns. What would they say if they found out about you and how I'd stolen you? And then that I was in their house looking after their children? No, I'd be terrified of them. Aren't you scared they'll find out who you are?'

'Yes.' Charlotte was dreading it. 'Forget it, Mum. It was a rotten idea.'

'Well, not entirely rotten – just absolutely impossible.'

Charlotte was ringing Glyn on her days off to see how they were at Plas Hafren. She gathered they were slowly getting over the shock, but still feeling low.

'And I'm still missing you,' Glyn said. 'More than ever now. Couldn't you come for another visit?'

'Would you rather come here to see me?' she asked. 'Gran has spare rooms now my uncles have left home.'

'I would like to see where you're living.' He sounded eager.

'Come for a weekend, then. I'll try to get the time off, and it'll do you good to have a change of scene. In a week or two, maybe? Hang on, I need to clear this with Gran and Mum. I'll ring you back.'

Mary was pleased when Charlotte asked her. 'It would be nice to see Glyn again,' she said. 'Enid, too. We could put them both up for a night or two, couldn't we?' she asked her mother.

'Why not? They were very kind to me while I was there. Though meals might be difficult.'

'They'll bring food with them,' Charlotte said. 'They produce food and understand how hard it is to come by in a city.'

'Give them a ring, Mary. Invite them both.'

Sitting round the big dining-room table later that evening over supper, Charlotte was pleased to hear they'd both accepted. They discussed what they should do while they were here and where they should take them.

'We'll have to go everywhere by public transport,' Mary lamented.

'I can't even use Dad's bike any more,' Charlotte said. 'I'm not entitled to a petrol ration and I've used up all the petrol coupons I took over with the bike.'

Mary said, 'I expect Dan could let you have a little petrol now and again.'

'I hope you're not going to ask him,' Edith said sharply. 'It's against the law.'

'I'd better ask him to put the bike up on blocks for the duration.' Charlotte pulled a face. 'Then I wouldn't be tempted to ask.'

CHAPTER SEVENTEEN

Now CLARISSA felt she was recovering the use of her limbs she was working harder at her exercises. She could walk with a stick, though she dragged her left foot a little, and was keen to get out and about again.

'I'd love to try going into town,' she said, 'but on my bad side I need someone to lean on.'

Polly wanted her to walk on her own and made her practise that way. However, Charlotte knew Clarissa would feel better if she could lead a less restricted life. At the moment, though, they could all see she'd need a good deal of help if she did.

'I'd love to go shopping,' she insisted.

'There's hardly anything to buy,' Jeremy told her. 'I'll take you and Charlotte out to lunch, and if you still have the energy, you could ask her to take you to a shop.'

A taxi was hired to take them to the Adelphi Hotel for lunch. Afterwards, Jeremy said he was going to visit his friend Walter Collingwood. He called a taxi for the women so they could go shopping.

Clarissa was flushed with excitement. 'I've had nothing new for eighteen months.'

'You asked Veronica to find you some new nightdresses,' Jeremy said. 'And a bed jacket.'

'Well, I'm not in bed all day any more. I'd like to have some new blouses and a skirt, something to wear. I've got plenty of clothing coupons saved up.'

She asked the driver to take them to Bold Street where the smartest and most expensive shops were. She pointed out her favourite and Charlotte took her inside.

'I'm afraid we have only utility wear,' the assistant told her as she brought out several blouses to show her. Clarissa did not seem impressed with the quality but she picked out two she thought might do. She was invited to try them on, but by then she was slumped back on her chair. Charlotte could see she was exhausted.

'You could take them and try them on at home,' she said, 'when you feel better. I'll bring them back if they don't fit.'

While Clarissa paid for the blouses, Charlotte went out to fetch the driver to help get her back to the car. Once home, Clarissa slept on the sofa for the best part of an hour, but after that, when she had had a cup of tea, she seemed quite exhilarated.

'I feel so much better,' she said. 'I feel as though I'm living again. To go to that restaurant and see other people walking about. For months and months, I've been incarcerated in a hospital and a rehabilitation centre, and then almost isolated in my own home. I'd almost forgotten what the outside world was like.'

She was making plans for further trips. 'I want to go into a bookshop to choose something to read for myself. I'd love to go to the theatre, and I'm certainly going to ask Jeremy to take me out for another meal. I've really enjoyed today.'

While his wife and Charlotte were looking at blouses in Bold Street, Jeremy took a taxi to Walter Collingwood's flat. It was in a block that had been built just before the war. Jeremy thought it was very comfortable; he liked the warmth of the foyer and the lift that took him up to the second floor. The rooms were not so different in size from his own, and Walter had a balcony to sit out on in the summer.

Walter welcomed him cordially. 'Tea?' he asked. 'I've got some short-bread to go with it.' Walter mostly fended for himself and seemed to get his share of luxury items.

'Tea on its own will be fine. I've just had a big lunch. The other night, you were going to tell me something. You seemed to think it was important.'

'Yes, about your yard. I think you should know.'

Jeremy settled into a comfortable armchair with his cup of tea. 'Fire away then.'

'Well, as I told you, my grandson Charles is with his ship in the yard while it's being repaired and refitted.'

Jeremy asked, 'He's not pleased with the standard of the work?'

'He's angry. He says the crew on his ship all pull together and work hard for the war effort, but the shipyard workers are a lazy bunch who won't work if they can avoid it. They stop to talk or smoke, and he's interrupted card games down in the engine room out of sight of the foreman. He says there's even a poker school in the radio room every afternoon. They lock themselves in and play until it's five o'clock and time to knock off.'

Jeremy's spirits sank. 'I've known for some time that Rod isn't running the place as he should. Well, so have you, but this sounds even worse than I imagined.'

'It means the ships are there far longer than they need to be,' Walter said, 'when they ought to be out bringing desperately needed supplies to Liverpool.'

'I've already talked to Rod about this sort of slackness. I told him he needed to gee up his foremen to keep the men at it. He was cross with me. "Things have changed," he said, "since the old days when the men were desperate to keep their jobs. They don't care if they are sacked now, because they can get another job at the drop of a hat."'

Walter got up to help himself to another piece of shortbread. 'He's probably right. What really infuriated Charles was that when he inspected the lifeboats with the captain, they found that food had been stolen from the watertight tins of provisions. This is food, Jeremy, which is intended to keep their men alive if they're torpedoed and have to abandon ship.'

'That's terrible!' Jeremy felt sick at the thought. 'Those workers ought to be put out in a lifeboat without food and see how they like it.'

'Charles says everything that isn't nailed down is stolen.'

Jeremy sighed. 'I have to hold Rod responsible,' he said sadly. 'He hardly seems to try. I don't think he has the ability. It's a terrible state of affairs in wartime.'

He was really distressed. However, he knew that if he went to Rod with this tale his son would fly off the handle and do little or nothing about it. Jeremy knew he would have to think hard and long about doing more than just talking about it. The only effect of giving advice to Rod was to make their relationship even worse.

Charlotte was beginning to wonder whether she'd found out all she was going to about the Barrington Brown family, and whether she ought to move on to a job that would help the war effort. But she'd grown fond of Clarissa and knew the older woman relied on her to make life more bearable.

She was doing more with the children, too. Most afternoons she took them upstairs to spend an hour with their grandparents. Clarissa said she was getting to know her grandchildren better and was enjoying their company.

Now that the weather was improving too, she took them out to the garden whenever they had a fine day. She was surprised at the size of the grounds. What she'd taken to be a nearby house in a paddock behind turned out to be the old stable block. The horses had long since gone and at some stage every scrap of hay and straw had been cleaned out. But there were still harnesses, saddles and horse brasses, now all dull and dusty with age and disuse.

There was also an attractive summerhouse beyond the shrubbery which could be turned round, so that those sitting inside could always be in the sun and out of the wind. Clarissa loved being out there watching the children play on the grass. They, however, preferred to play in the old stables, though it wasn't thought safe to let Becky go there alone; it would be too easy for her to hurt herself. She was trying to persuade Charlotte to take her one afternoon when Clarissa said it was years since she'd been inside the stables and suggested she go too in her wheel chair.

Once inside, Charlotte was enthralled; with the cobbled floors and wooden feeding racks it was like a journey back in time, though some of the cobbles were missing and the broken racks looked as though they might have woodworm. Becky was interested in a governess cart they found, and nearby was another carriage that Clarissa couldn't put a name to.

'When I first came here to live, I used to get a groom to take me out in that for afternoon drives. Such a long time ago.' The paint was flaking off and the leather trim was dry and cracked.

There were several cars here too, covered with dust. One dated from the twenties and two or three looked as though they'd just been taken off the road. It was another world.

Meriel had become more anxious and tearful since Roderick had vented his rage on Becky and Charlotte. She wasn't coping either with him or with the children. Clarissa thought she'd be less harassed if she had more help. She telephoned the local labour exchange several times. At last they sent a young girl round who was willing to act as mother's help. Her name was Joan and as she was not yet eighteen she did not have to do war work. Meriel didn't hesitate, but hired her on the spot. She was the eldest in a large family and was used to children. She sounded willing and said she'd be happy to live in and do a bit of housework too.

The shopping expeditions and the bridge sessions were now part of Clarissa's routine. Jeremy was inviting friends round for bridge at least once a week and sometimes twice.

'Doris has said she'll be pleased to come,' Charlotte heard him telling Clarissa. 'But I've just been on to Walter and he can't. His son is taking him to a concert tonight.'

'Try Veronica,' Clarissa said. 'She'll be happy to come if she isn't doing anything else.'

'Yes,' Jeremy returned from his study. 'Veronica and Doris tonight.'

'They're both good players,' Clarissa told Charlotte. 'Years ago we used to play regularly as a foursome.'

Mrs Shipley brought them upstairs. Charlotte had already met Doris Spalding. The other elderly lady was greeting Clarissa with a kiss. She had grey hair and wore a smart dress of lavender-coloured wool. Jeremy was setting up the card table as he introduced Charlotte to her.

'Mrs Veronica Terry,' he said. Charlotte shook hands. The woman was wearing several big diamond rings that bit painfully into her flesh.

'We feel very lucky to have Charlotte's services,' Jeremy went on. 'I don't know what we'd do without her. She's really got Clarissa up and going.'

Clarissa smiled. 'She's got you going too.'

Veronica's gentle eyes were scrutinising Charlotte closely. She said in tones of wonderment, 'How very like Alicia she is. Don't you think so? That dark auburn hair ... A very uncommon colour, except in our family.'

Charlotte felt the heat run up her neck and into her cheeks; the next moment she was coming out in a cold sweat.

'Alicia?' Clarissa said, and she was staring at her too. 'Yes, Alicia! You reminded me of someone, Charlotte, but I couldn't think who. It is Alicia.'

The strength ebbed from Charlotte's legs, which suddenly felt as though they were made of rubber. Alicia had been the name of the woman washed up on Glan y Mor beach, who Jonty said had been her mother. She collapsed back on the sofa. When she'd first come, she'd been scared she might be recognised, but as time passed she'd thought the danger was past.

'Are you all right?' Jeremy asked. 'You look as though you've seen a ghost.'

Her tongue felt too big for her mouth but she managed to say. 'I've something to tell you.' All four seemed transfixed and were hanging on to her every word. 'I think I might be Alicia's daughter.'

None of the four moved; their gazes didn't waver. Charlotte saw confusion, disbelief and alarm on their faces. She was trembling, and her voice shook as she said, 'I believe I'm Abigail Elinor.'

The intense silence continued a moment longer, then pandemonium seemed to break out. Jeremy and Clarissa were firing questions at her.

'How did you know about . . . ?'

'Why didn't you tell us?'

In the midst of the chaos, Veronica slid sideways off her chair and silently collapsed; a heap of lavender wool on the carpet.

That brought Charlotte down to earth. She rushed to turn the woman over. Her face was paper white but she was breathing and, yes, Charlotte could feel a steady pulse.

'She's only fainted,' she said. A few moments later, Veronica's eyes flickered open. 'Just lie still for a moment,' she told her.

'Veronica was Alicia's mother.' Jeremy's voice was shaking; he looked quite stunned. So, now, did Charlotte.

It took her a long time to recount the facts and they came out in the wrong order, mixed up and back to front. Everyone was questioning her. It felt like an inquisition, and the only one who seemed to believe her was Doris Spalding.

'Because no trace was ever found of Abigail, you've always worried about what happened to her,' she told them. 'Now here she is, a grown-up granddaughter to you all.'

Charlotte held her breath. Doris was the only one who was not a blood relation and the others still looked shocked. She fetched the little red book with the notes Jonty had made at the inquest, together with the cuttings from the newspapers of the time. They pored over them but seemed no more convinced.

She told them about Mary, who'd been desperate for a baby but unable to have one of her own. About how she'd found a baby washed up in a wooden cradle on Glan y Mor beach and how it had seemed like the answer to her prayers. How she'd given in to temptation and kept her.

Jeremy held his head in his hands. 'It's come out of the blue,' he said. 'And it sounds like a fairy story, and that makes it hard to take in. But knowing you, I'm inclined to think it could be the truth.'

'Believe me, it is.' Charlotte choked. She knew Veronica was watching her closely.

'If only we'd known Abigail had survived,' she breathed. 'It would have made such a difference to me.'

'And to us,' Clarissa said. 'And . . . I wonder if Roderick is home yet? Hadn't we better ask him to come up? This concerns him as closely as any of us. He was Abigail's father.'

'Is – in the present tense,' Jeremy corrected.

Charlotte got to her feet. 'I'll run down to see if he's there,' she said.

She was dreading this. Rod wasn't going to like it; he'd already taken a dislike to her. He'd have to know the truth now, but it could send him into paroxysms of rage.

When she saw his car was not parked outside the front door, her first feeling was one of relief. She found Meriel reading a bedtime story to her children, and couldn't bring herself to go into long explanations. It was only after she'd left a message saying his parents wanted Rod to come up as soon as he came home that she realised it would have been better to get it over and done with than have it hanging over her.

Back upstairs, she made a pot of tea. Her maternal grandmother looked as though she needed it. Everyone went on talking about the shipwreck, asking her the same questions over and over again. They wanted to know more about the family who had kept her, and about their little farm. And all the time, Charlotte's nerves jangled as they waited for Roderick to come up.

He appeared with a show of reluctance, and seemed irritable. 'What's the matter, Pa? I've had a busy day. Everything's fine at the yard.'

He stood glowering down at them, a dictatorial presence, before throwing himself down on a chair. 'Can I have a cup of that tea?'

'It'll be cold,' Charlotte said. 'It's an hour since I made it.'

'Then make some more.' His lordly expression showed he expected others to leap to satisfy his commands.

Charlotte was rising to her feet. 'No.' Jeremy caught at her arm. 'This is about Charlotte.'

'I'll make more tea.' Doris Spalding took the tray to the kitchen.

'So what about Charlotte?' Rod demanded, turning on her impatiently. 'Why get me up here? This has nothing to do with me.'

'It has.' Charlotte was frightened; her heart was pounding fit to burst as she fought to stay calm. 'I've just told your parents that I believe I'm Abigail Elinor.'

His eyes, full of disdain and dislike, glared into hers for a long silent minute.

'I'm dumbfounded. You're trying to tell me you're my daughter? Don't make me laugh.'

'I'm not trying to be funny,' she choked, and started to tell her story over again. This time she had a tighter grip on the facts and the tale came out in a more orderly fashion.

'Who are these people who brought you up?' Rod was aggressive. 'If what you say is true, it's abduction. They should be prosecuted.'

'No,' Charlotte said. 'The man I thought was my father died recently so there's nothing you can do to him. I loved him dearly. His wife is still alive and grieving, as I am. If it had not been for her I would have perished. I was nine weeks old, washed up on an empty beach during a raging storm. I was wet through and stone cold, hypothermic in fact. She saved my life by taking me to her home, warming me up and feeding me. I'll not have any harm come to her.'

'You'll not . . .' He choked. 'I'm not asking you.' A crimson tide ran up his cheeks. 'Pa, we aren't going to let her get away with this, are we?'

'Listen to what she says,' Jeremy said. But Roderick was gripped by fury.

'You've been here for months. Why didn't you say something before now? You take a job with my parents, pretending to be a nurse . . .'

'I am a nurse,' she said through clenched teeth.

'Yes, but now you're pretending to be a long-lost member of our family as well. You want us to believe you're my daughter? You're telling us she wasn't drowned after all?'

'Yes,' Charlotte said. 'That's about it.'

He laughed. 'I wouldn't bet on it. This reminds me of what happened to the Russian royal family. Is that where you got the idea? Several girls claimed to be Princess Anastasia, don't they? Is this your idea of a get rich quick scheme?'

'I don't want your money,' she spat out.

'So what do you want? And what proof have you got? It doesn't sound a likely story.'

That pulled Charlotte up. She hadn't asked Jonty for proof. She hadn't needed to; she'd known he'd never tell her a lie of any sort.

'You have no proof?'

Charlotte produced the red book with the notes Jonty had taken at the inquest, together with the newspaper cuttings. 'If it weren't true why would they have kept all this?'

Roderick glanced through it. 'I wouldn't call this proof. It's a few notes about the shipwreck copied from somewhere. Just a few details to base your story on. There'd be a transcript of the inquest in the archives – you could have copied it from there. If you grew up on Anglesey you could have seen the graves of those who perished and picked up the story that way.'

'We brought Alicia home and buried her in the churchyard here,' Veronica said.

'But Captain Merryhew and Joe Kelly were buried in Anglesey, and you could also have got those details from the Receiver of Wrecks. They'd have archives too.'

'The newspaper reports were cut from the newspapers at the time,' Charlotte pointed out. She was finding it hard to keep her temper when he was going for her like this. 'The woman I think of as my mother has my undying love and gratitude. She and . . .' she hesitated, 'she and my father gave me a very happy upbringing.'

'Don't you think she's like Alicia?' Clarissa asked.

'She is,' Veronica said. 'I saw it straight away. Her colouring . . .'

Roderick studied her suspiciously. 'Like Alicia? A little, perhaps. Just the colouring. I still think this is some sort of scheme to get money out of us.'

'I don't expect any of your money,' Charlotte said. 'I wouldn't accept it.'

'Then why?' His angry face was very close to hers now.

'My – the man I grew up believing to be my father only told me this on his deathbed. I was as shocked as you are. I didn't want it to be the truth. But I was very curious about what I understood to be my birth family.'

Roderick was breathing heavily but at least he was listening to her now.

She went on, 'We are all a combination of nature and nurture. My nurturing might seem strange to you but I'm very happy with it. But I was curious about my nature, and that's why I came. I needed to find out what you were like.'

'And now you have?' he sneered.

'I wish I hadn't bothered. I doubt you'd have shown me much fatherly affection.'

He laughed again. 'How could I possibly have fatherly affection for you? Don't be silly.'

'From what I've seen, you don't for Becky either,' she said, remembering how she'd seen him lambast her.

Roderick leapt to his feet. 'That's enough from you. As far as I'm concerned, Abigail died with her mother.'

'No,' Charlotte protested. 'No, it's twenty-two years ago, and what happened changed my life.'

'I'll have a word with my solicitor. I'm going to ask him to draw up a document and you will sign it. It will say you made up this cock and bull story as a means of extracting money.'

'I'd never sign that. It's untrue.'

'If you're telling the truth, I'll have this woman who took you charged with abduction. Make up your mind.' He hurtled out of the room and they heard him pounding downstairs.

Charlotte collapsed back on the sofa and felt angry tears stinging her eyes.

'Don't you worry,' Jeremy said. 'He won't do anything. I'll let him cool down and then talk to him again. No point now – he's in no mood to take anything in.'

'I believe you,' Veronica said. 'You look so much like Alicia. This woman who kept you, tell me what she's like.'

'She's a loving and kind person. I think of her as my mother.'

'Yes, well, does she have proof of all this?'

Charlotte shook her head. 'I think she sees the red notebook and cuttings as proof. What else could there be?'

Jeremy shook his head. 'After twenty-two years it's hard to say.'

'Or perhaps,' Clarissa suggested, 'you could bring her here to talk to us. If we heard the story from her, we'd all have a clearer picture.'

Charlotte knew Mary didn't want to face the Barrington Browns. There was no bridge that evening; Doris rang for the taxi to take her and Veronica home.

Mary could sense that Charlotte was bursting with news the moment she came home for her next day off.

She kissed her and said, 'Mum, they've found out. I had to tell them. They know I'm Abigail Elinor.'

Mary felt a spurt of anxiety. 'What did they say? I want to hear everything.'

Edith made a cup of tea and they sat round the sitting-room fire talking non-stop.

'I think Jeremy and Clarissa believe what I say and accept me.'

'And your – other father?'

'He doesn't. He thinks I'm a fortune-hunter trying to get a social leg-up. He's horrible, Mum.' Charlotte gave her hand a little squeeze. 'I don't like him a bit.'

Mary felt better. Roderick Barrington Brown was not going to eclipse Charlotte's memories of Jonty.

'He says I have no proof and my story sounds like a fairy tale. My grandparents would like you to come and see them, so they can hear your version, but I know you don't want to face them.'

'I've been thinking,' Mary said. 'I kept some of the baby clothes you were wearing when I found you . . . Would they recognise things like that, even after all this time? Oh, and you had a little gold bracelet on your wrist. I put that away too. Wouldn't that convince the Barrington Browns that what you're saying is true?'

'Yes,' she said. 'It ought to.'

'Come and see.' Mary took her up to her bedroom. She opened the bottom drawer of her chest and brought out a bundle wrapped in tissue paper. 'These are they.' She laid them on her bed.

Charlotte unfolded a little matinee jacket, yellowed and matted. 'It's hard to imagine myself wearing such a tiny jacket.'

Mary opened a cardboard box. 'This is your bracelet. When you were small these springy bracelets were fashionable for babies. I saw several silver ones but never before a gold one like this.'

It was a narrow engraved band, in a large enough circle to put her hand through now. Charlotte slid it on her wrist.

'It can be pressed smaller to fit even a baby, and the catch keeps it like that.'

'I see – so it's a double band part of the way.'

'Squeeze it again and it bounces back to its original size and can easily be taken off.'

'It's pretty,' Charlotte said, putting it back in its box.

'I put that away because it was something of a giveaway.'

'They might remember it,' Charlotte said.

Mary watched her run her hands over the shawl. 'That was hand crocheted by the look of it. You used it quite a lot. It was lovely when I first got it.' She was packing the things up again. 'When you go back to Burford House tomorrow, you must take them with you.'

The following evening, when Charlotte returned to Burford House, she found that Doris and Veronica were with her grandparents and a hand of bridge was in progress. She went to her bedroom to unpack her overnight bag and then took her baby things with her into the sitting room and sat down to wait for the game to finish.

Clarissa was dummy and noticed her immediately. 'Hello, you're back early. What have you got there?'

Charlotte unwrapped her bundle. 'Baby clothes. My mother said I was wearing these when I was washed up on the beach.'

The bridge game stopped, and there was a stunned silence. Clarissa was on her feet with more speed than she usually possessed. Charlotte held out the baby's bracelet on her palm. 'Do you recognise it?'

Clarissa lifted it, turned it over, incredulity on her face. 'Jeremy, look at this! We bought that for you, Charlotte,' she choked. 'It was a christening present. I wanted to have a message engraved inside but we never got round to it.'

They were all crowding round her, shaking the well-worn baby clothes out of their folds.

'I crocheted this shawl,' Veronica said in awed tones. 'You are Alicia's daughter. I knew it the moment I set eyes on you. You're my granddaughter.'

'And ours.' Clarissa smiled at her. 'It was a shock at first, but I want you to know I'm delighted.'

'We all are,' Jeremy told her. 'I was fairly sure but this has convinced me. We should get Rod up again to see these things.'

'I'll go,' Doris said.

He came at last, scowling aggressively at Charlotte.

'I hope you'll see these things as proof,' she said. He lifted the matinee jacket between his finger and thumb and held it out as though afraid it would contaminate him.

'These were Abigail's things,' Clarissa told him.

'They prove nothing,' he said. 'That shawl could have been washed up on the beach. Same with the bracelet. It could have come off the baby's wrist while she was in the water. Abigail was drowned and her body never found. This stuff could just be flotsam you found on the beach. It gave you the idea, something to hang your tale on.'

It was perfectly clear he didn't want to believe that Charlotte was his long-lost daughter.

CHAPTER EIGHTEEN

R ODERICK HURRIED downstairs seething with frustration. That
girl had a nerve, coming here and stirring up the past trouble of that
shipwreck. Everybody had blamed him, his father still hadn't forgiven
him. It had taken him years to get over his guilt and grief and to get back
in his stride. Now this girl was telling everybody she was his daughter and
accusing him of ill treating Rebecca. She was unbelievable, and he wasn't
going to put up with her.

'What did they want?' Meriel asked.

'That nurse is about to take over this place. Don't let her come in here
again.'

'She was kind, she helped me get Joan.'

Her pale blue eyes blinked at him. Why hadn't he foreseen how much
she would irritate him? She looked a bedraggled mess,

'What's that you've spilled on your jumper? On the shoulder?'

She twisted round to see. 'Robin brought some of his rice pudding
back at lunchtime. I think it must be that.'

'You mean he was sick on you? Surely you've had time to clean
yourself up?'

Meriel looked helpless and shook her head. 'It's hard to know where
the time goes.'

She had no go about her, no energy. 'You've got Joan here now. Don't
tell me you haven't got time to freshen yourself up before I get home. You
know I like you to look nice.'

'We took the children to the park this afternoon. They raced round
enjoying themselves but we were late back, and then they had to have
their tea. It was all a bit of a rush.'

'Surely you've got a watch?' Meriel was too dependent on others.

'Well, now you've got Joan you won't need that nurse to babysit any more. Keep her away from the children.'

Rod poured himself a stiff whisky, threw himself on a chair and surveyed his quarters with dissatisfaction. His parents described this as a flat. That was a euphemism. It was a series of draughty rooms with high ceilings that had been roughly converted from something else.

He'd wanted to have the library as his sitting room, because it was a pleasant sunny spot, but Pa had said no. 'What would we do with all those books?' he had asked. It was not as though anybody ever read them. Neither had he been all that willing to let him convert the billiards room into two bedrooms. 'We might want to use it,' he'd said, though he hadn't picked up a cue for years. Their bathroom had an enormous Victorian lavatory with a mahogany seat and lid, and a blue pattern of flowers down the pan. There was a mahogany chest of drawers with a lid that lifted to show the washbowl, and the room had been big enough to have a modern bath fitted. The floor was tiled and freezing cold.

This sitting room had once been the smoking room, and beyond it they'd made a playroom for the children. The tiny makeshift kitchen and dining room had been converted from goodness knows what. The windows rattled in the frames if there was a moderate breeze, and the luxury that his forebears had found here simply did not exist any more.

Mrs Shipley brought their dinner. It wasn't up to much. He and Meriel ate in complete silence. Then she followed him back to the sitting room and poured them both a cup of coffee from the tray put there for them. She took hers to the other side of the room, sat down with a magazine and opened it on her knee. She wasn't reading it, though; she was staring into space looking thoroughly cast down. He felt a prickle of guilt that he'd let his irritation get the better of him.

'Get yourself smartened up,' he said. 'We'll go to the golf club for a drink. Just for an hour or so.'

Her pale blue eyes raked him. 'All right,' she said, but picked up her coffee cup.

'Tell Joan we're going out and get yourself changed, Meriel. I can't take you looking like that. You're a disgrace.'

He could see she didn't really want to go with him and that infuriated him. He'd thought he was giving her a treat.

The expression on his face got her moving. She fled to their bedroom. Rod followed her. The money in his wallet was getting low and he'd need more if he went out. He kept his personal cash hidden in his vast Victorian mahogany wardrobe, which was fitted inside with mirrors and lockable drawers as well as hanging space. He took out his key ring and unlocked one of the drawers, careful to place his body between Meriel and the drawer as he took out the mahogany tea caddy. It was nothing special as tea caddies went but it held his cache of money. He didn't want her getting nosy and asking questions about it. He put the box under his arm, then to hide it he pulled his jacket round it.

'Will this do?' Meriel was asking him. She was dragging a nondescript blue dress over her head and buttoning the bodice.

'Yes. We're only going for a drink. It doesn't do much for you, though.'

'It's utility. There isn't much choice any more.'

'It'll do,' he told her, as he swept out of the room. 'At least it looks clean.'

He headed towards their bathroom, but Joan was bathing the kids in there. He changed course and went to their sitting room where he could be on his own.

He took out his key ring again and opened the box. Inside were three compartments, two of which had lids. He remembered Pa telling him that the centre compartment was for sugar and once it would have had a fitted glass container. He lifted the first lid, exposing bundles of five pound notes done up with elastic bands. Under the other lid the pound notes, being smaller, lay flat; he could get more in that way. This was his little secret, his little bit of comfort.

It was just his luck to be earning real money when there was little he could spend it on. He was stuffing as many notes as he could into his wallet when there was a knock on the door and his father looked into the room.

Rod jumped with surprise. He slammed the lid of the tea caddy down with one hand and with the other pushed the wallet and notes into his trouser pocket. He was trembling.

Pa must never see this little cache; it wasn't something he'd understand. Rod mustn't let him see he'd got the wind up. He was suspicious enough without that.

'Have you got a minute, Rod?' he asked.

Oh, hell, he meant to stay. What was he to do now? It had always been one of the problems of sharing the house: there was no way he could stop Pa creeping up on him.

'Yes, come in, Pa.' He made himself sound more affable than he felt.

His father sat down in what Rod considered to be the armchair reserved for his own use. He felt a wave of annoyance and he said testily, 'If it's about that nurse . . .'

'No, there's something else I need to talk to you about. Walter Collingwood says . . .'

Rod hated to hear Pa mention any of his old cronies. It always heralded trouble. This time was no exception. It seemed Walter's grandson, some little upstart working on the freighter *Atlantic Voyager* which was in for repairs, was criticising the way he was running the yard and thought he could do it better.

'He reckons your workmen are smoking and chatting when they should be working, which means his ship is being kept in dock far longer than it need be.'

Rod had heard it all before. It had always been like this, even when Pa was in charge. He was banging on about the emergency rations being stolen and what would happen to the brave sailors if they found the cupboard was bare after they'd been torpedoed.

'Pa, they always check the emergency rations before the ship puts to sea. If they don't, it's their own fault.'

'Roderick! It's downright theft and everything's in short supply.'

'That's why it's stolen. All right, Pa, I'll look into it,' he said to placate him. He wanted to get rid of him. 'Really, everything's going along all right,' he insisted. 'The yard's making more profit than it's ever done.' He knew he shouldn't have said that the moment the words were out of his mouth.

'Bring the books home for me tomorrow,' his father said. 'It's a long time since I looked at them.'

'No need, Pa, really. You don't have to work now.'

'I don't see it as work any more.' Pa was trying to smile. 'It interests me. It's bound to – it's been my life.'

The last thing Roderick wanted was to have him poking his nose into the books. 'Absolutely no need, Pa. One good thing about this war, we can't fail to make a profit.'

'There would be a better profit,' he said coldly, 'if you could speed up the turn-round. Bring the books anyway. What harm will it do to run my eye over them?'

Rod knew Pa wouldn't let him forget. It was by way of getting a dig back at him that he said, 'That nurse you've hired has a vivid imagination. I'd get rid of her if I were you.'

Pa gave a derisive little laugh. 'I can't do that. Your mother's fond of her. She's been good for both of us. Don't you think your mother's much improved?'

As far as Rod was concerned his mother never stopped moaning. She was always fussing, while Pa always seemed to be watching him. He wanted them both off his back.

'That girl's making trouble. She's trying to elbow her way into our family.'

'I want her to stay. Your mother's able to do much more now, thanks to her and Polly. Rod, I do think she's your daughter.'

'Well I don't. I think she's telling fairy tales.'

Pa had the grace to back down. 'Don't accuse the woman who brought her up of abduction. You must promise to drop any ideas like that.'

'All right,' he said. What did it matter?

Meriel came in then all ready to go out, and distracted Pa's attention with talk about the children. Rod wanted to send him back upstairs thinking all was well. He wanted him to forget about the books. Pa understood every nuance in the accounts, and the thought of him delving into them scared him.

Jeremy was more troubled than ever as he closed Rod's door and went slowly down the passage. He was shocked by what he'd seen. Rod must be breaking the law.

He was keeping cash in a mahogany box, a great deal of cash. Jeremy had not been able to drag his eyes away from that box all the time he'd been with him. What was wrong with the bank? He wanted to kick himself now for not asking Rod straight out, but he'd lost his nerve. At the very least, Rod would have flown into a temper and told him it was none of his business.

There was only one reason people kept money like that hidden in their homes, and that was that it hadn't been earned legally. Was it from the shipyard, or some other wartime deal? He'd heard there were lots of them, fuelled by the shortages of almost everything.

He went to the kitchen, where the pots had been washed up and left to drain. He was glad Mrs Shipley wasn't here, or she'd wonder why he was nosing round like this.

Rod made no secret about buying extra food, but he'd said it was legal. Most people had to queue for what was in short supply, but unrationed, when it went on sale. But Rod was one of the fortunate few who knew somebody who would put it his way, provided he was prepared to pay a little extra.

Of course, profiteering was illegal, but it was certainly going on, and the fines if one was caught were never heavy. Jeremy knew that was how Roderick got his cigarettes and Clarissa her supply of sherry; his own occasional bottle of whisky too. They enjoyed grouse and pheasant and salmon in season, and the occasional chicken or duck. The rationing system was said to be fair, but everyone knew it was easier to eat well if one had cash to spare.

There was a canteen at the yard, which he'd started in the Depression. Jeremy had believed that if men had a hot dinner at midday, they'd work harder during the afternoon. The canteen had always been popular with the workforce, but since rationing almost everybody ate there, including the office staff.

Jeremy opened the pantry door and peered round the shelves. A jelly had been put to set, no doubt for the children. There was part of the meat loaf Mrs Shipley had made for their lunch today. He knew she'd eked out the meat with breadcrumbs and herbs; it hadn't been that good. He hoped the staff would eat the leftovers tomorrow. It had been lamb's liver for dinner tonight – rather better, and offal was unrationed. There was very little butter, sugar and bacon in the house. It didn't look as though they had anything illegal here.

Of course, there was the petrol. Jeremy made a point of not asking Rod where he got his supply from – that surely must be illegal. He himself now used a car hire firm or rang for a taxi. He thought he was being charged more than he should be, but it was unwise to question the cost if he wanted the service to continue. Everybody was doing things like that. It was eroding standards of honesty but they had to to survive.

Polly had said he must walk more than he had been doing so he let himself out into the garden. The days were lengthening now and it was pleasant strolling round looking at the spring flowers which were all in bloom, everything looking green and fresh. He went to see how the roses were coming on, but found that many of the flower beds had been turned into what looked like a market garden.

He remembered now discussing this with Bill Dorking. Bill had been his chauffeur for more than twenty years, but when petrol rationing came in he'd had to mothball the cars. Dorking had always lived on the premises and it was impossible by then to ask him to move out. Instead Jeremy had asked him if he'd like to work as a gardener.

He admired the rows of beans and cabbages. Bill was making a good job of it considering they used to employ two gardeners here before they were called up. Fortunately, Bill was over retirement age, so there was no danger that they would lose his services.

Jeremy had been taking less interest in the garden over recent years. Once Clarissa had had that stroke he'd been unable to think of anything else, or leave her much on her own. Recently, he hadn't taken much interest in the shipyard either. No doubt there would be big changes there too.

Rod used to bring him the books so he could see how it was getting on, but he hadn't done that for a while. If Rod had some illegal scheme operating there, Jeremy had no idea what it might be.

By the following weekend, Charlotte's mind was focused firmly on her own affairs. Glyn was coming to Liverpool to see her and bringing Enid. With the visit in mind, her mother and grandmother had been planning menus and hoarding rations for a long time. Charlotte had her hair trimmed and as another page of clothing coupons had become valid she bought herself a new summer dress. The thought of Glyn's visit was bringing prickles of anticipation.

Now her connection to the Barrington Brown family was out in the open, and she'd convinced Jeremy and Clarissa that she was their grandchild, her mind was more at rest. She'd told them about the visit and been given both Saturday and Sunday off so she could spend more time with Glyn.

On Friday, Clarissa sent her home in mid-afternoon so she could meet her visitors off the Crosville bus. When she reached Templeton Avenue she found Mary getting ready to meet them too.

Not having seen Glyn for some time, Charlotte wanted to look her best. She was in high spirits as she changed into her new dress and put on some make-up. They went into the city centre together and the bus came in on time.

'There they are.' Mary was waving to Glyn and Enid while they were still inside the bus. Charlotte's heart turned over as Glyn came leaping down the steps like an athlete and strode over to wrap his arms round her in a great bear hug.

They were all talking at once and Glyn was the last passenger to drag their bags from the luggage compartment.

'How are you, Enid?' Charlotte asked. 'I'm sure the last few weeks must have been difficult for you.'

'Very.' Glyn pushed an arm through his mother's. 'Difficult for all of us to get over Kevin. But Dad made us promise to to think of other things this weekend.'

Mary was full of sympathy. 'I didn't know how I was going to survive without Jonty. Sometimes I feel he's still here with me.'

They had to catch a bus to Templeton Avenue then, and as it was rush hour Charlotte found herself standing crushed against Glyn in the aisle. His eyes flirted with hers.

'I've missed you,' he said softly. 'The place isn't the same without you up at Glan y Mor.'

She smiled at him. There was nobody she knew better or could be more relaxed with than Glyn. To stand this close to him was making her heart beat twice as fast as normal. She felt in a fever of effervescence, more alive than she had for months.

Edith was at home cooking cottage pie for them all. When Mary led the visitors to the kitchen to say hello Enid opened one of the bags they'd brought. It was packed tight with eggs and butter, a young cockerel dressed ready for the oven and jams and home-made cake.

'I know how hard it must be to feed visitors,' she said. 'These are things we produce so it's easy enough for us.'

Mary exclaimed with delight at such largesse and Edith said, 'We'll have the chicken for Sunday lunch.'

There was a companionable atmosphere when they sat down to eat at the dining table Mary had set several hours earlier. They caught up with the news about Glenys and Tegwen and the people in the village. It seemed very little had changed in Anglesey since they'd left.

Charlotte was watching her mother, half afraid she'd be upset at having her old life recalled with such clarity, but she seemed to be enjoying the company.

Glyn helped her to clear away and wash up after the meal. Then, wanting to have him to herself, she suggested a walk to the park. It was dark and no longer warm, and they huddled together on a bench, his face nuzzling hers. Charlotte put her lips up to his.

At breakfast the next morning, Mary and Enid seemed to understand they might want to spend the day on their own.

'I put it to Mum,' Glyn told her afterwards, 'that we needed time alone and that it was very hard to come by now you live here.'

Charlotte was pleased. It was Glyn's first visit to Liverpool and she wanted to show him the sights of the city. She took him on the bus to see the Royal Infirmary where she'd trained and the Barrington Brown ship repair yard.

He was horrified to see so many damaged buildings and craters in the ground. 'I'm shocked,' he said. 'All this bomb damage. I didn't realise there was so much of it. To have been here then must have been terrifying.'

'Yes, but we haven't had any raids for ages now,' she said as the bus took them back along the Dock Road. 'It's safe enough.'

At the Pier Head, he admired the great buildings on the river front, and was fascinated by the busy shipping on the Mersey. It was a mile-wide waterway busy with shipping. They took the ferry down to New Brighton at the river mouth, and as it was lunchtime by then they had a snack and a cup of coffee in a small café. It was a pleasant sunny afternoon and they strolled the length of the prom to Harrison Drive, where they sat on the sand to recover. There were few people about here, and he took her into his arms again.

Charlotte felt full of fresh air, sunshine and sand, and she wanted to return to Templeton Avenue to freshen up. When they arrived, Edith, Mary and Enid had just finished having tea in the garden. The shadows were lengthening and the warmth of the day had gone. Charlotte and Glyn sat at the kitchen table to have a fresh cup of tea while the others started to prepare their supper.

Charlotte's plan for the day had been that she and Glyn should go out for dinner on their own. Meriel, who knew about such things, had recommended they go to either the Adelphi or the Exchange Hotel.

'No restaurant or café is allowed to charge more than five shillings for a meal now, so you might as well go to the best,' she'd said. So Charlotte had booked a table at the Adelphi.

She hardly remembered what she ate but it was a very elegantly served meal and took a long time. She'd had a wonderful day. They'd spent it talking of their past, their present and what they might do in the future.

Neither of them wanted the evening to end, but it was getting late. The others were sitting round the fire waiting up for them when they got back.

When Sunday came, Charlotte was very conscious that they'd be parting that afternoon. Mary sent her and Glyn out for a walk in the morning, saying she'd have all the help she needed to get the lunch on the table from Edith and Enid.

They walked to the local park, where they sat on a park bench and she felt him slide an arm round her waist. 'I wish we could be together,' he said.

'I'll have two weeks' holiday in the summer.'

He smiled. 'Come and spend it with me.'

'I'm looking forward to that already.'

'You know, don't you, that I'll never be able to move from Anglesey?' His dark eyes were searching hers. 'Would you be happy to come back?'

Charlotte felt a prickle run down her spine. That sounded like a proposal. She was almost overcome at the thought of living with Glyn in the depths of the country, near beaches and the sea.

'I miss Glan y Mor,' she said. 'I loved living there. I'd be very happy to come back.'

'Good,' he said. 'Let's sort things out when you come for your holiday.'

Parting from Glyn was painful. When Charlotte got into her bed at Burford House that night, she couldn't get to sleep. Her mind wouldn't stop whirling. She knew she'd found real love, the sort that Jonty and Mary had had, the sort that would last a lifetime.

CHAPTER NINETEEN

A FEW DAYS later, Enid wrote to Mary saying she'd so enjoyed her weekend in Liverpool that she wanted the three of them to come and stay at Plas Hafren so she could return their hospitality. If it wasn't a convenient time for Charlotte, who had a job to consider, she suggested Mary and Edith come together for a week in early summer.

Mary knew it would do her mother good to have a change. For herself, she had to think about it for a while. She'd loved living on Anglesey but she wasn't yet over Jonty's death. Rarely did a day pass when she didn't mourn her loss. She was afraid that to return to the place she'd always associate with him might intensify her grief.

Nevertheless, she decided she would go. She missed Enid's company, and it seemed the Evanses might become Charlotte's in-laws. She must not avoid them.

'I'd love to come with you,' Charlotte said when Mary showed her Enid's letter. 'But I don't feel I can ask Jeremy to give me a week's holiday now. He asked me some time ago when I'd like to take my annual holiday, as he'd probably take Clarissa to a hotel while I was away. We agreed on early August, because I thought that might be a good time for Glyn. He can get time off from the Egg Marketing Board then, and the hay will already be gathered and the corn won't yet be ripe. There won't be so much work for him to do.'

Hearing her mother and grandmother planning their trip to Anglesey made Charlotte long to go with them. The week they'd be away, Barbara and Dan invited her to spend her day off with them.

When she got there, she found Tim, their younger son, was home for a week's leave, and the whole family was in a very upbeat mood. He was in the air force, an air gunner who had just successfully completed a full tour of duty flying raids over Germany. His parents were pleased because when he reported back he'd be doing a ground job for a while.

They were having an early supper because Barbara was going to a meeting of the Townswomen's Guild.

'Why don't you take Charlotte out dancing?' Dan suggested to Tim.

'What a splendid idea,' Tim said. 'Here I am with nights off and all my mates are down in Cambridge. Are you on, Charlotte?'

'You bet. Not that I've got a decent frock with me.'

'Go as you are,' Barbara said. 'You look very nice in that, even if it isn't very dressy. Nobody dresses up much these days anyway.'

Charlotte didn't care for it but there was little choice in the shops. Everything carried the utility mark which meant it was practical for its purpose. One style was made up in every size with a choice of three colours. This one was blue, rather skimpy and vaguely military in style.

They went to Reece's dance hall. Tim had been keen on dancing in his teens and was more practised than she was. He took her to a pub and then on to Chinatown for another supper.

'I've had a whale of a time,' she told him on the doorstep when they got home. 'It was quite a celebration. Thanks a lot.'

Tim had a lot to celebrate. His life on the airfield must be similar to what Kevin had known, but his luck had held. She hoped it always would. She was fond of Tim; after all, she'd been brought up thinking they were cousins. In a way, it seemed to make him so.

Mary and her mother were lucky with the weather; the sun shone all week. Mary had forgotten how beautiful the Anglesey countryside and beaches were. The island was quiet because it was so early in the season. It was the restful sort of holiday they both enjoyed.

They sat in the Plas Hafren garden and strolled along the beach. Glyn took Mary up to see Glan y Mor. His father had bought it because he wanted the land, and Enid had fixed up the house to rent to summer visitors. It didn't look quite as it had, but Mary could feel Jonty's presence there and it comforted her.

One day she said to Enid, 'I'd like to walk to the churchyard to visit Jonty's grave.'

'Pick some flowers to take with you,' Enid replied. 'There're plenty in the garden now. Jonty used to love the gladioli, I remember.'

'Thank you. Could I borrow a small hand fork? I'm sure there'll be a lot of weeds growing on the grave by now.'

'There aren't. I go up there once in a while to put flowers on my mother's grave, and since I knew you'd want Jonty's kept tidy I see to it at the same time.'

'Oh, Enid, that's so kind. Thank you.'

'We were fond of Jonty too,' Enid said gently.

It was rather a long walk for her mother and Mary wanted to go by herself. She found that Jonty's grave was indeed immaculate, and knowing that his friends here had not forgotten him was a great comfort.

It was Monday morning and Roderick felt fraught. Pa was still asking to see the company accounts and he didn't think he could put it off any longer. He felt sick every time he thought of what he would find.

All his life Pa had been on his back about making the firm pay. When war was declared he had seen it as an opportunity to come down on him even harder. 'In wartime there's plenty of business,' he'd told him. 'Ships are queuing up to be repaired. You should be able to make a good profit.'

But the profit had remained meagre, which made Rod feel inadequate. The last thing he wanted was for Pa to come back and take over again. That had made him look like an incompetent idiot in front of the whole workforce.

Rod knew very well that what he was doing was illegal. It had been Miles's idea, or Milo as he liked to be called. To start with Rod had been nervous about it but now it had been running successfully for two years they were all more confident. Pa had actually congratulated him on last year's results, saying he'd turned the business round. Rod thought highly of Milo's financial acumen.

Monday morning was the time he met with George Alderton, the company secretary, and Miles Morrow, his chief accountant, to work on the scheme. He counted them his personal friends. He'd made big changes in his senior staff once Pa's cronies had retired. These were his men: they saw things his way and he could trust them. Today, though, he had something to tell them that they would not relish at all, and his step faltered as he opened the office door.

'Good morning, Mr Barrington Brown,' said Pixie Kent.

'Morning, Miss Kent.' He could put on his usual show of authority for her. 'I'll see Mr Alderton and Mr Morrow for our meeting in half an hour. On no account are we to be disturbed, and order coffee and biscuits for us, would you? We shall be going to lunch directly after the meeting.'

She gave Rod his morning post and he took it through to his own office. Everything reminded him of Pa in here; he'd changed nothing since it had belonged to him. He'd thought there was no need; he'd always admired the red Turkey carpet and heavy mahogany furniture of the Victorian era. His sumptuous desk and glass-fronted bookcases had the polished gloss it takes generations to achieve. Two large windows looked out across his half-tide docks to the River Mersey. This morning it was mud-coloured under a dark sky and busy with shipping.

He could almost see his father sitting here with the accounts in front of him, his face dark with anger. He wished he'd changed everything to steel and glass, put his own stamp on the place.

He took his letters through to the boardroom which opened off his office, with its vast conference table down the centre. He always brought George and Milo in here on Monday mornings so they had space to spread out their papers and files. It also put them further away from the other staff, so nothing could be overheard. As the table was kept bare, nothing could be inadvertently left behind either.

He couldn't settle to reading his mail, he was too restless. Instead, he looked round at the portraits hanging on the walls; most recently put up was the present King George the Sixth. All the past managing directors of the Barrington Brown Ship Repair Yard were here: his father, his grandfather, his great-grandfather and his great-great-grandfather.

This morning, Rod didn't like being surrounded by his forebears. He was afraid that, like his father, they'd think he wasn't up to the job. He'd come to work here with the ambition to achieve bigger profits than any of those who'd gone before him, and though he was doing that now he knew these strait-laced gentlemen would disapprove of his methods. All the same, when he retired and had earned the right, he'd have his portrait painted to hang here.

His gaze came to rest on the large framed photograph of his older brother Nathaniel. Although he'd never been manager and never would be, his father had thought it appropriate to have that photo blown up to life size and hung here amongst the yard managers. It had been taken in his military uniform and Nat looked every inch a hero. He'd proved himself on the Somme, where he'd been awarded a posthumous medal.

Once he was dead there was no way Rod could get equal kudos. He'd been permanently outclassed.

As a boy, Rod was told he'd been born with a silver spoon in his mouth, but if he had his older brother had been luckier. He'd been born with a golden spoon in his.

Their parents had always favoured Nat, holding him up as a role model he must emulate. Nat had been better at everything: he'd played cricket and rugby for the school, he'd achieved better marks in class and he'd been better-looking. Nat had plenty of common sense, whereas Pa was fond of telling Rod he was sadly lacking in it. Nat had barely put his foot inside the shipyard but he was said to have a real flair for the business. Rod knew he was a disappointment to his parents.

It had always irritated him to see Nat's framed photo here, and now he unhooked it from the wall. He'd only allowed it to stay this long because his father was in and out of the office and might create if he missed it, but he hadn't been near the place since Clarissa's stroke. Rod wasn't going to put up with Nat lording it over him any longer. He carried the portrait to Pixie Kent's office and leaned it against the wall.

'Have this sent to the archives,' he told her. Then he paused at the door of his own office. 'On second thoughts, I'll take it myself. Leave it there until I have time.'

'Yes, Mr Barrington Brown.'

It had left an empty space on the wall. The surrounding paper had faded with time and the square stood out bright and fresh. It would remind him of Nat almost as much as his picture did; he needed to find something to take its place. He'd see if there was something he liked better stashed away in the archives.

He'd barely sat down at his desk when his internal phone rang. Miss Kent's voice told him Mr Alderton and Mr Morrow had arrived.

'Send them in,' he told her.

He led them into the boardroom and they sat talking about the weather while Miss Kent fussed with the coffee cups.

George was the son of one of Pa's cronies. He was well educated, went to a decent tailor and understood what the finer trappings of life were. Miles Morrow was the exact opposite; he could be a bit uncouth, and he looked like a wide boy, a spiv, which he was. But he had a good brain, he was on top of the job and he could see opportunities that were lost on Rod and George. When Pixie left, Rod locked the adjoining door.

'Another excellent week.' Miles opened the official ledgers of the firm on the table at their current pages.

Roderick said, 'My father's asking to see the books. Will they stand up to an inspection?'

Milo's smile slipped. 'By your father? I thought he'd given up doing that.'

'So did I. He hasn't felt too well recently and then my mother had that stroke. I thought he'd lost interest in the business.'

'It's not good news that he wants to look the books over again. It wouldn't be safe, Rod. He's spent a lifetime looking at the figures for this yard. He'd see too much.'

Rod pursed his lips. He could see his fingers trembling. 'He's going to nag me until I produce something.'

'Show him the trading account and the balance sheet, and the figures I draw up for management. There're absolutely no problems with them. They've been accepted by the Inland Revenue.'

There were many more ledgers showing the day to day accounts of each department, some of them giving a more accurate picture of what was going on.

Rod hesitated. 'Won't he have been sent those already? He still owns a big chunk of the business. He'll be expecting more detail.'

'Well, we can't let the books out of the yard, can we? The bookkeepers need them to make their daily entries.'

'We don't want him to come here, either.'

'Give him a set of management figures, Rod. And stall on anything else.' He opened the books he kept private figures in – those seen only by their eyes. 'It's all proceeding according to plan. Everything's very satisfactory.'

They sat together at one end of the table and Rod listened carefully to what Milo had to say about their profitability. His tone was upbeat, and he said they could expect more of the same.

He took three large heavyweight manila envelopes from his briefcase, and they all heard the coins tinkle inside as he laid them out in a row on the table. Names were not written on them. The profit was divided into three and each could take whichever envelope he liked. It was Rod's guarantee that Milo wasn't taking more than he should for himself. It was better that they could all see that everything was above board.

Miles had talked to them seriously when he'd made the first payout nearly two years ago. 'It's important that none of us arouse suspicion,' he'd said. 'The fewer people who know, the safer we'll be, so don't talk about it to anyone, not even your wives. Particularly not your wives. If at any time questions are asked, if they don't know, they won't be able to drop us in it. Keep them on a tight rein.'

'Agreed,' Rod had said.

'And we must all keep a careful watch on our bank accounts. Our salaries are paid in there and we must appear to use them. Don't allow big balances to build up because you're using this money instead. That's dangerous and could attract the bank manager's notice. And do be discreet about how you spend this. Being too free with it can also attract attention.'

'Does it have to be all in cash?' George had asked.

'I'm afraid it has to be in silver and notes of small denominations. It has to look as though it's going into wage packets for those phantom workers. You must look upon that as a benefit. After all, it's easy to spend and it makes it almost impossible to trace.'

All that was true enough, Rod thought, but his cash was building up into what looked like becoming an embarrassing amount. Because their business did not receive its legitimate income in this way, Miles had told them not to pay cash like this into their bank accounts as that too risked attracting the attention of their bank managers.

Rod paid for everything he possibly could in cash and that was most of what he wanted. Meriel could use it to buy her clothes and things for the children. The staff – such as it was these days – could be paid with it. He'd opened savings accounts in all the local banks and building societies, and regularly paid in small amounts to each.

He'd very much like to buy property, but he couldn't do that with cash. Solicitors and estate agents would expect a cheque or a banker's draft. He'd always hung on to the larger denomination notes that came his way. He stuffed them into deed boxes and had them stored in the strong room of the bank with his name on them. But he was getting more and more and he'd started hiding money about the house, locked away in the cellar and the attics where he hoped nobody would come across it.

'Black marketeers are happy to be paid with it,' Milo had told him. It seemed that was what he did with his share.

Roderick roused himself and looked round at his friends. 'It would be safer to forget all this. Return to normal business. We've had a good innings.'

Milo was affronted. 'Everything's going so well. No need. What d'you think, George?'

Rod could see George understood his feelings. 'I don't know . . . Once the war's over, and it won't go on much longer now, that'll be the end of it anyway.'

Milo said. 'It seems only sensible to carry on while we can.'

Rod felt he was being swept along by a current he could no longer control.

To run successfully, the scheme needed input from others not employed in their business. Roderick had suggested they keep in touch by having a monthly lunch well away from the yard.

'It helps to keep a tight control,' Milo had smiled round the table in the Adelphi at the first such meeting.

Today, Humphrey Caldwell, an official from the Admiralty whom Rod felt he was getting to know quite well, had brought along the officer from the Ministry of War Transport who was directing work to their firm.

The system was proving highly satisfactory. It gave them the chance to get to know the people engaged in the scheme, and to update arrangements and change anything that wasn't working.

The others had all enjoyed the meal. Rod hadn't slept well she last few night and felt very much on edge, but as a result of having a glass or two of wine he was back at his desk feeling sleepy. His chair happened to be in a patch of sun and he was on the point of dozing off when Pixie Kent buzzed through.

'Mr Alderton would like a word with you,' she said.

That surprised him. It was barely an hour since the lunch party had broken up and George, like everybody else, had held forth at length there. 'Send him in,' he told her.

As soon as he saw him, Rod realised that something had happened. George's smiles of satisfaction had gone, and he looked quite agitated.

'What's the matter?'

'It's Milo,' George said, in what was almost a whisper. 'I've just heard that two men came into reception and asked to see him. One of them flashed a police identity, and Milo's secretary thought the other was a government inspector.'

Rod's heart began to hammer. He pulled himself upright in his chair, wide awake in a moment. They all knew Milo's black market activities wouldn't stand much investigation.

'What did they want?' he asked, wondering how much the staff knew about Milo's affairs.

'I don't know. They spent about ten minutes in his office and then he went out with them.'

'They haven't taken him to the police station for questioning?'

'I don't know. He said nothing to his secretary, so nobody knows.'

Rod was shocked. He closed his eyes and tried to think. 'This could be dangerous for us. One thing can lead to another when the law starts probing.'

George knew that as well as he did. 'It's very worrying.'

'It could be disaster if they turn up something that points to the personnel department.'

'Why should they?'

Rod could think of half a dozen reasons. 'Milo's background won't bear much examination. He's on our staff records as being a chartered accountant though we know he's only some sort of accounts clerk.'

'There's nothing to prove we know that. He could have lied his way in. We needed someone we could trust as chief accountant, didn't we?'

'Yes. Steve Ripley had to go – we couldn't have him loose on the books. He'd have had the auditors in at the drop of a hat, or gone running to Pa.'

'This could be dangerous.'

'There's nothing we can do about it now. We've got to leave it to Milo. I'll ring for some tea to pull us together. I hope he's more on the ball than I feel.'

Rod felt as though a black pall was enveloping him as he sipped his tea and stared out of the window at the heaving muddy waters of the Mersey. They both knew Milo was a black marketeer and using the shortages of wartime to get rich as quickly as he could.

He'd told them, 'I don't come from the same background as you two. My dad was a welder, a skilled worker, but my family was at the bottom of the pile. I went hungry when I was growing up. During the Depression Dad was thrown out of work and couldn't get another job anywhere. Not any sort of job. We lived on the dole and what my mother could earn taking in washing and looking after other people's kids. It was never enough. We always had holes in our shoes and went without coats in winter – went without almost everything else too. I'm going to make sure I never go back to those days.'

George crashed his teacup back on its saucer. 'I can't stand hanging around here any longer,' he said. 'Let's go out and stretch our legs. We could take a look at that river-class frigate that came in last week that Humphrey was telling us about.'

'Why not?' Rod took out his file on HMS *Helmsdale* and put it on a clipboard. 'We might as well look as though we're working.'

Outside, it seemed a normal day. There was the sound of the riveters hammering and the flash of the acetylene torches. Beyond, in the river, an empty tanker was heading out to the Irish Sea.

George said, 'Milo will be able to handle it. He has an answer for everything.'

Rod began to feel better. They had another cup of tea in the frigate wardroom and an aimless conversation with the junior officer left in charge. They were back in George's office by five minutes to five. George rang Milo's secretary to see if he was back. The answer was no.

Rod was standing at the window when the five o'clock hooter sounded. He watched the torrent of workmen surging towards the gates. It looked as though a plug had been pulled. Within minutes the shipyard was deserted.

'We'd better go home too,' George said. 'We don't know whether Milo will come back now or not. Better if we do what we normally would.'

Rod drove home almost holding his breath, oppressed by the feeling that disaster was about to overtake him. He followed a hire car up the drive. Inside he could see his parents, together with that nurse who was claiming to be his daughter. She was an interfering busybody, come back to haunt him. She had red hair, but apart from that he couldn't see much of a likeness to Alicia. Surely she was just trying it on? She'd convinced his mother she was genuine, but he doubted it. He wouldn't feel an aversion like this if she was his own flesh and blood.

Rod did not feel sociable and wanted to go straight to his own quarters, but he knew he must not. They would expect him to pass the time of day. The nurse had taken the wheelchair out of the boot and set it up on top of the front steps.

'Hello, Ma,' he said. 'Have you had a good day?'

He watched the nurse and Pa help his mother up the steps. It was painful to see how slow she was, and that he couldn't help made him feel useless.

'Yes. Charlotte took me to a bookshop, and we had tea in town.'

She was surprisingly cheerful. Rod was glad to escape and go to his own rooms. He found Meriel stretched out on the sofa reading a book, and the baby asleep on the floor. The place was a tip as usual, with toys everywhere, but it seemed he'd have to get used to that. He strode through to his bedroom, taking off his jacket as he went, meaning to change into something more comfortable, and caught his daughter playing with his things. She'd dragged Meriel's dressing stool in front of his tallboy and had the top drawer open. This wasn't the first time. He'd forbidden her to come into their room.

'What on earth d'you think you're doing?' he thundered.

Becky was equally surprised to see him. She leapt down and tried to make her escape, but he caught her arm and swung her round.

'Haven't I told you to stay out of here?'

Her teddy bear was propped against his pillows with two of his tie pins stuck into its fur. His best cuff links were draped round the bear's ears.

'You naughty girl!' he screamed, as he caught sight of the box in which he kept all these things open on top of the tallboy. Three of his watches were laid out in a line, but he was worried because he kept his keys hidden in that box.

He dragged Becky across and rummaged in what remained inside. His key ring was not there. He panicked. Had Meriel found it and opened up his little cache?

His temper snapped. 'You little brat! Why can't you do as you're told?' He brought his hand down heavily against her firm little buttocks, and she opened her mouth and yelled.

That brought Meriel to the bedroom door, blinking helplessly. 'She's only playing, Rod. She's not doing any harm.'

'She needs to be taught a lesson. When I tell her not to do something, she mustn't. Where's Joan? She should be here looking after her.'

'She went to the kitchen to have her tea. She's only been gone ten minutes.'

Becky opened her mouth and cried louder. 'Shut up,' he screamed at her. 'If you don't shut up this minute, I'll give you something to cry for.'

Her cries reached a climax, and he raised his arm again to deliver his promise. Meriel whirled at him and tore his other hand away from the child, who ran screaming out of the room.

That was the last thing Rod had expected. Meriel never stood up to him.

'You don't know your own strength. You were hurting her.' Meriel was no longer soft and pliable. He'd never seen such determination on her face. 'Stop it. I'll not have this.'

He lashed out angrily at her, his blow catching her across the nose. 'Why can't you discipline that child? You let her do whatever she likes.'

Meriel screamed then and he was shocked to see blood pouring down her face. She was in tears.

'What's come over you? You're a horrible bully, belting me and little Becky.' She turned and ran from the room.

Rod's heart was in his mouth as he opened his wardrobe door. The drawer in which he hid his money was still locked. He was drawing a sigh of relief when he saw his keys on the floor. Had Becky dropped them there and Meriel not even seen them? Had nothing untoward happened to his private cache? He unlocked the drawer. Inside was his mahogany tea caddy, and he unlocked that too. Nothing inside had been touched.

He pushed a handful of notes into his wallet and locked up again. Then, carefully, he removed the two small keys and threaded them instead on the ring holding his car keys. All the time he could hear Becky, wailing as loud as she could.

Behind him a querulous little voice piped, 'Where's Mummy gone?' His little son came and pulled sleepily at his trousers. He picked up the teddy bear, tossed his cuff links off it and pushed it into Robin's arms.

He decided he'd go to the golf club for a drink. He could ring Milo from there to find out what had happened this afternoon.

Charlotte had made Clarissa comfortable and was helping her back to the little upright tub chair she found most comfortable in their sitting room. Jeremy was looking through the two books Clarissa had chosen for herself that afternoon.

'They both look good. I wouldn't mind reading them myself when you've finished.'

Charlotte knew they saw it as something of a milestone that Clarissa could go out to make her own choice. Jeremy put the books on the table beside her. 'How about a glass of sherry now?' he asked.

He was pouring her one when, after a perfunctory tap on the door, Meriel burst in. They were all shocked to see the blood and tears streaming down her face.

Jeremy was appalled. 'Did Rod do that?'

'Yes.' Meriel was so agitated she could hardly tell them what had happened.

Charlotte took her arm. 'Come and lie down on my bed, that should stop the bleeding.' She led her into the bedroom murmuring comforting words, tossed her pillows on a chair and threw her bath towel over the counterpane. Within moments she had Meriel flat on her back with a hand towel against her nose.

Meriel lifted the towel away for a moment to sob, 'I tried to stop Rod whacking Becky. I saw you do it, Charlotte. It seemed pathetic to stand by and let him hurt her.' Blood was surging out. 'But he turned on me.'

'Where is Becky?' Charlotte asked. 'And what about Robin?'

'There . . . With Rod.'

'Lie still. I'll be back in a minute.'

From the door, Jeremy asked, 'Is there anything I can do?'

Charlotte nodded at him. 'Get her some ice, if you would. Wrap it in a face flannel and put it across the bridge of her nose. It may help to stem the flow. I'll run down and make sure the children are all right.'

She could hear them both crying as she rushed along the passage. She hugged Becky and lifted her closer to Robin so she could put an arm round him too.

'Where's your daddy?' she asked.

'Gone,' Robin sobbed.

Chapter Twenty

ROD GULPED at his whisky and tried to unwind. George Alderton had been only too willing to join him in the bar. It had taken them the best part of an hour to contact Miles and get him to join them.

Now he sat between them sipping calmly at his drink, looking relaxed and at ease. 'I'm sorry, Rod. I didn't know you'd be worried.'

'Of course we were worried. What are we supposed to think when we find a policeman's been to the office and you've gone off with him?'

'Sorry. My wife told them I was at work, that's why they came. It had nothing to do with either of you. Nothing to do with the firm. It was to do with my brother, a petrol scam we run.'

Rod felt another stab of alarm. 'I've bought petrol coupons from you.'

'They aren't looking for my customers.'

'Not yet.' His mouth was suddenly dry. 'You told me to go to that garage on the corner of Drayton Road.'

'Not any more. I'll let you know when we've fixed up another safe outlet. We've been charged and we'll plead guilty. We'll both get a small fine and that will be the end of it.'

'But how can you be so sure?' George asked.

'My brother knows the police officer. It's all fixed, I promise you.'

Rod sucked at his teeth. 'Then the arrangements we have at the yard . . . ?'

'As safe as they've ever been. Nothing at all to worry about.'

Rod didn't share his confidence. Milo's plan to add to the yard's earnings was brilliant and had worked profitably for the last two years, but if Pa ever heard of it he'd have a fit. What if the police started to probe Milo's background? It wouldn't take them five minutes to turn up trouble and the obvious next step was to investigate the yard. If their scam came to light, the family would never forgive him.

'I've got to go.' Milo stood up. 'There's something else I must do. I'll see you both in the office in the morning.'

Rod watched him pause to pass the time of day with someone else before he went. Milo knew everybody and had too many fingers in too many pies. Rod felt he'd been badly frightened.

He asked for the second time, 'Do you think we should give up now, while we're still in the clear?'

'I don't know.' George drained his glass. 'Milo thinks it's still safe.'

'But is it worth the candle? There's a limit to what we can use small change for.'

'I don't know about you, but there's plenty I can use it for.'

'It isn't being put through your business, George. I've a lot more to lose.'

'Possibly. How about another drink?'

'Thanks. I could do with something to eat too.'

'A bite of supper then before we go home?'

'Yes,' Rod agreed, remembering then what had happened at home before he'd come out. He'd been afraid Meriel had found his cache of money. She hadn't but he'd thumped her, and he'd have some explaining to do.

He'd been under a lot of stress.

A few days later, Jeremy was just finishing his second cup of afternoon tea when Roderick came into his parents' sitting room.

'You asked to see our figures, Pa.' He put two documents down on the table beside him.

Some time ago, Jeremy had actually asked Rod to bring home the accounting ledgers, suggesting that if he brought them on a Saturday afternoon he could browse through them on Sunday, and they could be taken back on Monday morning. Now, after this long delay, Rod had brought him some of last year's printed figures: the trading account, the profit and loss account and the balance sheet.

'I think I've seen these already,' he said mildly. Rod knew he was still a shareholder; he'd surely know these would have been sent to him? He sat staring at them. They were good and showed a very healthy business. Unbelievably good. Too good? Was Rod massaging the figures? Why was he, Jeremy, so suspicious?

Rod looked pale and worried; he'd been reluctant to show him anything. If these figures were correct, he should be singing and dancing. He should have brought them to show him as soon as they'd been drawn up at the end of the financial year.

Instead, he was actually in a cold sweat. Jeremy could see beads of moisture across his son's nose and on his forehead. He was growing increasingly worried about Rod. He was very stressed and unable to hide it any longer. He didn't even seem comfortable in his father's company.

'Would you like a drink, Rod?' He could see he was tempted for a moment.

'No thanks, Pa. I've brought work home to do.' He was on his feet and away before Jeremy could press him again to bring the books home for him to see.

Both he and Clarissa had been shocked and worried when they'd seen Meriel and heard he'd used his fists against her again. Particularly when she said she'd been trying to stop him beating Becky. It was inexcusable behaviour. In their worst moments they'd never thought Rod capable of that. Jeremy had asked him if he had any worries and he'd said no, none at all. But quite obviously he had, and that he didn't want to talk about them made Jeremy even more suspicious. Things didn't add up.

Rod seemed at the end of his tether and Jeremy wondered if Charlotte's turning up had upset him. At Rod's age, he'd been on top of everything, but Rod wasn't. He'd spent his life trying to support his son, build up his confidence and teach him what he needed to understand to run the business. But he was beginning to see him as weaker and less able than he was himself. Not physically, of course, but in every other way.

He was sure Rod was trying to prevent him from taking a closer look at the business accounts, and that made him fear there could be something in them that he wanted to hide. He had to get to the bottom of it.

He would have liked to order a car to take him to the yard to collect the ledgers. But there were so many, he wouldn't be able to carry them all, even if he persuaded the staff to let him bring them away.

He made careful plans, because he was afraid he'd need help. Accordingly, he happened to be in the hall late in one afternoon, and saw Rod getting out of his Jaguar as he came home from work.

'How are things at the yard?' he asked. It was a question he asked too often. Rod was very reluctant to tell him anything these days. Jeremy followed him down the passage to his sitting room.

'It's my birthday next week,' he confided. 'My eighty-second.'

Rod swept a collection of toys off an armchair and threw himself on it. Jeremy moved a stuffed panda to the other end of the sofa and sat down facing him.

'I've been thinking it would make a bit of a treat if I invited old Walter Collingwood to take a look round the yard and then have lunch in the canteen with me.'

He saw Rod pull himself up in his chair. He looked shocked at the suggestion and said, 'I'll take you to have lunch at the Adelphi. You can ask Walter, and Ma too. You'll enjoy that more.'

'No, Rod, thanks. Your mother's planning a celebratory meal like that in the evening. What Walter and I want to see is how much harder the yard is working now. You have your own job to do; there's no need for you to bother about us.'

That didn't go down well either. Rod looked almost scared. 'Pa, there's much more security now there's a war on. I'm not sure . . .'

'Lots of people will remember us, I expect. I don't think we'll have any trouble getting in. Has that ship gone out yet? The one Walter's grandson was on?'

'What ship was that?'

'The *Atlantic Voyager*, a freighter. I told you about young . . .'

Rod was screwing up his face. 'I don't think it has.'

'It's been in some time, hasn't it? Walter has another relative on a frigate which he believes is coming in. HMS *Lagan*.'

'That came in today.'

'There you are then,' Jeremy said disarmingly. 'Walter was suggesting we might invite ourselves on to one or the other for lunch instead of going to the canteen. We old codgers just want something a little different to do.'

Rod sat silently staring straight in front of him.

'You don't mind us coming in for lunch? There've been such changes since we retired.'

'Pa, you won't find it interesting. It's all rush and noise these days. The hammering will give you a headache and nobody will have time to speak to you. In fact, most of the people you knew have retired. It's a very different place now. There's so much war work.'

*

When his father went, Rod got up and poured himself a glass of whisky, then threw himself back on the chair. He could hear Meriel in what passed as their kitchen, giving the children their evening meal. Becky kept saying she didn't like eggs, and was making more fuss than usual. Meriel was pleading with her to try them.

He got up and shut the door. They were getting on his nerves and so was Charlotte. He still found it hard to believe it was Abigail. She'd come back like a ghost from the past, raking up painful memories of his earlier troubles. The sight of her bustling round was enough to sap all his strength.

But even worse, Rod knew his father had every intention of visiting the yard on his birthday and nothing he could say would stop him. His palms were clammy with sweat; he felt everything was against him, as though a net was closing round him.

Pa said he meant to take Walter Collingwood to 'look round the yard'. That could be his way of saying to examine the books. Probably was. Rod's heart sank further. If Walter Collingwood had the accounts spread in front of him, Rod was afraid it wouldn't take him half an hour to spot the fraud he and Milo were perpetrating. Walter had been chief account-ant there for over a decade: he'd have no trouble. Pa could probably do it too, on his own. And worst of all, Rod couldn't see any way to stop him.

But today was Thursday, and Pa's birthday wasn't until next Wednesday. They still had a few days to think of some way round this. Perhaps Miles could work up an alternative set of figures to put Walter and Pa off. He was good at that sort of thing.

He went to the phone to ring him and managed to convey the sense of crisis he felt. Milo said he'd meet him in the bar at the golf club in half an hour.

Meriel's face was like thunder when he told her he was going out. 'What about your dinner? Mrs Shipley has managed to get pork chops for us.'

'I'm not hungry,' he said. How could he be with this hanging over him? 'Something urgent has come up that I have to deal with. I'll have a snack or something at the club. Don't worry about me.'

He had another whisky in the bar while he waited for Milo, and since he still hadn't arrived when he finished it he ordered a third. Morrow was apologetic when he finally appeared.

'Sorry,' he said. 'I was held up just when I was setting out.'

Rod felt a wave of horror. 'It wasn't anything to do with the police coming to the office the other day?'

'No. That blew over, just as I said it would. I'll just get myself a drink before I sit down. Another for you too?'

He came back a minute or two later with two glasses. 'What's this new problem?'

Rod told him, letting it all spill out.

Milo's face was stony. 'You'll have to choke them off. Stop them looking at the books. It's the only way.'

'I've tried, but Pa's suspicious, and he's got the bit between his teeth. I don't think I can.'

'You've got to, Rod. Don't let them near the books. It'll stick out a mile to them. Why don't you give them those sheets I had printed off? The balance sheet and profit and loss account . . .'

'I've already done that, but Pa had seen them before. He wants to see the day to day account books.'

'No, that's impossible. We'll all be in the mire if you let him near those.'

'Can't you doctor the figures a bit? Make it look OK?'

'No. They'd see through them. There isn't time to do a good job.'

'Five days . . .'

'The safest way is not to let that pair near the books.'

'But I can't stop Pa.'

Milo put his face near to Rod's. 'You've got to. Lose the damned account books if you have to. Burn them, for God's sake. Get rid of them any way you like.'

He could see Miles was starting to get impatient with him. 'How can I do that?'

'We've got the weekend. I'll sort out the books we don't want them to see and take them home with me. I'll bring them back when they've been and gone. If the accounts are not in the office they can't see them, can they?'

Rod was appalled. 'It'll make Pa even more suspicious.' He could see him sitting there demanding their return.

'Better to have him suspicious than certain we're up to no good. He's not the police anyway, nor the Admiralty.'

'He'll be worse,' Rod gasped. 'He'll bring it to a dead stop.'

'We must try to think up something better, then.' Miles stood up. 'Both of us. That's the best I can do on the spur of the moment.'

Rod felt desperate as he watched him go. Then he got himself another whisky and sat nursing it. Pa must never find out. He still thought of the shipyard as his own business, though he'd handed over its management and a large part of the stock to him. It was the family business that he was supposed to hand on to Robin in his turn.

There were all sorts of things Pa must never know. Things he'd done Pa wouldn't approve of and things he'd kept from him for years. But this fraud was the worst, and he was afraid he was about to be found out.

When the bar was about to close, he went round to George's flat. After all, he was the present company secretary, and if he and Milo went down, so would George. He needed to keep him up to date with what was happening. Fortunately George was a widower and did not go to bed early. He hoped they could put their heads together and come up with a better plan than Milo's.

George had no whisky; he preferred gin and tonic. Rod knew it wasn't a good idea to change, but he did. They spent several hours talking the problem through and came to the same conclusion, that they had a few days to think about it, and possibly they'd come up with something.

It was George who suggested it was time Rod went home, and offered to try to call a cab for him. There seemed no point when his Jaguar was outside and there was nothing on the roads at this hour. The blackout meant the city was as dark as hell, but he knew he'd have no difficulty. He turned into the drive of Burford House and heard the familiar crunch of gravel under his tyres. He wasn't sure how it happened – he'd meant to swing the car round and bring it to a stop as he always did. But somehow he misjudged it, and there was a resounding clash of tearing metal as he hit the stone balustrade running up the side of the front steps.

The sudden violent stop made him bang his head on the steering wheel and hurt his neck. Rod sat feeling dazed and a little sick, while everything eddied round him. It took quite an effort to open the door and get out of the car. Glass crunched under his feet. When he saw how much damage he'd done he was shocked. His car was a mess of crumpled metal at the front. He lost his footing on the front steps and fell, hurting his knee. When he reached the front door, he couldn't find his keys so he hammered on it with his fists and shouted for Meriel to come and let him in.

*

Charlotte knew something unusual had wakened her. She lay listening in the darkness until she heard Clarissa call her name. She quickly slid out of bed to pull on her dressing gown and slippers.

Clarissa was capable of getting herself to the bathroom nowadays, but Charlotte had told her to continue to wake her in the night if she should want to go. She was afraid Clarissa might fall if she were still half asleep.

When she reached her bedroom, she found Jeremy already there at the window, peering out into the night. They were more concerned about the noise outside than anything else.

'It sounded like Roderick.' Jeremy looked worried. 'But it's nearly three o'clock. What's he doing out there at this time?'

Clarissa said, 'Everything's gone quiet now.'

'Shall I pop down and find out what's happened?' Charlotte suggested, but as soon as she opened the door to the stairs they could all hear Becky crying. A distressed Meriel swept into their sitting room carrying her weeping daughter.

'Rod's drunk,' she sobbed. 'He's just come home and woken us all up. He's hurt himself – there's blood streaming down his face. Becky's frightened of him.'

Charlotte could see that she was frightened herself. She asked, 'Is Robin still asleep?'

'I don't know.'

'Don't worry, I'll go and see.' Charlotte was putting a brave face on it. They were all worried. It seemed something terrible must have happened to cause Rod to frighten them like this. 'If Robin's awake I'll bring him up.'

'Bring him even if he's asleep,' Meriel said. 'I'd rather he was here with us.'

Charlotte went nervously down to Meriel's suite of rooms. The door was ajar and the lights were on. She could hear Robin crying in his bedroom.

'Hello,' she called. 'Hello, Rod? Are you there?' Robin stopped crying at the sound of her voice and as she rushed through the living room there was no sign of Rod. Robin was standing in his cot, his face wet with tears.

'It's all right, pet,' she said, wrapping his eiderdown round him and picking him up. 'Let's go and find your mummy.'

Meriel always picked up his older sister first, which seemed hard on

239

Robin. He clasped his arms tightly round her neck as she carried him upstairs. Meriel had recovered somewhat, and put Becky down to sleep on one of the two sofas in Clarissa's sitting room.

'We'd better make a little bed for Robin on the floor,' Jeremy suggested, pulling cushions from the easy chairs. Charlotte tried to put the child down on them but he howled and hung on to her neck.

'He's frightened,' she said. 'Probably woke up and found himself alone. Rod doesn't seem to be there.'

Meriel cuddled her baby. 'You're all right now, darling,' she told him.

Clarissa said, 'Meriel was going to make us all a cup of tea, but there's no milk left up here. I expect Mrs Shipley has more in the fridge downstairs.'

'I'll go and see,' Charlotte told her. 'I'd better see if I can find Rod too, hadn't I? If he's been hurt?'

'Shall I come with you?' Jeremy offered. 'Don't you find the old house creepy? It doesn't seem right to send a young girl like you down alone.'

'I'll be all right,' Charlotte said quickly. Jeremy still needed a walking stick, and he didn't find getting up and down stairs easy. 'There's nothing to be scared of here, is there?'

'Of course not,' Clarissa said easily. 'While you're down there, take a look on the front steps, Charlotte. I'm sure what woke us up was outside. It sounded as though something fell off the roof. We can't see from the windows here.'

'It was Rod,' Meriel said.

Charlotte put all the lights on before venturing down the wide oak staircase. Despite what she'd said to Jeremy, she did find it creepy. She crossed the wide entrance hall, the wind and the moonlight making moving shadows on the black and white floor. It looked ghostly. She told herself she mustn't let Meriel's fears play on her mind.

She opened the front door and gasped with shock. Roderick's Jaguar was impaled against the stone balustrade at the bottom of the steps, its front wheels raised a foot off the drive. To get it like that, he must have driven straight into it at speed. Her heart was racing. The Jaguar was in shadow and she was standing too far above it to see inside properly. But it looked as though Rod was still hunched in the driver's seat. Had Meriel said he'd come indoors? She couldn't remember.

She hesitated, shivering on the step in the cold night air. For an awful moment she imagined she'd find Rod dead in the driver's seat. She had to find out one way or the other.

Taking a deep breath, she pulled the huge doormat forward to stop the door shutting behind her and crept down to look more closely. The car was empty. There was splintered glass all over the steps and the front bumper had been torn off. The bonnet was up and the engine was now a mess of twisted metal. She fled back up the steps, her head swimming with relief.

But after an accident like that, Rod must surely be hurt. Becky had been frightened by the blood on his face. Carefully closing the front door behind her, she went back to his rooms, to look round again. She even peeped in his bedroom to see if he'd passed out on his bed. There was no sign of him, so she switched off all the lights and went to see if she could find some milk.

The main kitchen was in darkness, except for a green glow from the light on the fridge, which was humming away. She felt for the electric switch and was shocked to see a manly bulk filling Mrs Shipley's Windsor chair. His arms were folded on the kitchen table, with his head and shoulders slumped on top.

She jerked back in alarm. 'Oh!'

Roderick slowly lifted his head and turned to look at her. His face was covered with blood and some had dripped down his shirt and jacket.

Charlotte went to him. 'You've had a nasty knock on the head. Are you in pain?' He stared back at her, his eyes expressionless. 'I'd better get some warm water to wash it off. Then we'll be able to see how much damage you've done and whether you'll need stitches.'

She was peering closer, wondering if she could see fresh blood welling up on his temple. Suddenly, his arm shot out and caught at the neck of her pyjama jacket. He dragged her closer, twisting it tighter and tighter. She screamed and tried to back away, but she couldn't shake him off.

'What did you have to come back here for?' he said through his teeth. 'This is all your fault.'

'My fault?' She thought he was blaming her for his car crash. 'Don't be silly, I was asleep when you did it, we all were.'

'Asleep? Yes, but you aren't now. You've come back, bringing bad memories to haunt me.'

Charlotte was struggling. Her cheeks were flaming, and she could barely speak. 'Let me go, you're choking me. What memories . . .'

'The shipwreck. I nearly drowned you, didn't I? I wish I had. That would have stopped you coming back.'

Charlotte couldn't believe her ears. It had to mean he meant to kill her. Her teeth were chattering with terror. 'I don't haunt . . .'

'I drowned Alicia and Captain Merryhew on the night of that storm. Others as well, so what would one more matter? The captain wanted to put into Holyhead harbour that night and wait till the weather cleared, but I persuaded him not to. I was impatient to get home. He said I was ordering him to sail on for Liverpool against his better judgement. As things turned out, he was right. If I hadn't done that you'd have been brought up here by Alicia and me in the bosom of your family. What do you think of that?'

Charlotte had managed to squeeze her fingers inside the neckline of her pyjama jacket and force it open wide enough to take the pressure off her throat. She could breathe again, think again, even speak.

'I thought you didn't believe I was your daughter?'

He looked up at her blankly then, his eyes rolling drunkenly in his head.

Was he drunk? He certainly smelled of alcohol. She tore his fingers away and twisted out of his grasp, backing towards the door. She wasn't going to let him near enough to do that again.

He pulled himself to his feet, glaring at her as though he'd never seen her before. 'You conniving bitch,' he swore. 'You're nothing but trouble.'

Charlotte thought then that, after all, he was not just drunk. She turned to flee upstairs, wanting to get back to Jeremy and Clarissa. He was shouting abuse after her and she understood only too well why Meriel and Becky were frightened of him.

CHAPTER TWENTY-ONE

CHARLOTTE COLLAPSED on the sofa, her face damp with perspiration. They all stared at her in amazement as, puffing and coughing, she tried to relate what had happened.

'I thought he was going to strangle me. He's in a very strange mood.'

'Oh, my God.' Meriel swallowed hard. 'I told you. He's gone for you as well?'

Jeremy looked shocked. 'What did he say?'

Charlotte had another fit of coughing. 'That he blames himself for Alicia's death.'

Clarissa's face went paper white. 'It's been playing on his mind, d'you think?'

Meriel's eyes were sparkling with tears again. 'Yes, he's been saying things like that to me for ages,' she said. 'He can't believe you're his daughter. He doesn't like you, but I told him everybody else does.'

'I think he accepts that I am his daughter now,' Charlotte said. 'But said I'm nothing but trouble.'

'Me too,' Meriel said. 'He keeps telling me that Alicia was a much better wife to him than I am.'

Charlotte tried to comfort her. 'I don't think he knows what he's saying.'

Clarissa was screwing her face up in thought. 'He seemed very strange after the shipwreck, but then he got over that. Recently . . .'

Meriel shuddered. 'I think he's mad. Mad as a March hare.'

'Mentally ill, you mean,' Charlotte said.

'I'm sure he is. Don't you?'

'I really don't know much about mental illness.'

It seemed nobody else did. They sat in troubled silence for a few moments, then Meriel said, 'I'm scared he's really going to harm somebody, particularly Becky.'

Clarissa asked, 'Do you think we should make sure he's all right?'

'Yes,' Charlotte agreed, but baulked at the thought of facing him again.

When Jeremy said, 'We ought to go together,' she stood up and took his arm.

'I'll come too,' Meriel said quickly. Clearly she felt she had to.

'Yes,' Jeremy said. 'Safety in numbers.'

The house was quiet as they crossed the landing. Charlotte suggested the back stairs so Jeremy could use the chair lift. She wanted him to have enough strength left to deal with Rod. They found him still slumped in the Windsor chair at the kitchen table, his head down on his arms. He seemed to be fast asleep.

'Whoever would have thought Rod would come to this?' Jeremy said sadly. 'We could just leave him here; he'll come to no harm.'

'He's unlikely to stay asleep sitting there. Not for the rest of the night.'

Meriel crept to the fridge without looking at her husband, giving him a wide berth.

'There's a couple of pints of milk here. I'll take one back and make some tea.' Her clattering footsteps sounded fear-driven as she rushed back upstairs.

Charlotte peered at the dried blood on the side of Rod's face and neck. She hesitated. She was employed here as a nurse and felt it was her responsibility to make sure he was all right. 'We ought to sponge this off so we can see what sort of injury he's got underneath. D'you think we should get him to bed first?'

'What if he turns violent again?' Jeremy asked.

'Then we get out of his way, but he's quietened down now. I'll go and switch the lights on.' Charlotte whisked off to do that and open all the doors between the kitchen and Rod's bedroom.

She came back. 'Come on, Rod,' she said briskly, putting a hand under his arm and giving him a heave. 'On your feet now. We're going to take you to bed.' She hoped they'd find the strength to manage it. 'You don't want to spend the rest of the night on that chair, do you?'

He only half woke up. With one each side of him he shuffled obediently between them to his bedroom. She whipped away the eiderdown so he could sit on the edge of his bed. She took off his tie and he fell back against the pillows. His father undid his shoes and took them off.

'Shall we leave him?' he suggested. Roderick was breathing deeply and seemed instantly fast asleep again.

'Hang on a sec.'

In the bathroom she wetted a flannel under the tap, took a towel back to the bedroom with her and tried to wash away the dried blood. He moaned and moved his head away.

'Leave him,' Jeremy said anxiously.

'Here's the cut . . . it's quite deep. Probably it will need a stitch or two, but it's not bleeding now.'

'I don't want you to wake him again, Charlotte. We'll get the doctor to come in the morning.'

'Right.'

She covered him with the eiderdown and put off the light. 'It's now half past four. He looks as though he'll sleep through till morning.'

She felt spent, and after a cup of Meriel's tea she settled down for what was left of the night and slept until eight o'clock.

Meriel and her family had slept in the sitting room, but now the children were awake and running about in their nightclothes.

'I'll have to go down to get our things,' Meriel worried. 'Will you come with me?'

They crept down like mice, but Roderick hardly seemed to have moved. He was still asleep on the bed. Meriel snatched up their clothes and they ran back upstairs to safety.

'He's still flat out,' Charlotte reported to his parents.

'Will you ring Dr Staples?' Clarissa asked. 'Tell him what happened and ask him to come and see Rod.'

Charlotte did so, and told the doctor he'd had an accident in his car and had a cut on his head that would probably need a stitch or two.

Jeremy rang the garage and asked them to tow the Jaguar away for repair.

'We'll have to wait and see how much damage he's done to the front steps and the balustrade.' He sighed. 'But we're going to need a builder to fix that too.'

Meriel was wary of taking the children down to their own rooms. She was afraid Rod would turn on them again. When the doctor came, she wept as she told him Rod had been very aggressive and she thought he was mentally ill.

245

It was Charlotte who went down with the doctor. They had to wake Rod so he could have a few stitches put in his head and the wound dressed. He hardly seemed to notice, and was soon fast asleep again.

Upstairs once more, the doctor told Clarissa and Meriel, 'There's no history of previous mental illness, and none in the family. He's quite comatose now. I think he's just had too much to drink.'

Jeremy was a very troubled man. He'd felt absolutely exhausted as he'd ridden upstairs on the chairlift last night. He must have looked it because Charlotte had said, 'Why don't you go straight back to bed?'

Meriel had poured a cup of tea for him and Charlotte had carried it in and put it on his bedside table. But when he got into bed, sleep seemed miles away.

He was desperately worried about Rod. He knew he'd been drinking, he could smell it on his breath, but Rod wasn't a heavy drinker. Jeremy had never known him come home drunk before. He must have been really under the influence to hit the front steps like that.

Even more worrying was the violence he was showing to the girls, hitting Becky and attacking Meriel and Charlotte. They were suggesting he was mentally ill. Usually, he didn't give much credence to Meriel's opinion, but to tell your present wife you much preferred your first was the height of folly, and cruel to boot. Surely no man in his right mind would do that?

Jeremy was afraid something might have happened to cause Rod to act in this way, and decided not to wait until his birthday. Tomorrow, Rod would be sleeping off this bender. He and Walter would be able to go to the yard and look at the books without him fussing round them.

Dawn was breaking when he finally dropped off to sleep, and it was later than usual when he woke up, but he felt better. Well enough to put his plans in hand. He felt sufficiently driven to ring Walter before he had breakfast. Walter was not convinced they'd find evidence of fraud in the books, but he was willing to go along with him.

He came to pick Jeremy up in his taxi and Jeremy tried to tell him on the journey what was making him suspicious.

Walter said, 'If it's last year's balance sheet that's bothering you, we should look at last year's figures, not those for this year.'

'But that wouldn't tell us if the problem was still ongoing. Really we need the books for last year as well as this.'

'Last year's ledgers will all have been closed and archived, and if the staff know we're going through two years' figures they're bound to think we suspect something.'

'If we can get a key to the archives, you could fish out what you need. Who would know we had both years?'

'I hope you're right. It'll take us ages, though, to work through two years' figures.'

'I'll try to get the books for the present financial year. It ends in April, so we'll have figures for almost a complete year there. It shouldn't take too long to see if there's anything to be worried about.'

Walter was frowning. 'If there is a fiddle going on, Miles Morrow and George Alderton must know about it. As chief accountant and company secretary, they'd have to be in the know. I'm worried they might try to stop us getting anywhere near the books. There could be other people involved too that you don't know about.

'By coming sooner than I told Rod we would, I hope we'll take them by surprise, and have it all over and done with before they realise we're on the premises.'

'Easy enough to say,' Walter told him. Jeremy knew he had butterflies in his stomach too. It was getting on for ten thirty by the time they arrived at the yard and it seemed busy.

'Busier than in our day,' Walter said.

'We can see that from the figures Morrow drew up for last year. Business is booming, income is growing.'

'They're doing better than we ever did.'

'Only because of the war. Everybody's got more work.'

Jeremy found it exhilarating to think he wasn't past working, not yet, but he could sense Walter's unease and it was rubbing off on him.

Jeremy looked round Rod's office. It was quite grand for a company engaged in ship repairs. He felt at home here. Miss Kent didn't look a day older, but she never had seemed young. She was pleased to see them and gave them a warm welcome.

'Rod isn't well this morning,' Jeremy told her. 'I don't think he'll be in today. He and I decided it would be a good opportunity to take an overall look at the profitability of the company.' She didn't seem to see anything strange in that. 'Do you have the keys to the archives?'

They were produced and Walter set off to see what he could find. Jeremy started by ringing the manager of each department. He had a little chat to those he knew and introduced himself to those he did not.

'I'm in the office today to run a general check through the company accounts. I want you to send over all your permanent day to day records, and all the ledgers from which the management accounts will be prepared at the end of the financial year.'

'Everything?'

'Not the petty cash books, but everything else.'

Jeremy moved into the conference room, deciding they'd have more space to work there.

Walter returned and started studying the documents Roderick had given to Jeremy, the profit and loss account and the balance sheet that Miles Morrow had drawn up.

As the books were delivered, Pixie Kent brought them in and spread them out on the conference table.

'We'll have room to work in here. Nobody else is planning to use this room today?'

'No, Mr Barrington Brown.'

She brought them coffee and they settled down. Both Jeremy and Walter were familiar with the current accounting system. It hadn't been changed since they'd run the business.

'The figures look extremely good,' Walter said.

'Too good?'

'Not necessarily.' Walter wasn't yet convinced. 'We'll soon see, anyhow. The true picture of what is being earned and spent is in these day to day ledgers.'

Jeremy knew that was true. At the end of the year, those figures would be added together by Miles Morrow to show the overall management picture.

Fortunately, it was Friday. On Saturdays, the yard usually worked a half day unless they were very busy. It would be possible to keep the books here until Monday morning, if they needed to.

Half an hour later, Walter said, 'The Ministry of War Transport is providing most of the income.'

'That's what you'd expect, isn't it? Most of the repair work is the result of war damage?'

'Yes, but in the Great War I always divided the company income into what was earned by repair work and what came from wartime allowances.'

'How d'you mean?'

'The Ministry pays the wages for men to work on ships urgently needed for convoy duty.'

'It's done that throughout the war.'

'Yes, but that isn't made clear. It's Morrow's duty to list and detail all sources of income. Why doesn't he do it? We ought to be able to see all that at a glance from the figures he's bringing forward to the profit and loss account.'

'In fact,' Jeremy said, 'there are monthly sums coming in to cover wages. Big sums, but it doesn't say for how many men, nor can I see where the figures are added together for the year.'

'There must be another ledger somewhere. Each workman should be named and the capacity in which he is employed given – welder or riveter or whatever – together with the hours worked and the amount paid.'

'And the name of the vessel on which he worked.'

'Hang on.' Walter whistled through his teeth. 'Here's something from last August. Wages for two thousand men to work on HMS *Kale*, HMS *Itchen* and MV *Wayfarer*, urgently needed for convoy duty. Two thousand? That's a prodigious number.' Walter was shuffling through the documents spread in front of him. 'And why isn't that information given in the profit and loss account? And I can't find how much is received annually from that source. It's beginning to look a bit iffy.'

At that moment, the whistle blew for the lunch break.

'We ought to have something to eat,' Walter said. 'It keeps the energy levels up. Unfortunately, the *Atlantic Voyager* has gone out now, and my nephew on HMS *Lagan* has been given leave. So it looks as though the canteen is the only place we can go.'

'It might be better if we didn't,' Jeremy said. 'We don't want Rod's cronies to know we're here. They might come and throw us out.'

Miss Kent knocked to ask if they intended to go out for lunch. 'No. We don't have much time and we'd like to get this done as soon as we can.'

'If you're hungry, I could ask Mrs Cuthbert, the canteen manageress, to send you some lunch over.'

'Yes please,' Jeremy said. 'That would be very helpful.'

Fifteen minutes later, two ladies in white overalls brought in covered dishes on trays and set the other end of the conference table with a cloth and tableware.

'Smells good,' Walter said. 'I'm hungry.'

As soon as the ladies were gone, they moved up and began to eat. They were just finishing their meal when Mrs Cuthbert came to see if they were happy with what they'd received. She'd worked as canteen manageress for the past twenty years and remembered them both.

'The beef stew was excellent,' Jeremy told her.

'Your apple brown Betty and custard was good too,' Walter said. 'I really enjoyed that. Congratulate the cooks for us.'

Mrs Cuthbert's bulging figure showed she enjoyed the food here too. 'I will. Thank you, Mr Collingwood.'

'The food's as good as it's ever been, despite the rationing,' Walter said. 'Have you been busy today?'

'A full house. We're always busy. And why shouldn't we be? A good hot meal for ninepence and a cup of tea to follow for another penny. It's not only good value but it saves the rations at home.' She was beaming at them. 'We served seven hundred and thirty meals yesterday.'

'How many today?' Jeremy asked.

She laughed. 'We have to add up our figures before I can tell you that, as you very well know. But it doesn't vary much. Since the war, they all come every day, and most of the office people do too.'

'So you cater for virtually the whole staff?'

'Yes.'

'And how many is that these days?'

'Around seven hundred and seventy. There's always a few off sick or something.'

'What about last August?' Walter asked. 'You had more people working here then, didn't you?'

'Not as I remember. In fact we'll have had fewer to feed then, there's always so many on their summer holidays at that time of the year.'

As soon as she'd gone, Walter moved back up the table and opened the canteen accounts. 'That's right. She's providing between seven hundred and thirty and seven hundred and fifty meals a day.'

'Yet wages for two thousand workmen were being claimed from the Ministry of War Transport in August – and possibly every month for all we know.'

'Where are the figures for wages and salaries? They should be broken down into different departments.'

'We don't seem to have any books from the accounts department. I asked for bank balances and . . .'

Jeremy took a deep breath. 'I think you've cracked it, Walter. Is Roderick charging the Ministry of War Transport the cost of wages for two thousand men to work on ships, while actually employing and paying less than eight hundred.'

'That's what it looks like.'

'But wages for two thousand? How much would that amount to?'

'Possibly twenty thousand a week.'

'But the business isn't earning that much. Figures like that aren't reflected in these books.'

'No.' Walter looked shocked. 'Those in the know must be embezzling huge amounts week after week. It's a colossal fraud, Jeremy. Goodness knows how long it's been going on. Miles Morrow and George Alderton. Rod too, of course. I bet there are others from the Ministry in it, and naval officials as well.'

Jeremy felt as though he'd been kicked in the stomach. Rod had been using the family business to defraud the government – in wartime too! The thought of it made his toes curl with embarrassment and shame. That a son of his could do such a thing made him feel sick. 'Oh, God!' he said. 'No wonder Rod's worried.' He closed the ledgers he'd been studying and lay back on his chair. He was angry. 'Damn Roderick. I could wring his neck!'

He'd been dimly aware of voices from Miss Kent's office for the last few moments. Suddenly the door burst open and Miles Morrow rushed in looking irate, with George and Miss Kent in tow.

'Who gave you permission to come in here and send for our books like this?' he demanded.

Jeremy was about to let fly at him but Walter stood up and took over.

'We were just coming to pay our respects to you and Milo,' he said to George in his pleasant cultured voice. 'I'm glad you've popped in to see us. We're very impressed with what you're doing in the yard these days, aren't we, Jeremy?'

Jeremy thought there was something menacing about Milo and knew Walter was doing his best to get them out without conflict. He nodded and smiled. 'We are, and it's been a great pleasure to spend an hour or so looking round the old yard. Quite like old times.'

Walter was closing the account books he had in front of him. 'With

251

profits like these you can say you've turned the yard round after the depression we had in our time. And I have to say I found the the bookkeeping exemplary.'

Jeremy could see Walter had taken the wind out of Morrow's sails. Milo didn't know now whether they'd found anything amiss with the bookkeeping or not.

'Miss Kent, would you be good enough to call this number?' He handed her a card. 'It's the taxi service I usually use. They know me. Tell them we'll meet them at the north gate in about fifteen minutes.'

'Yes, sir.'

Jeremy smiled at the two men. 'We have enjoyed our day out, haven't we, Walter? Such a pleasure to come back and see so many faces we know still working here.'

George was closing the remaining ledgers on the table and piling them one on top of the other.

'Where's Roderick today?' Milo managed to get a word in at last.

'He had a bit of an accident last night,' Jeremy said.

Miles jumped on that. 'Heavens! I've been wondering where he was.' He asked sharply, 'What sort of accident?'

'In his car. I don't think he's too badly hurt, but he needed a few stitches in his head.'

As soon as the words were out of his mouth, Jeremy knew he shouldn't have said that. They needed Miles to think they'd come with Rod's knowledge and blessing. His heart began to pound. Milo was staring at him.

Walter was hurriedly taking his coat and hat from the bentwood stand. He unhooked Jeremy's coat and held it out for him.

'Why didn't you ring through to let us know?'

'Didn't Rod do that? I'm sure he said he would. As I mentioned, he isn't badly hurt.'

Walter had him by the arm and was hurrying him out.

'Good day to you both. How is your father keeping, George? Well, I hope? Give him my regards.'

As soon as they were out in the yard, Walter said, 'Did you see his face change as soon as he heard about Rod's accident? He's a villain, that one.'

Walter took Jeremy to his flat to talk over what they'd discovered and have a cup of tea and a slice of cherry cake. His slow and steady voice listing the problems they'd found, and the legal consequences, brought Jeremy out in a cold sweat. The situation was worse than he'd imagined it could be. He was tense with anger.

'What are we going to do? We can't let it go on.'

'If you report this to the police and accuse Milo and George of fraud, your son will be charged with them.'

Jeremy shivered. 'I know, but he's in it up to his neck.'

'In addition,' Walter said, 'the company's good name is involved. We none of us want Barrington Brown's Ship Repair Yard to get a name for dishonesty.'

That was going to be the hardest part. Jeremy was shocked and upset that Rod could do such a thing.

Feeling sick, he took a taxi home. The Jaguar had been towed away. The balustrade on the front steps had been demolished on one side. It had enhanced the entrance of the family residence since 1872, and Roderick had damaged that as he had their business. Fortunately, the steps could still be used.

He found Clarissa and Charlotte having their afternoon tea. He refused the offer of another cup himself. 'How has Rod been?' he asked.

'Dr Staples had to wake him up to check him over. He put five stitches in his forehead but he went back to sleep straight away. He says he doesn't think he's mentally ill, or anything like that. He reckons he was just drunk. Meriel took the children downstairs. She said she'd arranged to take them to see her sister. I think Rod's stayed in bed.'

Jeremy inveigled Clarissa into his bedroom to tell her what he and Walter had found out. He didn't want to say anything to Charlotte about it yet. He told Clarissa that he was going downstairs to have it out with Roderick right away.

CHAPTER TWENTY-TWO

As JEREMY WENT downstairs, he could feel his anger welling up again. Rod had abused the trust he'd put in him. There was no sign of Meriel or the children and the rooms were silent. He went straight to Rod's bedroom. The curtains were closed and the room was in semi-darkness. It riled him to see Rod still asleep at this time of the day. He flung the curtains open.

'Wake up. Come on, Rod, get up now.'

Rod pulled the bedclothes over his face to subdue the afternoon light. That infuriated Jeremy even more. In one angry movement he ripped them right off him.

'It's no good trying to hide under the bedclothes,' Jeremy spat out. 'I hear Dr Staples has been to see you. I know he's put five stitches into your head, but he thinks the only thing wrong with you is a bad hangover.' A dressing was held on Rod's temple with sticking plaster. His eyes looked up at his father, full of pathos. The air seemed fetid. Jeremy strode back to the window. He wanted to fling it wide open, but it was stiff and old and he had to struggle to open it a few inches.

Rod's eyes were closing again as he turned round. 'It's no good looking to me for sympathy,' he bellowed. 'Sit up, can't you?' Jeremy was suffused with anger now. 'Get up. Come on, get out of that bed. I want to talk to you. This is important and I'm not having you dozing off while I do it.' He pulled Rod off the bed and reeled him round into a small tub chair. Then he paced back and forth, too angry to stay still.

'Now you listen to me. Walter Collingwood and I have looked through the company accounts and I'm appalled at what we've found. It's fraud, isn't it? For how long have you and your cronies been milking funds from the Admiralty?'

Rod's eyes were pleading for sympathy. 'Things have been hard for my generation. Harder than for . . .'

'Rubbish. I brought that company through the Depression. It was making a profit when I handed it over to you. I came back once to sort out the mess you'd made. Now there's a war on there's more than enough work for all ship repairers to make a living.

'This business has been run by our family since 1864. You are the present caretaker, and you should be nurturing it until Robin takes over. Instead, you've been dishonest in your dealings. You've ruined our good name. What you've done is despicable.'

Jeremy said a whole lot more in the same vein. Always before, he'd held back, not wanting to rob Rod of the last vestige of self-respect. Now he was so angry, he couldn't exercise any restraint. Rod didn't deserve self-respect after this, nor was he showing signs of remorse for what he'd done.

'Whatever made you do it? Surely not for the money?'

'Yes, of course.'

'What? The firm is paying you an adequate salary, isn't it?' Jeremy thought of Rod's extravagant ways. 'You could pay yourself more.'

Rod turned agonised eyes up at him and said, 'Pa, you don't understand. I did it for you.'

That took Jeremy's breath away. 'What d'you mean, for me?'

'You want the business to make a big profit, don't you? It's all you ever think about. I knew that if I could push the profits sky high, you'd count me a success. Worthy of the Barrington Brown name.'

'Oh, my Lord,' Jeremy sank down on the edge of the bed. Rod was seeking his approval. 'But not if I knew how you were doing it. You must have known I wouldn't approve of that?'

'I'm sick of being labelled a failure, an inadequate.'

Jeremy shivered. Rod wasn't thinking straight. 'There are two victims of your fraud. The first is the Admiralty but the second is our own family business! The good name of the Barrington Brown Ship Yard! How could you be so stupid, so lacking in judgement, as to allow that to be associated with fraud?'

He saw Rod double up as he heard that, and said more gently, 'How did the scheme work?'

'It was Milo Morrow's idea.'

'Oh, I've no doubts about that. He's a crook, a wide boy, you shouldn't be employing people like that. Whatever made you get rid of Steven Ripley? Walter thought he'd make an excellent chief accountant.'

'He didn't want to stay.'

'I'm not surprised. It would have been difficult for an honest man.'

'It's standard practice to claim the cost of wages from the Ministry. All the yards do it. George thought . . .'

'George is weak, he can be talked into anything, but it's no good blaming others. It's your responsibility to make sure your business dealings are within the law. So come on, how does it work?'

Sulkily, Rod said, 'You said you knew.'

'I know you're defrauding the Ministry of War Transport by claiming wages for two thousand men while actually employing less than eight hundred. Exactly how much you put in your back pocket from it, or who is involved, I don't know. So what are you doing with these ill-gotten gains?'

Rod stared back silently at him.

'You're obviously reaping a large reward from this. Milo and George will be too. So where is it?'

'I have some of it here.' Rod got up and unlocked his wardrobe. Taking out the Victorian mahogany tea caddy, he opened it up.

'You'll have to hand back all the money you've taken.' Jeremy ran his fingers through the silver coins. 'Is this all?'

'No, I have more in strongboxes in the bank vaults.'

'Which bank?'

'The Midland and Barclays and . . .'

'Oh, God! I can't go along with this, Rod, it's too big. On Monday morning, you must call the auditors in. I want this matter cleared up right away. You must inform the police and hand all this money back. You can tell them exactly what you've got in your special deposit boxes and where you're storing them.'

'Pa, I can't just drop Milo and George . . .'

'Stop that,' Jeremy said firmly. 'No arguments. Either you do it, or I will.'

With that he turned on his heel and rode back upstairs on the chairlift. His stomach was churning, and he felt sick. He had to rush to his bathroom, where he lost Walter's tea and cherry cake. He was trembling, and tears were streaming down his face. He wept for Rod and the agony he'd seen in his eyes, and for all the hopes and dreams that had come to naught.

After a few minutes he pulled himself together. It was no good being a silly old man. No good expecting things to be as he wanted them; he'd have to cope with things as they were. He washed his face in cold water and dried it well before going back to Clarissa and Charlotte.

Roderick watched his father leave, his head held high, his back straight and determined. The outer door clicked quietly behind him, showing his control.

Into the silence that followed, Rod opened his mouth and screamed with anguish, again and again and again. There was no one to hear him except the family ghosts, the Barrington Browns who had run the shipyard with such success.

He screamed till his throat was sore and his mouth was dry. The sound, echoing round the high-ceilinged room, was frightening in its intensity. His eye caught the tea caddy standing on the rumpled bed where Pa had left it, its lid still open. He shot out of the chair, grabbed it, and spun the contents round the room. Coins and notes rained down on the floor and the bed. What use had this money ever been to him? Then he hurled the box at the wardrobe. He heard a smash and saw a jagged crack ran up the full length mirror.

Sobbing with frustration, he collapsed back on the chair, pressing his aching body back into the cushions. He was appalled at what his father had said.

'There are two victims. The first is the Admiralty but the second is our own family business! The good name of the Barrington Brown Ship Yard! How could you be so stupid, so lacking in judgement, as to allow that to be associated with fraud?'

Rod had a thumping headache and his face was wet with tears and sweat. He wiped it with his handkerchief. For more than two years, he'd been living in dread that this fraud would come to light.

'It won't.' Milo had always been confident about that. 'It's government money that's being handed to us. Nobody will ever be as careful with that as they are with their own.'

That had given Rod a prickle of anxiety. Milo was nominally in charge of his company's money, though he personally kept a watchful eye on the cheques being sent out.

'It's not as though we're billing a private company for these repairs,' Milo maintained with a smirk. 'Government money is unlimited, isn't it?

There's always plenty more where it came from. Once their top brass have sanctioned a few payments, it sets a precedent. Now the documents I send in to claim the money are hardly looked at. There's a war on and wars are expensive.'

Milo might well have been right about that, but something had made Pa and Walter Collingwood suspicious. Rod didn't know what it had been, but he'd known that once they started scratching round they'd see what Milo was doing. Pa was mustard when it came to the damn business, always had been. He still owned a large part of it and so Rod couldn't stop him snooping round.

Rod knew now he should not have allowed himself to be talked into allowing this. After all, he had more to lose than either Milo or George. They were just senior employees. He was the managing director and owned a part of the business.

Pa knew how to hurt him. He'd always expected him to fail. Rod had never been able to do anything that pleased him.

There was no way he could go to the police and tell them about the scam. To hear Pa put it in words and see his disgust had been mortifying, but even worse would come.

How was he going to tell Milo and George? They'd be furious, to say the least of it. Milo referred to it as a good little earner; he wouldn't want to lose it. But there was no way round it.

Would this mean prison for him? He was afraid it might. Possibly prison for Milo and George too. Roderick let out another wail of distress. There seemed no way out of this mess now. If he didn't go to the police, Pa would. He was in no doubt that his father meant what he'd said.

Rod had slept off and on all day and was no longer tired. He couldn't cope with any of this. There was only one thing he could do. He'd thought about it many times over the years.

He wanted to get his own back on Pa, who'd dogged him all his life. He wanted to get his own back on the whole family – he was sick of running their blasted business. Sick of this awful house too. They all thought they were so superior to him, but he was going to show them.

At some point during the day he had changed into his pyjamas, and now he reached for his dressing gown and slippers. He wasn't well – he had the mother and father of a headache and when he stood up he was shaky – but he'd do it. He went out to his car to start getting things ready and was shocked to find it gone.

He stood swaying at the top of the steps. Had his Jag been stolen?

No, there at the bottom the balustrade was a heap of stones. He remembered running into it last night. He hadn't been well. The Jag would need to be repaired. No matter, there were other cars in the stables.

He shivered and went back inside, closing the front door. There was a shorter way to the stables through the old kitchen. It was warmer here, but what a dump this place was. He couldn't understand why Pa thought so highly of it.

Mrs Shipley was cooking at the stove. 'I've got a nice bit of cod for you tonight,' she told him as he marched past. 'With mash and parsley sauce.'

'You know I don't like fish,' he told her.

'Lucky to get this. There's a war on, you know.' The stables were cold and depressing, but there were cars here he could use. Pa's old Rover had been here since the early days of the war. When the petrol shortage had begun to bite, Pa had stopped driving himself. The Bentley limousine dated from the year dot and carry one. Rod paused as he caught sight of the red MG Midget, half covered with a canvas. It had been a prized possession of his youth. He'd driven this old Standard a lot at one time, too. All the cars had been put up on blocks for the duration, to take the weight off the tyres. It was said to preserve them.

A good job he happened to have petrol. He could thank Milo for that. Since it had been rationed, Milo had been giving him petrol coupons so he could buy the stuff from a garage, but he'd also given him a couple of full jerricans he could use in an emergency. And there could be no greater emergency than this. He'd need a full tank, so he moved one jerrican near to the Rover. He could think of a use for the other one, too.

Rod leaned against the car. Pa wouldn't like him using that one but all the more reason to. Pa had never given him a chance. He was always measuring him against some hero and finding him wanting.

Rod didn't have the energy now to get the car ready to use. He'd ask what's his name to do it. Old Bill Dorking who'd worked here for donkey's years and used to chauffeur his father round at one time. When the gardeners received their calling-up papers, Pa had let him stay on to keep the garden tidy. He was living in the flat above here that had once been occupied by a groom.

Old Bill answered his knock. 'I want to use the Rover tonight,' he told him. Dorking looked less than pleased. 'Check that the battery's connected, would you? And run the engine over to make sure it'll go.'

There was a strong smell of fish as he went back through the kitchen and no sign of Mrs Shipley. He knew she'd be taking Pa's supper upstairs. If it was something like fish, she would usually cook it in two lots.

Rod was shivering by the time he reached his bedroom again and it was almost dark. He should not have gone out in his pyjamas and dressing gown. He felt stiff and achey too, after lying in bed all day.

He'd have a hot bath. He went to the bathroom and started to run it. A good long soak might help. He looked round for bath salts, the medicinal sort that would help take away his stiffness, but there was only the cosmetic stuff that Meriel bought. Fancy bottles half used, covered in the dust of ages and decorated with bows of fading ribbon. He stripped off his pyjamas, dropped them on the floor and left them there.

To help the war effort, one was supposed to use only five inches of hot water in one's tub, and early in the war Meriel or someone had painted a blue line at that level. When the water was lapping near it, Rod got in. He'd never been interested in economies like that and to ease his aches and pains he needed much more. He turned the tap full on and lay back. Within moments he could feel the water running cold. Angrily, he sat up. It was tepid now and would do his aching joints no good. He hauled himself out on the bath mat and shivering looked round for a towel.

They were piled one on top of the other on the towel rail so they never would dry. He tossed them all on the floor. Meriel had no idea about housekeeping. He returned to his bedroom and started opening drawers. There must be clean towels somewhere. He was still wet and would catch his death of cold at this rate. At last he pulled out two clean bath towels and started to rub himself dry.

He heard the door slam and a moment later his wife was in the doorway looking shocked at the state of the room.

'What's happened?' Meriel asked. 'Why are you starkers? Where's all this money come from?'

Becky was busy picking it up, chortling with joy. 'Look, Mummy. I'll be able to buy more crayons.' Robin started to do the same.

'Stop that,' Rod bellowed. He caught Becky by the arm and flung her across the room. She collapsed in a heap beside the bed and let out an ear-splitting cry.

Meriel was gripped by sudden panic. 'Rod! Don't you dare hurt her.'

Becky scrambled up and came running towards her. She clasped her in her arms, but he was turning on Robin. 'Don't!' she screeched at him. 'Don't you dare touch either of them. Have you gone stark raving mad?'

If Charlotte could stand up to Rod, Meriel felt she had to find the courage from somewhere to do the same. She mustn't let him hurt the children. They were both wailing with distress.

'Stay away from us. Don't come nearer, not even one step.'

He came bounding over with fists flying, taking not a blind bit of notice. She saw him coming and stepped back, but even so his fist caught her shoulder and sent her reeling. She was crying too, from pain as well as terror.

'What's the matter with you?' He'd always been ready to wallop Becky but it was only this year he'd started striking out at her. 'We're not staying here to be your punch bag. I'm taking the children to Francine's, where they'll be safe.'

The phone was in their sitting room, and she lifted the receiver and spoke to the operator. She heard her sister's voice. 'We're coming back,' she wept. 'I'll call a taxi and bring the kids straight over.'

She looked up to find Rod's snarling face close to her own. 'You aren't taking them anywhere.' She saw him tug the telephone wires out of the wall and the line went dead.

Becky gave a terrified scream. Meriel's legs turned to jelly. She snatched up Robin and, grabbing Becky's hand, ran upstairs with them to the grandparents and safety.

Charlotte had a lovely day. That morning, after Dr Staples had left, she'd put Clarissa through her exercise routine; she was doing them with enthusiasm now she could tell she was reaping benefit from them. She was feeling stronger and finding it easier to get about.

Veronica Terry had invited them both to have lunch with her, and Jeremy had booked a taxi for them before he left for the shipyard.

'Veronica and I used to lunch almost every week,' Clarissa told her. 'She lives in a hotel in Southport, so it's no trouble for her.'

'In a hotel?'

'Yes. She used to live in Gatacre, but her house was damaged in the raids. She was already a widow and was lonely living alone, and she

261

couldn't get any help in the house. She was scared of the raids and thought Southport would be safer, and a hotel would be the answer for her.'

'Is she happy there?'

'Yes, I think she is. It took her a while to settle – it was bound to, losing so many of her possessions like that. But now I'm sure she thinks it was the right decision.'

Veronica has met them in the foyer of the Royal Gardens Hotel looking very summery in a floral silk dress. She took them out to a wide terrace overlooking the gardens, which were magnificent at this time of the year. With so many flowers in bloom they were a riot of colour.

Sitting under a striped sunshade, they had drinks first and a lovely leisurely lunch of several courses. Charlotte looked from one to the other, amazed to think they were both her grandmother and she'd not known them until recently. Edith had always been her grandmother; not many people managed three. What a complicated family she had.

Afterwards, Veronica took her up in the lift to see her rooms. As well as a bedroom and bathroom, she had a small sitting room with a balcony overlooking the gardens, with a view beyond of the sea. On this sunny day, it all looked very comfortable and serene.

'I'm so glad I've been able to get to know you,' Veronica told her. 'Alicia was my only child. I think you're my only living relative.' She hesitated, looking diffident, 'I'd like to keep in touch.'

'Of course,' Charlotte replied, giving her cheek a little kiss.

It was mid-afternoon when they returned to Burford House. The telephone was ringing as they went upstairs, and Charlotte ran to answer it. Hearing Glyn's voice sent a thrill running down her spine. She was in a buoyant mood as she told him about having lunch with her two grandmothers.

'You're having a lovely time there,' he said, 'while I'm missing you terribly. I can't stop thinking about you. I love you so much.'

Charlotte wanted to melt into his arms.

'Am I getting too impatient? You've sorted out where you stand with your relatives, haven't you?'

'More or less, I suppose.' She dropped her voice. 'But I don't feel I can leave them yet. They can't manage on their own.'

'But eventually they will?'

'Yes, I'm sure, but I'll need to find them someone to take my place.'

'Sorry, love, I didn't mean to be pushy. I just want to marry you and keep you here with me.'

'I can think of nothing I want more,' she said. 'Just give me a bit more time to settle things here.'

'Of course, love. Forgive me.'

Charlotte was happy, with her head in the clouds. For her, the future was bright.

She and Clarissa were having afternoon tea when Jeremy came home and the atmosphere seemed suddenly very different. He was angry and upset. He'd spoken to Clarissa in private and then gone downstairs to see Roderick, who was still in bed, apparently. Meriel had taken the children to see her sister. Half an hour later Jeremy had returned, looking white and drawn.

She made tea for him, but he didn't want it. She got out the sherry bottle and poured a glass for each of them. They usually had a drink about this time, before their evening meal, but it seemed nothing would calm Jeremy down. Now she was setting the table, ready for their supper. Mrs Shipley would be bringing it up soon.

At last, Jeremy relaxed a little. Mrs Shipley came up on time with her trays of food. 'Cod with mash and parsley sauce,' she said as she put the dishes on the table. Charlotte wasn't hungry after her large lunch, and neither was Clarissa. Jeremy was pushing the food round his plate too. Little was said.

They were about to start on baked apples and custard when Meriel came rushing in with the children, both of whom were in floods of noisy tears. She came to a stop by Clarissa's chair and burst into tears herself.

'We can't live here with Rod any longer,' she wept. Clarissa put her arms round Becky to comfort her, while Jeremy lifted Robin to his shoulder and patted his back.

'Come through.' He led the way to their sitting room and nursed Robin on his knee.

Charlotte followed, pulling Meriel down on the sofa beside her. She put an arm round her shaking shoulders. 'What's happened?' she asked.

Meriel lifted up her face. It showed raw terror. 'Rod's off his head. He's gone berserk.'

'Dr Staples thought he'd just drunk too much,' Clarissa said.

'He was wrong. Rod's in a real frenzy. He's throwing money and clothes all over the floor. He's shouting and hitting out at me and the kids.' She sobbed on Charlotte's shoulder.

Jeremy handed her his handkerchief.

'Thanks. I told my sister Francine about him this afternoon. She said if we're scared of him, or he wallops Becky again, I must go and stay with her. I tried to phone her to say I was coming, but he tore the phone wires out of the wall. He's insane.'

'What do you think?' Clarissa turned to Jeremy.

He covered his face with his hands. 'Have I caused this? Is it what I said to him? I blamed him . . .'

'I think it's his mind,' Charlotte said. 'He must have some sort of mental illness.'

'We'll get him sorted,' Jeremy said. 'I'll tell Dr Staples we want Rod to see a specialist. Meriel, the best thing for you would be to take the children to stay with Francine until he's better. Why don't you ring her now and tell her you're coming tonight? She'll need time to get the beds organised. Go on, use the phone in my study.'

When she'd gone, Clarissa said, 'I never thought it would come to this, Meriel having to take refuge in her old home. It'll be a squash for her. I gather there're only three bedrooms and her sister has a family of her own.'

Meriel looked subdued when she came back. 'She says to come right away.'

'Hadn't you better have supper first?'

'I'm not hungry. I couldn't eat anything.'

'But the children?' Clarissa asked. 'They've not eaten?'

She shook her head.

'Better if you all eat before you go. Your meal will be ready now.'

'I can't take them down there.'

'Of course not,' Charlotte said. 'I'll ask Mrs Shipley to bring it up here.'

She collected some of the empty dishes from the table to take with her. This place was making her nervous. She'd be as edgy as Meriel if this went on much longer. It was dark now, and although the lights could be switched on in the passages, some of the rooms that were no longer used had had their light bulbs taken out to be used in other places because of wartime shortages. It would be impossible to see Rod if he were to hide in one of them.

The chairlift was at the top of the back stairs. She rode it down and was glad she'd only been asked to go to the kitchen. It was empty when went in but an irate Mrs Shipley was close on her heels.

'Where is Mr Rod and his family? They aren't in their rooms. Their supper's going to be ruined.'

Charlotte told her Meriel and the children would eat upstairs. 'But Rod isn't there,' she said. 'Are you sure he isn't in his rooms?'

'Yes. I did call him, but he didn't answer.'

Charlotte wasn't convinced she was right. Rod could have gone back to bed. She helped carry the food upstairs and got the children to the table while Mrs Shipley dished up.

Meriel wouldn't even go to the table. 'I'll need to take our clothes and a lot of things for the children.' Charlotte saw her pleading eyes look straight at her. 'Will you come down and help me pack?'

'Mrs Shipley doesn't think he's there.'

'He can't be far,' Jeremy said. 'He has no car and no phone.'

Meriel's eyes were still appealing for her help. Charlotte felt her stomach muscles contract. She was scared of Roderick too. 'Yes, all right. If he's not there, this could be a good time.'

Jeremy stood up, 'We'll both come with you,' he said. 'Clarissa, you keep an eye on the children. We won't be long.'

With fingers crossed that Mrs Shipley was right, Charlotte headed downstairs. If Rod was about and as aggressive as he'd been earlier, he'd soon overcome them – two frightened girls and an old man who was little better than an invalid.

They were almost creeping past the library. Meriel let them into her suite.

Jeremy called, 'Hello, Rod? Are you there?'

In the silence, Meriel went slowly to their bedroom. Charlotte was close behind and gasped when she saw the mess of money, clothes and towels tossed everywhere. She had to be sure Rod wasn't about, and she made herself look round. He'd had a bath and not pulled the plug; the water wasn't quite cold. He'd left pools on the bathroom floor and made a general mess, but the children's playroom and bedroom were reasonably tidy. In the dining room, the table was set for supper. It looked inviting, and the kitchenette hadn't been used. She breathed a sigh of relief. There was no sign of Rod.

Meriel already had suitcases open on the bed and was tossing her clothes in. Jeremy was throwing toys on to a sheet he'd ripped off Becky's bed and was bundling them up. He said, 'I don't know what clothes the children will need.'

Meriel was picking up money from the floor by then. 'Pack all you can,' she told Charlotte, pushing two bags at her. 'We'll need bedding too, Francine doesn't have enough for us all.'

Charlotte stuffed everything she could into the bags and took what they'd packed and piled it by the front door.

'Where can Rod be?' Jeremy worried as he brought out another bag. 'Go and ring for a taxi, Charlotte. It would be better for them to be gone before he comes back.'

She had the children bundled into their coats and shoes by the time the taxi came. She and Jeremy helped the little family and their baggage into it and saw them off.

Jeremy stood staring after it. 'Where can Rod possibly have gone?' Charlotte could see he was very concerned. They headed towards the kitchen, and found Mrs Shipley and Joan washing up.

'No,' they said, 'he's not here.'

'He was out in the garden earlier this evening,' Mrs Shipley said. 'I saw him come in.'

'But it's dark now.' Charlotte peered through the window. 'He can't still be out there.'

'Well, at least we've got his wife and family safely out of the way,' Jeremy said as he rode the chairlift upstairs.

Chapter Twenty-Three

'NEITHER OF you finished your dinner,' Clarissa said. 'I saved some pudding for you.' There were two bowls left on the table. 'I had mine with the children.'

Jeremy shook his head, 'Just coffee for me, please.' Charlotte went to the kitchen to make it. She couldn't eat any more either.

They were all very uneasy about Rod. 'He must be here in the house somewhere,' Jeremy said. 'But where, and what's he doing? Perhaps we should take a good look round.'

'You're doing too much,' Clarissa said. 'You'll exhaust yourself. Rest for a while.'

He sounded impatient with her. 'How can I rest?'

'At least sit down and drink your coffee.'

'I'm going to ring Staples. He's got to help. Rod doesn't know what he's doing. He's mentally ill.'

Jeremy had been in his study for some time when Joan came running up to tell them Rod was back.

'We saw him come in,' she said breathlessly. 'He's in the kitchen.'

Charlotte felt her heart somersault as she rushed to tell Jeremy.

He stood up and said, 'I'd better see if he's all right.' She followed him. At the top of the stairs he said, 'You're coming too?'

She felt fluttery but she couldn't let him go alone. 'I might be able to help.'

'Thank you. Rod's my son. I need to make sure he's all right.'

'He's my father,' she said. 'I'm worried too.' But she was also a nurse and it was looking more and more likely that Rod was ill.

'You're a great help to us, Charlotte.'

Before she was halfway down the back stairs she could hear Rod shouting, 'I want my dinner. Steak and chips. A large T-bone steak.'

Mrs Shipley was trying to reason with him. 'I cooked your dinner same as usual. I took it to put on your table at quarter to seven, but you weren't there. I made you cod and parsley sauce.'

'I told you, I don't want that tasteless pap. Steak and chips, I said.' He was bent over her table, his head supported on his hands, and didn't look at all well.

Jeremy took his arm, 'Come to your rooms, Rod.'

'I'm hungry . . .'

'Mrs Shipley will find you something to eat. Good gracious, you've been outside with nothing on except your dressing gown.'

Charlotte took his other arm. 'Gosh, yes, you're cold. Your hands are frozen. Joan, could you fill a couple of hot water bottles for him? Why don't we get you into bed?'

'You'll be more comfortable there,' his father said. 'Where've you been?'

'To the stables. Somebody's taken my Jag and I need a car. Old Bill's fixing another for me. Got it down off those blocks. Turned the engine over.'

'Of course,' Charlotte said. 'Why didn't we think of that?'

'There's no petrol,' Jeremy said.

'Yes there is.'

'Well, you don't want to go out now, do you? Let's get you warmed up and get you something to eat.'

'Steak and chips.'

'There's a war on, Rod. I doubt if Mrs Shipley can stretch to that.'

Charlotte was glad Jeremy was with her. He could talk to Rod and keep his attention away from her. She found some pyjamas in a drawer and while his father persuaded him to put them on, she hastily made his bed and picked up the things he'd strewn round the room. She left the dirty clothes and towels in a heap by the door ready to take out to be washed.

They'd got him into bed when Joan came to the door with two stone hot water bottles. She looked frightened and would come no nearer. Charlotte pushed them against Rod's feet, which felt like ice.

Mrs Shipley came with a tray. 'It's the best I can do, Mr Rod, we finished the cod.' She'd set out a bowl of soup and a sandwich.

Charlotte plumped up his pillows and sat him up. 'Here's your supper.'

The tray had legs. Mrs Shipley settled it at a comfortable distance in front of him.

'You'll feel better with something inside you.' Jeremy was sympathetic. 'Eat up now, then you can go to sleep. You'll feel more yourself in the morning.'

Rod was glowering at them. 'What's this?' He gripped the tray with both hands. 'I said steak and chips.' With one powerful swing, he flung the tray and dishes off his bed. Charlotte took the full force of the tomato soup down the front of her white dress. The bowl broke against the dressing-table leg. Mrs Shipley clucked with distress and started picking up the bits, while Charlotte wiped the excess of soup from her uniform on one of Rod's damp towels.

Jeremy strode to the sitting room. Charlotte could see he was very upset. 'Has he been drinking again?' He was opening the drinks cabinet.

'I don't think so,' Charlotte said.

'Meriel's right,' he sighed. 'He's been tipped over the edge. I'm afraid this is my fault. I shouldn't have been so outspoken.'

'You mustn't blame yourself.'

Mrs Shipley was leaving with her tray, Joan was collecting up the washing. Charlotte and Jeremy went back to see Rod. He'd curled up against his pillows and his eyes were closed. Charlotte drew the curtains and then Jeremy ushered her out and switched off the light.

'It looks as though he'll go to sleep,' she said.

'I'm going to ring Dr Staples again and tell him what Rod's like. He's got to do something to help. We can't go on like this.'

Clarissa was on tenterhooks and it didn't help that Jeremy came out of his study in an even greater state of frustration.

'Dr Staples's wife says he's been called out to a maternity case and she doesn't know when he'll be back. I said I thought Rod might go to sleep now, and she said, "Ring again if you need him, but otherwise I'll tell him you called again, and I'll get him to come first thing in the morning."'

'What if Rod doesn't sleep?' Clarissa worried.

Charlotte helped her to have a bath and get into bed. She made malted milk for them all and ate her helping of baked apple and custard. She'd intended to get into bed and read but she felt exhausted. After ten minutes, she closed her book and settled down to sleep.

*

Charlotte woke when she heard Clarissa calling her softly. She needed to get up to the bathroom. 'I'm so worried about Roderick,' she said. 'I haven't been able to get to sleep yet, and it's after two o'clock.'

The moon was full. It was a fine night and silvery light was streaming into the flat. Charlotte was sympathetic. 'Would a cup of tea help? Or some more malted milk?'

'Tea would be nice.'

Still half asleep, Charlotte went slowly to the kitchenette to put the kettle on. It was at the front of the house over the main entrance. Looking through the window, she saw that the moonlight seemed less bright and silvery and sensed that something was wrong. Leaning over the sink, she drew the curtains further back to peer out. From here, it should be possible to see up the east wing where Rod had his rooms. But tonight she couldn't. Fog was swirling in. Or was it smoke? Then she saw a flicker of orange . . .

Could that be fire? For a second she felt paralysed. Rod's rooms were on fire! She was jolted back to full wakefulness and went flying back to Clarissa's bedroom.

'The house is on fire,' she said, sounding calmer than she felt. 'Rod's flat. Wake Jeremy and get dressed. I'm going to phone for the fire brigade.'

Clarissa was aghast. 'Oh, my God! What about Rod?'

By the time Charlotte had got through and given them the information they asked for, Jeremy and Clarissa were at the kitchen window in their nightclothes.

'Get dressed,' she told them. 'Hurry up.' She ran to her own room to pull on trousers, a pullover and a jacket, and push her feet into shoes. She felt panic-stricken and couldn't think straight, but the elderly couple seemed almost paralysed. 'Get some warm clothes on,' she urged them.

'Are you going to see to Rod?' Clarissa asked, her eyes wide with fear. Charlotte understood: she was hardly mobile herself and certainly couldn't help others.

'Yes, but first I'm going to wake Mrs Shipley and Joan,' she said.

At one time the staff rooms had been in the attic, but since the war she knew they'd moved down to rooms in the east wing, above Rod's flat. Charlotte wasn't sure exactly where they were or how to reach them, but she was afraid they were in great danger.

She could smell the smoke as soon as she reached the top of the staircase. It was suffocatingly strong. She stood holding on to the banisters as a fit of coughing shook her. She could see little spirals of smoke eddying up, and, worse, she could hear the crackle as the flames fed on the old dry wood.

She went to where the corridor led into the east wing. Suddenly, the lights she'd switched on went out, leaving her looking into a black void. Her knees turned to water, and she had a terrible impulse to turn and run. She couldn't make herself put one foot in front of the other and go into that black hole.

'Joan,' she yelled. 'Mrs Shipley. Where are you?'

She heard a faint answer and sweating with relief she saw two dark shapes coming towards her out of the darkness. 'Thank goodness,' she breathed. 'You're all right?'

Joan was crying as she lugged a suitcase. Mrs Shipley grasped her arm and said, 'Glory be, the place is going up like a tinderbox.' She doubled over in a fit of coughing. 'Can we get out of here?'

'Yes, yes.'

Charlotte looked down the main staircase and could see the dancing lights of the fire. It no longer looked safe that way.

A thousand questions were thudding through her mind. Where was Rod? The fire was raging in the rooms he used; he could be in mortal danger now. It was providential that Meriel had taken the children away last night.

What had started this? Had she and Jeremy left the electric fire on when they'd made that hurried exit earlier this evening? Had Rod knocked it over?

'Down the back stairs,' she said, pushing them along the landing.

'We'll get out through the kitchen.' Mrs Shipley was seized with another bout of coughing.

'What about Rod?' Charlotte said. 'I've got to get him out.' Would it still be possible to reach him? She pushed at the baize door, knowing she could get through the garden room and the gun room and to the entrance hall that way. Mrs Shipley grabbed her arm and swung her round.

'No!' she screamed. 'No, it's not safe. It's too late, the whole place is ablaze. And what about the master and mistress?'

Charlotte turned and ran back upstairs. What was she thinking of? If the electricity cut out in the west wing as it had in the east, the stairlift wouldn't work and Clarissa would have difficulty getting out. The air was clearer in their flat when she got back, but there was enough smoke to make Clarissa cough. She was dressed and had made bundles of her possessions.

'I've got to get you out of here,' Charlotte said, snatching an eiderdown off her bed and wrapping it round her shoulders.

'No, no.' Clarissa was jittery. 'I ought to wait for Jeremy. He said he'd come back for me.'

'Where's he gone?'

'He went off to save his pictures. He wouldn't listen to sense.'

Charlotte was horrified. It wasn't like Jeremy to panic. Didn't he realise how dangerous that could be? 'For goodness' sake! I'll come back for him. Let's get you to the chairlift.'

Mrs Shipley was at the bottom. Her voice shook as she called, 'Thank goodness, you've found her. I'll help her off at this end.'

Charlotte got Clarissa on the seat and sent it on its way. Then she ran back to grab basic necessities for her patient. She hoped Mrs Shipley would understand the need to send the chair back. Yes, it was coming. Charlotte balanced the wheelchair precariously on it, and loaded Clarissa's bundles. She saw some of these falling off as it went slowly down.

It was more important that she find Jeremy now. She felt desperate. Clarissa would be bereft if Rod hadn't got out. She'd failed to reach him and she'd heard the flames roaring through the rooms he used.

The smoke was worse on the landing, making her cough, but she could hear Jeremy coughing too. She guessed he'd be in the room where she'd seen him gilding picture frames on the day she'd first come here. Jeremy's face was glistening with sweat. He'd stacked some of his pictures against the wall.

At that moment they heard the fire engines arrive. 'Thank goodness,' he gasped. 'Let's hope they'll get it under control now.'

Charlotte was afraid it might not be possible. 'It's dangerous. Come on,' she urged. 'We've got to get out.'

'Not yet. Help me with my pictures.'

'Damn the pictures, come on.'

'We're all right for the moment.'

He was carrying them out. She tried to help, thinking she could carry two, but found it impossible. They were big and heavy and very awkward to carry.

She heard Jeremy say, 'Am I glad to see you, Bill. We badly need a hand.'

Charlotte realised old Bill the gardener had come to help. The two men loaded several pictures on the chairlift and Charlotte found a toe hold and rode down holding them in position. Mrs Shipley and Joan helped her unload at the bottom.

'We've got more waiting here,' Jeremy called down. 'Send the chair back.'

Charlotte scrambled back upstairs to help. 'You've got to get out,' she said. 'You shouldn't be doing this.'

After what seemed an age they got his pictures to the ground floor. 'Take my pictures to the old stables,' Jeremy told Bill. He seemed more controlled than any of them. 'That's far enough away for them to be safe. Be as careful as you can with them.'

Mrs Shipley gasped. 'Are they valuable?'

'Some are,' he said, helping to carry one through the kitchen. 'It looks as though I might lose everything else.'

A fireman came in. 'Everybody outside now,' he ordered. 'It's not safe to stay any longer. How many people were there in this house? Is there anybody not accounted for?'

'There's Roderick,' Charlotte remembered, feeling a flood of misgivings. 'He was asleep in the east wing.'

Jeremy's expression changed.

'I couldn't reach him,' she sobbed. 'I'm so sorry.'

Charlotte was coughing and choking and filling her lungs with cool fresh night air. She thought it would make her feel better but instead she couldn't rid her mind of the image of Rod being burned alive. Now the need to stay calm and keep her wits about her had gone, she was trembling and in a torrent of tears.

Everybody else was busy, rushing hither and thither, but she could do no more. When others seemed to be going to the front of the house, she followed. Someone pointed out the flames behind the first floor windows of the east wing, but tears were distorting her sight. She could see and smell the billowing clouds of black smoke and feel the pandemonium all round her. Figures were running out hoses, jets of water were spraying into the burning rooms. Another fire engine came clanging up the drive.

She knew it was Jeremy who put an arm round her shoulders. 'Rod,' she wept. 'I couldn't reach him.' The flames had almost devoured the ground floor. She knew he was crying too.

'You were marvellous,' he said. 'You kept your nerve. You're a real heroine.'

'Is Clarissa all right?'

'Yes, she's safe. She's been taken to hospital for a check-up. They think we should all go.'

'I'm all right.'

'No, you must come. Smoke inhalation is likely to be a problem. The ambulance is coming back for us.'

'Sir, sir . . .' Bill was rushing towards them. 'It's Mr Roderick, sir. We found him in the stables when we took the pictures over.'

Jeremy jerked back to life, and set off towards the stables. Charlotte hung on to him. She'd never seen him move so quickly.

'No,' Bill puffed, trying to keep up. 'No, sir, don't go. Wait, let me tell you.'

She knew Jeremy couldn't wait. He barked, 'Is he all right? Is he safe?

Bill said, 'He wanted a car to drive. He asked me to get your Rover ready.'

'But why is he here in the middle of the night?'

Charlotte saw the police car and an ambulance waiting outside the building. There was a cluster of figures round the car and she couldn't at first see . . . But she could guess. Cold horror ran through her. Jeremy clutched her to him and burst into sobs that shook his whole body.

In the cold light of dawn, Charlotte was waiting in the hospital with Mrs Shipley and Bill Dorking for transport to take them home.

They'd all been checked over and found not to be suffering from injury or smoke inhalation, but been told to rest. Joan had gone to get a bus to her mother's house. Clarissa and Jeremy were being kept in for observation, but were said to be reasonably comfortable.

Charlotte was going home to Templeton Avenue. She'd telephoned, and her mother was expecting her. Bill's flat in the stables was undamaged; he'd offered his bed to Mrs Shipley and said he'd sleep on his sofa. They couldn't stop talking over the terrible events of the night.

Bill said, 'The master told me to store his pictures in the tack room. He'd organised us to carry them over to the stables and we'd stacked them outside, but he couldn't get his breath and was ready to drop by then. I made him sit on that bench in the garden and rest.

'I could hear an engine running as soon as I opened the door,' Bill went on. 'But there was so much noise outside and so much to do. Everybody else disappeared.'

'Joan and I were trying to salvage some of the silver,' Mrs Shipley said. 'We were in the butler's pantry.'

'As you know, there's no electric in the stables, never has been. I had to light the hurricane lamp before I could do anything. I carried in three pictures . . .'

'What about the engine?' Mrs Shipley asked. 'If it was running, didn't you wonder why?'

'When I realised it was the Rover, my first thought was that I hadn't switched it off. Last evening, Mr Roderick told me to turn it over, and make sure it would work after standing still for so long. It was quite a job to get it going.

'I couldn't believe my eyes when I saw Mr Roderick sitting in the driver's seat, and I didn't at first see that he'd piped the exhaust fumes into the car.'

'You should have switched off the engine and got him out as soon as you could,' Mrs Shipley was still agitated.

'I did that, but I'm not so quick these days. I'm getting on a bit, you know,' Bill complained. 'I pulled at him and he almost fell out on to the floor.'

'Go on, then what happened?'

'There was a half-empty bottle of whisky on the seat beside him, and an envelope addressed to his father.'

Charlotte shivered. 'Oh, Lord! I was so sure Rod had been overcome by smoke while he slept, and I'd been too slow to help him.'

'You'd have gone in if I hadn't stopped you,' Mrs Shipley told her. 'You could have been killed, and that's not all.' She gripped Charlotte's arm. 'One of the fireman told me they thought the fire had been started deliberately, that petrol had been sprayed round Mr Rod's rooms.'

Charlotte couldn't get her breath. 'Deliberately? Rod did that?'

'Nobody else would have.'

'He was a strange one,' Bill said slowly. 'He had everything, didn't he? Yet he killed himself and wanted to take all of us with him.'

*

The hospital transport took a long time getting to Templeton Avenue as it dropped others off on the way. Charlotte was almost asleep on her feet when she got out at the gate. The front door was pulled open before she reached it and Mary came out on the step to throw her arms round her.

'What a terrible thing to happen. You're sure you're all right?' she asked.

'I'm fine, Mum. Just dead dog tired.'

Edith came to kiss her. 'You must have been frightened.'

'Scared rigid.'

'Such a shock, to wake up and find the house on fire,' Edith said. 'My, but you do smell of smoke. Anybody could tell you've been close to fire.'

'Come and tell us what happened.' Her mother led her indoors.

Charlotte tried but it was a garbled account. She told them about Rod and what they thought he'd done.

'It doesn't bear thinking about,' Mary said. 'Burned down the family home, endangered the lives of his parents? Are you sure?'

'Jeremy said there'd be an official investigation, but we think so.'

'Oh, dear!'

'Would you like some breakfast? We've got eggs.'

'No thanks, Gran.' Charlotte could hardly keep her eyes open. 'Just tea. I've had two cups and I'd like another, please. I've never needed it more.'

'A hot bath, perhaps?'

'Yes, please. I stink of fire. I'll have to wash my hair. Then I'd like to go to bed.'

It was after midday when Charlotte woke up and by then she felt hungry. Mary told her lunch was on the table. She pulled a coat over her pyjamas and followed her mother down stairs.

'Where's your dressing gown?' Edith wanted to know.

'At Burford House. I didn't have time to pick up my things. I don't know whether they're burned or not – all my uniform and my best coat.'

'At least you're safe.'

Charlotte smiled. 'And I've got a home to come to.' It was lovely to be fussed over by her family. 'But I'm worried about Clarissa and Jeremy – they must feel awful. Their son committing suicide, and then setting their house on fire.'

'He could have killed you all,' Mary said. 'It's too dreadful to think about. I feel quite sorry for them.'

'You've grown fond of them, haven't you?' Edith asked Charlotte.

'Yes, they're older than you, Gran, and quite frail. They're my other grandparents, after all.' Charlotte sighed. 'I don't know whether they'll be able to live in their house after this. They may not have anywhere to go.'

'Don't they have other relatives?'

'There's Meriel and the two children. Thank goodness they went to stay with her sister last night, but I gather she doesn't have much space. Not enough for them to stay permanently. I'd like to go to the hospital this afternoon and see how Clarissa and Jeremy are.'

'If they've nowhere else,' Edith said slowly, 'we could put them up for a while, couldn't we, Mary? We've got enough room and Charlotte could look after them here.'

'Well . . . I'm not sure that's a good idea. We don't know them and they're used to better than a room in Templeton Avenue. Think of the extra work they'll make.'

'I'll take care of the work, Mum. Don't you worry about that.'

When Charlotte reached the hospital she found the Barrington Browns had rooms in the private wing. She was shown into Clarissa's room and found Jeremy sitting with her, together with Meriel and Mrs Shipley.

'How are you?' she asked. The elderly couple looked shaky and unwell.

'Feeling as though I had a very hard night,' Jeremy said.

'It makes me feel ill every time I think of Rod,' Clarissa said. 'For him to die like that at his own hand and set fire to our house first . . .'

Charlotte put a comforting hand on her arm. 'But do you know definitely that's what happened?'

'I'm afraid we do,' Jeremy said. 'He left a letter for me.'

'It's as though he wanted to kill us all,' his wife wept. 'I'll never get over it.'

'I thank God I'd taken the children away before it happened,' Meriel said. 'The east wing is completely gutted. We could all have burned in our beds.'

'But if Rod had known you were there,' Charlotte said slowly, 'perhaps he wouldn't have set fire to the house at all.'

'He hated us,' Meriel said. 'I doubt if we would have made any difference. He wanted us all to go to hell.'

Jeremy shook his head. 'He was in such a state, who can say?'

'What about the west wing?' Charlotte asked. 'Is it badly damaged?'

'Yes. We won't be able to go home,' Clarissa said. 'Not immediately.'

'Mrs Shipley, you'll have seen it, what's it like?' Charlotte asked.

'It'll need a lot of work to get it right.'

'I've seen it too,' Meriel said. 'I went on the way here. It's a real mess. There was a fire engine standing by in case flames broke out again.'

'We managed to save some of your furniture and things,' Mrs Shipley added. 'Bill and I have carried load after load over to the old stables. It's dryer there now and I thought it better to check through your things and pack them away properly in boxes. Most of your belongings are safe, but the house has been badly damaged.'

'But in time, will it be possible to live in your flat again? Can it be done up?'

'That remains to be seen.' Jeremy shook his head.

Meriel said, 'There's nothing much of the east wing left. The roof has gone. The other half of the house is standing; there's a few slates off the roof but most of it's there. Most of the windows are out and everything is smoke-blackened.'

'It sounds as though we'll need to get a surveyor to find out if it's still sound.' Jeremy sighed. 'I'm afraid it's going to mean a hotel for us.'

'That'll be better than a nursing home.' Clarissa wiped away a tear.

Charlotte said, 'I could take you home with me. It's my grandmother's house and she suggested it. She's taken me and Mum in but there're several empty bedrooms. Mum had three brothers and they've all got homes of their own now. I could look after you, just as I did in your flat. Of course, our house is nothing like as grand as Burford House, but you might like it better than a hotel.'

For a moment, they stared back at her silently. 'I don't know what to say.' Jeremy looked embarrassed.

'You're so kind.' Clarissa pulled her down to kiss her. 'Thank you.'

'Are you sure? I don't want to be a burden to your family.'

'Gran offered. It was her idea, not mine.'

'She's very kind. Thank you both. They want us out of here fairly quickly. If we could come for a few days, it would give me time to look round for something permanent.'

Charlotte smiled. 'Right. I'll go home and get your room ready.'

CHAPTER TWENTY-FOUR

JEREMY FELT overwhelmed. There was so much he needed to see to, he hardly knew which way to turn. There was the funeral to arrange, but first there'd have to be an inquest.

He was grateful to Charlotte for offering to put a temporary roof over their heads; that was one less thing he had to worry about. She'd promised to fetch them after lunch today. She'd even helped him book a taxi for the journey.

Yesterday had been a black day. He'd had to call the police once Bill Dorking had found Rod's body. He and Clarissa had been in such a state then that they'd said they'd return this morning to talk to him.

He couldn't get over what Rod had done. Why hadn't it occurred to him that he might kill himself? It should have done; after all, Clarissa kept saying how like her Uncle Simon he was. A real chip off the old block. But to burn down the house he'd inherit before many more years were out and to ruin the business that had nurtured their family for their lifetime? It made no sense.

Handling it like a hot potato, he took out Rod's letter. The first time he'd read it, it had felt like a knife being gouged into his side. He'd been shocked to the core. Rod was so bitter.

Dear Father [he'd scrawled],

I've had enough. I can't cope with being a Barrington Brown any longer. I'm sick of you telling me how fortunate I am to inherit what my forebears have built up, and how I'm to be the guardian of their assets until it's time to hand them on to Robin.

You're always throwing in my face that I don't come up to the standard set

279

by my dead relatives. You make me feel a failure. I resent being ordered about. My life has never been my own.

Neither do I delight in the house they built. It is too big, too old, too cold and too draughty. If I can rid you and Robin of that, you should look upon it as a favour.

I refuse to tell Milo and George. You can tell them and you can do whatever you like about the business. You can run it in your way from now on.

Jeremy blinked angrily. He was not going to break down again. He'd ordered Rod to deal with the fraud at the shipyard, but he hadn't been able to face it.

That meant that he'd have to do it himself; there was nobody else. But yes, there was. He'd ring Walter Collingwood – he'd give him a hand. They'd get those fraudsters out as soon as they could.

He set out to use the public telephone on the landing but met the two policemen on their way up. Back in his room, they asked after Clarissa.

'Very upset,' he said. 'I'd like to do as much of this without her as I can.' He took Rob's letter from his pocket and handed it to the one in charge.

Mary had offered to help Charlotte make up the spare bed, but she knew she'd not done it with good grace. She wasn't sure she wanted the Barrington Browns here.

'We'd better use the linen sheets and the embroidered pillowcases,' she said, burrowing deep into the linen chest to get them. 'They'll be used to the best.'

'They'll be happy with anything, Mum.'

'I'm sure after Burford House Templeton Avenue will seem a come-down.'

Charlotte had asked Dan to come round on his way home from work yesterday to help her move furniture around. They'd collapsed the bed in the next room and moved in a couple of easy chairs and a small table from which they could eat. Edith had gone round the house looking for other things to make the room more comfortable, and come up with a bright hearthrug and a small desk.

'You're making a private suite for them?' Mary had asked. 'They won't want to eat downstairs with the likes of us?'

'Clarissa will find the stairs difficult,' Charlotte told her. 'They had a chairlift at Burford House.'

'Well, we certainly can't run to a chairlift here.' Feeling exasperated, Mary went to find the Hoover.

'They won't expect it, Mum. This is just a stop-gap until they can get their own place fixed up.'

Mary knew what they'd be like. All those years ago, Jonty's description of the family had been burned into her mind. Rich and opulent, not like us. He'd watched them drive off in a chauffeured limousine and then showed her articles in the newspapers about them.

They'd described the Barrington Browns as merchant princes, a powerful family owning a large and successful business. Jonty had been in awe of them. He'd been horrified to find they'd taken Charlotte away from a family like that. He'd believed she would have had a better life with them. Now it seemed the wheel had turned full circle and she'd been drawn back into the family.

Charlotte put a hand on her arm. 'They're old, Mum. Clarissa's had a stroke. She was a real invalid, hardly able to do anything for herself. She's better and doing more now, but she still needs help.'

Mary felt full of guilt. She'd persuaded Jonty to abduct their baby granddaughter. She didn't want to meet this family. They were going to blame her for their loss.

Charlotte took the bus to the hospital. Neither of her patients looked well. Jeremy's hair was singed at the front and he had a dressing on his arm where he had a burn. She was not surprised to hear they wanted the taxi to take them to see Burford House before going to Templeton Avenue.

'We want to see what we've got left,' Clarissa said. Her cold hand gripped Charlotte's as the taxi swung towards the imposing iron gates, and as the house came into view she heard her gasp of horror. Yes, the west wing was still standing, but it was a smoke-blackened virtual ruin.

They both wanted to get out and there was no persuading Clarissa to stay in the car. Charlotte helped her into the entrance hall. The black and white tiles were running with water and broken glass crunched under their feet.

Clarissa was in tears as they drove to Templeton Avenue. Jeremy sat silently staring out of the window.

*

Edith called, 'They're here, Mary,' as she opened the front door and went out to meet their guests.

Mary had already heard the taxi pull up at the gate. Her heart was racing. She had to force herself to go out to meet Charlotte's real grandparents. She was expecting to see a confident couple sitting bolt upright in the car, but they both had bowed heads.

Charlotte got out and turned to help the woman. Mary caught sight of a tear-stained face as she was helped into her wheelchair and felt a hot rush of sympathy. She'd got it all wrong. This poor woman had her own very recent troubles; she was not concerned about Charlotte's history now.

Charlotte wheeled her into the hall. 'Do you want to go up and see your rooms first? We've made one into a little sitting room where you and Jeremy can be by yourselves, but you're welcome to use the main rooms down here when you feel like it.'

'I'd like to go up now, and perhaps have a little rest.'

Charlotte wheeled her to the bottom of the staircase. It was wide and did not rise steeply. She saw Clarissa assessing the staircase as she helped her to her feet.

'I'll manage that. I'm much better now, thanks to you and Polly.' But she was slow, and so obviously finding it difficult that Mary's heart went out to her.

She followed with their bags and found that her mother had already taken Jeremy to see the rooms they'd prepared for them.

'I'm delighted with them,' he was saying. 'Look, Clarissa, we'll be very comfortable here, won't we? This is a lovely big room.'

Their bedroom had one window overlooking the back garden and another to the side that caught the morning sun. It had always held a double bed, but Charlotte had persuaded them to take in Noel's old single bed when they'd collapsed it from the room next door.

'They used separate rooms at home,' she had told Mary, 'but whether that's only since Clarissa had her stroke I don't know. They might prefer separate beds, but if she wants to get up in the night he's close enough to help her.'

'You've gone to such a lot of trouble,' Clarissa said when she saw their sitting room next door. It was smaller than the one in Burford House but it caught all the sun. 'I hardly know how to thank you.'

'You already have,' Charlotte said. 'Several times.'

Jeremy was shaking his head. 'I'm afraid it'll take a long time to make Burford House habitable again, and it might prove impossible. It upset us both to see it in such a state.'

'You're very welcome to stay here for as long as you need,' Edith told them.

'But we can't impose on you indefinitely. Burford House will need virtually rebuilding, and finding workmen and materials to do it now will be nigh impossible. I think we'll have to forget it for the time being and look for something else as a stop-gap.'

'I understand that's quite difficult,' Edith said. 'So many houses were damaged in the Blitz.'

'I know. I'll try ringing round the estate agents later to see if there is anything on the market.'

'You're very kind to open your house to us,' Clarissa said, still near to tears. 'I'm sure we'll be very comfortable here for the time being.'

'There's only one bathroom between us, I'm afraid. And a downstairs lavatory.'

'We'll manage,' Jeremy said.

In the days that followed, he was out and about, kept busy with his business affairs and the many other things he had to deal with. Clarissa was left at home in Charlotte's care and appeared to be devastated with grief. Having the Barrington Browns under the same roof, Mary felt drawn into their affairs.

She understood how Clarissa must feel, and she wanted to help this poor woman. She'd envied her, and so had Jonty; they'd believed she had everything in the world she could possibly want. But she'd lost two sons and her home, and the intensity of her grief was frightening.

Charlotte had gone to the chemist for more medicines for her patients, and knowing Clarissa was alone Mary asked her if, today, she'd like to come down to have her lunch with them.

She shook her head sadly. 'You must forgive me for being unsociable,' she said. 'I'm not very good company.'

'I understand. I know things must be very difficult for you. I'll bring your lunch up here on a tray.'

Clarissa lifted a ravaged face. 'It's very hard to take, both my sons dead before me. In the natural order of things they should both be in their prime, although to me they'll always be my little boys. Can any mother ever get over the death of her children?'

Mary didn't doubt Jeremy grieved for his son too, though she'd gathered Roderick had been difficult to live with. She understood they blamed him for the wreck of the *Priscilla* and the resulting loss of life. She'd watched the sea smash the yacht against the rocks on their headland, and couldn't help feeling sympathy for him. To lose one's spouse because of one's own negligence must be the hardest thing in the world to bear.

Jeremy felt more on top of things now he'd told the police about the fraudulent dealings he suspected were taking place in the shipyard. On Monday morning, he arranged for the auditors to go into the office straight away to establish exactly what was going on. Then he had a long telephone talk with Walter, who promised to help him put the business back on track once the police had dealt with the problems.

At lunchtime, he heard that the Admiralty were sending in their own auditors that same afternoon and that the date for the inquest was fixed for the following week.

Within a few days he had two pieces of bad news. The fire service confirmed that the fire had been started deliberately, and when he asked a firm of surveyors to establish whether or not it would be possible to repair Burford House their report said no. What remained of the east wing should be demolished to make it safe, while the main supporting timbers of the west wing showed evidence of wet rot as well as fire damage. In their opinion the house was beyond repair.

Jeremy was devastated, but he immediately telephoned several estate agents to see if it would be possible to buy or rent other accommodation. None of them seemed hopeful. The 1941 Blitz had reduced Liverpool's housing stock to such an extent that there was little on the market. He wanted both the inquest and the funeral to be over and knew neither he nor Clarissa would be able to relax until both things were behind them.

The day of the inquest came. Jeremy wanted Clarissa to stay at home. He thought it would be too painful for her to attend, but she insisted.

'I'll be all right,' she said. 'I want to know what's said about Rod.'

'I'm going to be called as a witness. Will you come with us, Charlotte? I'd like you here in case Clarissa wants to be taken out and I can't leave.'

'Yes, of course.'

*

Charlotte had never been to an inquest before. She could feel Clarissa's stress. She and Jeremy were being torn apart. Roderick was her natural father, but she couldn't see him as that. She hadn't even liked him, and at times she'd been frightened of him. She didn't feel as involved with him as his wife and parents were. She could be objective and stand apart.

It didn't last very long; the facts were conclusive. Dr Staples was called and told the court that in his opinion Roderick was psychotic at the time.

Clarissa was gripping Charlotte's hand so hard it hurt. 'What exactly does that mean?' she whispered.

'He was mentally ill, and his contact with reality was highly distorted.' A pity, she thought, that Dr Staples hadn't come to that conclusion when she'd first suggested it to him.

Meriel stood up to give evidence and said she thought he'd been mentally unbalanced for the last year. She described, graphically, his sudden unprovoked rages, and how he'd hit her and his children. 'I was frightened of him and the children were terrified.'

She was asked if previously he'd been a good husband and father, a calm person.

'Never calm,' she said. 'He'd always been strict with the children but he hadn't flown into rages and struck them in the same way.'

A police officer was called to describe the problems of criminal fraud at the shipyard. Charges had been brought against two senior employees of the firm as well as several other people and Roderick had been involved.

Jeremy was asked to describe the events of the evening leading up to the fire. Charlotte could tell from his voice that he found it difficult.

A fire officer then described the evidence that Roderick had started the fire deliberately by sprinkling petrol about the rooms he'd occupied.

Bill Dorking described how he had found Roderick's body inside the Rover in the old stables and the letter he'd left there was read out.

Charlotte was shocked by the words Rod had used. They showed such hatred of his family. Clarissa was crying openly. Charlotte felt for her hand.

The evidence that Rod had started the fire deliberately must surely mean he was not thinking straight, when his parents and staff were asleep in the house.

As they'd all expected, the verdict given was suicide whilst the balance of his mind was disturbed. His body was released for burial.

The funeral took place quietly two days later on a very wet morning. Charlotte went with Clarissa and took charge of her wheelchair. Only the doctor, the staff, the family and their few close friends attended. Mary looked after the children at Templeton Avenue.

Over the following weeks, Mary thought the Barrington Browns were settling in with them. A routine had been established and they were getting on well together.

Mrs Shipley came every morning to tidy the rooms Clarissa and Jeremy used, make their lunch, and take home their washing. She'd brought their ration books so Mary could register them in the shops where she bought their own groceries. On several days each week she returned in the evenings to cook a meal for them all which they ate together in the downstairs dining room.

Meriel regularly visited her in-laws, bringing the children with her. She told Mary she was not finding life easy with her sister's family.

'We're all crammed in together, packed like sardines in a tin.'

Mary thought she was exaggerating. 'Didn't the house belong to your parents?'

'Yes, I grew up there,' she said. 'Legally I own half of it, but it's just a sunshine semi.'

Hadn't Charlotte told her Meriel had not come from a wealthy family?

'I believed I'd never need to live there. When Rod and I were married we had a dream house and I loved it. But then we were bombed out, and although Rod complained about the rooms we had at Burford House, they were spacious and we had every comfort. I more or less told Francine she was welcome to my share of the house, but now I've had to push in too.'

'But it's not for ever,' Mary tried to point out. 'When the war's over and they start building again . . .'

'That seems like for ever.' Meriel brushed a tear from her cheek. 'Why did Rod have to burn Burford House down? It had been his family's home for generations; you'd think he'd want to preserve it, wouldn't you? I can hardly believe he did it, knowing it might kill Gran and Grandpops. And what if I'd been there with the kids? I go cold every time I think of it.'

Joan was going daily to help Meriel with the children. Mrs Shipley had heard and reported back to the grandparents that the children were at loggerheads with their cousins. Derek, two years older, Jason aged four and Paul, aged three, were fighting Becky on every possible occasion. There was hair-pulling, kicking and sometimes biting. Joan was doing her best to keep them apart, but the only space for them to play was the garden, and in poor weather it meant things were difficult.

'That nursery class isn't enough for Becky,' Jeremy said. 'She needs to be in full time school. Have you decided where you want her to go, Meriel?'

'No . . .'

'Perhaps if you look round and get some brochures,' Clarissa said. 'If you want me to, I could come with you to see them. I think we should make arrangements for September.'

'It's not just that. I want Becky to go to school, but I want to find somewhere else to live, a place of my own, and that complicates things.'

'We'd all like to find a place of our own,' Clarissa sighed. 'But in the meantime, would you mind, Edith, if Meriel brought the children here more often in the afternoons? They can be a bit noisy but I do enjoy seeing them.'

Mary was enchanted with the children. Robin was plump and cuddly with big brown eyes. He wanted to be picked up so he could put his little arms round her neck all the time. Becky was like quicksilver, full of energy, but Mary could cope with her better than anybody else.

It seemed almost impossible that these pretty children were Charlotte's half-siblings. They were nothing like her. Becky was more like Meriel, with fine white hair blowing about like dandelion fluff. Even more impossible to believe was that Meriel, who looked so young and had so ineffective a manner, was Charlotte's stepmother. Meriel was impractical and seemed much in need of help and guidance. Charlotte was a far more capable person.

On several mornings each week, Mary walked up to their nearest parade of shops and carried home heavy bags of food. Having the Barrington Browns in their house gave her more work but she found she was enjoying their company. She'd always been a busy person and the more she had to do the happier she was.

One morning, she was returning up Templeton Avenue when, on the opposite side of the road and some hundred yards or so from Edith's house, she saw a woman unlatching her garden gate on her way out.

'Hello,' Mary said, putting down her shopping bags. 'It's Iris, isn't it? Iris Fry?'

'Iris Morgan now.' The middle-aged woman looked at her more closely and smiled. 'Goodness, it's Mary Shawcross. I wouldn't have known you . . .'

'I wouldn't have recognised you except that I know you lived here. I used to come and play with you when we were children.'

'So you did.'

'Decades ago now.' Mary remembered how Pa would never let her take her friends home to play. Always she'd had to go to them. Iris's parents had been more welcoming. 'How is your mother?'

'Pretty low at the moment. My father died a few months ago . . .'

'Oh, I'm so sorry.' Mary tried to picture Mr Fry and failed.

'Well, Mum can't go on living here alone. It's a big house and she's finding it lonely. I'm taking her to Chester to live with me and my family.'

'She'll be happier with you.'

'And how are you, Mary? The last I heard . . . Didn't you run away with some fellow your family disapproved of?'

Mary laughed. 'Was there a neighbourhood scandal? I was nineteen and Pa refused to let us marry.'

'But you're married now?'

Mary pulled a face. 'Unfortunately, I'm a widow, that's why I've come back home to live with Mum. Pa's dead too, so it made sense.'

'Everything changes, doesn't it? Do you have children?'

'One daughter. What about you?'

'Two sons.'

'Iris . . .' Mary had wanted to ask since the moment she'd mentioned it. 'What are you going to do with this house?'

'We're putting it up for sale. I'm just going to see an estate agent now, to ask him to come and value it.'

'Oh, Iris!' Mary took a deep breath. 'I know somebody who'll think this is a godsend. We have an elderly couple staying with us who have nowhere else to live. My daughter works for them. I'm sure they'd be interested.'

'Really? We'd like a quick sale, and now the raids have stopped I don't think that's hard to get.'

'It isn't, but please don't put it on the market until my lodgers have seen it. When can I bring them?'

'Well, any time.'

'What about now? Jeremy was at home when I came out.'

'All right.'

'I'll fetch them. Fifteen minutes – Clarissa's in a wheelchair so it'll take me all of that.'

Mary picked up her shopping and almost ran home. She dumped her bags in the kitchen and rushed upstairs. Jeremy was reading the morning paper and Charlotte was putting Clarissa through her exercises. She had only to mention there was a house about to go on sale just across the road for them to be keen to see it.

'If it's the same as this, it would suit us fine,' Jeremy said.

'Not exactly the same, but similar.'

'Is it as big?'

'Yes, I think so.'

Mary led the way, Charlotte pushed Clarissa's wheelchair and Jeremy brought up in the rear.

'It's been well looked after,' he said, pausing at the gate to study the building.

Iris met them at the front door and Mary introduced them.

'There's no front step here.' Clarissa sounded quite excited. 'That makes it easier for me.'

The house was slightly bigger than Edith's. There were two small attic bedrooms and six of a more generous size with a bathroom on the first floor. On the ground floor, Clarissa thought the large sitting room with three windows was lovely. She wanted Charlotte to push her round rapidly to see the dining room, another smaller sitting room, a study, and a generous kitchen with a scullery.

'What's that door there?' Charlotte opened it. It was a downstairs lavatory and washbowl.

'Big enough for me to get the wheelchair in.'

The stairs were much the same as those at home, and Mary knew Clarissa was learning to manage them. She went up slowly under her own steam to see the bedrooms.

Jeremy had already been round them all and stood at the head of the stairs surveying the landing.

'I like it,' he said to Iris. 'I think we could make ourselves very comfortable here. I'd be delighted if we could agree a price.'

'Yes, of course.'

Jeremy said, 'I want you to have it valued by at least two estate agents and I'll offer you whatever they suggest.'

'Well, gosh, you can't say fairer than that.' Iris wore a wide smile as she shook hands on the deal.

Back home, Mrs Shipley had their lunch ready. Usually Clarissa and Jeremy had it upstairs but today they all sat round the dining room table and couldn't stop talking about the house they'd just seen.

'What d'you think of making it into two flats?' Jeremy suggested. 'We ought to think of Meriel and the children. She isn't happy with her sister. I'd feel guilty if we took over the whole of that house.'

Clarissa nodded. 'We can't leave her where she is.'

'That downstairs cloakroom is big enough to fit a shower in, and nowadays you find that easier than a bath. The smaller sitting room would make us a reasonable bedroom, and Meriel and the children would have plenty of room upstairs.'

'Six big bedrooms to convert,' Charlotte said, 'and there's a bathroom there already.'

'I think we must offer it. Until the war's over she'll not find anything else.'

For the next few moments the only sound was the scraping of knives and forks on plates. Then Jeremy said, 'Please, Mrs Shawcross, don't think we aren't grateful to be here. You've made us very welcome but we make a lot of extra work and your home is not your own any more.'

'I've been a bit worried,' Clarissa said, 'about overstaying our welcome.'

'You'd never do that,' Edith told them.

Mary said, 'I enjoy having you here. You've livened us up.'

CHAPTER TWENTY-FIVE

August 1944

JEREMY HAD bought number 34 Templeton Avenue and moved his family there. Clarissa was improving and Meriel was thrilled with her new quarters. They'd managed to salvage most of what they needed by way of furniture from the ruins of Burford House. Mrs Shipley had moved into one of the attic bedrooms and was looking after them. She was happy because the house was much smaller than Burford House; easier to manage and keep warm.

They were all finding it hard not to dwell on the terrible events of June, but knew they must be put them behind them. Jeremy had been afraid that criminal charges of fraud against his senior staff would drag the name of Barrington Brown through the mud and ruin the yard's reputation. He'd hoped to keep it quiet, but that proved impossible.

This was a white collar crime: public funds had been stolen and that was considered unusual. The sheer scale of the fraud, and that public servants and Admiralty staff were involved, guaranteed public interest. Already it had made the front pages of the national newspapers. Miles Morrow and George Alderton together with officials from the Admiralty and the Ministry of War Transport had been charged and were awaiting trial. There would be another burst of publicity then.

But further publicity overtook Jeremy long before then. As a result of Morrow's involvement in the shipyard fraud, his personal affairs were being investigated by the police. Several incidents of illicit trading in food and petrol came to light, but what really shocked Jeremy was that Milo had had an extension built on his house using timber and other materials supplied unwittingly by the shipyard, and this too had been charged for as work done for the Admiralty.

He and Walter Collingwood were going into the yard every day to keep the business ticking over. They were trying to find replacement staff and work to keep the yard busy.

It helped to keep Jeremy's spirits up that the war news was improving and the future seemed brighter. The Russians had invaded Germany's eastern front, and the D-Day invasion of France was under way. It meant Germany was now fighting on two fronts.

Joan was unable to move into Templeton Avenue with Meriel. She'd had her eighteenth birthday and had to register for war work. Her departure reminded Charlotte that she should be doing war work too, and not enjoying an easy job with Clarissa. Especially now that Clarissa was able to do so much more for herself.

It was now possible for Charlotte to live at home and walk across the road to work. This arrangement suited her as she was able to spend more time with Mary and Edith. But her summer holiday was almost on her. She'd been looking forward to it for months.

While she was to be away, she'd organised Mary to go across in her place to help Clarissa, and also keep an eye on the children for Meriel. Meriel was more relaxed now Becky was separated from her cousins and the noisy squabbles were a thing of the past. Becky would be starting school in September.

Charlotte couldn't wait to see Glyn again. She found herself thinking about him last thing at night as she was drifting off to sleep and he was still in her mind first thing in the morning. Almost every day she received a letter from him and sometimes they spoke on the telephone as well. She felt blissfully in love as she boarded the Crosville bus at the start of her holiday, and her excitement grew as the miles that had separated them were swallowed up.

As the bus pulled to the stop in Bangor, she had her cheek pressed hard against the window. She could see Glyn waiting for her on the pavement as he'd told her he would. He looked fit and healthy, poised for action, a man at the peak of his form. The breeze was fluttering his dark curls.

He caught sight of her and waved and could no longer stand still. He was at the door before she reached it, waiting impatiently for others to get off. He lifted her down from the step, his arms tightening round her, and his mouth found hers.

'Hello, love,' he said. 'I'd almost forgotten how beautiful you are. Absolutely gorgeous.' He gave her another hug.

Charlotte had forgotten his rosy cheeks and how his skin crinkled up at the corners of his brown eyes. He kept his arm round her waist as she waited her turn to claim her suitcases.

'I've left the car in Moelfre,' he told her. 'Sorry, I didn't have enough petrol to bring it this far. I could have come on the motor bike but I knew you'd have suitcases. It's the Anglesey bus, I'm afraid.'

'It doesn't matter. Nothing matters now I'm here.'

Every turn in the road was familiar; it was like coming home.

'I've been thinking about this holiday for months,' Glyn told her. 'About what we should do while you're here. Is there anything special you'd like?'

'If the weather's going to stay hot and sunny,' she stretched back in her seat, 'I'd like to relax on the beach, swim and sunbathe.'

'How about going out on a fishing trip? I could arrange that. Or we could go up Snowdon in the train?'

She sighed contentedly. 'Both. I've never been up Snowdon. I believe you can see for miles.'

'On a fine day, if there's no mist or heat haze.'

When they reached Plas Hafren, Enid gave her a big welcome and so did Glyn's father when he came in from the fields. That evening after supper, Glyn suggested a walk along Hafren Sands.

'What I'd really like to do,' Charlotte said, 'is walk up to Glan y Mor.' She could feel it drawing her like a magnet. 'Will anybody be there?'

'I'm afraid so. This is the holiday season and it's rented out. But it's Saturday tomorrow: the visitors will be moving out and new ones coming. Mum and I usually go up to strip the beds and clean up.'

'I'd like to help with that,' she said. 'I can't go back to Liverpool without seeing the old place again.'

In the meantime, she gave herself up to a stroll along the sands as the sun was going down. She was very conscious of Glyn's arm round her waist pulling her against his body. She'd been longing for his kisses for months.

The next morning, she told Enid she'd go up to Glan y Mor in her place, and found that the rough track leading up the hill had been improved and a car could now get to the house.

'I told you,' Glyn said, 'didn't I?'

'Yes, but . . .' She hadn't envisaged the road would be as good as this. Glyn drove his tractor up, pulling a trailer with clean towels and bedding for three beds.

293

This week's visitors were on the point of leaving as they arrived. She heard them say they'd had a marvellous time and ask if they could book again for next year. Charlotte heard Glyn say he'd have to let them know. While he was dealing with them she couldn't resist running up to the headland to see the view from there once more.

Today she gloried in it. The sun was glinting on the calm sea. Already there were sunshades out on the long stretch of Hafren Sands and children splashing in the shallows. She could see several local fishing boats working out in the bay as well as pleasure boats sailing peacefully along the coast.

Charlotte lay down on the grass and looked down over the cliff to the waves that splashed over the rocks below even on a day like today. Their own little cove, mostly pale shingle with its rim of golden sand, seemed to beckon.

She heard the visitors' car pulling away and ran back to help Glyn tidy up. Once inside the house she found much of the furniture and fittings had been changed, but there was still an atmosphere of welcoming warmth, of love and contentment. Memories of her childhood came flooding back. Love for this place had been ingrained into her during those happy years; she'd come back to where she belonged.

They spent time bed-making and dusting and taking the week's rubbish and dirty laundry out to the tractor. The house had been well cared for and not much was required to make it gleaming and fresh again.

'While I'm up here,' Glyn said, 'I need to look round the sheep and the calves we're fattening to make sure all is well.' Charlotte followed him and then trailed nostalgically round the buildings. There was hay in the barn and grain ripening in the field.

'You're looking after Glan y Mor very well,' she told him. 'Taking good care of it. It's what Jonty would have wanted.'

He smiled, 'It makes good business sense, to look after your animals. And the land too, of course. I'm getting hungry.' Enid had filled a Thermos and given them sandwiches for their lunch.

He took her arm and led her back to the headland, This was where Charlotte had picnicked as a child. The breeze from the sea was stronger now, ruffling her hair. It was lovely to see it all again. When they'd finished eating they stretched out on the turf and Glyn sucked thoughtfully on a blade of grass.

'Charlotte' he said, levering himself up to look at her. 'I've told you I

294

love you, and I've asked you to marry me, I think you've said yes, but we don't seem to be getting any nearer. Is it that city life offers more?'

'No, don't think that.'

'But you want to stay there?'

'No, I do love you. Oh, Glyn, there's nothing I want more than to marry you. I want to stay here with you for ever, but . . .'

'But what?'

Charlotte could see he was uneasy, expecting the worst. She knew she had to try to explain, and frowned in concentration.

'When Dad died . . . I knew he was terminally ill, of course, but it happened so quickly after I came home. I'd come to nurse him and I wasn't prepared. Neither was I prepared when he told me he wasn't my real father. I hadn't the slightest idea. He told me the night before he died – it was almost as though he stayed alive to get it off his conscience. For me, it was a bolt from the blue.'

'I was shocked too when you told me.'

'I was dumbfounded. It threw me, and then I began thinking about what he'd told me, about my natural father.

'I was very curious about the family I'd come from, and desperate to find out more. There were things I needed to find out about myself, too. I've done all that now and I know nobody can replace Jonty. Certainly not Roderick Barrington Brown. I even feel sorry for him now. He must have felt tortured in the days before he killed himself.

'I've got to know my grandparents well, and I've grown fond of them. I wanted to help them; that's one reason I stayed there so long. There's Veronica, too – she says I'm the only living relative she has. They've all gone through so much.'

'But they're all right now?'

'They're better and I've done my best, and now, well, I don't want the sophisticated life of the rich, I want to be with you. This is where I belong and where I want to live.'

He put an arm round her shoulders and pulled her close. 'Thank goodness for that.'

Charlotte kissed him and melted into his arms content that he understood. It was some twenty minutes later that he asked, 'So when are we going to get married?'

Charlotte clung to him enchanted. 'As soon as possible,' she whispered into his ear. She felt his arms tighten round her again.

'Very soon, then. I hate us being parted, you in Liverpool and me here.'

'Let's tell everybody, make it official. Announce our engagement.'

'Yes, as soon as we get home.'

'I'd like us to be married here.'

'So would I. Should I ask your mother for your hand first?'

Charlotte laughed and sat up. 'She'd like that. We'll ring her together and tell her. She'll be thrilled; I know it's what she wants.'

'It's what my family want too.'

'My mum will want to know when and where and all practical things like that.'

'So will mine. With the war and rationing, we won't be able to have a big do.'

'A quiet wedding is what I want.'

'Me too,' he said, and Charlotte felt overwhelmed that it was all going to happen at last. 'Just our families and a few friends.'

They stayed out on the headland until the car bringing the new visitors pulled into the farmyard. Glyn went to let them in and show them round.

Charlotte sat staring out to sea, feeling heady and exhilarated. She wouldn't be able to go on working for Jeremy and Clarissa for much longer; she hoped they wouldn't feel she was letting them down.

When they returned to Plas Hafren, the house was silent.

'Mum and Dad will be out with the animals. Let's ring your mother now.'

He led Charlotte up the hall to a seat by the phone and she asked the operator for the number. While they waited to be connected, he said, 'Don't forget I want to speak to her.'

'Mum? It's Charlotte. How are you?'

'We're fine, love. I didn't expect to hear from you so soon. Is everything all right?'

'Everything's wonderful, Mum. Glyn wants a word with you.'

He was standing beside her, suddenly stiff and formal. 'Hello, Mrs Jones. I want to ask you for Charlotte's hand in marriage.'

Charlotte heard Mary's little squeal of delight. 'You're engaged?'

'Yes, I've asked her . . .'

'Glyn, of course you have my approval. You must have known I'd be delighted.'

'Mum?' Charlotte took the phone from him.

'Oh, Charlotte, I'm so pleased, so excited.' Charlotte could hear it in her voice. 'I know you'll be happy with him. When is it to be?'

'We haven't decided yet, but soon. Tell Clarissa for me. How is she? I'm excited myself.'

'Glyn's a lovely person. He'll look after you. Jonty would be very happy for you.' There was a catch in Mary's voice then.

'We've decided to have the wedding here. You'll all have to come.'

'Of course, love. Tell Glyn I couldn't be more pleased with my future son-in-law.'

Charlotte put the phone down with a broad smile on her face. 'I'm so happy.'

'I know.' Glyn kissed her. 'But it's milking time. I feel I ought to give a hand with it.'

'Hang on, I'm coming too.'

He took her arm on the doorstep. 'We'll wait until later to tell them. Mum might be in the dairy, and anyway we can't shout news like this across the byre.'

They were all round the supper table that evening: Enid had just sat down after filling their plates with slices of home-cured ham that she'd baked with the first wild mushrooms of the season when Glyn laid down his knife and fork. He met Charlotte's eyes and smiled at her.

'I've asked Charlotte to marry me,' he said. 'And she's agreed.'

There was a moment's stunned silence, then Enid leapt to her feet and went to Charlotte's chair to kiss her cheek. 'I'm delighted. Not that we haven't been expecting it.'

Glyn's father too came to kiss her. 'Couldn't have a daughter-in-law I'd like more if I'd chosen you myself.'

'You'll have the reception here at home, won't you?' Enid was too excited to eat.

'Won't it be too much for you?' Charlotte asked.

'No, I'd love to do it, really I would. When is the wedding to be?'

Glyn said, 'Almost immediately.'

'Hang on,' Enid said. 'There'll be a lot to get ready.'

'Not before the end of September, I hope,' his father said. 'The grain's almost ripe. If this weather holds, we'll be opening up next week and cutting the week after.'

'And I'm kept busy here cooking for the men during harvest.'

'October then?' Glyn asked.

Charlotte saw Enid look at her. 'I'll need a week or two to get things ready, and I need to go to Bangor to get myself a new outfit. Glyn's the first of our children to be married from home, so I want to have a bit of a party.'

Ted said, 'Tegwen's married, of course, but she met her husband in Cairo and they couldn't come home. They aren't even together any more; he had to move on with the Eighth Army.'

His mother smiled. 'Glenys is older than you, but we're still waiting for her take the plunge.'

'November then?' Glyn asked, looking round the table. 'Early November?'

'Yes,' Charlotte said. 'That will give me time to give notice to Jeremy and Clarissa, and look for someone to take my place.'

'You'll have plenty to do too,' Enid said. 'You'll need to get your trousseau together and choose your wedding dress.'

Charlotte groaned, 'I've spent all my clothing coupons, and even borrowed some from Edith.'

'Have you told your mother?' Enid asked.

'Yes, and she's thrilled to bits. Couldn't be more pleased. But I'd like to ring her again to tell her it'll be in early November, now we've decided.'

'Go and do it now,' Ted said.

When Charlotte came back, feeling her head was in the clouds, Enid lifted her left hand. 'You haven't bought the engagement ring yet, Glyn? No? You must.'

'I will, but tomorrow we need to see the vicar, to book the marriage service,' he said. 'We'll go to church in the morning.'

'We'll all go,' Enid said.

The vicar knew them, of course, and there was no difficulty. Charlotte couldn't believe everything was being organised so quickly. Her wedding day was fixed for 4 November.

'We'll go to Holyhead tomorrow and see if we can find you an engagement ring,' Glyn said. 'And while we're at it, we might as well choose your wedding ring too.'

He took her to a jeweller's shop. They looked at the rings in the window, but they seemed rather ordinary. They went inside and asked the man behind the counter.

'We don't have a wide choice at the moment,' he admitted. 'Not much jewellery is being made because of the war.' He brought a velvet tray to show them what he had. 'We do have a few second-hand ones you might like better.'

They were brought out and put before them, but Glyn shook his head. 'I'm not keen on any of them,' he said. 'What about wedding rings?'

'Yes, we have eighteen carat and twenty-two carat.'

'Twenty-two carat please.'

More rings were brought out. This was easier. Charlotte chose a slim gold band, and it was wrapped up for Glyn to put in his pocket.

They tried to buy an engagement ring in Llangefni too, but it was the same story there. 'It can't be helped,' Charlotte said. 'I shall be quite happy to wear just a wedding ring.'

'Till the war's over,' Glyn told her.

When they returned to Plas Hafren Enid was almost ready to put their supper on the table. Charlotte brought them up to date with the events of the afternoon.

'One good thing,' Glyn's father said, 'if you put your wedding off until November, the last visitors will be gone from Glan y Mor. Your mother and I have been talking about it. You can move in, live there. It'll be a good home for you.'

Glyn said, 'You mean for the winter?'

Charlotte could see Ted looking from her to Glyn. 'We mean permanently. You won't want to keep moving.'

Charlotte was thrilled. 'Thank you!' She'd hoped she'd be able to live at Glan y Mor for some of the time, but as a holiday home it was providing income for Glyn's family. 'I can think of nowhere I'd rather live. That's marvellous.'

'It's your old home,' Enid said. 'We knew you'd be pleased.'

'Dad, I'm thrilled too. I knew we could stay there part of the time – after all, it's empty for most of the winter – but to have it to ourselves . . . A place to call our own, that's wonderful.'

'It's ideal,' Enid said. 'I'm so glad we bought it. It'll be handy for you, Glyn, seeing you'll have to come here to work every day.'

'What I'm trying to say,' Ted said, 'is that your mother and I have decided to make it over to you and Charlotte as a wedding present.'

Charlotte felt bowled over. 'It's a most marvellous wedding present. I hardly know what to say. It's very generous of you.' She kissed Enid and then Ted. 'Thank you, thank you.'

Ted smiled at her. 'We thought that if we gave Glyn a little farm of his own, he wouldn't hanker after buying one, and looking all over the island. We need to keep him close so he can go on working here.'

Mary had been singing in her bath ever since Charlotte had phoned. There could be no more suitable husband for her. Edith too was delighted and they could talk of little else.

Mary had missed having Charlotte about the house since she'd gone on holiday, but taking over her job had brought her benefits she hadn't foreseen. She really enjoyed crossing the road each morning to help Clarissa and Jeremy. Having work to do put structure into her day.

She'd been somewhat in awe of the Barrington Brown family, but now she'd got to know the older couple she liked them and was full of sympathy for what they'd gone through. She was full of admiration for Jeremy too, for the way he'd taken up the reins of the family business again.

She had half expected to feel superfluous when Charlotte returned wanting her job back, but Clarissa was so much better she didn't really need a trained nurse to look after her any more. Now that Charlotte was to marry, it seemed there'd be a permanent opening for her with them and Meriel.

Everybody wanted to help Meriel. She seemed a nervous wreck and kept dissolving into tears. They all understood now that her relationship with Rod had not been the norm between husband and wife and that her life had been difficult for some time.

'I do feel better now,' she said. 'I don't have to worry about him flying off the handle. I lived in dread of what he might do to the kids when he was in one of his rages. I tried to keep them quiet, stop them getting on his nerves, but I couldn't. Then to think of how he killed himself . . .'

Clarissa had told Dr Staples she was worried about Meriel, and he'd had a long talk with her and given her medication. After he'd gone, Meriel had come downstairs to discuss the consultation with her in-laws. Mary was with them.

'I don't want his pills,' she said. 'He seems to think I'm as mad as Rod was. But he won't listen to me. He wouldn't listen when we told him what Rod was like, would he?'

'I wish Charlotte was here,' Clarissa said. They were having afternoon tea. Mary poured a cup and put it in Meriel's hand.

'What I'd really like to do,' Meriel said, 'is go back to work.'

'Meriel,' Jeremy said, 'there's absolutely no need for that. We haven't sorted out Rod's financial affairs yet but I can assure you, you and the children will be well provided for.'

'I'm not thinking of the money,' she said. 'You know exactly what I earned and it wasn't much. It's just that working in your office with other people seemed to suit me.'

'You need to rest,' Clarissa told her. 'Perhaps later on. And what about the children? They need you.'

'I've no patience with the children, you know that. I feel so restless and can't settle to anything. I hardly know what I'm doing. No, I need an ordinary routine job now.'

Clarissa was shaking her head. 'I don't think you're right. It would be another thing for you to worry about.'

'You don't understand,' Meriel wailed.

'If that's what you want,' Jeremy said, 'you can come to work with me tomorrow.'

She got up to drop a kiss on his cheek. 'Thank you, Jeremy. I'm sorry about the kids, but they run me ragged. Wind me up. I love them, but I'm not as kind to them as I should be.'

'It's just that you're on edge, dear.'

'I'll look after the children,' Mary offered quickly. 'I'd love to. Besides, they're so closely related to my Charlotte.'

'Half-siblings,' Clarissa said. 'I've marvelled at that. If they turn out half as well as she has, we'll all be proud of them.'

'There's always the typing pool for you, Meriel, if nothing else. Though I don't know whether you'll be able to settle back into that. Still, you can always change your mind and stay at home if you want to.'

'I was a working girl, Grandpops. Looking back, life seemed so simple and easy then.'

When she'd gone, Mary said, 'It's been a traumatic time for her too. Perhaps this will help her get over it.'

Since then Mary had spent most of the day looking after Becky and Robin. While she tidied their rooms they helped her make their beds; she gave them dusters to polish round and she got them to put their things away. She taught them nursery rhymes, which they loved; they drew and they painted and she played little games with them. After lunch, she put Robin down for his rest and taught Becky to make simple dishes in Meriel's kitchen. Then she'd take them on an outing to the park or the library or the shops.

Mary loved caring for children. Becky had been taught to form the letters of the alphabet and to count at nursery school; Mary found books for her that built on what she already knew. It was what she'd done with Charlotte all those years ago.

Charlotte was keeping in touch by telephone, and Mary told her how well they were managing without her. 'Of course, it does mean Clarissa is getting less help than she did from you.'

'Not a bad thing,' Charlotte said. 'It'll push her into being even more independent. And if she really can't manage, you're just upstairs.'

Because things were going so well in Templeton Avenue, Charlotte rang Clarissa and asked if she might extend her holiday. They all knew she didn't want to tear herself away from Glyn, and now the need to do so was gone.

When she finally came home she was fizzing with high spirits, which gave them all a lift. She said, 'Mum, it's better now if I don't interfere too much with what you're doing. They're already relying on you.'

One thing she did do was to consult Polly Carr about finding a lighter wheelchair for Clarissa, of the sort she could manoeuvre herself. When this arrived, Polly came two or three times to teach her to use it. Clarissa had more use in her left arm now and could manage, though kerbs and road crossings could sometimes prove a problem. After that, she quite often joined Mary and the children on their outings.

Mary was happier than she had been since Jonty died. She felt she had a job she really enjoyed, and one of the best things about it was that she could run back across the road and be home in minutes. Edith usually prepared supper and had it ready, so they could sit down and eat together in the evenings.

'You don't mind, do you, Mum?' Charlotte asked. 'That I persuaded you to leave Glan y Mor and now I'm going to live there?'

'No, you were right. I couldn't have coped there without Jonty, and I'm needed here now. But you'll have Glyn. It's your turn to have what I so much enjoyed. You'll be working together on that little farm.'

'It won't be exactly like that for us, Mum. I feel I ought to get a job, with the war and all that. There's a small hospital in Llangefni. I've been to see them. They're short-staffed and said they'll be glad to have me. I'll start at the beginning of December.

Edith said, 'I wondered whether you would.'

'You must both come and visit often. It's a lovely place for a holiday.'

The weather had turned autumnal now, and late one evening they were sitting round the fire discussing preparations for the wedding, and how to manage with all the shortages that five years of war had brought. It made Mary remember Charlotte's laughingly saying she and Glyn had not been able to find an engagement ring that pleased them. She went upstairs and fetched the jewellery Edith had given her so hurriedly before she'd left with Jonty.

'We have plenty of family rings you could have,' she said, setting them out in front of Charlotte. 'They're very pretty and they've hardly been on my fingers.'

Charlotte said, 'I have seen them before. Don't you remember? You got them out from time to time, just to look at.'

'This sapphire and diamond ring, now. Do you like it?' Mary slid it on her daughter's finger.

'It's absolutely magnificent,' Charlotte gasped.

'It's a Ceylon sapphire,' Edith said. It was a large octagonal stone flanked by two graduated baguette diamonds.

'There's this sapphire brooch too. They aren't part of a set or anything but they seem a good match.'

Charlotte picked up the brooch. It was a large square-cut stone surrounded by rose diamonds. 'When you had your wedding photographs out to show me the other day, I noticed you were wearing this brooch then.'

'Yes. I wore the ring too – on my right hand.'

'They belonged to my mother,' Edith said. 'I believe she wore them quite a lot, but none of us have done so since.'

'Mum, I couldn't take these. Glyn couldn't afford to buy me jewellery like this.'

'All the more reason why you should have it.'

'But Jonty . . . I remember him saying he wanted you to keep them.'

'He didn't want me to sell them. He said they were our security, something to fall back on in time of need. That won't happen now. I know he'd want you to have them. You are our family and he'd like to think of things like this being handed down through the generations to you.'

'That's a lovely thing to say, Mum. That I'm still your family. I've been afraid you might think I'm showing more affection to the Barrington Browns than you.'

'Of course you're our family,' Edith said. 'Always have been, always will be.'

'The sapphires are lovely.' Charlotte twisted the ring on her finger. 'But so are the others. This diamond solitaire. It's gorgeous . . . so big.'

'You can choose,' Mary said. 'Take the one you want.'

'Though it would be rather nice,' Edith said, 'if you wore the sapphire ring and brooch on your wedding day as your mother did.'

'You're both being very kind and generous.' Charlotte looked quite moved. 'I do like the sapphire and diamond ring best.'

'Then I want you to have them. We all like to make a fuss of a bride to be.'

CHAPTER TWENTY-SIX

THE NEXT day, Charlotte phoned Glyn to tell him about the jewellery she'd been given. She said, 'Aren't we lucky? Don't you think it's a lovely idea to hand things like that down through the family?'

'I must thank your mother,' he said. 'She's saved me a big expense.'

Charlotte laughed. 'We couldn't find anything we liked in the shops.'

She was wearing the ring on her engagement finger when she took Clarissa shopping and she noticed it.

'It's a beautiful ring,' she told her. 'One you can be proud of. What about your wedding dress? Have you chosen that yet?'

'No, but I really need to make up my mind. There are wedding gowns in the shops but they all have the utility mark in them, and they aren't anything special. These days most brides wear a suit or a dress they'll be able to get some wear from later. I'll have to do that. Not that I've got any clothing coupons to spare – I must get myself a new macintosh and some wellingtons. I'll definitely need them when I move to Glan y Mor.'

'Isn't there a bridal gown tucked away in mothballs somewhere in your family?'

'Not that I've heard of, but that's an idea. Barbara, my sister-in-law, was married in white. But no, hers wouldn't fit me. She's small and dainty while I'm a big strapping lass.'

'I'm your size,' Clarissa said. 'Or I was years ago when I was married. Would you be interested in borrowing mine?'

Charlotte was overwhelmed. 'Thank you. Yes, that might be the answer.'

'I haven't seen it for years, but I packed it away in layers of tissue paper. There's been the fire, of course, but it might be worth asking Mrs Shipley if she could look for it.' Clarissa did so as soon as Charlotte had helped her wheelchair over the front step.

'I've seen it,' Mrs Shipley said. 'I emptied all your cupboards and wardrobes. I remember taking your bridal gown and old dance dresses from the house and storing them with all your other stuff in the old stables.'

Charlotte said, 'That sounds hopeful.'

'You mightn't like it, Charlotte, or it might have rotted. We got married in 1891. That's, let me see . . .

'Fifty-three years.'

'More than fifty years old. Well, we might as well see what it's like. Perhaps you could fetch it, Mrs Shipley?'

'Thank you,' Charlotte said. 'I'd love to.'

That same afternoon, Jeremy came home from the shipyard with a newspaper already folded open.

'Read this,' he said, handing it to Clarissa. She felt for her reading glasses.

It was a report on the trial of those implicated in the fraud at the shipyard. Miles Morrow and George Alderton had received heavy fines as well as prison sentences.

'It's over and done with now, as far as we're concerned,' Jeremy said.

'Thank goodness.'

'The police have been searching through Rod's financial affairs. They've checked everything that went through his bank accounts, and he had several. They also found deposit boxes with his name on them in several other banks, with large amounts of cash hidden in them. They confiscated it all, of course, so that has been paid back and those involved have got their deserts. It's been hard work sorting things out, and I hope that's the last we hear of it.'

'What about the yard? You seem to be spending so much time there. It'll tire you out.'

'It already has. Walter too, though he says it's made him feel young again. We're going to go alternate days just for an hour or so to keep an eye on things. We've got new staff in place and I think they'll be all right. Now the German U-boats are no longer damaging so much of our shipping there isn't the same amount of work coming through, but it's enough to keep the business ticking over. It'll have to do that until Robin's old enough to take over.'

Clarissa sighed. 'I can't help thinking Rod paid a higher price than anybody else.'

'He could have said no,' Jeremy said shortly, 'and it would never have happened.'

It was Charlotte's wedding day, a cold raw morning. Mary was sharing a bedroom at Plas Hafren with her mother. When she parted the curtains, she saw the fields had been touched with overnight frost, but one couldn't expect sun in November.

Outside, the farm work had started and already she could hear the clatter of dishes from the kitchen beneath. Mary got back into bed and a few moments later there was a knock on the door.

'Good morning.' Enid bustled in with a tray of tea and toast.

'You're very kind, but you must have so much to do today you shouldn't have bothered.'

'I wanted to bring breakfast up for Charlotte,' Enid said. 'This is her day, and besides, Glenys is home, so she's helping me. It's lovely to see her after all this time. Tegwen couldn't get leave.' She sighed. 'I wish this war was over.'

'The second front is going well; the Allied forces are closing in on Germany. It should be over before too much longer.'

When they got up, the house was in a ferment of excitement. The wedding was to be at eleven o'clock that morning and Enid was putting on the reception at lunchtime.

'We'll all have enormous appetites by then,' she laughed as she spread starched white cloths over tables in the dining room and kitchen.

Mary spent a long time getting herself ready. She'd bought a dark red tweed suit, and to dress it up a bit had stitched on a chinchilla collar that had done duty for five years on her mother's winter coat. She was pleased with the way it had turned out and it would keep her warm today. Edith had brought the Persian lamb coat Percy had bought for her over twenty years ago; she meant to wear it over her Sunday best blue wool dress.

'Who will notice what I wear?' she asked. 'All eyes will be on the bride.' Edith had given Charlotte her full ration of clothing coupons, so she could set herself up for her new life.

Charlotte had said yesterday, 'I think I'll need a hand to get dressed. The gown is very grand and rather heavy, there's so much material in the skirt.'

Mary crossed the landing to Charlotte's room. She was sitting at the dressing table wearing the long petticoat of white parachute silk Mary had run up for her. Her hands were deftly twisting her long hair into a French pleat.

'You're so good at that,' Mary marvelled. She'd never had that skill. She'd had her own hair cut short the moment she'd come here and never regretted it. 'You have such lovely hair.'

Charlotte smiled. 'From the other side of the family. Right, I'm ready to put on Clarissa's wedding dress.'

'Your wedding dress now.'

When Mary had first heard of this dress, she'd been a little sorry that she had no wedding gown to hand on to Charlotte. But Clarissa's had been dry cleaned and pressed, and when she lifted it out of its box she couldn't stop the little gasp of pleasure and surprise.

'It's made of silk velvet,' Charlotte told her. 'I'm delighted with it. Clarissa's dressmaker has made it fit like a glove.'

It was a traditional style with a tight bodice buttoned up the front with long sleeves and a Mandarin collar. The skirt was full and the back was cut into a pretty bustle and a small train. It was lined and stiffened in places to give it shape; the fastenings were quite complicated and the sleeves buttoned at the wrist with a fancy covering for the back of her hands.

'I was afraid you'd feel the cold today, but in a heavy velvet dress like this you shouldn't.'

'Clarissa said she was married in December and it snowed on her wedding day. She showed me photographs of herself, with snow on the trees and on the ground. She looked spectacular.'

'There'll be no snow today.' Mary lifted out the headdress and veil. She knew this wasn't what Clarissa had worn. She'd told Charlotte that hers had gone yellow and looked like curtains that had been up to a kitchen window for years; and that there was too much of it for today's fashion. She'd taken Charlotte to Bold Street and insisted on buying her this new veil and headdress. 'It's lovely.'

'She said she chose a short veil because she wanted the back of the dress to be seen in church.'

The last thing Charlotte did was to pin the sapphire brooch to her dress and slide the Ceylon stone on the ring finger of her right hand.

'I'm glad you invited Clarissa. She's grown fond of you.'

'I'm fond of her too, Mum. She sees herself as another grandmother. The other side of my family, but she understands how I feel about Jonty. He was a better father to me than Roderick would ever have been.'

'You've brought us together,' Mary said. 'It's almost as though they're my family now.'

Veronica Terry and all the Barrington Brown family had been invited, they were staying at the hotel in Beaumaris. Becky was to be Charlotte's one attendant.

Several cars could be heard pulling up on the farmyard below. Enid came up and put her head round the door, 'Charlotte, you look absolutely beautiful. That gown! You wouldn't be able to get anything like that today. It's out of this world.'

Charlotte could only nod.

'I came to tell you that not only is Meriel here with the children, but your Uncle Dan is too.' Dan was to give her away. He was staying in a nearby guest house with Barbara and Len and Noel and their wives. Charlotte was sorry her cousins Simon and Tim were on active service and unable to come.

'Is it time for me to come downstairs?' she wanted to know.

'Hang on a moment. Glyn is just leaving for the church. Let's get him out of the way first.'

Charlotte went to the window and watched him get into a car with the friend who was to be his best man.

'We're filling every car up,' Enid said from behind her. 'Those are Ted's sisters going with him. The others will start leaving now. Come on, let's get you downstairs.'

'You'll need help with that train,' Mary said. 'We mustn't let it drag on the floor.'

Down in the parlour everybody told the bride how beautiful she was, and that her dress was splendid. Becky was there swinging on her mother's hand.

'You look very pretty in your wedding finery,' Mary told her, 'almost as beautiful as the bride.' She and Charlotte had taken Meriel to help choose the tartan kilt, black velvet jacket and ankle strap shoes Becky was wearing.

'Robin has a new outfit too,' Becky said, but he was asleep in a corner of the sofa.

Mary thought Meriel looked much better. Going back to work had suited her. She'd pulled herself together and was making friends of her own age. Today she looked very smart.

Mary couldn't resist peeping into the dining room. The table had been extended to its maximum length and as there would be too many for a sit down meal it was laid out with a festive buffet. She congratulated Enid on putting on such a spread.

'There's no wedding cake, unfortunately,' Enid said. 'I couldn't get any sultanas or currants. But I managed to get a pound of icing sugar, so there is a big iced sponge cake as well as some iced fairy cakes.'

There was cold roast chicken, pork pies and boiled ham, and a big selection of trifles and syllabubs, puddings and pies.

Glenys had spent much of the morning making a posy of fresh flowers for Charlotte to carry. 'Not easy at this time of the year, I'm afraid.'

'Glenys, it's beautiful. I wouldn't have believed you could achieve anything as lovely as this.' Beads of moisture clung to the roses and winter jasmine. Glenys had fastened a paper doily and cellophane round them and tied the posy with trailing satin ribbons. 'It smells wonderful and you've made it look very professional, just as good as if it was made by a florist.'

'I managed to make buttonholes too, but I had to plunder several of the neighbours' gardens.' Glenys laughed. 'Last night's frost didn't help. Fortunately, there were a quite a lot of late roses. The outside petals were spotted and brown but they peel off and the inside flowers are perfect.'

'Everything's turning out to be perfect,' Charlotte told her.

Charlotte sat beside her Uncle Dan on the back seat of the limousine. Jeremy had hired it to bring his family to Anglesey and it had already dropped him with Clarissa and Veronica at the church before coming on to collect the bride.

It was a dark morning with heavy cloud. For Charlotte, everything was beginning to feel unreal. Her gown certainly looked gorgeous but it felt heavy and it restricted her movements, reminding her that it dated from an earlier age. She was glad it was a big car because getting in and out was not an easy feat. She hung on to Dan's arm for support.

Mary was waiting for her in the porch, holding Becky by the hand. The child was all smiles, and so excited she couldn't keep still. Charlotte knew her mum had schooled her in her duties.

'Wait a moment for Mary to get to her seat,' Uncle Dan whispered. She could hear the harmonium playing softly. The music was fading and after a moment's silence struck up again on a brisk welcoming note.

'Are you ready, Becky?' she asked. The child was gripping her train as though her life depended on it. The tip of her pink tongue was peeping through her teeth, showing her concentration.

Uncle Dan pushed the porch door open and they set off up the aisle. The church was full. Charlotte was conscious of Clarissa turning to see her come, of Jeremy smiling affectionately, of Megan Lewis and her other school friends, and of people she hadn't seen for ages. Then she saw Glyn smiling at her from the front of the church and could think only of him. This was their moment. She was not nervous. What had she to be nervous about?

Today heralded the beginning of a new life for her, and yet she'd be returning to what she knew and loved. Glan y Mor was all ready for them to move in, but first there was to be a three-day honeymoon in Liverpool. Charlotte thought her heart would burst as the voices of the congregation soared to the rafters in the opening hymn.

Then she was listening to the familiar words of the marriage service. 'Wilt thou have this woman to be thy wedded wife . . . Wilt thou love her, comfort her, honour, and keep her in sickness and in health?'

'I will.' Glyn was looking at her; his face was serious, his voice strong and positive. She knew it was a promise he would keep.

They were husband and wife and walking down the aisle together to the triumphant strains of the wedding march. It took only a few moments to take the photographs, because film was almost impossible to come by, but Jeremy took some and so did Ted. Charlotte heard him telling Glyn to take her back to Plas Hafren so that they could stand at the door to receive their guests.

'Just one moment,' Charlotte said. 'There's something I want to do first.'

She led Glyn to Jonty's grave and the congregation followed her, clustering round. For a moment she closed her eyes to concentrate on all that Jonty had meant to her, then slowly she laid her wedding posy at its head. The priest who'd married them stepped forward to say a brief blessing. When she looked up, her mother smiled at her, but there were tears in her eyes.

'Dad would want to be here to share this with us, if he could,' Charlotte whispered.